Amity

We gratefully acknowledge the support of the Canada Council for the Arts and the Ontario Arts Council for our publishing program. We also acknowledge the financial support of the Government of Canada through the Canada Book Fund.

Cover design: Val Fullard

Library and Archives Canada Cataloguing in Publication

Pejvack, Nasreen, 1954–, author
        Amity : a novel / by Nasreen Pejvack.

(Inanna poetry & fiction series)
Issued in print and electronic formats.
ISBN 978-1-77133-237-8 (paperback).– ISBN 978-1-77133-238-5 (epub). -- ISBN 978-1-77133-240-8 (pdf)

        I. Title. II. Series: Inanna poetry and fiction series

PS8631.E4147A64 2015   C813'.6   C2015-904993-8
                                                   C2015-904994-6

Printed and bound in Canada

Inanna Publications and Education Inc.
210 Founders College, York University
4700 Keele Street, Toronto, Ontario, Canada M3J 1P3
Telephone: (416) 736-5356 Fax: (416) 736-5765
Email: inanna.publications@inanna.ca Website: www.inanna.ca

MIX
Paper from
responsible sources
FSC® C004071

Amity

A NOVEL

Nasreen Pejvack

inanna poetry & fiction series

INANNA PUBLICATIONS AND EDUCATION INC.
TORONTO, CANADA

To the victims of revolutions, wars, and conflicts.

AUTHOR FOREWORD

If I believe my country is the planet Earth, then my loyalties lie there. I was born in the Middle-Eastern region, in the large province of Iran, in the city of Tehran. Throughout much of my adulthood, I have lived on the north side of my country Earth, in the province of Canada, in the city of Vancouver. I have also lived in other provinces of this blue country, such as Greece and America, and in each I have learned much from the people and their culture.

In my childhood, I thought that religion meant peace. I heard and read the representatives of each religion preach kindness and a better life for all. However, as I matured, I saw that they had lied. Each religion killed many to convert others, or punished their own if they did not obey. So, my religion developed into a simple love for humanity, and for this blue home as my country, and for all life that accompanies us here.

We have advanced to a point in time where there are spaces where we can be free from being told what is right, what is wrong, and how to live. As intelligent beings, we all need to learn our histories, and from them gain wisdom and the knowledge of how to achieve peace and harmony. We must move away from the contention created by those who are blind to anything but the desire to exploit and control. We should strive without hesitation to establish universal amity.

Unfortunately, the wars and conflicts seen all across this world tell us that we are not there yet. We either contribute to the atrocities, or we have learned to ignore them.

It is with hope and conviction that I call for the protection of all humanity. Our global society can easily achieve this goal if we work together. I strongly believe that people matter. Everyone should be happy, healthy and secure, not just those in some fortunate parts of the globe.

This book is a window into the hearts and souls of those ruined by conflicts, revolution, and wars. It is a glimpse into the lives of these people who survive and go on, or do not. It is about lives lived beyond and within the wreckage of contention.

CHAPTER 1 **ENCOUNTER**

DARK NIGHT RETREATS, and now the austere greyness of dawn fades as sunrise brightens a new day. The air is fresh and cool. A few cottages dot the shoreline on this magnificent inland water of the Pacific Ocean. Nearby, a fishing village awakes and begins its bustle of activity. The cottages, each surrounded by a good acre of beautiful flowers and greenery, face the water with their backs to a deep forest. The door of one opens and Payvand slowly emerges, putting a note on the small table next to the door to let her love know that she did not sleep well, and that she needs to walk alone this morning. She puts on her shoes, stands tall, and takes a deep breath as she looks out at the horizon.

She listens to the birds and feels the soft breeze on her skin. She smiles at the movements of life stirring within this new morning.

Payvand has a profound connection with nature. It is the place to which she retreats when she needs to disappear and gather her strength once more. With all the challenges and anguish in her life, if she did not have this bottomless bond with nature, she would fall easily into a deep depression. Nature is her redeemer. It has been her greatest help whenever she needs to rejuvenate, before once more facing inevitable challenges, and of course, disappointments.

Payvand looks up. It is still dark enough to see stars shimmering in the sky. She wonders how far away they are. She gazes at the sky for a long time, happy in her certainty that there are other philosophers living their lives in orbit around their own sun up there somewhere. She whispers, "I hope they are doing better than us. Are they living like us? Are they more advanced or more primitive?" She contemplates how far humans have come with science and how much has been discovered about the universe above and around them. She values how much has been understood about the cosmos, yet she fears how vulnerable humans are in this vast ocean of space and, most of all, she despises how horridly people treat one another.

She sits briefly on a chair in front of her cottage to enjoy the peaceful tranquility of the ocean embraced by the dark arms of evergreen mountains. Listen to the birds chirping! She closes her eyes with a relaxed smile as if those birds are singing only to her. They make no requests or demands; they simply soar, dance, and sing to complement the new day. She takes another deep breath and looks out at the horizon as the sun comes up to craft a shimmering display on the water. Only when she is in nature does Payvand feel removed from the pain, anger, and aggressions of the human world. Perhaps that is why she always hated curtains — they only hinder her view of sky and trees.

She begins her walk among the trees that are swaying quietly in the breeze. She loves to watch as the rising sun first turns the tip of the mountains a soft yellow, then moves to blanket the tops of the trees with its golden rays, and, as it climbs up higher and higher, coaxes reflections of colour from the water. She breathes in and fills her lungs with fresh air. "I am alive! I am part of this loveliness!" she says just loud enough for herself. Then, she smiles and repeats it as she walks to the nearby woods.

As she strolls along the edge of the forest near the water, she spots some movement among the trees. She moves closer and discovers a middle-aged woman on the path just ahead of her. *Ah, another early bird who enjoys a morning walk,* she thinks. Payvand greets the woman and comments on the pleasant morning. The woman acknowledges the greeting with a curt nod, then turns her face away to stare out at the water. *She looks so sad*, Payvand thinks.

The melancholy that pervades the woman will brook no communion, so Payvand continues her walk near the water and listens to a loon filling the morning air with its clear, distinctive call. She feels that the loon also takes joy from the sunrise.

She walks for over an hour, feeling the breeze and enjoying the warming sun, all the while doing her best to wash away last night's nightmare. Returning to her cottage, Payvand notices the same woman, now sitting on a log and still staring out at the water. She seems oblivious to Payvand's return, so lost as she is in her misery. Payvand decides to rest for a moment on a nearby rock to make sure the woman is fine.

The woman appears to be a bit younger than herself; in her mid- or perhaps late-forties, though the lines of pain in her face make her appear much older. *What happened to her?* Payvand wonders. Finally, the woman looks up with tears in her eyes and gives Payvand a faint smile. Payvand takes the opportunity to ask if she is all right, and would she rather be left alone. The woman shrugs as Payvand moves towards her. *Is she ill, is she confused? Is any of this my business? She looks awful*, she thinks. But, no, the woman is speaking now, telling her that she was forced to come here because her family and friends thought it would be good for her.

"But that's true," Payvand says brightly. "It really is nice here, don't you think?"

The woman replies, "Oh sure, it's quite nice. No, by 'here' I meant back in the city. Whatever. It doesn't matter. Life just isn't worth living anymore!"

"Oh, I am so sorry to hear that you feel so down. You look so exhausted."

"I'm all right," says the woman. "Well, I'm fine. I'm just tired…. I am … it is … it's too … too much for…. Well, who are you anyway? Go away!" she turns her face, covering it with her hands, mumbling incoherently and crying.

Payvand wants to leave, but it does not seem right. She stands up and asks the woman if she can call someone for her as she does not look well.

"No! Please don't call anyone," the woman says, and as if that opened the floodgates, she starts to talk passionately, a look almost of desperation on her face. She talks non-stop, with a tormented voice and a slight foaming at the corner of her mouth. Her emotions are overwhelming everything she says as she stumbles over the pain and sadness in her heart. Though the woman's English is flawless, the speed at which she is talking makes it difficult to catch what is being said. But Payvand can see that the woman's words are honest and heartfelt in the midst of her misery and sorrow.

Payvand stares and wonders at what she is seeing. She feels fortunate to be here, to have provoked this strange woman, to help her start carving up her grief. She feels it is best not to stop her. Maybe she needs a sympathetic stranger to listen to her, rather than familiar faces who do not heed, and think they know what is best by spouting platitudes like, "It's okay," or "There are situations worse than yours."

Then suddenly the woman stops talking, looks over at her and says, "I'm not making sense, am I?" Payvand smiles and assures her that she is happy to listen and eager to understand as much as possible. Then they sit next to each other in silence, allowing the beauty of the place to soothe their minds and calm their nerves.

Finally, Payvand asks, "You have a beautiful accent. What part of our world were you born in?" The woman looks sidelong at her, and tells her she was born in Croatia, one of six republics in the former Yugoslavia. She briefly relates a few impressions of childhood, and as she gets to her college years and marriage, her words are again tumbling out faster and faster. She mentions a lost child and her emotions get the better of her, and Payvand's heart aches once more to hear the pain and suffering in the woman's voice. Soon the woman falters as she becomes aware that Payvand is staring and intently trying to understand her. The woman stops again and sheepishly concedes, "I am not making sense again, am I? You look confused. I'm sorry." Payvand nods, but tells the woman not to worry and to feel free and comfortable to say whatever she wants to say. "But at the same time, I would really like to understand what you are trying to tell me. I am intrigued, and I want to hear your story."

Then, impulsively, she asks the woman if she has had breakfast. They gaze at one another over a lengthy pause. The woman says she does not remember when she last ate.

Payvand invites her to the cottage to have some hot tea and a chance to start the discussion over again. "I really do want to hear about your life; I want hear it from your true beginning, from when your genuine life began."

The woman contemplates Payvand warily and asks, "What do you mean by starting with my genuine life?"

Payvand explains her belief that each person's real life begins when she becomes aware that she is on a journey and should be giving thought to meaning and values. Sure, we were all born to a family and grew up with our parents and siblings or whoever was around; but when we begin to learn of love, pain, and adventure within our own circumstances, that really is the time when we start to make sense of who we are. That is, when we start to ask questions like, what is our involvement in this world, what are our goals and what are we trying to accomplish within one life, the only one we have? "Start from there. When was it that you thought, this is it, this is what I want, and my life's adventures and goals begin from right here. Who were you then, and what path led you to become who you are now?"

The woman smiles and after a prolonged silence, yields to the plan. "Actually, a tea would be nice, but on one condition only. After we are done talking, you must walk with me right back here, kiss me goodbye, and then please leave me to my own devices."

Payvand smiles and agrees, asking if her family will be picking her up here. "No, no one knows I am here," the woman says. She looks at Payvand suspiciously, but assents to her wishes. She has difficulty getting up and when Payvand rushes to help her, she is shocked at how heavy the woman is.

"How long have you been sitting here?"

"Quite a while now...." Her physique seems small, yet she moves with a peculiar weightiness. Payvand looks at her suspiciously. The woman becomes conscious of that and stops. Then, with a tender smile, she starts to empty her pockets of bulky rocks.

Payvand frowns. "What were you trying to do? Did you want to walk into the ocean with these in your pockets? Were you trying to...? Oh, my!"

There is a long stillness. Then the two of them calmly continue to remove all the rocks that have almost split the seams of the pockets of two layers of jackets. They do not say a word as they finish the task, after which they begin walking to Payvand's cottage.

After a few minutes, the woman stops and firmly states, "I will come back here and you will forget about what you have seen or who you have seen! You promise me, or we part ways right here."

Payvand says, "Look, there it is, my little place. Let's go eat something. Then we will talk about it."

The woman holds Payvand's arm so strongly that it hurts. "No." She again insists that Payvand not call anyone or make a scene over her concerns.

Gently, Payvand takes the woman's hand and places it between her own. "Your life is yours and yours alone, and your choice to carry on or leave it is entirely up to you, I promise. Now, shall we go in?" she asks. Payvand then turns and, without looking back, opens the door and enters the cottage. After a long moment's consideration, the woman finally follows her inside.

Payvand's other half, her love, has tea ready and is surprised to see a second person walking in. But he smiles and greets them both, then follows Payvand into the kitchen where she quickly explains the situation and suggests she should be alone with the woman. He understands, as is his way, and says he will go into town for a few hours.

After the man leaves, the two women sit in silence for a while. Payvand decides not to talk about the rocks in the woman's pockets and what she wanted to do. She understands that the woman had not made her decision lightly as she had been sitting in the same spot for several hours. She even accepted help in emptying her pockets of the heavy rocks. She obviously was in no immediate rush to walk into the water with no hope of return. Maybe she was not that serious.

Payvand decides to begin a general conversation about the former Yugoslavia, and how Tito was able to keep the country unified in relative peace. But the woman is not happy with Tito's policies, and refers to him as a dictator. Payvand doesn't want to argue with her; in a way, she agrees with the lady. However, to keep the conversation going, she admits to his authoritarian style but asks if it was not true that he did lead a fairly successful economy and tried to develop the country for all citizens.

"Somewhat," the woman concedes.

Also, was he not a popular public figure both in Yugoslavia and abroad?

"Sure," the woman admits.

Did his internal policies and strategies not successfully maintain a relatively peaceful coexistence of Yugoslavia's diverse ethnicities?

"In a way," the woman says quietly. She looks at Payvand and seems to relax slightly. "Look, Tito did many things for my country, and indeed was vigorous in advocating for tolerance and respect between those coexisting groups, but he never implemented policies that were effective in actually educating the people toward those goals. If he had, then the population of that country would not have so easily drifted down the slippery slope of recourse to ancient grudges and historical resentments." She pauses for a bit, and then continues. "Tito was born in Croatia; so was I. My family liked him and respected him, but not everyone shared that sentiment. Some hated him, but did not dare express those feelings or share their ideas. People should not have such anxieties or fear about their leaders." She pauses and looks into the distance.

Payvand takes the opportunity to ask for her name.

The woman smiles, "Ragusa. My name is Ragusa."

"Does it have a meaning?"

"As a matter of fact, Ragusa was the old name of Dubrovnik, the city where my family has lived for generations. My parents loved the old Latin name for Dubrovnik, city of poets and artists, so they named me Ragusa."

"How beautiful," Payvand says.

Ragusa asks for her name.

"Payvand, my name is Payvand! And does it have a meaning? Indeed it does, and the story of how I got the name is special to me."

Ragusa smiles, "I am listening."

"Well, my mother gave me that name while I was still inside her. She told me that when she was a couple of weeks away from giving birth, she still did not know what name she wanted for me. One day, she was at a river with her feet in the water. She was rubbing her belly and talking to me, telling me how far she had travelled, and how lonely and frightened she felt at that moment, and how dangerous her last trip had been, and what a beautiful May day it was.

"Apparently, I kicked and moved anytime she spoke. My mother said she held her belly and then talked to me some more.

'Ah, baby of mine, how delightfully you have been connected to me for all these months. What a great honour it has been to carry you for all this time. I don't want to let go of you; you are so much safer in my womb. I love this connection.'

"My mother said she repeated the word 'connection' to herself and liked it but realized that eventually she would have to disconnect and let this little human out. She knew that physical resemblances, genetic inheritance, and emotional attachments will always represent connections to me, so she resolved to name me 'Payvand,' the word for 'connection' in her language, Farsi.

"As she relaxed by that river, anytime my mother sang a soft melody or caressed her belly or repeated my name, I would move or push out with my elbow or foot. To test the effect, she would wait for me to calm down, then, in a different voice, talk to me and tell that she wanted to call me Payvand. Again, I would push and move around. She told me she did that several times, and each time, I kicked and showed signs of excitement. My mother always laughed and talked about my name with joy."

Payvand laughs softly and shakes her head, "Yes, that's how my name was bestowed upon me. Of course, any baby likes to hear their mother's voice no matter what she says, but I like the story nonetheless."

The two women chuckle in amusement, for a moment contemplating the joys of motherhood.

Ragusa's eyes are now shining and she seems energized. Payvand notices how beautiful Ragusa is when she smiles. Payvand is happy that she was able to change Ragusa's mood, and is thrilled that two women, born in two different parts of the world, should meet in yet another part of the world and begin to develop a trust without feeling the barriers that can normally keep cultures apart.

"Come on," Payvand says, "let's get something to eat." As they walk back and forth between the kitchen and the patio, bringing their meal, Payvand continues to comment on her name and how it also refers to "grafting," whereby two plants can grow as one.

They continue to discuss names and their meanings in different cultures, and the sound of cheerful laughter fills the air. Then, abruptly, Ragusa becomes serious and looks intently at Payvand. "Thank you," she says, "for inviting me to your place. You seem to be a very nice person. You are different, and I like your differences. I feel comfortable talking to you and it is relaxing being with someone who doesn't know me and thus doesn't pre-judge, criticize, or advise me. I think I'd like to talk out loud about what is eating me alive inside and try to remember it all one last time. Then I am sure you will understand why I do not want to live anymore...."

CHAPTER 2 **RAGUSA**

PAYVAND LOOKS AT HER with apprehension as Ragusa sits back with a beautiful and proud smile on her lips, and begins her story. "I was born in Dubrovnik in Croatia, one of the most delightful parts of this world. It is a land of poets and writers; a place where such people can thrive and connect with nature and create magnificent stories or poems. I had a happy childhood there with my younger brother, and we were raised by kind, hard-working and loving parents.

"I remember my high-school years were not much fun. I had ugly teeth, though my mother always said that I was beautiful."

"Oh, but you are beautiful!" says Payvand.

"Well, my mother wanted me to do work on my teeth. Later I eventually did. But at the time, I resisted. I said that that I did not care how I looked and that people had to like me for who I was."

Ragusa chuckles, "It sounds so cliché now. But there was no denying my teeth were so bad that when I smiled it did the opposite of enhancing any beauty I might have had. My self-esteem suffered because of it, and I was a natural target for teasing by others.

"One day, a group of boys and girls were making fun of me, and one of them pushed me down. I felt so dejected that I just didn't have the energy to get up. Then something was poured over me, and the indignity began to fire up a will to fight back. But before I could get to my feet, I heard a strong kind voice shouting, 'Enough! Get lost, all of you!' And then a generous hand was offered to help me up. It was Dragomir, one of the most popular students in the school, especially amongst the girls. I was taken aback and a bit embarrassed that he was helping me, defending me, and showing concern for me.

"He walked with me to the girls' washroom where I went in and cleaned myself up. I don't remember what was on me or how I cleaned it off; all I cared was that Dragomir was there, helping me. I even held his hand, which was the dream of any girl in our school. I rushed out of the washroom, thinking he was probably gone, but there he was, waiting for me, asking me if I was okay. Then, he offered to walk home with me, so we did.

"That day, I told my mom that I had decided to get the work done on my teeth."

Payvand interjects, "Dragomir already seemed to like you and didn't seem to care about your teeth, so why did you do it?"

"Well, it hadn't mattered before because I never thought it would make any difference. But I now feared that other girls would keep pointing out my teeth to Dragomir, and that mortified me. So I did it!" Ragusa replies.

They both laugh again, and joke about how superficial they were when they were young.

"We struck up a friendship. But it's important to note that Dragomir was a Serbian, and I was a Croatian. Even though it was during Tito's era, most people were not happy about mixed relationships. I knew my family wouldn't be tough on us, but I didn't know about his.

"From then on, all through high school, we were never apart. We studied side by side, hung out, and went to parties. We were together practically all the time, inside school and out. I had my own set of friends as well, but I soon realized that Dragomir did not seem to have that many male friends. He did well in school and had a very sociable attitude and good manners, but he didn't seem to have even one close friend. As we became closer, he talked more about his personal life. He told me how some students were bothering him because he was not local, or better to say, he was a Serb. He said they would call him names and shun him at every opportunity."

Ragusa pauses and looks sadly off into the distance. Then she looks at Payvand, smiles, and continues. "He was two years ahead of me, which made him a good tutor for me. By the end of high school, my teeth were rearranged and I looked rather good. The boys started to notice me, but I didn't care; I knew Dragomir was the one.

"There was another young man called Josef who never could understand that no meant no. He was frequently after me, showing interest and asking me out. I constantly rebuffed him and assured him that I was with Dragomir, which of course made him angry, rude, and violent. I always ignored him and walked away, but one day he cornered me and insisted that I had to stay away from Dragomir. He said that a Serbian man was not for me. As a Croatian woman, he said, I must date a Croatian man and other such nonsense. I pushed him away, shouted at him, and ran. He followed me looking vicious and spiteful. I was frightened and ran away as fast as I could until I couldn't see him anymore. I never mentioned any of these incidents to Dragomir as I did not want to worry him, or be the cause of any conflict between them.

"We eventually introduced each other to our families. Mine liked him, and his family liked me, but no one took us very seriously. Neither family knew much about what we were doing and how affectionate and passionate we were for one another. To them, it was just teenage fun and it would soon be over.

"Dragomir graduated a couple of years earlier than me, went to a local college, and worked part-time. When I too graduated, we moved to Sarajevo where we went to university."

"Oh, you went to the University of Sarajevo. I have heard good things about it," Payvand says.

"Yes," Ragusa says with a deep smile. "I really miss those

days. You see, Sarajevo was socially and politically a vibrant cultural centre, and much more ethnically diverse than other major cities in Yugoslavia. We were attracted to its rich history and its cultural, political, educational, entertainment, scientific, and artistic variety. Being from two different ethnic groups ourselves, the choice of Sarajevo was natural. Moreover, it was a beautiful city in the middle of the Dinaric Alps, with the marvelous Miljacka River running right through its heart. So we moved there, and I have many beautiful memories of our time in Sarajevo. Dragomir found a good part-time job and helped set me up with some part-time employment of my own where he was working. Our families were sending money occasionally, so we were doing well. In a rather bold move, and without letting our parents know, we moved in together and found ourselves a small, cozy apartment near the university. We studied and worked and enjoyed life among our circle of friends, who were from almost every cultural group in our country."

Ragusa takes a breath and smiles grimly, "At that time, I never focused much on the ethnic differences in that circle; we were just friends who respected one another. I didn't think that could change.

"I was in my senior year in 1980 when Tito departed from this life. Of course, it was a profound shock to all of us. We took a trip to Belgrade and went to watch as they brought his body through the city. A huge crowd followed it and chanted that they would continue to follow his path. Looking at that crowd, I had an uneasy feeling and wondered if this hopeful sentiment was possible or if this was a turning point and the start of some sort of political change in the country. Well, it soon became obvious that his death was only a transition to another authoritarian regime and the beginning of a long-feared era of disorder.

"Within a year, an economic crisis started as it did in many other countries in Eastern Europe. It was in 1981 that Albanian nationalists demonstrated in Kosovo, renewing long-simmering demands for the status of a republic. Soon, separatist rumblings were heard in every part of Yugoslavia. For instance, Albanians protested in 1981 for the autonomy of Kosovo province, a move suppressed by Serbian authorities. From every corner of the country, flare-ups of ethnic tensions were bursting from smouldering ashes. They were suppressed and condemned by the Yugoslavian government of the day, but these events turned out to be precursors to a countrywide blaze of turmoil."

"Such a chaos it was," Payvand observes. "I suppose that means the previous era of Tito's 'brotherhood and unity' must have been secured by quelling such conflicts. I imagine anyone talking separatism must have felt the heat. There were political prisoners, right? I remember hearing about his suppression of ethnic pressures and how easily he used military or police powers anytime he needed to keep things stable."

Ragusa nodded. "Yes that's true, after all he was a military man, and for thirty-five years in his capacities as Premier and President, that indeed was how Tito maintained his peace."

Payvand shakes her head. "Ah, it's so frustrating to hear how time and again dictators around the world act that way. They just can't see any way to build on the natural yearning of people to live in peace. Imagine using those kinds of desires as a springboard into directing ethnic groups toward cooperative habits of respectful coexistence, instead of just hammering people into submission and ignoring simmering hatreds."

With the fervour of one passionate for a better world, Payvand foresees where Ragusa's story is going and decries war's destructive effects, not only on infrastructure or on the air and water, but also on the human spirit as people lose livelihoods and loved ones. "Look at your Yugoslavian region. It certainly seems more fractured and weaker now than when the six republics were united. I mean, what were the underlying reasons for war in your country? Was it just nationalism or was there some sort of struggle for resources or profits?" Payvand rises from the table and moves about, her hands busy with emphasis as she talks despondently about the world's aggressions. "Ah, what does it matter?" she adds. "Will the people of this planet ever realize that war, no matter how it begins, can only bring tragedy and disaster?"

Ragusa gets up and holds Payvand tightly, whispering, "Such a great passion you have. It is as if you are voicing my thoughts. I couldn't agree more." Then Ragusa lets go and walks to the window to look outside. She turns around and sits on the window ledge, looking appreciatively at Payvand. "You know the history: after Tito died things went steadily downhill and eventually fell apart into open conflict. Things went from tolerable to bad to worse, and sometimes I think if the people of Yugoslavia had turned the guns on the ones who were arming them, we would have had a much better result. I don't know what to think.... Yes, I suppose people's ignorance does allow tyrants to rule," she says.

Payvand wrings her hands and says, apprehensively, "You see, I am worried to death thinking about Iran's situation as I can smell a similar war being prepared there. It will proceed the same way as with the Yugoslavia you knew. We also have many different ethnic groups: Pars or Fars, Azeris, Kurds, Arabs and some others. Ethnic passions can run as high and hot there as anywhere else on the planet."

Payvand continues. "I once heard a woman who considered herself an Iranian Azeri nationalist, declare that 'Iran belongs to Iranian Azeris, and they own Iran from Khuzestan to Azerbaijan.'" She smiles. "The joke is that Khuzestan is where the oil is, and each region loves to claim that they own Iran from Khuzestan to their state!"

The two women look at each other with bemusement and Ragusa shakes her head before continuing with her story. "So, by 1986, after three years in Sarajevo, Dragomir had completed his economics degree and already had a good job, and I had graduated as a radiologist and soon had stable employment as well. However, things were changing fast and people were not as well behaved as before. Occasionally, some people would give us a hard time about our informal relationship, so we made the decision to go to Plitvice Lake and get married."

"Why at Plitvice Lake?" Payvand asks. "Why not in Sarajevo where you were living?"

Ragusa frowns. "We just were not comfortable there anymore. Granted, as I said before, Sarajevo was one of the better cities in Yugoslavia for ethnic diversity, as was reflected in our own relationship. However from 1983 to 1986, more and more nationalistic rumblings were heard, with strident speeches and slogans about who owned what in Yugoslavia and who was better than whom. With tensions in the air and heated discussions on every corner, we did not want to start our marriage in such an environment.

"Plitvice Lake is a National Park and one of the most beautiful places in this world. It was recognized in 1979 as a World Heritage site." Ragusa smiles with the memory. "It is a magnificent place where many people loved to go on May 25th, the national Day of Youth, to get married. We didn't actually go on that particular day, but we decided to tie the knot in the Plitvice Lake area in June of 1986. Our friends were worried that with the situation becoming worse than ever, we were a bit crazy to be doing this, but we were determined.

"So, in spite of the cautionary advice from our friends, on June 10th, we stood near a particularly attractive collection of waterfalls beside one of the most astonishing lakes in the world and exchanged our vows. We then travelled in the area, visiting the large number of lakes and forests in that beautiful natural monument. It was our honeymoon, and we took an absolutely mesmerizing drive along the coast of the Adriatic Sea and had our most beautiful experiences together." Ragusa sighs and whispers, "I miss it so much."

Payvand seizes the moment and softly says, "Something to live for? I would love to visit such a collection of amazing waterfalls and lakes. You can show me that magnificent place of yours." Payvand smiles as innocently as she can, but Ragusa eyes her with such a long and penetrating gaze that Payvand shrinks sheepishly in her chair.

After a while, with a sly grin on her face, Ragusa continues her tale. "After getting married, we decided to go home to Dubrovnik and tell our parents, and then have a ceremony with them. That way they would know it was done; that we were a married couple, and they would have to accept us.

"I am glad to say that both our parents accepted our marriage with joy, though they were quite worried. They had actually recently learned about it, having heard rumors from friends and family. They had come to understand how committed we were to one another and were happy for us.

"Both families suggested we should stay in Sarajevo, as they thought it would be safer there. My parents told me that Dragomir's family were being bothered by people and that they were thinking of moving to Belgrade. But they never did as they still felt strongly that Dubrovnik was their home. 'It is a sad situation,' my father said. 'But, enough gloomy thoughts for now. We have a wedding to plan!' And with a big smile on his face, he went out to see Dragomir's father to work things out.

"My mother and I forgot our worries for a while as we started making plans about food, guests, my dress and other details. But then reality set in as my mother choked and said, 'Oh dear, how we are going to invite the guests? Our family may object to Dragomir's family and his family may have issues with ours.' Mother began to sob and held me tight, and said, 'Oh my child, what troubles await you?' I kissed her and held her tight. I too was frightened. As she held me, she said, 'And you know what makes it hard for me? He is such a fine young man, and I really like him.' There was such honesty in my mother's voice and such sadness in her eyes.

"Across the country animosity and hostility were rising among the people. The situation was becoming more chaotic and hopeless, with conflicts and tensions increasing between ethnic groups. Nationalism and independence seemed top-of-mind for everyone though the largest group, Serbians, aspired to maintain Yugoslavian unity. Everyone was right, and everyone knew the truth. Everyone argued and fought for what they believed. Of course, the saddest part was that no one listened anymore. People just shouted at one another.

"We soon found a nice place for our ceremony. I bought a beautiful yet simple dress, and Dragomir looked absolutely stunning in his suit; even more handsome than usual. Our immediate family was there, but from our large extended family only about fifteen guests showed up. The rest took issue and boycotted our wedding. Well, their loss, we thought. It was a wonderful ceremony and those that came all had a great time. We stayed a week or so with our family, then we went back to Sarajevo to our work and our married life."

Ragusa has a sip of her tea and stares at a distant point for a few minutes. She does that from time to time, and Payvand resists saying anything at those moments, not wanting to disturb her as she plumbs the depths of her memories. Payvand watches her and ponders her emotions and her motives for wanting to kill herself. Ragusa's story has not given her a good reason so far, though Payvand can guess that this sad face is hiding much more than she has heard thus far.

After a few minutes, Ragusa resumes her narrative. "We had been away from Sarajevo for only a month or so, but it felt as though a year had passed when we saw the scale with which tensions had grown. In this corner we were hearing speeches about 'expelling all Croats, Albanians and other foreign elements from holy Serb ground.' In that corner, we were being informed that 'Croatia should be for Croatians,' and suddenly Serbs there were being pressured to leave. In every corner of Bosnia, Serbs and Croats and Bosniaks were drawing lines on the map to see who should have what. This was all quite frightening stuff and everyone was rapidly losing the habit of thinking in terms of a unified Yugoslavia. In Belgrade, Zagreb and other cities, nationalist sentiment was growing daily and additional police forces were everywhere trying to contain problems.

"Meanwhile, we endeavoured to move on with our own lives in the hopes that all this nonsense would soon resolve itself into a return to some sort of stable political settlement. In 1988, we had our first child, and we called her Danica, our morning star. She was such a joy."

Payvand jumps in. "Oh, my daughter was also born in 1988."

"Oh, what a coincidence! How she is doing now?"

"Very well, thank you. She is happy and busy with school and work."

Ragusa smiles, but it seems to come from a heavy heart. She pauses as if to regain strength and then continues. "By 1990, uprising, war and dissolution was thick in the air and ethnic tensions were everywhere now. People became hostile to one another; people who had been living and working together side by side and socializing for years. I would ask myself where they had kept all this anger and animosity? Had all the years of smiles and friendliness been an intentional mask, hiding internal resentments and hatreds that were just biding time for an opportunity to burst forth? We had a wonderful circle of friends: Serbians, Croatians, Bosnians, Slovenians, and others. Our dearest one was Nicolae, a photographer born and raised in Moldova, and who had travelled widely. We were a mature, trustworthy, and reliable group; all friends and colleagues since university.

"Nonetheless, our weekend gatherings were no longer so fun. We seemed to be arguing all the time, taking sides, and having antagonistic discussions. Soon we found ourselves trying to stay away from each other. We still maintained relations with one Serbian couple, as well as two Croatian couples; people we had known since childhood. We also stayed close to our dear Moldovan friend, Nicolae. The rest either drifted away back to where they were born or migrated as skilled workers to Western countries.

"Our families were encouraging us to emigrate as well, believing that it would be safer for our little family to leave while we could. We disagreed. We did not want to leave the country where we had been born and raised and where memories of friends and families were still fresh and strong. It was the only home we knew, and we had worked so hard for the successful careers that we were building. We didn't want to abandon all of that. We felt that we belonged here, and it didn't seem wise to have to start all over again somewhere else.

"Our family agreed with our arguments, but their unhappy faces showed that they were worried about us. Indeed, it was around this time that Slobodan Milosevic emerged as a strong political figure, and he quickly rose to power in Serbian circles, becoming popular among Serbian nationalists. Similarly, Franjo Tudjman in Croatia and Alija Izetbegovic in Bosnia became leaders within their ethnic homelands as separatist sentiments hardened and flourished on all sides. My father said that things had changed, that people had taken sides, that the country was getting ready to tear itself apart, and that it was going to be difficult for a mixed couple to deal with demands for loyalty from radicals with guns."

Payvand leans back in her chair and says, "Ah, your father was right! Yugoslavia broke apart not only into two, but several countries. What a tragedy!"

"That's very true," says Ragusa. "Everywhere, people felt less and less like their country was the safe, beautiful place we used to know. Tensions among ethnic groups were everywhere. In the end we couldn't ignore the threat to our safety and our child's future and we did decide to leave Sarajevo and go back home to our families. Both of us were professionals and were sure we could find jobs in Dubrovnik.

"We weren't the only ones in a Serb and Croat mixed marriage. Other people in our extended family had to make difficult decisions too. One of my first cousins had recently married Dragomir's sister, and they had quickly moved to Canada. My brother and his wife did too.

"People more and more had to determine who they could or could not trust. Soon, armed resistance groups were being organized, which caused conflicts between the police and residents. Sometimes even the police provoked localized armed conflicts as happened in Slovenia and Bosnia. In short order anarchy was rife in many parts of Yugoslavia, which soon played host to one of the most brutal wars of our time, destroying many lives and causing the largest refugee crisis in the area since World War Two. The conflict caused mass migration of terrified people all across the country; people who did not want to fight and just wanted to go where they thought it might be safer. We were part of this unwilling displacement. We had thought that because Dragomir was Serb, we might be better off moving to Belgrade. But we realized that wasn't realistic as Dragomir's previous protections were no use to me now with the rising tides of intolerance and jingoism directed at anyone not displaying strict cultural allegiances. And mixed marriages such as ours certainly topped that ludicrous list of taboos.

"Allegiance to Yugoslav unity seemed to evaporate, and the bonds of schoolyard friendships, college camaraderie, and colleagues in the workplace appeared to lose all meaning as the heat of sectarian rhetoric filled the air. Dragomir and I were pacifists who did not believe in killing. With people thirsty for each other's blood and looking for weapons, we decided it was time to leave Sarajevo. But we had left the decision too late as sporadic shooting had already begun by the summer of 1991. The killing machine was up and running. Nowhere was safe anymore."

Ragusa is quiet again, this time for a longer stretch. Payvand makes her a little sandwich and gives it to her. Ragusa sips her tea and takes the sandwich, but she moves mechanically, almost unaware of her surroundings. Her face seems empty of expression.

Finally Ragusa shakes her head, as if forcing herself back to the present. "I am sure you have read the history about how, in a few short years, each republic, one after another, declared independence and created a new country. But what is forgotten is who paid the penalty for that autonomy.

"Early on, it was proposed that Yugoslavia be transformed into a loose confederation of six republics. The congress worked to set up multi-party elections and voted for an end to the one-party system. However, with a Serbia, Montenegro, and Kosovo voting alliance guaranteeing political dominance from Belgrade, the Slovenian and Croatian delegations walked out and the 'brotherhood and unity' that Tito had worked all his life to establish began its disintegration.

"With everyone seeking autonomy, nationalist Serbs also claimed their right to self-determination. Milosevic's version of this included either territorial consolidation of all Serb populations or at least strong protective autonomy for Serb minorities, which clashed with the nationalist plans of other republics. For instance, in 1989, almost a year before the Croatian leadership made a move towards independence, attempts were made to form Serbian independent areas within Croatia.

"Demonstrations against Milosevic sprung up, prompting police and military actions to 'restore order,' which led to clashes that killed several people, thus leading to sporadic open conflict between ethnic groups.

"Soon, people on all sides were being attacked or arrested. Nobody knew where people were being taken, and a terrifying chaos ensued. If you read or watched Serbian news, you learned all about how Croats were killing people just like they did in the fascist days of World War Two. There were calls for revenge and the propaganda machinery groomed people for a bloody war. Similarly, you would read and watch the Croatian news to find it exclusively featuring Serb atrocities, including attacks on villages, the raping and killing women, and ethnic cleansing. Bosnian media kept everyone informed about the evils of Croatian and Serbian actions. The news was so provoking that everyone wanted to go to war to defend their people, but all that was really accomplished was to set cultural groups against one another and to melt away decades of authoritarian but sincere efforts to move beyond the passions of old historical insults and outrages.

"I felt so hopeless, constantly asking myself what was happening to us. Just a few years ago we were all working together, building one of the most beautiful countries in Eastern Europe. Where had all this animosity come from? How had we forgotten our unity and strength? Ironically, anyone you talked to would agree with you, but the madness continued as if nobody listened, as if nobody knew what they were doing.

"We resigned from our jobs and planned our return to Dubrovnik, our childhood home. Just a few days before our planned departure, we put our Danica to bed and started to pack. All of a sudden a squad of about ten or fifteen soldiers came to our building, shouting and making noises. They ordered the tenants of two units to leave their apartments for the night because both units gave the soldiers a good view of one of their targets. One of the tenants argued with the officer, saying he had no right to evict him. As we were watching, we could not believe our ears when we heard one of our neighbours shout out, 'You should leave the Serbs alone. Send that one out. She's a Croat. Purge her apartment.' She was pointing at me.

"The officer brushed her off and continued to evict the people in the two units he wanted. Most of the squad piled into the units with their weapons, but one of the soldiers came at me in an offensive manner, trying to touch my hair and mocking Dragomir that he was not man enough to make a Serb woman happy.

"I don't remember everything. But Dragomir pushed him

away, telling him to shut up and be off, and then he drew me inside and closed the door. The solider kicked at the door, cursing at us until his superior officer called him out and ordered him back to their mission.

"I was shaking as Dragomir tried to calm me down. Ten minutes later, just as I was regaining my composure, the same soldier aggressively banged on our door and pushed himself in. He came at Dragomir kicking, swearing, and calling him a traitor. When he landed a punch on Dragomir's face I panicked and couldn't breathe, holding my chest as I gasped for air. Dragomir saw that and ran to me, shaking me and shouting, 'Breathe, breathe,' but the soldier came and grabbed him from behind, and they got into a vicious fight.

"I couldn't follow what was happening but suddenly the soldier fell back and hit his head on a chair. He did not move and started to bleed from his head.

"With a gasp one of our neighbours rushed in from the hallway and ran up to the soldier to take his pulse. 'He's alive,' he said, 'but we have to take him to hospital.' At that point, another soldier ran into the room, demanding to know what had happened here. Our neighbour said he didn't know, but that he had heard the sounds of fighting, and when he came to investigate, he saw the soldier hitting Dragomir and Dragomir pushing him back in self-defense.

"Then, I heard my Danica crying frantically as the shouting and commotion had awoken the poor child. I ran to her room, picked her up, and tried to calm her.

"The injured soldier now regained consciousness, so the other one dragged him to his feet and hustled him out, berating him for lack of discipline.

"We thanked our neighbour, who warned us that the soldier would return to cause trouble, possibly with others. 'There is no law governing our country anymore, and my wife and I are leaving early tomorrow morning. You should leave before they come back.'

"We knew he was right. The soldier had looked like a wounded animal and had mumbled something like, 'We are not done here,' as he was hauled away. We knew we were in danger, so we decided to leave our little home immediately and try to find a safer place for the night. We dressed our terrified little Danica in the middle of the night, packed whatever necessities, documents, and valuables we could fit into two large suitcases, left everything else behind, locked the door and began our journey.

"We called on our dear Moldovan friend, Nicolae, who took us to one of his closest friends on the other side of the city that night. Nicolae explained to his friend what had happened, and they agreed that we should stay with him for a while and that we should leave Sarajevo as soon as possible. We told him that our goal was to join our family in Dubrovnik and perhaps find jobs and start a new life together there. Nicolae got us settled, and the next day went to try and retrieve more belongings from our apartment.

"He returned around noon without anything, and he was very upset. He had not found any of our packed bags, and indeed the entire apartment had been torn apart. Apparently, the soldier who had hit his head went into a coma soon after he left and died early the next morning.

"His superior officer was very angry, and his inquiries soon led him to our building in search of 'Dragomir and his Croat wife.' He wanted to know why his soldier had died at the hands of another Serb. His soldiers broke into our apartment looking for us, and for any evidence that showed how the soldier had died. In their fury, they destroyed or took everything they could.

"Dragomir was devastated. We all tried to convince him that it was an accident and that it was the soldier's fault for invading our home and initiating a violent fight, but he still was so upset. I had never seen him that way before. Of course, he also was worried about me and our child. We had to leave Sarajevo as soon as possible.

"Two days later Nicolae returned with fake documents and food and asked us to get ready as we would be starting on our way that night. So, we made our preparations and waited for night to fall. Guided by Nicolae, we carefully moved from street to street and alley to alley, encountering nothing in a city where nobody dared to come out at night anymore. Danica was agitated as we moved carefully through the darkness, and sometimes she cried, which made our journey even more dangerous. But how could we continue to move once dawn broke when the army might be searching for Dragomir? Not only that, but any number of newly minted nationalists could cause serious trouble to a Croat and Serb couple.

"Nonetheless, when daylight came, we decided to press onward. Gunfire crackled throughout the day as the army of the new order sought out subversives. Our child was crying fitfully, feeding off our anxiety. We had to give her a mild sedative to calm her and keep her from making noises. The second night, Nicolae left us with another one of his friends, a very kind man and his wife, both from Kosovo. I was worried as we were still near Sarajevo and I didn't feel safe. We were to stay with the couple for a few days while Nicolae went to prepare our next move away from Sarajevo and toward Dubrovnik.

"He came back as he promised and announced that he would be coming with us. He had secured a car, and that night we drove slowly with no headlights, carefully making our way along moonlit roads. We drove the whole night and the next day travelling through the Bosnian countryside, but we didn't feel any safer for having left Sarajevo. We passed many small towns and villages along our way, and I still have nightmares from the scenes of violence I witnessed along the way. People did not know who to trust and found themselves seeking the company of their own cultural groups for protection, which only reinforced the segregation of communities from one another. Fear and panic would lead to fights and battles, and sadly, every village had a tale to tell of intolerances leading to horrific consequences.

"Passing through one village, we saw an agitated cluster of people, so we approached to see what was going on. There was a young girl, perhaps twelve or thirteen years old, sitting against a wall and screaming frantically. If anyone tried to get close to her, she would attack them or start to hit her head against the wall. There was a pool of blood under her feet.

"I looked around at the people who were there and asked what had happened to her. People said four or five soldiers took her behind that wall, and she had been like that ever since. Then one woman said, 'She is not one of us; she is Bosnian.'"

Ragusa takes a deep breath and snarls, "I wanted to slap that woman for her ignorance. I spat at her and shouted that the girl is a child whose mother was surely desperately looking for her. The woman said nobody was looking for her as the soldiers had killed her whole family before turning their attention to her. The tone of cruelty and nastiness in that woman's voice convinced me that she couldn't be a mother and still have so little sympathy for that child.

"Dragomir shouted, 'Shame on all of you. You watched all that happen and did nothing?' Just then the land beneath us began to shake, which meant army tanks were coming, so everyone scattered to a safe place. The girl seemed to be staring at me as she leaned quietly against the wall, and I wanted to go get her, but then her lifeless body slid down and rested in her own blood. I became frantic with rage and despair, but Dragomir grabbed me and pulled me to safety."

Ragusa stops talking and stares at Payvand's frozen pale face. After a short pause she whispers, "You know, I was actually happy that the child was gone. The sound coming out of that throat, her screams of anguish, were just too much. She could never have had a normal life again, and the experience of that day would ruin her for as long as she lived. Her death was a cruel relief. After all, she had no one left in this world to hold her and ease her pain."

Ragusa gets up and walks around a bit, then looks at Payvand, who has tears in her eyes and is shaking slightly. Ragusa goes over to sit beside her, and they hold each other tight. "You should understand why some need to go," Ragusa says.

She then lets go of Payvand, and paces the room anxiously, before she finally sits on the floor and leans against a wall. It is well into the afternoon.

Payvand goes to the bathroom and washes her face. She goes into the kitchen for a glass of water and sees that her love has come in by the back door. He holds her tenderly and asks if she is okay. Payvand whispers, "Oh, Brian, did you hear what Ragusa said?"

He tells her he overheard the last part about her journey out of Sarajevo. "What a brutal experience," he says. "Do you want me to leave?"

She thinks about that, but then assures him he should stay. "Just don't let her see you." He goes to sit by the garden window, and through the slightly open door, sees their guest slump in despair.

Payvand returns to the living room and sits quietly beside Ragusa on the floor and waits in silence until she continues.

"In Mostar, we stayed in a hotel only for a day as the war was spreading everywhere. The Bosnian population was splintering and factional fighting was erupting all over that region."

Again Ragusa paused, staring off into a corner with indescribable misery. "I still cannot comprehend any of it. The people of one country all of a sudden becoming each other's worst enemy. We were travelling through districts in Yugoslavia, but at that time, it was as if we were going into different, hostile countries.

"From Sarajevo to Mostar we witnessed the atrocity, brutality, and inhumanity of human beings, which has kept my soul in turmoil ever since. I often have nightmares and wake up sweaty and shaking. I feel as if nothing looks beautiful or vibrant anymore. If people can so shamefully and hideously destroy and torment, then I have trust neither in humanity nor in the human spirit."

Once more Ragusa pauses to recover, then continues. "From Mostar, we travelled cautiously through several other small towns on our way to Dubrovnik. We stayed in Zaton for a few days, sending someone to Dubrovnik to see if we would be safe there, and to let our family know that we were coming.

"The messenger returned saying nobody in Dubrovnik knew what had happened in Sarajevo with the soldier, so he had not said anything about the event to our families. The next day, we completed our trip home. It felt so safe with our parents and all our relatives around us. It seemed like a different universe to be with two families, one Serb one Croat, treating each other with respect. They were so happy that they had their children and their grandchild home with them."

"We rested for a couple of days and then started to look at our options. We talked about going to Italy. From Pescara on Italy's east coast we knew our way, and we had friends in Rome. My father said that we were more than welcome to stay with him for now. This was nice as I needed my mother's help with updating our passports, and seeing what other paperwork we might need for leaving the country.

"It was wonderful to be home, and our daughter was happy, playful, and healthy, as any child should be. We felt more secure and comfortable though we were still worried about the events in Sarajevo. We wondered constantly whether the army was still looking for us or whether perhaps the war was keeping them busy enough that they had no time to investigate the death of one soldier."

Ragusa sits back and asks for more water. Payvand rushes into the kitchen where she sees Brian sitting patiently. He looks at her warmly, assuring her as always that he is right there for her. Payvand feels a bit better seeing him there, and she hurries back out into the living room with the water only to find her guest crying again.

Payvand takes her hand and gets her comfortable on the sofa where Ragusa sips at her water and struggles to recover herself. "It was near the end of September, and I was on my way home when I ran into Josef on the street."

Payvand says, "Refresh my memory; who was he?"

"Ah well, he was that old class mate who kept asking me out and who hated Dragomir. He seemed to know all about me as he ran up and angrily lectured me on what my husband and his people were doing to our country, how they were massacring women and children. I won't mention the colourful language he used, but the gist was that I was a traitor who didn't deserve to live in Dubrovnik. I knew it was useless to argue with him, so I just walked away and went home. I immediately told Dragomir about the incident and said that we were delaying things too long and that we had to leave. He agreed, and we decided to prepare for our trip as soon as possible.

"We put our little girl to bed and talked far into the night, analyzing our options. Our beautiful little daughter was a healthy, talkative three-year-old who seemed happy to be in Dubrovnik with her loving grandparents. However, by then, we knew we could not comfortably live among Serbs or Croats. Although our city seemed better than others, as our trip across the country had shown us, people could boil into intolerance with very little notice. Furthermore, both Serbs and Croats seemed antagonistic towards us in particular, despite the fact that we were obviously happy together. Unfortunately, it seemed that it was *because* we were happy that we attracted the small-minded bigotry that was so thick in the air those days.

"Accordingly, we talked more and more about leaving the country, and we worked out what our best route to Rome would be. It was the most distressing decision of our lives, but we both were jobless and so we didn't have that much to lose. Time might be running out if the army was getting closer to capturing us for the death of the soldier in Sarajevo. We decided that going to Italy directly across the Adriatic Sea was the most feasible option.

"We went to bed that night feeling a bit more optimistic, especially because we loved Italy. We hoped to stay there for some time and wait out the events in our country. We told stories, talked about our happy memories, and kissed intensely as we realized we hadn't been together for so long. With the hectic and frantic turbulence of the previous weeks, we hadn't had time for each other anymore. He kissed me head to toe, and we made passionate love, reminding one another of our shared affection. Then we slept in each other arms, relaxed and with a great hope for the future."

Ragusa's tears stream down her face. She is sobbing so hard that it worries Payvand, who moves closer to her and wraps one arm around her tenderly. Payvand asks her what happened that she is crying like this. "Talk to me." Ragusa's face is like a death mask again, and Payvand runs to the kitchen for some more water. Brian is there and he looks at her anxiously, but says nothing. Payvand hurries back in and they sit quietly for some time. Then Payvand says, "If it is bothering you too much, let's not talk about it anymore."

Ragusa looks at her with a long and piercing gaze, then shakes off her grim mood and softly says, "Hey stranger, you asked me to tell you who I was then and who I am now. I want to remember one last time, and you must forgive me for the apprehensions and anxiety I fall into occasionally."

Payvand smiles. "Sorry. I just don't want you to be this upset."

Ragusa holds her hand and continues, with a deep grief in her eyes and a faint smile. "We woke up happy, still in each other's arms. Exhausted as we were from our constant worries, we had slept well. We got up and quickly prepared for our next move.

"Nicolae was still in town, and he felt that we could not leave legally as the authorities may have become aware of the search for Dragomir. So our only option was to stay under the radar and travel illegally, which we weren't happy about. Nicolae took us to the harbour district and introduced us to a fisherman with whom we arranged passage to Pescara. He asked for a lot of money, but there seemed to be no other choice.

"As we all left the harbour, we saw Josef going by. He glared at me so viciously that he really scared me. Dragomir saw that and moved in to challenge him, but before anything was said, Nicolae and the fisherman both jumped in and pushed Dragomir and Josef apart. The fisherman did not want to draw any attention to his operation, so he and Nicolae kept Josef busy while we walked quickly away and out of sight.

"We went home and told our families about our plan. They were glad that we were getting away to safety but sad that they were losing us. We all gathered at the home of Dragomir's parents and had our last dinner together. We had a wonderful time with everyone, and went to bed with optimism in our hearts.

"The next day our plans drastically changed. That was the day the army chose to come out of the hills and attack the city.

"Dubrovnik is one of the oldest and most beautiful towns in the region; a tourist city nestled on the coast of the Adriatic Sea. It hadn't experienced the same turmoil that the rest of Yugoslavia was going through then. The city was about eighty percent Croatian and not particularly prone to ethnic animosity; however, as troubles developed around Yugoslavia, tensions inevitably rose in Dubrovnik as well. Over the course of the summer of 1991, rancour grew between the Serb and Croat communities as the Serbian army moved closer to the region.

"Then, on the very October day in 1991 when we had planned to make our escape to Italy, we were attacked from land and sea.

"We woke to the all too familiar sounds of shooting, shelling, and the screams of a terrified population. We all ran to my father's cellar where he kept his wine and other valuables. The ground shook and we cursed and cried as our beautiful, peaceful city was visited with the same spectacle of senseless violence as the rest of the country."

Ragusa sighs. "As always, you wonder why a species so intelligent couldn't just sit and negotiate a settlement between all these resurgent political aspirations. Why couldn't we prevent bloodshed and work out some form of stable regional agreement? Who was stoking the hatreds and aggressions? Who was bringing in weapons? Who was selling them? Who was profiting? As night followed day, the aggressions of one army just meant the creation of another to challenge it. Sure, everyone talked about the need to protect the vital national interests of the newly forming Republic of Croatia and to defend its sovereignty and territorial integrity. But in the end, it was just another crowd of men with guns keeping the misery in motion.

"By noon, during a lull in the shelling, my father and Dragomir carefully hurried over to Dragomir's parents' home and brought them to our house as theirs did not have a basement or cellar for protection. They reported what they saw: disorder and confusion in an unarmed city with no preparation, training, or protection. The hospital was getting full as the number of injured people increased. Volunteers soon appeared from all over the city to help, bringing whatever supplies they could.

"Our own plans had to wait as the army was attacking from land and sea. I was so fearful that they would come and ask my love to take sides, to join the army, and help kill me and my family. Dragomir was distressed, and he did not want to leave the home at all, thinking that the army would arrive any day and take over the town. For the time being, they only seemed capable of firing artillery shells from the surrounding hills. As the days went by, people feared that grand, historic Dubrovnik would become yet another ruin in war-torn Yugoslavia. Though only a few buildings were completely destroyed, more than two-thirds of all buildings in the Old Town, by the end of the siege, suffered some artillery damage.

"Eager to defend our home should the army enter the city, our fathers diligently sought weapons. On the fourth day, the two older men went out on their search, and in due course returned with a few rifles. My father said he had heard that trucks full of new weapons were being distributed to people. We wondered where they came from and who was selling them.

"My cousin said that it didn't matter because we just needed them. But my father and I both feared that maybe the ones selling the guns were largely responsible for inflaming this war. The other important point I saw was that our people, Yugoslavs, were avidly buying them and using them against one another. However, if people chose to not play into these merchants' hands, there would be no customers for them. As a result, an opportunity might be available for a critical mass of responsible citizens to take control of the dissolution of old Yugoslavia. If this happened, we could work to forge a reasoned and thoughtful transition to whatever could be peacefully negotiated: a loose federation or a collection of newly minted nations.

"As if to give voice to the narrow sectarianism that was causing all the current misery, my cousin indignantly swore at the Serbs for starting the war. I held him tightly and said, 'No, no, we all did this; it was not just the Serbs but everyone in Yugoslavia. We should not play into the hands of the war mongers.' My cousin was morose, 'I just don't understand what is happening.' My Dragomir went to my cousin, put his hand on his shoulder, and said, 'Young man, you are not the only one. It appears they have already succeeded because every corner of Yugoslavia is now demanding independence. Perhaps we should ask ourselves if it was because our Yugoslavia did not cater to the needs of the "world order" and arrangements for a weaker and divided region had to be made.?'"

Payvand nods in agreement. "There are studies that show that the conflict was supported by a massive and complex pattern of weapons shipments to the region, funded and organized by

German corporate interests. Furthermore, there is evidence that Austria and perhaps even some other NATO allies were involved with selling arms, which clearly violated international embargo protocols against the supply of weapons into conflict zones."

Ragusa sighs and says, "I will always dream of the day that people learn to be the owners of their own destinies and refuse to be fooled or used by those attempting to manipulate them for crass personal gain. Look what happened to our Yugoslavia. Sure it never was perfect, but it was certainly more stable and successful than it is today. We now have six diminished republics, each proudly trumpeting its glorious new independence. Together, they could be a much stronger regional entity than they are now separately, and I hope they are beginning to realize that."

Payvand nods. "A big problem is that not many of us pay attention to what is going on in our world, so we don't seem to learn anything from past mistakes. Look at Syria, where the army and an opposition, each claiming to be loyal to Syria, Islam, and anything else that sounds good, are grimly killing one another. They each assert to be the legitimate voice of Syrians, and so they each feel authorized to massacre the other for political power. Do they know the history of their region? What about the Egyptian revolution? Did it achieve anything but a change in the board of directors? To start, how did the al-Assad family in Syria come to power? Just like our Shah, how did they attain leadership of the country and inherit power? Why have the Palestinians and Israel been fighting for so long? Who is fueling these conflicts and what do they gain from them? If the people of Syria knew their own history, they would know that whichever side wins, they will lose. They will once again end up with a country controlled by geopolitical interests that ensure regions of any importance are under careful management. Perhaps these interests are in some way pleased with the added bonus of eliminating some of the seven billion people in this overcrowded world." Payvand crosses her arms as if to hold herself back. She knows this is Ragusa's time to talk and that in-depth discussions can come later.

Ragusa smiles and says, "Your words resonate so well with my heart! I like you more as time passes."

Payvand encourages her to continue with her story. "Let's share our opinions after you are finished."

Ragusa continues, "Well, a little later, Dragomir's father appeared with a few more guns, and we asked him how he came by them. He smiled and related his adventure of going up the hill to where the army had placed their artillery, where he introduced himself as a local Serb in need of protecting himself and his family in this hostile Croatian town. We laughed at his clever scheme and joked about whether we were safe living under the same roof as a Serb man with so many guns. We certainly knew we had nothing to fear from a father who had raised Dragomir to be such a decent human being.

"The men examined the guns and set about training the women on the most modern ones that were easiest to use. Dragomir's mother chuckled and said, 'Just point and shoot, eh? You better hope we never have to use these.'"

Ragusa's smile is bitter. "There we were. As much as we disagreed with the militaristic spirit of the day, there we were, learning how to use guns to defend ourselves. How ironic was that?

"For over a week, our city was bombarded in every corner. But there were no enemy soldiers actually in the town yet, so we would take our chances and move around cautiously. One day, my mother and I went on a volunteer run to the hospital to bring some sheets and other items that my mother had put together. Artillery projectiles occasionally passed over our heads on the way to distant parts of the city.

"Quite suddenly, the bombardment moved much closer and became heavy, noisy, and frightening. We rushed to conceal ourselves behind a wall and squeezed into a doorway. I held my mother. There was a storm of debris, and a flurry of dust and bricks surrounded us. As it cleared, I brushed away the dust that was all over us. I looked up. The sky was cobalt blue and beautifully bright. A stiff breeze helped push away the dust and bring back the aroma of trees and flowers but with it came the smell of blood. I smelled blood? Why did I smell blood? I turned to my mother to ask if she smelled blood too, only to notice that she was pale and shivering. I called her name, and then she looked at me blankly, just like that young girl who had died before my eyes.

"I panicked and screamed for help. With a crash, someone ran up and kicked in the door where we had taken shelter and dragged us into a courtyard. It was Josef. He put his finger to his lips and urged me to keep quiet. He gathered my mother from my arms and sheltered her under a balcony. I ran to her and held her, weeping, howling, and calling her."

Payvand comes closer and puts her arm around Ragusa firmly. Ragusa lays her head on Payvand's shoulder and continues, "I was crying like a baby, sobbing and calling my mother. Josef held me, trying to calm me.

"Darkness began to fall as I continued to sit over my mother's body, crying and talking to her and hopelessly asking her to get up. We were alone in that house where we had taken refuge, but we began to hear shouting and running noises outside. Josef again put his finger to his lips and urged me to keep quiet. We were alarmed that perhaps soldiers had entered the city and were searching for residents. Josef did not look so tough anymore; he was as scared as I was. Who was running? All I was thinking about was what the Serbs soldiers would do to us. I don't remember everything. It was all a blur. Josef held my arm tight and moved us to the corner of the courtyard where we sat quietly. After a few minutes, there was silence. We waited several more excruciating minutes, then he said it would be best to stay here for the night. In the morning, we could better understand what we should do. I angrily got to my feet and disagreed, saying I had to go get my father and husband to help bring my mother's body home. Josef pleaded with me, insisting that soldiers were still outside roaming around. I couldn't hear anything anymore, and I insisted that I would go out when it was dark. I went to my mother and held her in my arms, and Josef brought a sheet and put it over her.

"As I held my mother and caressed her hair, I looked up into the blue-grey twilight. There were some beautiful patterns of puffy, white clouds moving with the wind, drifting freely as if nothing was happening down here. I stared at the sky, a sky that had witnessed so many bloody wars. Then I started to make up stories about the puffy clouds, as I used to do with my mother when I was young, where from time to time my mother would purse her lips and blow at the clouds as if she could make them drift away. As I held her body tight under the shelter of the balcony, I blew at the clouds and begged for the darkness.

"As soon as night spread over that desperate town, I got up to leave. Josef tried to argue that we should stay there for the night, but I insisted on leaving. His demeanour then changed, and he began swearing at my husband and muttering that I shouldn't be with those monsters. Before he could continue with his predictable tirade, I swore at him and yelled out that Dragomir was the kindest and most decent human being I had ever known. I told him to hold his tongue if he had nothing sensible to say, and that he was not worthy to mention his name.

"I guess that did it. He became very angry and cursed rudely. I realized I was trapped there, and I tried to get away, but he lunged at me and knocked me to the ground. Then he pulled me into a room, closed the door and started to hit me while trying to undress me. I fought back and hit him, throwing at him whatever came to my hand. He was losing control, crying out that I shouldn't have married that Serb, that I had to be with him instead, and that Croats should stick together and get rid of all the Serbs in Dubrovnik. I guess all the noise attracted enough attention, and suddenly the door burst open. We both jumped to the back of the room, terrified of who had discovered us. To my great relief, there he was — my love, Dragomir.

"He said one of the neighbours had seen us take shelter in the house. He thanked Josef for helping us, but then wondered why he had heard fighting noises here. I cut him off and angrily scolded him for coming out into this hostile city to look for me; 'Why not my father and my cousin?' Dragomir laughed and said he came out thinking that it might actually be safer for him as a Serb in a city possibly occupied by Serbs. I couldn't bring myself to reproach him further as he was so happy to find me. But he was concerned that my clothes were torn and that Josef was bloody, and he asked what had happened here. I rushed to cut off a conflict between Dragomir and Josef, but then Josef furiously screamed that he was claiming what was his.

"I felt so angry and dishonoured by Josef's insult, that I grabbed the first thing my hand found — to this day, I don't remember what it was — and hit him in the head so hard that blood gushed out like a fountain. 'You worthless ignorant monster, I have had enough of you,' I roared. He moved like a drunken man back and forth and then fell to the ground. Dragomir rushed to him and put his hand on the wound to stop the bleeding. Josef was moaning like a cow. I headed for the door, calling for Dragomir to follow and for the rapist to die.

"Dragomir looked quickly around for something to staunch the blood. He grabbed a discarded sheet and brought it to Josef to bind his wound. He then sprinted after me and kissed my hand saying, 'Why are you upset about that little jerk? You are a strong and powerful girl. He couldn't hurt you, if that is what you are distressed about. Look at him, he is the bloodied one.' He winked at me and told me to go get my mother ready while he went out to see if it was safe to go.

"While he was gone, I wrapped my mother's body more securely and kissed her, promising that I would return for her as soon as possible. When Dragomir came back, I started to break the news to him about my mother's death, but Josef yelled out that my mother had been killed by Serb artillery. Dragomir cried out and ran to her side, threw off the covers, and burst into tears as if his own mother had been killed. We both wept and together held her in a communion of despair. Josef watched us in dismay, urging us to keep quiet or to go, fearful that the whole army might be outside the door in the street.

"Dragomir got up, cleaned his face with his sleeve, then went to Josef to help him up. But Josef refused to budge, turning his back almost like a child. Dragomir shrugged his shoulders and pointed out that he might be safer on army-controlled streets in the company of a Serb man. As Dragomir took my hand and lead me to the door, Josef relented and called out to wait for him.

"Stealthily we moved out of that house, leaving my mother covered in the corner of its courtyard. We feared that the army might already be roaming the streets of the city, so we moved as silently as possible towards our home through the back alleys of a city darkened by lack of electricity. From that area to my home would normally take twenty minutes, but our cautious pace turned the trip into a two-hour expedition. We first went to Josef's home, where Dragomir sent him flying through his door with a solid punch to his arm. 'That's for disrespecting my wife,' Dragomir said, and we left Josef sprawled on the floor as we headed back out into the streets. I remember feeling grimly satisfied at that small measure of revenge for all the times Josef had demeaned me," Ragusa says as Payvand nods her head in sympathy.

"We arrived home exhausted. My father ran towards us and asked about my mother. I did not know what to say, but I guess my pale frantic face said it all, and he went down on his knees and sobbed like a little boy. I held him and whispered what had happened. In a few minutes, he got up, looking fatigued and wretched, and declared that he was going out to retrieve her body. He was afraid the army would take over the city any time now, and they might just bury her anonymously with other found bodies. 'No,' he affirmed, 'I will not wait for tomorrow.' Despite his determination, Dragomir and my father-in-law convinced him to wait for morning light. Since it might be a Serb-controlled town by morning, they would accompany him. 'Let's stick together brother,' Dragomir's father said.

"At dawn, the three of them took the car with a couple of guns and drove off. We all just sat there and stared at that door. It took them less than an hour, but it felt like we sat and stared at that door for ages. Finally, it opened, and my father entered carrying my mother's lifeless body. They said the streets were quiet and they had no problems carrying out their grim task.

"My father washed the blood and grime from his wife's body, and Dragomir's mother dressed her while kissing her and talking to her. After our marriage, the two mothers had become very close. By noon, we were ready, and we buried her in our courtyard as my father wished, so his love would be safe nearby. During this process I took Danica to our neighbour's house because I didn't want her to witness what was happening. However, she felt something was wrong, and every morning after that, as soon as she was up, her first question was 'Where is Nana?' That was the most difficult little phrase for my father to hear.

"After that day, my father went to volunteer and help in any way he could to support his wife's legacy. In only a week, the city had become badly damaged. Artillery and fire damage was everywhere, and reminders of the human cost could be seen in the bloody stains around the city. Every day my father went out on his mission, and every day he returned more gloomy, depressed, and withdrawn.

"Dragomir also went out more and more with me to help with my volunteer work at the hospital. Around noon one day, two volunteers came with food for all the hard-working volunteers. As we ate our sandwiches I told him that my period was late. He seemed puzzled at first, but then both of us smiled and remembered our beautiful night together just a few weeks before. We had always talked of having another child but knew this was definitely not a good time. We went home upset and angry at the imposition this conflict had on our family life. We held our daughter and played with her a bit before putting her to bed."

Ragusa pauses. "I don't really wish to go through more gruesome details of those days. I am just telling you enough so you know who Ragusa was then and who is she now. I don't want you to think I am a weak coward for what I am contemplating now."

Payvand reaches out for her hands, and says, "Never! Not even when I met you and found out what you were trying to do, did I ever judge you." They then hold each other's hands quietly on the sofa, and all the while Brian monitors them anxiously from the kitchen.

After a few minutes, Ragusa starts speaking again, with tears in her eyes and a tremulous voice. "One morning, as we were having breakfast and getting ready to go to the hospital, we heard a violent commotion right outside our home on the street. Dragomir cautiously went to the door to see what was going on. A young Serb boy was being attacked and beaten by a small crowed of young Croats. Dragomir shouted for them to stop and, with my father, ran out to break up the fight and help the boy up. 'He is only a boy,' my father shouted. The mob of youngsters surrounded him, yelling out, 'That boy killed your wife, old man.'

"The boy was bloody and frightened and leapt up shouting, 'No, no, I haven't killed anyone. I am a citizen of this city too. This is not true. My father went up the hill to join the Serb army, and he forced me to go with him. I refused and ran away. I didn't want to help hurt anyone. I was running from my father when you stopped me and attacked me for no reason. I did not, I cannot kill anyone.' He said it all with such a passion and cried so hard that the gathering crowds of onlookers were touched.

"The emotion and anger in his words began to shift the demeanour even of the young Croatians. One of them approached him and tried to clean his dirty clothes. Another one gave him a handkerchief to clean his bloody nose, and I went and held his hand and brought him into our courtyard. A few of the boys came in with him and we all sat around and told stories of what they each had experienced in the past few days. A consensus emerged that we shouldn't let these events turn us into the same monsters that were responsible for all the tragedies we saw around us.

"I think maybe an hour had passed, when all of a sudden our door was kicked open and in rushed some angry armed Serb men accompanied by a few Montenegrins, who we later found out had directed much of the shelling of Dubrovnik. They demanded to see the young man and wanted to know who had touched him or hit him.

"With the help of my father, the boy stood up on his still-wobbly legs. He asked them to be calm, and insisted that there was nothing to worry about. 'I am okay now and we were actually sitting here and having a good conversation.' Dragomir's father sided with the boy and assured everyone that we were all fine and that the boy could stay with us as long as he wanted. One of the intruders, whose wild eyes I will remember as long as I live, pushed him back and said, 'Shame on you, you are a traitor as well. Why haven't you joined us?' Dragomir's father said that he did not believe in war. This enraged the man even further and he shouted, 'You are an old man, and you should remember the forties when these filthy rats massacred our people.' Dragomir's father said, 'Yes I remember it well. A neighbouring Croatian family hid us in their home for months. You see young man, what you and I have each learned from these events is not the same. I do not believe in any kind of war. It does nothing but destroy the human spirit.'

"The man came closer to Dragomir's father, glared at him for a long time, then pushed him down and screamed that he had no time for this nonsense. Dragomir ran to his father to help him up, and the man asked, 'Is this your father? You haven't joined us either?' The man was furious that there were Serbs who didn't share his bloody ideas. He started cursing everyone in the house. Then another member of the gang shouted out that I was a Croat married to Dragomir.

"In terror, I hid behind Dragomir and held his arm as our new nightmare faced Dragomir and shouted, 'Is she a Croat? You are a despicable disgusting man. What is wrong with our women?' His look of fury and shameful words told me that he was callous brute with no moral compass. Before we could move, he had my hair in his hand, and he was dragging me around the courtyard, shouting and cursing us all. I cried out, not because I was in pain, but because I feared for Dragomir who ran towards the man. Two of the thug's companions intercepted him and hit him with their rifle butts. I saw Dragomir fly up against a wall and fall motionless to the ground.

"Our daughter started to scream and run towards me, dropping herself onto me and crying, 'Mommy, Mommy!' I wanted to hold her, but the man holding my hair lifted her little body up and threw her against the same wall where her father was slumped."

Ragusa pauses, breathless. Payvand, with a feral look of smouldering rage, stares at her wanting to say something but is unable to utter a word. Ragusa puts her hands on Payvand's shoulders, and then sighs loudly. "Right before my eyes, my child's skull opened, and she dropped to the ground bleeding. Furiously, I reached around and bit my assailant's hand so hard that I felt the disgusting taste of his blood. He screamed, but then the sound of a gunshot overwhelmed everything, and he plunged to the ground and lay motionless. In absolute silence, everyone looked around to see what had happened.

"It was my father. During the moments of disorder and confusion, he had gone in for our guns. He was holding one, and Dragomir's father was holding another. I don't know who shot the Serb man. I crawled towards my baby and picked up her lifeless body and held her to my chest. Then I crawled to my love. His eyes were closed but he was breathing, though bleeding from his head and left ear. I shook him and begged him to open his eyes. I knew it was bad, but I was desperately relieved that he was alive. I dragged him and pulled him up so that his head was on my lap. And there I sat, rocking my baby. There were shouts and gunshots and a violent blur of commotion....

"I remember that bloody day so vividly. My legs were numb, and my whole world was in my arms and on my lap as I rocked my baby and mumbled nonsense to block out the bedlam. People came and attended to Dragomir, then someone hauled me up and tried to take my daughter, but I screamed and clutched her even tighter. I looked up; it was Dragomir's mother, so I relented. Others lifted Dragomir up and took him inside. My father held me tight, sobbing. I could barely breathe as I looked around to see what had happened.

"There were several men dead, and the floor of our courtyard was stained with blood. The young Croatian men and the Serb boy were cleaning up the mess. My mother-in-law was holding my daughter Danica, and a young man was talking slowly with Dragomir. I ran to them. My love's eyes were open, but he was weak and nauseous. I held him so tight, and he whispered that we had to leave immediately.

"My father-in-law brought a truck and loaded up the bodies. A couple of the young men helped him take the dead men away. The Serb boy was so sad, and apologized to everyone. My father gripped his shoulder and assured him that the incident was not his fault.

"I helped Dragomir get up onto his feet. Holding and leaning on each other, we went to my mother-in-law and took our Danica back. We held her tight and went to wash her."

Payvand's husband tiptoes into the room and brings water for the two dejected women. Ragusa looks up and thanks him with a warm look of gratitude. Her shaky voice breaks the tense silence that had fallen over the room. "My baby's eyes were open and I did not want to close them. I wanted to see that beautiful cobalt blue as long as I could. Dragomir held both of us, and the three of us sat under the shower. The red and then pink water ran down our bodies and over the tiles as we sat there sobbing with our lifeless baby in our arms. We washed her and her glassy eyes seemed to watch us. I don't know how much time passed. Dragomir's mother knocked on the door to say things were ready. We came out wet, dripping with water and blood. My mother-in-law took the baby and wrapped her in a clean sheet and then took her out to the courtyard. I ran out after her and I saw that my father had already opened my mother's grave. He had pulled aside mother's covering and lowered Danica into her arms. Then, he covered them together with another sheet. I threw myself into that small grave on top of them. That is the last thing I remember of that day."

Payvand is shivering. Ragusa looks up, and in the dark, reaches out for Payvand, who takes her hands and with a tremulous voice says, "I am here." Ragusa wipes the tears off Payvand's face with the back of her hand. Payvand cannot find any words to say. How can one endure such a loss? She stares at Ragusa. Then they hold each other and cry softly.

"Please stop," Payvand says. "I cannot watch you suffer like this."

But Ragusa insists that she wants to remember, and to repeat her life story one last time. "When I opened my eyes, I was in a truck lying beside Dragomir. He was looking at me lovingly and with concern in his eyes. As soon as I saw him, I remembered we had lost our child and I wept in his arms.

"After a long drive, the truck stopped. Nicolae came to assist us once more. 'Our saviour is with us again,' I whispered. He smiled and helped us out. We were on a mountain road along with my father and my in-laws, as well as the Serb boy who had no place in that city anymore. He had Serbs and Croatians both to hate him and hunt him. I told him that I was happy to see him. He smiled though his eyes were sad and frightened.

"The area we were travelling through was beautiful, with lung-tingling fresh air. On one side, green forests climbed the mountains as far as the eye could see. The other side offered a panoramic view of the wide Adriatic Sea shimmering in the afternoon sun. 'Where are we?' I cried. 'Why have I never heard of or seen this extraordinary place?'

"Nicolae said, 'People are so busy with their hectic daily lives working to support home and family that they never look around to see what this stunning blue planet has to offers us.' We all silently looked at him; yes, he was right. I then remembered my baby who would never see these beautiful things, and I could hear her lovely giggling laugh. Dragomir came towards me as if he knew what I was thinking; he held my hand and helped me forward as my knees went weak with grief. We rested for an hour to recharge our spirits in those majestic surroundings. I found refuge in my love's arms and together we shared pleasant memories of our child's short life. We then climbed the mountain for the remainder of the daylight hours, and at nightfall we arrived at a small village.

"Nicolae and our guide took us to a small rustic house. Our hosts were a kind couple who made us feel right at home, setting us up comfortably in various corners of the house and a nearby converted shed. We stayed there for a few weeks, working and living all together. I will never forget that area, and I have never seen anything like it since."

For the first time, Payvand sees a smile on Ragusa's face as she says, "I will give you a map for how to get there. I am sure you will love it." Payvand kisses her hands and returns her smile.

Ragusa continues. "Dragomir was not recovering well from his head injury. He had a bad and tenacious headache and was in a foul mood much of the time. I had never experienced such a temper in him before, and it was all because of that excruciating pain. We couldn't help him, so we had little choice but to leave the mountain and return to the city for a doctor. Also, after discussing the overall situation, we all concluded that all our parents should now accompany us to Italy because their friendship would probably put their lives in danger.

"We had no proper news about conditions in Dubrovnik, but Dragomir needed medical attention, and so our journey down from that captivating mountain village began. Once more Nicolae went ahead to scout the conditions, and he reported back that the Dubrovnik medical community was too overwhelmed by the war crisis to be of sufficient help to Dragomir, so he had re-established our plans with the fisherman to sail away as soon as possible to Italy. But this time, it was even more money as, with the Serb boy and our parents, we were now seven people.

"Uneventfully, we came down the mountain and waited for nightfall before entering the city. We then cautiously went to our home and found that the Serb gang had returned and trashed the place. Thankfully, they had not found the gravesite. My father had hidden it well.

"We sat at the grave, holding each other's hands and soothing ourselves, each with our own thoughts. My father quietly wept and whispered to my mother. Dragomir had his head on my shoulder crying softly. I thought how down there in the cold ground, the one who gave birth to me and the one I gave birth to were holding each other and resting together. It felt such a waste. My mother wasn't old enough to die and my daughter hadn't even started her life. Why? I was so angry. I lost them both, and for what? Who was responsible? Then, I heard my father's happy voice, and I looked up at him in surprise."

Ragusa smiles once more and adds, "He was happy that the thugs had not found the savings that he had hidden for getting his daughter and son-in-law to Italy. 'They could not find this one in our cellar either,' he said as he threw a package of even more money to my father-in-law.

"By midnight, we were at the pier where the fisherman was waiting for us. Nicolae had found the Serb boy's mother and she was there too, which was brilliant because we had worried about what we should do with our young charge. Apparently, her husband had left her in order to join the army and all that was left for her was that boy. So, we became eight people and more money was given to the fisherman. We all boarded his vessel and silently sailed in the dark out into the Adriatic Sea, lying down, hidden in the boat's cabin. After a couple of hours, the fisherman started up the engine and said that we were far enough from shore that it was safe to come up.

"Dragomir and I went up on deck. It was dark, but the water was shimmering in the light of the half moon. I had never been at sea in the middle of the night. It felt scary at first. Then I looked up into a sky that was so full of stars that I thought I would weep with the beauty of it. I have looked up at the night sky many times, but I had never seen so many stars as I saw that night. It was truly a profound experience."

Payvand smiles and holds Ragusa's hands. "It is cathartic, isn't it? When I feel hopeless or deeply sad, I love to drive out of the city where the lights cannot dim the stars. There, lying on some high ground, I stare up in admiration of the universe. I sometimes see a shining meteor or two passing through, some small, some big. I ask myself, what would happen to our population if one of them hit today — one as big as the one that wiped out the dinosaurs millions of years ago? Sadly, it seems such threats, and others like global warming or poverty, are not a priority for the world's elites who are too busy scouring every corner of this planet for its resources. They are already billionaires, yet greed has them ever on the hunt for more, even if the price of their greed is human suffering such as yours, or the destruction of the ecosystems we depend on for life."

Ragusa puts Payvand's cold hand to her cheeks and says, "Yes, if we all could direct our passions to the appreciation of beauty such as this, perhaps people would make more compassionate decisions about what is important in this world. I certainly share in your anger."

Payvand smiles grimly and encourages Ragusa to continue. "Well, for a long while we just sat down on the deck, held each other, and stared at the glittering sky quietly without a word, waiting for Danica, our morning star. As dawn approached, we pointed at the brightest stars, wondering which it was. By noon, we had reached the small island of Vela Palagruza, where we anchored off the coast and rested on the boat for the remainder of the day. The next day, we completed our journey to Pescara. From there, we travelled to Rome, and immediately sought medical attention for Dragomir's head injury.

"The doctors found a blood clot in his head and a blockage in one inner ear. They didn't touch the blood clot because it would have required a dangerous operation, but they cleaned out his ear, and he was better for a while. But then the pain returned again for a few days. After that he was all right for about a week, but then the severe headaches returned. He was tormented like this for weeks, and I could do nothing but watch him suffer."

Raugsa gets up and goes to sit on the floor, leaning against the wall by the window. As Payvand joins her, Brian comes in and turns on the light. Payvand is leaning against Ragusa as she listens. Brian brings them some fresh food, and then takes back the tray he had brought them earlier for lunch. He frowns with concern for the two women, for they have not touched their lunch. However, he decides not to intrude on their discussion.

"My belly was showing," says Ragusa, "and a new baby was moving in my body, but not as strongly as Danica had done. I dreamt about her some nights. Some were sweet dreams of playing with her, but at that time, they were mostly nightmares of the day she was murdered. Still today, I dream of her murder, sometimes over and over."

Payvand is lying down with her head on Ragusa's lap. Tears stream down Ragusa's face again as she strokes Payvand's hair.

"By mid-1992, the newly formed Croatian army counterattacked and lifted the siege of Dubrovnik. Around that time, our son Mladen was born in Rome. He was a beautiful boy but underweight and somewhat sickly. The doctor kept him in the hospital for a week, and then we brought him home. He cried a lot and was not as effortless a baby as his sister Danica had been."

Payvand says, "Well, with what you had gone through during the pregnancy, you were lucky that you didn't lose him."

"I wish I did," Ragusa says.

Payvand is so surprised at such an admission that she sits upright to say something, but the look on Ragusa's face changes her mind, and she sits back to listen solemnly.

"My father and Dragomir's parents wanted to return right after the liberation of Dubrovnik, but they encouraged us to either stay in Rome or go to some other Western country, promising to send us money until we got on our feet. However, we were worried about how safe things really were back home, so we convinced them to stay for a few more months to be sure everything was okay. Eventually, they returned to Croatia and we applied for immigration to Canada. Of course, we could have gone back home with our parents, but I couldn't face the thought of going to my father's home, and every day seeing the courtyard where my mother and daughter were lying lifeless.

"It was bad enough for me there in distant Rome with all the horrible memories of those ghastly events: the violated young girl screaming as she died; the deaths of my mother and daughter; all that I had seen on our journey between Sarajevo and our hometown. Of more immediate concern, of course, were Dragomir's worsening headaches that required ongoing specialized medical attention, which could not be had in war-torn Dubrovnik at that time. My sister in-law and my brother, who were already in Canada, helped us with our admission process. Being a Croatian refugee helped, so by early 1993, we were in Canada. We stayed with my brother as he had a big house and a good job, and I was so happy to be with his wife who was a close friend of mine."

Payvand asks where her brother is now. "In the city, and I am living with them again," Ragusa says.

"Ah, he must be worried for you," Payvand says.

"Yes. I left the house two days ago, got on the ferryboat, and came to this island." They look at each other warily. Ragusa pulls out her phone to check that it is off.

"It is better this way," she says.

Her smile is thin as she continues. "When we arrived, we first saw to my love's headaches. Scans showed a large pooling of blood in his head near his right ear. The doctors in Canada called it a subdural hematoma. As the doctors had said in Italy, the operation was considered dangerous, and now the formation was even bigger. The Canadian doctors said they would have to remove it, but there could be complications as the area was sensitive. There was a possibility that he would not survive the procedure, or that there might be incapacitating complications. An operation at the time of the injury would have been much easier, and they asked us why we hadn't done it earlier. We explained the violent and isolating circumstances that had prevented us from accessing immediate adequate health care. They scheduled his operation three months away to give us enough time to think about it.

"I had a job and it was keeping me busy, and I also tried to spend more time with our Mladen. But I was still having nightmares, and Dragomir's headaches were so debilitating. Yet he refused the operation because he was worried about us should he not survive. As time passed, though, the severity of his headaches made it difficult for him to eat or sleep, and impossible to work, so eventually he was convinced to go ahead with the operation. 'I am not helping you anyway,' he said, 'I am only making your life more difficult. If they operate, I either become healthy and work and contribute to our life together or I go and let you move on with your life.' It terrified me every time he talked that way.

"After our decision, we locked ourselves away for a few days just to hold each other and play with our baby. We kissed endlessly and tried to enjoy each other and just luxuriate in our moments together.

"The operation took over six hours, and the doctors said that they had removed everything. Unfortunately, he fell into a coma and never opened his eyes again. I was crestfallen, and for days I pestered the doctors to try whatever they could do to bring him back to me. They sympathized, but could offer no assurance that he would ever regain consciousness. Eventually, I concentrated on being with him every night: reading to him, lying down beside him, whispering in his ear, and recounting the beautiful memories we had together. I kissed him and begged him to open his eyes. I pleaded with him not leave me alone in this cruel world.

"I stopped caring about anything else. Soon, I lost my job. I did not see our son for days at a time and I did not know how he was or what he was doing. As the weeks went by, Drago-mir's condition worsened, and he had to be put on life support to survive. I was at his side twenty-four hours a day and had pretty well cut myself off from the outside world. My family and the doctors became concerned about the situation and told me that his condition was terminal and the best decision was to stop life support and let him go. For weeks I challenged my family and the medical team, but in the end I had to concede to their reasonable judgment and give my consent."

Ragusa falls into silence again, and Payvand waits as she holds her hands. After several minutes she sighs, "I went into a deep depression, and ended up being hospitalized myself for about a year. I just wanted to die. I had lost the will to live.

I didn't even see much of my son Mladen that year as I was heavily medicated and sleeping much of the time.

"I eventually got a hold of myself and decided I had been around hospitals too long. I improved my behaviour, told the doctors what they wanted to hear, and ate properly in order to improve my health. Soon, my family was delighted to hear me inquire after my son, and they wasted no time in bringing him in for a visit. He was then about four years old and tall for his age. He recognized me and rushed to give me a big hug. But he did not cry. When I saw him, I stared at him. I had never seen anybody so closely resemble one of his parents. He was the spitting image of his father with the same kind, assuring, and calm look in that beautiful face and warm smile. I couldn't believe it.

"I thought perhaps my mind was tricking me because I just wanted to see him like that. I kept repeating, 'It cannot be!' My brother said, 'Hard to believe, hey?' He showed me a black-and-white picture of Dragomir when he was our son's age. My in-laws had sent it thinking it might help in my recovery. I held my son so tight that he squirmed away in irritation. I kissed him and tried to make sense of everything that had happened to us. What was our future together going to be like? Was the resemblance of this boy to his father a good thing or bad? Was it going to be a painful reminder of what I had lost every time I looked at him, or could I rejoice in the company of this precious living echo?

"Shortly after that, the doctors released me from the hospital. I told them nothing about my nightmares or my feelings of depression. To get away from them, I just let them think that my prospects were rosy.

"Since then, I kept myself going with sweet memories of life with Dragomir and time spent with my son, the dearest little being you could ever imagine. On the other hand, I still endured nightmares inspired by the atrocities of the war that tore my family and my homeland apart."

Payvand's face is drained of emotion, reflective; thinking of the times in her life when she had gone through similar situations, and how painful those episodes had been. She labours to breathe, but calms herself and looks at the floor.

Ragusa lets out a reflective sigh. "As Mladen was growing, he seemed to be getting weaker. We were constantly in and out of hospitals for days or weeks at a time. We would come back home only to return a month or two later. But I never complained, nor did he. Unable to keep up with his school work, he did not even get a chance to complete his high school. Mladen was the only shining light left in my life. Then two years ago he deteriorated and became worse than ever. They kept him in hospital for good, and three months ago he too died."

With despair in her eyes, she stares motionless at Payvand. "I do not want to go through the details of his sicknesses as I know why he suffered so much. During my pregnancy, I was exposed to all kinds of war-borne chemicals in the air, as well as constant fear, stress, and restlessness. Also, we were often not eating properly, at a time when I needed a steady and healthy diet the most. He was a child of war, bearing the toxic fruit of strife. You tell me, do the ones who foster wars ever ask the people of the affected areas for permission? No, never. Do they concern themselves with the effects war has on the regions hosting the conflicts, or on the land and its people? No, never. It is as though we do not exist. And so, as they have for thousands of years, too many people suffer during war, as well as after, just like my son."

She sighs again. "I wish it was I who had taken the fatal blow, not my mother. I wish I had had my head smashed against the wall, not my daughter. I wish it was I who had died in hospital, not my Dragomir. And I wish I had not given birth to that beautiful vulnerable child who lived such a short and pain-filled life. Oh my boy, how he suffered to his death. Yet he possessed such strength and always had a smile on his face and never complained.

"After I buried him beside his father, I went home and made a milkshake into which I mixed all my son's leftover medications. I drank it all, but it didn't work and I opened my eyes to find myself once more in the hospital. The good doctor was telling my family, 'She is suicidal and we have to watch her for some time.' Once again I found myself confined and medicated. Then I was provided with a therapist to help me search for meaning in my life. No one had any idea how well I understood the meaning in my life. My therapist would say, 'We cannot avoid suffering but we can learn how to cope with it, find meaning in it, and move forward.' I truly wanted to slap her sometimes.

"I argued with my therapist. I attacked the idea that we should accept and move on. Suffering has many causes, many levels and many faces, much of it caused by the Western world's careless and selfish lifestyles. If more people paid more attention and educated themselves about the conflicts that plague this world, such as the one in Yugoslavia then, Iraq later, and Syria today, they could work collectively to push their governments to pursue policies that actually prevent the turmoil and suffering of people in war-torn areas, instead of promoting them. I told my therapist it is impossible for her to understand people like me, let alone be able to help me. I told her my stories in each session. She would be truly saddened and say, 'Yes, your life was very difficult, and I am sorry for what has happened to you, but it remains true that you have to move on.' I couldn't believe how easily she could just brush off all my pain and anguish and simply instruct me to go on with my life.

"Once, I tried to listen and see what she really wanted from me. I do not exactly remember what she said, but it angered me so much that I got up to leave. Standing behind my chair, I delivered a final rebuke. 'For you to understand me, you must lose your loved ones, one by one, after watching them suffer greatly. You must endure life in a war-torn area where armed gangs overrun your neighbourhood and then tell you how to live. After losing all you have, I will ask if you are able to find meaning. I will use your theories on you. After what people like me have gone through, telling individuals to find meaning in life is not the answer. The response to such barbarity is to use your knowledge and power to stop elites from committing atrocities just to control "their" populations or resources. Do that, and we will all be fine. I will not and I cannot find any private little meaning in all the suffering that was imposed on me, or on any other human being, in the name of prestige or profit. As for moving on, I am quite capable of that, and I did so with my son. Now he is gone too but not before suffering so much that I willingly let him go. At this stage of my life, I simply choose not to move forward anymore. There really is a limit to how much one can tolerate!' Then I slammed her door and never returned.

"I have nothing left in me, and at my age who are they to tell me how to live? I have more insight than they could ever find in their theories. I lived a life that too many people only know about through their movies as entertainment. How dare they call me 'sick' or 'psychotic'! If I want to go, I will go. It is my life. I pity them and their superficial opinions and empty knowledge. They try to analyze me with their laws of psychology. They have to learn that the only way you can understand people like me is to walk in their shoes into total devastation, and come out the other side.

"I am away from their ministrations now, and I will decide my own destiny and leave this fake world of blissful ignorance to them."

The women are leaning against one another, sitting in the dark. Both are quiet and breathing softly. They look exhausted and restless. The food and drink on the table is still untouched. Brian comes in and takes it away, then returns from the kitchen with some wine. The two women smile weakly in appreciation, but nobody says a word. The room is dark; they do not want light in a world that seems so empty.

Payvand says, "After what we all learned from World War II, one might think that humanity would never want to experience such madness again. Yet, all around us are man-made disasters, wars, and conflicts with no end in sight."

She sits up, then adds, "I feel your pain, and I will not stop you. I understand now. But I would ask that you not go just yet. I'd like you to give me the chance to talk about my own life. Let me tell you who I was then and who I am now. Do you care to hear me?"

Ragusa says nothing, only looks at her.

"There are stories in my past that I never talked about, at least not to everyone. Maybe a bit here and there with Brian, especially after nightmares, when I had to explain and tell him why I am so disturbed. In time, he heard most of my stories, so we are not strangers to your pain, Ragusa. I hope you are willing to listen to me, and that you will give me the chance to talk to someone who doesn't know me. It will allow me to recount my unspoken history."

Ragusa looks at Payvand with unconcealed admiration and nods.

"Look," Payvand says, "the sun will be rising soon. I will walk with you to where I met you and say farewell to you as I promised. I will understand and empathize with any decision you make. However, it would mean a lot to me if you came back here and let me talk to you about the events that have brought me to this day and this place, and what my life has taught me. I have been honoured to hear your story, and I would count it as a further blessing to tell mine to a person with such a story as yours."

She then holds her tightly, and Ragusa hugs her back, the two of them silent for several minutes.

Although they had intended to get up and prepare for their walk, the intensity of the night's discussion has exhausted them both so much that they simply fall asleep in each other's arms as they lean against the wall on the floor. Brian comes in and gently covers them both with a blanket. Then, he sits in the armchair and watches over them in admiration.

They sleep through the morning until the phone rings. Ragusa awakes abruptly, "Ah, sorry, I slept." The two of them yawn and stretch and laugh about how they nodded off. Brian brings a small breakfast and tea for them, and they get up and go to the table to eat in silence. He sits in the armchair and looks at them apprehensively, but with undying affection.

Refreshed, the ladies don their coats and step out into the bright day. He remains seated, choosing not to say anything. Payvand and Ragusa take the little path that leads to the water. They are holding hands and walking in silence. They arrive at the big log where they had met the previous day and Payvand helps Ragusa up onto it. Then she sits down on the sandy beach, wraps her arm around the back of Ragusa's legs, as if to hold her in place, and puts her chin on her own pulled-up knees. They both gaze out at the water and listen to the loons.

Payvand says, "Yesterday when I met you, I was actually walking around here trying to wash away my nightmare from the night before."

Ragusa leans forward quickly. "Are they bad, your nightmares?"

Payvand nods silently. She then looks into Ragusa's eyes and says, "I really admire you. I do not know many people who could go through what you have experienced and survive. You have become strong in living through such tragedy. You have become a history book that the world can learn from.

"My dear Ragusa, it is okay to be this angry. Of course, you are greatly hurt. That ugly war did not determine any winner or decide who was right. Just like any other conflict in this world, it was the average person who lost everything. The ones who started the war have perhaps gained what they craved; their resources or profit or power. But we shouldn't let them get away with the suffering they inflicted for it. I am sure you know that you are not alone. You can help others

who are not as strong as you. Those others can then go on
to help expose to the world those governments, people and
policies that ruined their lives. Always we must challenge evil
and fight for a better world. "

She continues. "I am not going to preach and tell you what
to do. I will leave now, and let you decide. But you should
know that in only one day you have become a valuable part
of me. As you related your story, I felt as if I was your companion in those beautiful times and those horrible ones too.
This made me feel as if you were my companion in my own
struggles. I really wish to see you again and I want you to let
me talk about my life."

After a long pause, while staring into Ragusa's eyes, she says,
"Who knows, maybe one day we will decide to go down into
that cold, dark water together."

She then stands up, kisses Ragusa on the forehead and cheek,
holds Ragusa's hands, and says, "There is no excuse for the
world's charlatans and war criminals to put so many in such
misery." She then releases her hands and walks away without
looking back.

CHAPTER 3 **AMITY**

AS PAYVAND WALKS towards the woods, she feels Ragusa's gaze on her back, but resists the urge to turn around. Her heart is pounding so hard it is almost audible as she continues down the path to her house. A debate rages within her. *Is it right leaving her alone there? Yes, she has every right to determine her own affairs; it is her life. No wait. Perhaps I agreed to this too quickly. Oh, stop it! I must respect her decision.*

Payvand has always loved the sights, sounds, and smells of these wild woods, but now she is barely aware of her surroundings as she wrestles with her predicament. She returns home exhausted, and finds Brian waiting anxiously for her at the door, and he gathers her into his arms fondly.

"What did you two do? Where is she?" he asks.

"I left her there, where I met her yesterday. It is up to her now."

"What?" He rushes to the phone saying, "You cannot leave her there, she may kill herself! We should call the police."

Payvand charges over to him, grabs the phone, and hangs it up. Her voice is firm. "I do not think of it as a suicide. I have offered her a reason to come back and be with me, and now she just needs some time to rest and think. If, in the end, she wishes to let go of her misery, her agony, then she should!"

He holds her kindly and speaks softly, "What we know is that a woman is sitting at the beach and perhaps filling up her pockets with heavy rocks, and planning to walk out into the depths. We are responsible," he says.

Payvand moves out of his arms, pushes him away and cries out, "We are responsible for what? The real responsibility is on the political engines of destruction that devastated her family and brought her to this point. The same engines that talk 'democracy' and 'working for the people' to the cameras, but arrange global economics to pit one region against another, thus stoking regional strife, and surprise, surprise, we see an ethnic cleansing here or a genocide there, with elites interfering only if it suits their own agenda and with little regard for the thousands of lives ruined by their actions.

"Or maybe you are right, and we are responsible for the way her whole family perished one by one because of a war that you and I watched on the news but did nothing to stop or that others watched briefly before changing the channel in discomfort. Yes," she cries, "We are responsible as a society when half of us don't even watch the news in case we might have to care. And with most news being corporate vehicles for entertainment and distraction, we sometimes cannot even know what we know.

"Even so, we have no excuse for not helping Ragusa and others like her before they are destroyed. You know as well as I do that there are many well-researched documentaries and books that clearly reveal the cynical manipulations of governments and corporations in gaining and keeping power and resources, no matter the cost to societies, ecosystems and individuals like Ragusa. So with all that information available, why can we all not work together to stop this ongoing villainy of the elites? Do we want to continue to collude with their evils by our apathy and inaction?"

She is pacing back and forth, not knowing what to do with herself. Old torments from her past, both experienced and witnessed, flood back in clear memories, as do the righteous passions born from them that have informed a lifetime of seeking a better world. It is as if Ragusa was a mirror that reflected Payvand's own life starkly before her eyes. The combined power of all those years has thrown her whole being into distress. Breathlessly she continues, "From earliest times to today, humans have fought for peace and liberation. Spartacus was a symbol against authoritarian control. And here we are, so many centuries later, in a world we view as the 'most advanced' yet, and still slavery is pervasive: wage slavery, sex trafficking, child soldiers. People across the world are still being crucified with the same abuses and insults.

"Brian, it is not only Ragusa's problem that bothers me. Look at the wreckage of Iraq and how many years that country has suffered. How many mothers are there living shattered lives like Ragusa? September 11th has unleashed a whole new round of xenophobic militarism and destruction from all sides. Somebody's happy about that. Who? Who is benefiting?

"Before the West attacked Iraq, Saddam was just a weak and petty tyrant used by them as a plaything. First they set him up with weapons of mass destruction so he could be a proxy bully to Iran. Then, they took those toys away when he misbehaved. Then, they accused him of having the very things they ensured he did not have, and proceeded to attack the country. It all looks like a mean joke at the expense of a victimized and exploited people."

Payvand is striding about, shouting and waving her arms to emphasize her observations. Brian is dismayed to see her in such a state of despair. He has seen her like this before and loves her strong passion as much as ever, but at the same time, he does not want her to be so distressed. Her vigour is undiminished as she continues her audit of humanity's transgressions. "Because of the sanctions, Iraq was already weakened militarily. So, what was the purpose of attacking them? Can you tell me?

"The majority of every population around the world, including many Americans, disagreed with the invasion of Iraq, but since when have managers been concerned with the wishes of the managed? Especially when the media, enslaved to power, plays on people's unawareness and has them blindly following government propaganda into disaster. Sure, after all these years people look back and realize it was an unjust and senseless war, but still there is no focus on the legacy of victims: Iraq's children, mothers and fathers. Do we have any idea about the daily lives of those people as they deal with the mess created by that conflict? Not that we care, as we are all too busy with our sitcoms or where the next bargain is!"

She is still pacing in an excited manner, completely consumed by her anger. "Just wait and see how history repeats itself in Syria and all that is left there with yet another shattered country. We all just follow the news without taking proper action against such atrocities. And the Syrian people are being duped by or are playing into the hands of bullies; they have forgotten that both the soldiers and rebels are Syrian brothers."

Payvand is breathless and exhausted. Brian is worried for her. He feels he should comfort her but for now does not dare come between her and her fury.

"Is it because we are talking more than listening? Analyzing more than acting? Are our observations and understandings guiding us towards any meaningful accomplishments? How do we find one another and work in unison to create a compassionate world? We have to work globally to solve all these problems, because only united will we have such a voice. Alone we are already defeated. But what am I saying? Sure, we can find others who share the same ideas of how the world should work. The problem is, who leads the newly developed unity? Soon there is a struggle over who will guide the new model society, and the same vicious cycle of control and manipulation takes over the process.

"Here's another example! It was right around the same time as the Yugoslavian crisis that Rwandans were being massacred, and again we were following that news. Do you remember?" she shouts. "Yes, we were responsible because once more we did nothing! Perhaps we think of ourselves as caring people just because we keep up with the news. What good does that do for the people in the midst of the terror?

"And now we have heard the story of this miserable woman who was our guest. She was a daughter, a mother, a lover, and the only survivor of a beautiful family. Now she has nothing, and she doesn't know how to live anymore! Can any psychologist or psychiatrist take her nightmares away?

"If so, how? Drug her? Can you do it? You couldn't take mine away over all these years. Nobody could. I still have nightmares!" She jabs at the air in frustration.

Then she stops, and compassion returns to her words. "It is too late for that woman; her spirit is broken. Her life is hers to keep or abort. Who are we to decide for her? The only thing left to her is that physical body. What will calling the police do? They would put her in psychiatric care where she would be drugged and confined. That is not the help she needs."

She drops into a chair, holding her face in her hands. "All of us. All the people of this planet are responsible for all the wars across the world. It is we who must find a way to stop these incessant and futile wars. Did you hear how her therapist told her to look for meaning in her misery? How ironic!"

Brian pulls up a chair next to her and tries to wrap his arms around Payvand but she will not let him. He stubbornly reaches for her again, and this time she leans into him and lets the tears flow. Then, she pushes him away again as if fearing to betray her mission. She goes on angrily, "What a perfect mess societies and nations get themselves into. Trapped by abusive economic and political straitjackets imposed by overpowering institutions of westernized globalization, people feel compelled to fight each other for jobs and resources. From there it is too easy to tap into old ethnic hatreds and, *voila!* Another fractured country with a long list of antagonists that corporations and other elites can pick and choose from as allies to help in exploiting local resources.

"And now, as we speak, the same is happening in Syria. While different religious or ethnic groups kill each other for a while, we watch and wait to see who might be useful in promoting the Master Agenda. Then, with great displays of wisdom and compassion, the West will leap to the rescue and bomb its way to a resolution. What kind of a rescue is that?

"Libya before; Iran next! So many people in the Middle East alone are killing each other and playing into the hands of the overlords waiting in the wings to divide and conquer. Has anyone learned anything from Yugoslavia's nonsensical war? No! Because so many people really don't follow what is happening around them; not in their country with their own people, nor in nations around the world. They are too busy with their petty feuds, their shallow daily lives, or their empty momentary amusements.

"You do not dare call anyone!" she yells as she goes into the bathroom and slams the door.

Brian stands in the middle of the room wondering what to do. He knocks at the bathroom door, but through her sobbing she tells him to go away. He decides to go out and walk quickly to the beach with the idea of talking to Ragusa and convincing her to return to the cottage. He arrives at the beach but can see no one there. He calls her name, but there is no response.

He spots a man sitting in front of his cottage further along the shore, so he runs to him and asks if he has seen a woman around the beach. The man says, "No. I have been sitting here reading for about an hour and I haven't seen anyone."

Brian runs back toward his cottage just as Payvand is coming out. "Where were you?" she says. "What were you trying to do? Where is she?"

He takes her hands and tries to calm her down. Together they walk to the beach. He asks, "Where exactly was she sitting yesterday?"

"Right there, on that log."

They look around there and find nobody.

"Look," Payvand says. "Those rocks are the ones she had in her pockets. We pulled them out together."

They look grimly at each other and search the area. They walk to the woods close to the shore then back to the beach, anxiously looking for any sign of Ragusa.

Payvand goes back to the log and starts to count the rocks. "Maybe she took different rocks this time." She walks to the edge of the water and stares out at the horizon. "It's so peaceful," she says. "The loon is still there, quiet though."

She has her feet in the water and feels its chill rise up her legs and into the small of her back. Payvand turns slowly and goes back to sit dejectedly on the same log. Brian sits beside her and holds her affectionately as they stare at the dim water.

Ragusa sits on the log and watches Payvand as she walks away; she likes her and appreciates her special kindness. As tears run down Ragusa's face, she wants to get up and run after her, wants to stop her and thank her, but she cannot move. Payvand disappears into the woods and onto the trail and cannot be seen anymore.

She sits and stares at the water. She believes she eventually will go into the depths to find her peace away from the nightmares. *I cannot continue without him, without them,* she thinks. *Still, maybe, in fairness to Payvand, I should listen to her stories. Maybe she needs me as much as I needed her.*

Ragusa feels that she has nothing to look forward to, and she is certain that Payvand now knows that. And that Payvand understands that the past two decades in Canada have been as harsh as Ragusa's last year at home. Mladen was sick most of the time before Ragusa lost him, and her husband, Dragomir, suffered so much before he passed. It was unbearable for Ragusa to witness their pain. She smiles to herself as she remembers that there were some men interested in her, but Dragomir had always been the only one for her. She is sure that Payvand understood that as well, and that she is aware that Ragusa needs to rest now.

She sighs out loud, remembering that her brother is likely worried and that she needs to call him. She takes her phone out of her handbag, turns it on and fixes her gaze on the pale green water. She tells her brother that she has met an old friend and would like to spend some time with her. Her brother is indeed worried, and wants to know where she is, and if he too can come and meet her friend. She says that she will call him back, and hangs up. *As long as he knows I am fine, it's good enough.*

She rests a bit longer on the log, then gets up and walks to the road leading to the fishing village nearby. It is a charming town. There are a few interesting boutiques that cater to visitors. She enters one that catches her eye with its appealing artisan crafts and decides she wants to buy Payvand a gift. Ragusa wants the gift to convey her appreciation for their sweet short time together; her gratitude for the kindness Payvand has shown her, and it has to be something that matches her beautiful spirit.

From the corner of her eye, she spots a sparkling object shining with reflected light. She leans towards it. It is a pendant. At its centre is a colourful gem, but she cannot think where she has seen anything like it before. It is not a sapphire, a ruby, or an emerald. It seems to be a combination of all those beautiful stones. It appears to have captured all the colours of the rainbow, and shines like the stars.

The shopkeeper asks if he can help her, and Ragusa eagerly asks him about the gem. "Yes, that one," the shopkeeper says as he brings it out of the case for her. "It's a clever combination of a few gems. You see, everything in this store is handmade by artists, and each item is unique."

Ragusa cheerfully says, "Well, then this is the perfect place to buy a gift for a unique person. Can you tell me about the stones?"

"In the middle is a spinel gem. It has shades of ruby red, and, as you can see, there are also subtle shades of pink, purple, and blue, plus some delicate tones in-between. The spinel gemstone is one of the most unusual in the world, yet not very expensive. The artist has shaped it to fit three other stones around it. These are the apatite gem from Madagascar, jeremejevite from Namibia, and aquamarine from Brazil, which is the one that causes most of the sparkles, and distributes the light so well. The delicate tracings of blue are star sapphire from Sri Lanka that the artist embedded in little holes between the cuts. If you look closely, you can see that they all come together in the shape of a dove with open wings. It's a beautifully crafted pendant, and with this white-gold chain it would make a stunning necklace. What do you think, Madame?"

Ragusa's eyes are sparkling just like the gems in the pendant. She sighs and murmurs, "Ah, it is so beautiful, just like her. Are you able to engrave something too?" she asks.

"Indeed," the shopkeeper says. "The gem frame is platinum, and I can engrave on the back." He offers her a pen and paper, and Ragusa takes it, writes a brief line, and gives it back to the shopkeeper. He gives her the bill and says, "It will be ready tomorrow."

Ragusa hesitates at the price, and then chuckles when she realizes that she no longer needs money. "Okay," she says, handing her credit card to the shopkeeper. As he is processing the transaction, he says, "This artist is an amazing woman. She travels to many remarkable places, and she works and lives with the people of each area, gathering objects unique to each region. From time to time, she brings me a new, exquisitely handmade piece of art that she has put together, and it always sells very quickly. This piece came in yesterday, and you got it today."

Ragusa smiles and asks, "Does she have anything else here?"

"No. As I said, once in a while she brings one piece of art, and that is it!"

Ragusa bids the shopkeeper farewell then leaves the store and walks back to the beach and to the trail that goes to Payvand's cottage.

It is getting dark, so she walks briskly. She knows how worried Payvand could be at this very moment. Along the way, she encounters a boy running and playing with his dog. The boy's mother follows close behind, shouting for him to slow down and be careful.

Ragusa stops and watches them wistfully. *My son loved dogs, though he could not even go near them with his allergies,* Ragusa thinks. *How sick he was, and how much he suffered. How much he loved life and how brief it was.* Overcome by emotion, she runs into the woods, collapses against a tree, and sobs so hard that the sound echoes back from the surrounding trees. She is once again gripped by an overwhelming urge to throw herself into the water, but then she remembers Payvand and holds on to the tree as if to anchor herself to the earth. She waits for her panic to subside, then gets up. Determined, she walks to Payvand's house.

As Ragusa gets closer, she sees the couple sitting on the patio and she walks faster. Payvand sees her, pushes herself up, and runs to Ragusa. They hold each other tight and long. There are no words of "Where were you" or "What are you doing here?" Finally, arm in arm, they walk into the house as Brian holds the door open for them.

They sink into the sofa in the living room, and hold hands. Payvand turns to her, and with a tender voice says, "I will never deny the deep-seated devastation that vexes your soul. I am truly and deeply sorry for the pain and misery you had to experience and witness. You have every right to be angry, and it breaks my heart that you may never find peace again. You have been afflicted with much more than your fair share of what this unjust world can dish out. Be that as it may, I don't want you to relinquish your spirit and surrender. We can change things, together, and with others just like us." She stops, exhausted by the power of her desire to communicate exactly the right words to convince Ragusa to stay with her in this world. She looks into Ragusa's eyes, searching desperately for an answer.

Ragusa looks intently back at her and says compassionately, "What you say is all true, and I have thought about it. I have tried to rationalize my pain and loss, but reasoned arguments do not ease my loneliness and the despair of being robbed of my loved ones. I can scream at the top of my lungs and demand to know, 'Who is responsible for all the pain and agony that so many like me have gone through?' And the same pragmatic answer always comes back to me with a pat on my head: 'Oh, it has always been like this. War and its aftermath have always been a stain on our history. It's just part of our nature.' But such pat and intellectually weak drivel melts away in the heat of the reproach that perhaps a species priding itself on being so elevated above brutish instincts should have a good answer for how to end conflicts. Intelligent beings so accomplished in the arts and sciences should be wholly consumed with no better task than to fashion a beautiful peaceful Earth." She places a gentle kiss on Payvand's forehead and says, "Then I look around me at the world and concede, 'That's only a dream.'"

Payvand pauses for a few seconds, then takes Ragusa's hand and puts it on her heart. She says, "Not if you share your experiences, enlighten the oblivious, and hold the feet of those who are corrupt and barbarous to the fire. Don't take away from us such a strong moral force as yours. There are many other compassionate people around the world who understand your pain and who share your ideas. There are plenty like me ready to join you, in moving the world forward to a better place. We just have to find one another and work together, as one, to stop this madness."

They look at each other quietly for some time, and then Payvand breaks the silence and asks her if she has eaten. Ragusa says that she has not and that she is not hungry. Then, she says, "I called my brother to let him know I am all right, but he became angry with me and wanted to know where I was."

Payvand gives Ragusa her phone and asks her to call him again and comfort him. "I will talk to him if you wish."

Ragusa makes the call and assures her brother that she is fine, then passes the phone over to Payvand. After a short and courteous introduction, he says, "My sister is not fine, she is suicidal."

"I know," Payvand says as she leaves the room. "But I don't call it that."

"What do you mean? Call it what?"

"Suicide," she says. "She is just profoundly weary of her ordeal, and she has lost so much to the ignorance of this world."

He says, "Well, we are here, and we love her."

"Of course," Payvand says, "but you are not her husband and her children, each of whom she lost one after another by the most vicious means."

"Well, I try to understand, but I know I can't fully appreciate the depth of Ragusa's torment. During the war I was here, and I really only witnessed the breakup of Yugoslavia through the news media."

"Yes, just like the rest of us here," Payvand says. "That certainly makes it difficult to comprehend what the people in war zones really have to deal with." She gives him her phone number and describes where her cottage is on the Sunshine Coast north of Vancouver. He is surprised that Ragusa went to so much trouble, travelling by bus and ferry to get that far away. Payvand also gives him her address in Vancouver and promises that she and his sister will be there tomorrow. Satisfied, he thanks her and says farewell.

Payvand returns to the living room and informs Ragusa of the conversation. Surprised, Ragusa asks, "Do you not live here?"

"No, I come here whenever I can no longer tolerate the big city and the pervasive culture of greed. I come here to get away and to be left alone. We both work in Vancouver, so that's our main residence, and we will return tomorrow. You know, I would dearly love to show you my little garden there."

"I would love to see it," Ragusa says.

They sit serenely for a time and quietly enjoy each other's company. Then Payvand gets up and asks her husband to prepare something for dinner while she takes a shower.

"My pleasure," he says. Ragusa follows him into the kitchen where she apologizes for her imposition into his life.

"Oh, please don't worry about that," he says. "Actually, to be honest, this has been a most interesting affair. You two met each other just yesterday, yet it feels as if you have known one another for years. Payvand has had many experiences that are similar to yours."

"Many?" Ragusa asks.

"Yes, she has lost several loved ones as well. She still has nightmares if anything triggers some particular memories. Then, we will have a few days of distress, but I am used to it now, and happy to be present for her." He takes vegetables and fish out of the fridge and begins preparing them. Ragusa asks if she can help. "By all means," he says as he pushes an assortment of vegetables over to her and hands her a sharp knife.

"What do you think of what is happening around the world?" Ragusa asks as she starts chopping.

He considers the question, "Well, I was born and grew up in a pretty safe part of our world; one that hasn't faced much conflict in my time. Of course, the long-standing legacy of disgrace here in North America arises from the expropriation of the continent by Europeans and the consequent desolation of its First Nations and their cultures. It's an issue that still is a long way from being resolved."

Ragusa nods her head, "Well, I hope our modern immigrants, who come from all over the world, aren't contributing to that."

"Well, no, it's interesting. In a way, new immigration has the effect of raising people's awareness of a multicultural world and of diminishing that great 'fear of the others' that keeps cultures battling each other. First Nations are real cultures too but with unique and legitimate claims that are quite capable of being accommodated within the enormous abundances of North American economies. As long as we—the older European immigrants and the newer immigrants — understand that we are guests here, everyone should be able to live together." He pauses and realizes he has forgotten to introduce himself. "By the way, my name is Brian." He smiles as he reaches his hand out to Ragusa. "And it means 'noble and strong' in Irish!"

They both laugh, and Ragusa says, "So, Payvand has told you about our love of names."

"Yes," Brian says as they both chuckle. "Today's migrations are quite different from those of the past," he adds. People flee war zones and economic privation with doctorates or trades under their belt, but end up in Western countries as menial labourers. It's interesting to compare that with the great migrations of prehistory that began sixty or seventy thousand years ago. They were largely quests for natural resources like food and water. Entire tribes might seek out better or less crowded hunting grounds. However, with the more complex societies of today, migration tends to be about escaping exploitation or ideological strife. It may even be that moving to a Western country is not necessarily helpful for many who simply trade one set of difficulties for another. Unfortunately, migration today often results in a modern form of slavery."

Ragusa says, "By today's migration you mean the last few hundred years as opposed to sixty thousand years ago, right?"

Brian says, "Yes and no. I mean of the last few decades."

"What about your family?" Ragusa asks.

"Well, my ancestors went to America in the 1790s. Apparently they did not like it, so they moved to Canada in the early 1800s. I heard many different stories from my great-grandfather while growing up, about the family's history; their move and their troubles."

Ragusa listens keenly as Brian continues, "As a species, we were animals who developed a powerful intelligence. But now we think too much of ourselves, and we assume we can run roughshod over nature and take whatever we want. Then there are those among us who are so smug as to believe that they can run roughshod over humanity itself by policing the whole world and dictating the proper economy within which people should live. They like to enforce their own ideas of a trivial freedom everywhere possible in order to secure their own freedom to maximize access to markets and resources. This bothers me a lot."

Brian pauses and looks at Ragusa. "I overheard some of your story when I was in the next room, and then Payvand filled in the blanks. I am so sorry for what you have gone through. I cannot even imagine your anguish. However, by killing yourself, you just concede the space to the parasites and make life easier for them. Sorry, maybe I shouldn't say that."

Ragusa stares at him wretchedly. "Maybe you are right," she says, "but I cannot bear the nightmares anymore or this feeling of emptiness. Furthermore, I despair at knowing that the vast majority of people in this world are careless and selfish, deaf to the harm and destruction they may be doing to others and nature. This too makes me feel utterly hopeless, and I just do not want to be part of the chaos anymore." They look at each other and then continue preparing the meal in silence.

Soon Payvand comes into the kitchen, her hair wrapped in a towel. She asks Ragusa if she wants to take a shower. Ragusa thanks her and says, "Perhaps I should." Payvand gives her a towel and some clean clothing, and then returns to help Brian finish the preparations and set the table.

When Ragusa is ready, they sit around the table and begin their meal. The women compliment Brian's cooking, and they all engage in some light-hearted banter and playful joking. As is their habit, Payvand and Brian progress into politics, and Ragusa joins the discussion. They clean up from their meal and settle into the living room with some wine. They talk about the history of humankind, the great migrations, scientific and technological advancements, and the unending litany of wars and conquests. They marvel at how such significant progress in ethics and the sciences has not been matched by an ability to keep the peace and coexist, as civilized societies should. They discuss how the greedy, resentful, and competitive "Self" now appears to be Master of the world.

The good wine and stimulating conversation eventually make them sleepy. Brian gets up to go to bed and Payvand makes up a bed for Ragusa in the spare room. She tucks Ragusa in, kisses her forehead, and says, "You know, these kinds of discussions bother me the most. We sit around a table drinking and having insightful discussions, but what does it do? Nothing. We shouldn't just talk. These ideas should be proclaimed to the world and should occupy people's attention."

"How?" Ragusa asks. "People in the Western world are so immersed in their comforts that they don't want to know, or they know but don't care. How do you want to make them pay attention?"

"Well, let's see. Maybe if we could replace the all-encompassing bombardment of profoundly meaningless commercial advertising with an equal volume of reasoned arguments and factual information and proofs, they would eventually listen," Payvand says.

"Who? Who would listen, and what are you guys talking about?" Brian shouts from the other room.

Ragusa and Payvand laugh. "I thought you were tired!" Payvand shouts back.

Brian comes into Ragusa's room, "I am not going to be sleeping if there is an interesting conversation happening within earshot!"

Payvand laughs again, then returns to her thoughts. "Do you remember how people across the world went out into the streets in protest to prevent the American and British armies from going into Iraq? We were on the streets every few Saturdays for months. In countries all over this world, millions of people made their voices heard. Suspicious of the claim that Iraq was swimming in weapons of mass destruction, together they had only one thing to say, 'No war in Iraq!' Remember the arguments that the protesters made worldwide? Sanctions had already crippled Iraq and were killing hundreds of children a day. The people were already living in misery; why did they need more?"

Brian says, "And yet the invasion began, and they bombed them anyway. There were no weapons of mass destruction found in Iraq, but the conquerors shrugged their shoulders and said, 'Oh, well. Now, where's that oil?' And that was it."

Brian asks Ragusa, "Have you seen pictures of the destruction that occurred in Iraq, and how the people there continue to endure the consequences of the war, such as the after-effects of depleted uranium?"

"Yes, and it is a criminal shame," Ragusa says.

"Okay then, let's give up, and let the tyrants do as they wish," exclaims Payvand as she throws herself into an armchair. She fumes about the disastrous environmental consequences and psychological effects that war in any shape or form inflicts on the people within war zones. She rails against the cynical exploitation of insensitive soldiers, who end-up fighting wars that are not theirs and that they do not even understand. And yet it is they who directly cause all the harm. She criticizes the scandalous negligence of warmongers who obliterate ecosystems and scatter chemicals into war zones, subjecting populations to birth defects, chronic illnesses, long-term disabilities, cancers and more. "We must get through to a citizenry that carelessly allows their governments to engage in warfare without paying attention to its huge implications!" She turns to Ragusa. "Here she is, a signature example of a human life ruined by the callousness of militarists. Every member of her family violated and destroyed by some capricious by-product of combat!"

Brian brings some water for Payvand, and tries to calm her as he softly says, "You know I agree with you and with what you are saying, but, as Ragusa says, the indifferent outnumber those dedicated to the serious work of reforming the way our world works. And that won't change in the few minutes between now and the moment near to hand when our guest passes out from exhaustion. So how about we go rest, and let dear Ragusa rest too." He then wishes Ragusa a good night's sleep as he guides Payvand to the door and switches off the light.

As they go into their room, Payvand says, "You know you kind of contradicted yourself in there."

Brian raises his eyebrows, "What did I say?"

Payvand points out that he supported the millions of people who came out into the street to tell the world's self-appointed police not to invade Iraq, and he even participated in the marches.

"Yes, so?"

"Well," Payvand says, "then you said that the number of indifferent people is more than those who care."

Brian kisses her and says, "Oh, you don't let me to get away with anything, do you? What I meant was, think of all the people who agreed with our position but did not join us. They could have made our voice stronger but they remained indifferent. They gave up before they began."

Payvand says, "No, that does not mean indifference. It means they can't give us their time because they may be too busy scraping a living." They close the bedroom door, but Ragusa hears them still discussing passionately. She falls asleep smiling.

Ragusa wakes up to the sound of birds chirping and a breeze caressing her face. She gets up, pushes the window open all the way, and takes a deep breath as she gazes at the incredible view. She marvels at how beautiful this perfect getaway is and how little she appreciated it yesterday with all the talking they did. She hears her hosts walking about and talking, and bets they are continuing their debate about last night's discussion. She smiles, looks out, and breathes deeply as she puts on her clothes.

Payvand and Brian have set a wonderful table for breakfast and are waiting for her. They both greet her cheerfully, and Payvand asks how she slept last night. Ragusa looks at her warmly and says, "I don't remember when I last slept so deeply. Thank you both."

They have a quiet, enjoyable breakfast, each reflecting on her or his own thoughts. Payvand mentions that they will do some cleaning around the cottage before they leave in the early afternoon.

Ragusa agrees, "Sure, I have no plans. And nobody is waiting for me."

"Your brother is," Payvand says.

The time comes when they are all packed up and ready to leave their little haven. As they drive to the ferry, Ragusa asks if they can stop in the village as she bought something yesterday and needs to pick it up. Surprised, Payvand and Brian blurt out, "Sure," in unison. Ragusa guides them to the gift shop and asks them to wait for her.

As she disappears into the shop, Payvand and Brian look at each other with a smile. "Are you thinking what I'm thinking?" Payvand asks.

Brian guesses that she has bought a souvenir for a relative.

"Perhaps for her niece?" Payvand suggests with glee.

Brian assents with a shrug of his shoulders.

Payvand looks happy. "Whoever, as long as she is thinking of family like that, it's a hopeful sign to me.... Hush, she is coming."

Ragusa gets in the car, thanks them again, and sits quietly, fixing her gaze out the window while Brian drives on. Payvand can barely contain her delight at this sign that this fine woman can indeed find something in this life to hold on to.

She looks forward to the coming days and anticipates further positive omens.

Several hours later, they finally arrive at Payvand and Brian's Vancouver home, a modest bungalow with a generous living and dining area, a spacious study filled with books, and two tasteful, well-designed, bedrooms. Payvand gives Ragusa a tour of the house who compliments the simple yet elegant arrangements. But her greatest praise comes when they step into the garden at the back of the house. "Wow, this is beautiful!" she exclaims. "Ah, such an exuberant variety of beautiful plants! Who waters them when you are not here?"

"My daughter," Payvand says.

Brian calls out from the kitchen, "I put the tea on."

"Thank you, Brian," Payvand replies as she offers Ragusa a chair facing the roses. "How red and beautiful that one is. And so many roses in such a small place!"

Brian joins them with a platter of cookies and says, "All this is her creation you know."

"It is absolutely beautiful," says Ragusa.

Payvand smiles. "Working in the garden makes me happy. Each part was created with a happy or angry or sad memory, reflecting episodes in my life. This garden takes me home, causes me to reflect on my life past and present, and reminds me of what was there for me once and what is here for me now. Where did the journey begin that led me to today?"

Ragusa gets up, takes Payvand's hand, and says, "You asked me this question just two days ago: 'Who were you then, and who you are now?' In just two days, I have become so involved with you that I have told you about some events in my life that I never shared with anyone before. So now, I wish to know more about you. Talk to me."

Payvand looks at her seriously. "And then what?"

"What do you mean?" Ragusa asks.

Payvand right away regrets her words, bites her tongue, and says, "Nothing. It certainly is my turn. But you should know that I am over two hundred years of age, and I cannot rush through the story in one day, as you did." She grins at Ragusa, who laughs and says, "Two hundred years old, huh?"

"Yes," Payvand says, "Because it is not only my life. I have been involved with many others, especially women."

"How?" Ragusa asks.

"Well, early on in my teens, an interest in feminism and the social welfare of others was awakened in me. I came to understand how poorly the majority of people —mostly women, workers, and minorities — were served by societies structured along exploitative and patriarchal lines. I noticed how improved their lives were in societies with some level of regard for social welfare, labour laws, and universal suffrage. I was always especially concerned, given my personal history, for the welfare of women. I worked to support their struggles for workplace and educational equality and to remove them from abusive relationships by accompanying them into whatever situation required my support. I would argue and champion for a woman's right to make her own choices and determine her own fate."

"Was that your job?" Ragusa asks.

"No, though seemingly as a consequence of where I was born and grew up, I chose it as an important calling. Using principles learned from historical and contemporary heroes of social activism, I developed my own skill-set in advocacy, counselling, and activism, all geared to the unique cultural setting found in a strongly patriarchal Iran.

"You see, each stage of my life was its own journey that built and shaped my character and gave me a clearer understanding of the political environment I was living in. When I was younger, I thought education and skills training were important for laying a strong foundation for a subsequent serious and successful career as you and Dragomir did by pursuing higher education. But I soon learned that, yes, a good degree will help bring success and perhaps a comfortable life, but it will not necessarily bring an appreciation for the value of life or a respectful understanding of the world around us. It seems some people use education as a tool for gaining power over other people and resources. I began university in pursuit of a degree, but like so many others, I was there because my parents expected it of me. However, as soon as I stepped onto campus I met many young students like myself interested in refashioning and improving society in their beloved Iran."

"Ah, were you involved in the Iranian revolution?" Ragusa asks.

"Yes, I was politically involved in the years leading up to the revolution. How about this? I am going to give you one life a day. Know that several of the people that you will hear about are gone, either killed or disappeared. Are you ready for that?"

Ragusa raises her eyebrows, "I am, but what do you mean by 'one life a day?'"

"Well, you told me your story in one day. My life only has meaning within the context of several people vitally important to who I am today. You will need to hear their stories as well. Is that all right with you?"

Ragusa stares at her, trying to discern Payvand's meaning as Brian brings the tea and asks Payvand to give him a hand in the kitchen. They leave Ragusa in the garden to sit and wonder how long Payvand's story may take. She bends over to look more closely at the roses and thinks, *I like her very much, and I want to let her talk, but I need to leave this world soon.*

Brian pulls Payvand into the kitchen and asks, "What are you trying to do?"

"Nothing Brian, I just want to prolong the life stories as long as I can every day. In doing so, perhaps I can change her mind about killing herself. Not, of course, by lecturing her, but by portraying people whose lives were every bit as painful as hers yet who chose to continue living."

Brian looks at her fondly, then folds her into his arms and says, "Be careful, my darling."

"I will," she says.

They join Ragusa in the garden and Payvand pours the tea as Brian serves the cookies. They are interrupted by a knock on the front door.

Brian opens it to a middle-aged man with a young woman. The man introduces himself. "Hi, I am Andelko, Ragusa's brother, and this is Nada, my daughter."

"Welcome, come on in," Brian says, and then calls Payvand. The two women come in from the garden, and Andelko greets his sister with open arms. Ragusa lets him embrace her and says she is sorry to have troubled him and his family. Nada comes in close and whispers, "We were so worried, Aunty." There is sincerity in her voice.

Payvand says, "Such a beautiful young niece you have, Ragusa."

Ragusa nods her head with tears in her eyes as she hugs her niece, apologizing again for the pain she has caused them.

Payvand guides everyone out onto the patio while Brian brings out extra chairs, and soon everyone is gathered around the table, drinking tea and admiring the garden. Then Payvand asks Nada if her name has a meaning as beautiful as that of her aunt. Andelko looks quizzically at his sister, and the two ladies laugh. Ragusa says, "Names and their meanings have been a bit of fun for us these past couple of days."

Andelko says, "Well, Nada means 'hope.'" He smiles. "Ironic hey? We called her 'Nada' in hope for a peaceful world."

Everyone loves it, and for a while they play with names and their meanings, as they laugh and enjoy the sunny afternoon. Eventually, Andelko asks his sister if she is ready to go.

Payvand and Ragusa look at each other, and Ragusa says, "Sure, but I intend to come see Payvand daily for some time. We have untold stories to finish."

Andelko smiles, and Nada says, "That's wonderful. I will drive you back and forth if you will allow me, Aunty."

Brian walks Andelko and Nada to the door as Payvand

and Ragusa finish talking. "She is such a fine young lady," Payvand says.

Ragusa has tears in her eyes, "You know, when she was two years old, they sent us a picture of her. If I hadn't known better, I would have sworn they had sent Danica's picture to me. They look so alike. Now, anytime I look at her I think of my daughter. Would she be as tall and as beautiful as Nada if she was alive? Looking at my brother's daughter is sometimes the most painful part of my day though I love her very much. She is a very smart and kind young lady."

Payvand takes her hand and says, "You can also think of it as a good thing. But it must be also very painful. I can see that."

Ragusa places her hand on Payvand's shoulder and says, "Is tomorrow morning at ten o'clock good?"

"It is perfect," Payvand says, and they hug goodbye before Ragusa leaves with her brother and niece.

Payvand is sitting in the garden when Brian joins her. "You should tell her brother what she was up to," Brian says. "He seems a very nice man and obviously loves his sister. He is neither police nor psychiatrist, and he has a right to know how seriously she is considering taking her own life."

"I know," Payvand says. "But you tell him, please. You can tell him one of the days that she is here. But don't you think that if she knows you have told her brother about that, she will lose her trust in us, and she may not come here anymore? She is happy with me, at least for now. Don't ruin it. Let us be."

Brian gently kisses her on the lips and then rises to take the dishes inside. She sits in the garden and waits for night to fall.

CHAPTER 4 **MINOO**

PAYVAND WAKES UP to the sound of the kettle whistle, and looks out the window to a bright day. Then she looks at the clock and sits up, "Oh, it's after nine! Did I sleep that long?"

"Yes, you did indeed," Brian says, his smile wide and affectionate.

"Why didn't you wake me up?"

"I never wake you up when you are sound asleep. You're fine. You have about forty-five minutes to get ready, and breakfast is already prepared. Get up lazy-bones!"

She leaps out of the bed and chases Brian into the kitchen waving her hairbrush. They laugh as she messes up his hair. "You are so kind and wonderful to me," she says. Then she kisses him and begins brushing her own hair as she makes her way back to the bedroom to get dressed.

When she returns to the kitchen, Brian bows mischievously and pulls out her chair, beckoning her to sit. "Here, look," Brian says, "Even some toast with your favourite jam on it." He pours some tea for her and leans in to kiss her.

As she eats, she thinks about the day ahead. "I hope our talk goes well today. I'm a bit worried!"

"I know you are."

The doorbell chimes, and Payvand is happy that Ragusa is ten minutes early.

"How do you know it's her?" Brian teases as he goes to open

the door. "Aha, Payvand was right; it is you! Good morning, Ragusa. And good morning, Nada!"

Payvand rushes to them as they enter and first plants a kiss on the young lady's cheek. Then she hugs Ragusa tight and kisses her too. "So good to see you, dear Ragusa."

Brian offers them tea and breakfast, but Nada says, "We already had our breakfast. Besides, I can't stay. Good to see you both though." At the door she asks, "Is five o'clock good for picking you up, Aunty?" Ragusa looks at Payvand, who mentions that she has an appointment later in the day and they may have to finish up by three. "Sure, no problem," Nada says and blows the women a kiss as she leaves.

Ragusa makes herself comfortable in the garden while Payvand clears the breakfast dishes. Brian comes into the kitchen and gives her a hug and a kiss before heading off to work, "Do you think you two will be all right? Will you please call me if you need me?"

"Don't worry, I will." She kisses him back and holds him tenderly. He then pokes his head into the garden and wishes Ragusa a nice day, but he leaves the home with a worried expression on his face.

Payvand finishes tidying up the kitchen and joins Ragusa in the garden. She sits directly across from her, face-to-face, with a big smile. "Enough of sad things, just for one day," she says. "Allow me to tell you a cheerful, heartening story. Can I start with that?"

"Is it about you?"

"No, but I was very involved in it."

"Okay," Ragusa says smiling.

"Let's see. If you remember, I told you I worked as an activist before and after Iran's revolution. I will tell you a story about one of my activities, but first, let me tell you who we were. Our organization had many teams around the country, and our members were from all walks of life: doctors and nurses working in hospitals, lawyers working for labour and women's rights, university students, government workers, and many others. Everyone had their normal day jobs and, at the same time, had hidden occupations working without pay for the people of their communities."

"What was your job at the time?"

"I was a university student studying sociology. I had a rich daddy who adored me," she giggles. "Well, I graduated from high school a year early and passed the entrance examination for the University of Tehran on the first attempt. My father was so proud of me. Both my parents were activists themselves and they were a great influence on my learning and upbringing. They knew that I was working with other young activists, but did not dare talk about it or question me as they feared the extent of my involvement. I was an only child and my parents indulged me," she says grinning. "They were both very well educated and they lived together for more than thirty-five years, in a profoundly loving and respectful relationship."

Payvand talks about her parents joyfully, but she gets up quickly to hide the tears in her eyes and hurries into the kitchen to get them some snacks and something to drink.

"How are they doing now?"

"We will talk about them later," Payvand calls from the kitchen. Soon she returns to the garden with a tray full of refreshments.

"Wow, wine in the morning?" Ragusa asks.

Payvand sticks her tongue out at her and says, "On special occasions it's okay. Can I go on now?"

Ragusa laughs, gently slapping the back of Payvand's hand and says, "Okay, okay, please do go on."

Payvand pours some wine and picks up a piece of cheese. "Our organization helped the powerless and trapped people of society. We also assisted those who had financial problems such as young people who were anxious to learn and study but did not have the money for education. Our main concern was the training and educating of people who had no clue as to why a resource-rich country like Iran, with an immense income from oil and tourism, should have the majority of its people living in crippling poverty. We helped them to find the answers themselves by providing books and other resources they needed to learn and recognize the political realities that were controlling their lives.

"We believed that before people could decide whether to join a movement that professed to present them with the truth, they had to be educated about their world, their country, their city, and the very community in which they lived. There were many adults who could not even write a sentence or read a simple book. Some had been child labourers who had never had the opportunity to be children. The most sensitive aspect of my own work was dealing with abused women, usually ones with marital issues. Many of these women were not able to save themselves or leave their miserable situations."

"Didn't you have social workers?"

Payvand shakes her head. "No. In Iran, then and still today, society was rife with corruption, and those in need really had no one trustworthy they could turn to. We fundraised ourselves, or donated a part of our salaries for team needs. Don't ask about my team. I will tell you about it later. Today is just about a young woman that I met one day and how she became a part of my life for a good number of years. Her name was Minoo, which in Farsi means 'heaven' or 'heavenly.'"

Ragusa smiles and repeats the name, "Mee-noo, did I pronounce it right?"

"You sure did, and that 'minoo' is just one of several words that mean 'heaven.' So, I met Minoo one day after Shokat, one of the lawyers I knew and worked with closely, called me and explained that she had just received a call from Fattaneh, one of our nurse activists. She was a strong member of our team and she often found such miserable individuals in the hospital where she worked, which is where beaten or abused women usually ended up.

"Fattaneh would talk to them about our safe house, prepare them, and then call us to bring them in. Mind you, this was all before the revolution. It was much easier to work at that time if your group was not armed. We were all about education and did not believe in assassinations or violent insurrection, so groups like ours had good opportunities to blend in with the people and work with them and for them. The government's special police had their hands full with two rather more threatening partisan groups, one religious and the other leftist.

"Anyway, back to this new victim, whom I was told was a very young, injured woman in a lot of danger. I hurried over and there and she was indeed in very bad shape. A broken arm, a couple of fractured ribs, and her face was so puffed up that you couldn't say if she was a person or a beast! The skin around her eyes was purple and green, her lips were swollen, and her right cheek was inflamed.

"Fattaneh filled me in on the details. This was the work of her husband, and it was the third time in two years that she had been admitted to the hospital. The husband was in jail for the incident. They were supposed to keep him there overnight, but apparently, he got into a fight with the police, so they were going to incarcerate him for more than a week. It was a great opportunity for us to prepare Minoo who was terrified of losing her children.

"Fattaneh introduced me to Minoo, and I sat by the bed and talked to her briefly. She could speak, but she was in great pain so most of her answers were a simple 'Yes' or "No'. For that reason I let her rest, and instead I began to sing for her. This was an approach that I had found worked very well. I had a good voice, and my singing seemed to take these frightened and confused women away from the dark places in their minds, at least for a while. It was a good tool for getting people into a more positive frame of mind."

"Will you sing for me too?"

Payvand laughs. "Sure I will. But you have to wait; it has to be the right time. I don't like to sing if it is not the right time or if it's not in me."

"Okay, but I have your promise now!" Ragusa teases.

Payvand smiles and then continues. "I sat by her bed and sang a poem by Nima that I had put to music."

"Who is Nima?"

"Nima was the father of modern poetry in Iran. So, after a few minutes of staring at me, Minoo slowly moved her good arm toward me. I stroked her hand lightly, and continued singing to her. Tears streamed silently down her face, and I whispered to her, promising that things would be different from now on and that she would never see that monster ever again.

"As I softly and quietly went over the plan, I felt a hand on my shoulder. I jumped, but it was only Fattaneh with another woman. Fattaneh introduced me to Minoo's mother, who had been visiting every morning and evening, bringing food for her daughter and bathing her. She was wonderfully helpful but very upset at herself for not being able to protect her child from harm. She would sit by her daughter's bed, crying silently. After bathing her daughter, she would go to the nurses and beg them to look after her when she was not there. She brought homemade pastries for everyone every day, and the whole ward loved her.

"I took the mother aside and told her my plans to take Minoo to a safe house. She was so worried, holding my hands and pleading that Minoo was too badly injured and needed a doctor. I told her not to worry as we had our own doctor and nurses. She wanted Fattaneh to come with us, but I put my finger on her lips and told her that no one could know."

"But I thought Fattaneh was a member of your organization too," says Ragusa.

"Yes, but to protect Fattaneh, we had to pretend she was just another nurse in the hospital. The next day, when the mother was to release her daughter from hospital, we had her bring Minoo's kids for a visit. We had Minoo up and ready, and I made noises about helping them to get a cab. But when we were out of the hospital, we loaded them all into our car and drove off to our safe house.

"Now I had time to turn my attention to Minoo's adorable children. She had three girls, ages six, four, and two. They were polite, though abnormally quiet, which was understandable given their mother's situation. The older one sat tightly by her mom, holding her hands. The other two watched her with apprehension.

"I tried to joke and play with them, but I realized they did not understand what I was saying. Minoo's mother explained that they didn't speak Farsi. She said, 'We are Turk and their parents only spoke with them in Turkish.' That was no problem as we had friends who could communicate with them in Turkish.

"By the time we arrived at the safe house, other team members had set up the big room for Grandma and the kids, and the smaller room for Minoo so she could have quiet and rest. Grandma was worried, saying that this wasn't going to work because Minoo's husband's family would find them and demand her back. We tried assuring her they were safe, but she just couldn't be convinced. So I posed a question to her: 'Can you tell me where you are?' She didn't know and admitted that the twists and turns along the route had confused her. I told her that is the way we keep the place secret and not to worry.

"We asked Minoo's mother to stay for a few days to help us care for her daughter and get her grandchildren used to us. 'You see, we are only here to help. Now, once you leave, you will never see us again until the court day for the divorce, which our lawyer will inform you about. That lawyer will tell Minoo's husband that her father, meaning your husband, is hiding her and that he wants justice for his daughter.'

"I told her we would drop her near her home, and that she must go prepare her husband for this story. She assured us that her husband would help with the plan. 'The last time that Minoo's husband hit our daughter, my husband went to that man's work and smacked him in front of his co-workers, telling him that if he ever touched Minoo again, he would bring her back to our home.'"

Ragusa impatiently asks, "So, did you help her with the divorce?"

"Excuse me, you have to wait. Actually I am going to cut short the divorce proceedings, including the ludicrous court wrangling that took about two years to process. I'm going to concentrate on the fun parts. Now, bear with me!"

"Okay. Go on. Sorry, Madam!"

"After a week or so, I had another mission that took me away for a few weeks. There were nurses, including Fattaneh, our doctor Kaveh, and other friends taking care of Minoo and the kids. They were teaching the kids games and how to read as well as helping Minoo to recover.

"After several weeks, I returned to find an absolutely gorgeous woman standing in the middle of our hallway. She greeted me by name, but I had to ask who she was. She smiled and said, 'Minoo, I am Minoo.' I stared at her, speechless. So it was left to Fattaneh to say, 'Isn't she something?'

"Ragusa, I have never seen anybody more beautiful in my entire life. I have travelled a lot and I have seen many beautiful women from different cultures, but this woman was incredible. Her big, almond-shaped eyes had a colour impossible to describe. Were they yellow? Green? Hazel? The eyelashes were so long and dark, and an amazing contrast to her eye colour. She had a cute little nose, flawless skin, and pouty lips like red rose blossoms."

"Do you have a picture of her?"

"Not from that time; how could I? We didn't keep pictures of one another as it was too dangerous. However, I have pictures of her when she was older. I will show you later. Believe me, there's no difference; she remains absolutely gorgeous.

"So, once I hugged Minoo and sent her on her way, Fattaneh said, 'Yes, she makes quite an impression on people when they see her for the first time. You should see Shayan around her. He is awestruck every time he sees her.' I asked her, 'Our Shayan? What does he have to do with her?' 'Well, he is our teacher now!' Fattaneh said. 'He is teaching her, and she is so smart and learning so fast. What a waste! She only went to school up to the sixth grade before they forced her into a marriage.'

"You know, even though I was the one who was supposed to take care of them and teach her, I was glad that I had to go on that trip because then I was able to see all the wonderful things that had happened in my absence. She had recovered so well physically, and Shayan's teaching had made all the difference for her and her three kids.

"Our lawyer continued working on Minoo's case, filing legal documents and going to court, as well as presenting photographic and testimonial evidence of the many beatings and abuses she had endured. The lawyer brought Minoo to the court only once, two days after we brought her to the safe house from the hospital. She had to appear before a judge, with her father escorting her. We were there too and watched as Minoo's father declared that he would now be taking care of his daughter and that he would not allow his daughter to go to her husband's home ever again. The judge recognized how badly Minoo was beaten and he quickly signed the papers allowing Minoo to stay with her relatives during the court proceedings.

"So, we let our lawyer do her job as she slowly but surely won the fight to get Minoo a divorce. As the days and weeks went by, we learned more and more about Minoo's story. Minoo was only twenty-one when we met her, meaning she was only thirteen years old when she got married to that monster Ahmad. The circumstances leading up to that marriage were that Minoo's father owed money to Ahmad's father, but he could not pay him back because he had just been laid off and couldn't find another job. They were living in very poor conditions in the city of Tabriz, but Ahmad had a good job in Tehran at a shoe factory and supported his own family well. On one visit to his family, he caught sight of our beautiful Minoo and demanded that his father ask for her hand. His father disagreed, saying that Minoo's family was too low class and other such nonsense. But Ahmad threatened to cut off support to them if they did not arrange this marriage. That solved that problem; his parents agreed and promptly asked for Minoo's hand.

"But now it was Minoo's parents who disagreed, saying that their only daughter was too young, and they didn't want her going to Tehran. The monster Ahmad solved that problem too by threatening to land Minoo's father in jail for not paying back his own father's money. He promised to support Minoo and her family in his house in Tehran and that he would wait for her to grow older before taking her into his bedroom.

"Poor Minoo was so afraid of her father going to jail that she convinced her parents that the marriage was okay with her. Doesn't get much more romantic than that, does it Ragusa?"

Ragusa sighs, sympathizing with Payvand's cheerless sarcasm.

"Of course, what young Minoo at age thirteen did not understand were the implications of a long life in a joyless marriage. Her only innocent thought was, *I will save my father from jail and make Mother happy*. She was an inexperienced child as are so many young brides in marriages just like that in Iran. When there is no social system to protect young girls, marriage is often seen as the only way to solve a problem.

"So, the family moved to Tehran and lived in Ahmad's house. He helped Minoo's father get a job in the same factory where he was working, and Minoo was supposed to go back to school and complete her the seventh grade. Unfortunately, Ahmad did not like the idea of his striking wife going to school, especially in those relatively liberal days before the revolution when most girls dressed in modern fashions and without a head scarf. So, after only a week, Ahmad called the school to reveal that

Minoo was married, which automatically got her expelled. Remember, I said it was 'relatively' liberal in those days.

"Minoo went home crying, but Ahmad took the family out and bought them all new clothes. Then, he gave some more money to her father, and, in a way, he purchased her. He then promised to hire a tutor for her, which he never did.

"A few weeks after that, he came home one day acting as if he was sick and sent Minoo's mother off to buy medicine from the pharmacy. The naïve mother did as she was told and left her daughter alone with that monster Ahmad.

"Minoo told a psychologist later that her husband had then entered her room where she was looking at a book. His eyes were scary and he was acting strange. She said, 'Normally he would ask if he needed something, and he certainly never came to my room. I was confused right up to when he reached out and touched my hair. I jumped, and he grabbed my arm and said he could not wait; I was his wife and had to obey his wishes.'

"Minoo told her doctor how she pushed him away, screaming that he had promised to wait for her fifteenth birthday. 'I called for my mother, and I felt a shiver down my back when I realized, by his sickening smile, that it was only the two of us in the house. I screamed again, and that's when he hit me for the first time. He struck me across the face so hard that I felt the blood in my mouth. Then he pinned me to the ground, hit me again, and raped me.'

"She then told her psychologist that her next memory was of opening her eyes in the hospital where her mother had brought her with the help of neighbours after she returned home and found out what had happened."

"What did they do to her husband?" Ragusa asks.

"Nothing; he was her husband. For Minoo's protection the doctors told him she had stitches and that she needed to recover for a few weeks before she could be his 'wife' again. Apparently, the doctors were not happy with him, but legally, there was nothing they could do."

"How disgusting," Ragusa says furiously. She gets up and paces around the little garden. "I cannot believe it. You mean there was no law to protect that child?"

"Law? If there was a law to protect these kids, he could not have married her in the first place." Payvand gets up and pours some more wine for Ragusa and herself before going to the kitchen to bring out some more food.

Ragusa follows her and says, "Where is the fun in this story? This has been awfully sad."

Payvand smiles and says, "If I didn't tell you the beginning of her life, you wouldn't know who the heck I am talking about. Furthermore, you wouldn't enjoy what I am about to tell you."

"I suppose that's reasonable. You go on then," Ragusa says as she begins slicing some tomatoes, pickles, and avocado. "I will make sandwiches for us. You go on."

Payvand looks at her affectionately, and continues. "When Minoo's father found out, he argued with Ahmad, and from that moment, her parents made sure they never left the couple alone together again. But as I heard from her mother, Minoo changed from that day. She was sad and rarely smiled or spoke. She would sit alone and stare into the distance. After a few months, when Minoo had just turned fourteen, her father came home one night and told Ahmad that he had earned the money he owed to Ahmad's father, and he wanted him to divorce his daughter. Ahmad refused and said if anyone talked about it one more time, he would make sure that her father lost his job. Minoo, for the first time, stood up for herself and said, 'That is fine father. Give the money to them. Forget the job, and let's go back to Tabriz.'

"At that moment Ahmad got up and swore at Minoo and her father. He said that without his permission, Minoo could not go anywhere. Then, he stormed out of the house. Her father didn't argue with Ahmad, but when they were alone, he told Minoo, 'If we leave, you will become a divorcee, and who is going to marry you later?'

"A few weeks after that conversation, Ahmad came home one night pleasant and civil and showing no sign of hostility. He had bought gifts for everyone and asked Minoo to go out and see a movie with him. Minoo rejected the offer immediately, and Ahmad became visibly upset. But Minoo's father pointed out that Ahmad could not bother her in the cinema, so she should go out and have some fun. So Minoo finally agreed.

"They did go to see a movie of Minoo's choosing, but after that, instead of driving her home, Ahmad forcefully took her to a motel, raped her, and kept her there for two days. This time he made sure that she didn't end up in a hospital.

"The rest is obvious. She got pregnant at age fourteen and again every two years or so, and when we met her she was twenty-one, with three kids, the oldest being six years old. He hit her regularly, not only because he wanted to disfigure her and erode her self-esteem, but because he knew that Minoo hated having sex with him. It never ever occurred to the donkey that she hated him because he was an abusive bully.

"This was Minoo's life before we rescued her. Now let's come back to our team and what happened after her arrival. The deep involvement of our team in Minoo's particular case was a phenomenon. It had never happened before Minoo's time nor did it ever happen again. As I said, in my absence they chose a teacher for Minoo and two tutors for her daughters. Shayan, Minoo's teacher, was twenty-five and a medical student, and he was a member of our team. He worked with me on our underground magazine as well. I had a literature section where I wrote short stories, poems, and fictionalized accounts loosely based on cases like Minoo. Such accounts were heavily altered so as to be untraceable to real people. Shayan made scientific articles on topics of general interest, and also about such things as health and hygiene accessible to ordinary people by rewriting them in simple language. The two of us generally had about six to ten pages in each issue of our underground magazine. He was smart and good-looking but extremely shy. He had never had a girlfriend and was socially awkward around women. For this reason, our group thought that he would be the best choice as Minoo's teacher because we assumed he would not flirt with her. Well, he was shy all right, but any human being with an appreciation for nature's beauty would not fail to notice Minoo. Shayan was no exception.

"Minoo was happy with Shayan because she had had enough of all the years of leering lecherousness from her husband and she appreciated the fact that Shayan always looked at the ground or the sofa or the wall in front of him whenever he talked to her. He was too shy to look at her directly!

"They soon learned to relax in each other's company, and when I returned from that mission of mine, I could see that he was killing himself trying to steal glimpses of her without her noticing, and she was killing herself to look at him without him noticing, and they were both killing themselves to keep other people from witnessing their furtive glances at each other."

Ragusa and Payvand laugh out loud at the couple's innocence.

"I seemed to be the only one in the house to clue in to all this. Minoo, obviously for the first time in her short life, had finally met a true gentleman, and she was constantly looking at him sideways. She was clearly attracted to him, but she had no understanding of her own strange feelings or what to do about them. And then there was our shy little Shayan who was mad about Minoo, but as you might have guessed, he had no clue about Minoo's feelings, or what to do about his own. They were a perfect match!"

Ragusa laughs out loud again. "You are kidding me!" she says, playfully slapping Payvand's hand.

"No, I mean it. She was too young when she married that monster, and her normal feminine affections were crushed, not awakened. Now, there was Shayan's gentle manner, good looks, warm and respectful behaviour, all conspiring to awaken her feelings for the opposite sex.

"I did not say anything about my observations to anybody, fearing that the group may separate them, which could possibly crush her again. So, sneaky Payvand secretly kept an eye on them both."

"You devious scamp," Ragusa teases.

"Well, I started to take the children out more often to give the two of them space to get to know each other. A few months passed and the kids were learning more and more Farsi with us, but still speaking Turkish with their mother. It was lovely watching them switch between the two languages and open up to everyone. Minoo's progress was amazing, and Shayan, who had in the process put some weight on his skinny body, looked even better.

"One day, when I returned with the kids from a matinee, I saw Shayan walking around the room anxious and frightened. I asked him, 'What is wrong? What have you done? Where is Minoo?' My other friend, who was parking the car, came in and asked what was going on, and I asked her to take the kids away. Then, I turned to Shayan again and demanded to know what was happening. 'I don't know. You go and ask her.' So, I knocked on the door of her room and she said to wait and give her some time. I returned to Shayan and said, 'You are killing me. What happened?'

"'I do not know, please believe me,' Shayan said.

"'Okay, let's start from the beginning. What is going on between you two? Don't deny it; I've been watching you both since my arrival.'

"'Yes, yes, we know, and we both appreciate that you are covering for us.'

"'Oh, so you are "*we*" now, are you? Explain please.'

"'Well, as you know she is so keen to learn, and keeps asking questions. She is very organized, and every morning, I come in for lessons and we go straight to math, then science, then English. We eat lunch, and then we go to history and then geography, which is her favourite subject. So, last week, I told her that fall is coming and because I have to go back to university, I won't be able to come here every day. I told her she may even have a different teacher, perhaps. Well, she said she doesn't want to have another teacher, and she started to cry. Looking into those beautiful eyes, I started to cry too and I held her hands. She did not say anything, but she blushed, and I blushed, and we both pulled back.'

"'So what happened then?' I asked. He repeated, 'We held hands, and...'

"'Hush!' I blurted out quickly, holding up my hand and looking away."

"What did you mean by 'hush'?" Ragusa asks. "They were just holding hands."

Payvand laughs and says, "I know that now, but back then I was as naïve as those two."

"Get out you silly girl. Are you serious? How old were you?"

"I was twenty-three and I had never held anybody's hand, so I did not know or even think about touching or physical attraction."

"What year was that?" Ragusa asks.

"It was just two or three years before the revolution. Yes, yes, I know, can you believe it? It was a more permissive time in the Western world, and even among the hipper elements within Iran, however, there were people on this planet at that time for whom a shallow, physical lifestyle meant nothing. We were entirely focused on preparing for a revolution and busy helping the weak and oppressed. How could we know how it feels to hold the opposite sex's hand?

"Anyhow, I decided to be brave and let Shayan tell me what happened next. He said, 'Well, I told her I would make sure that I could come twice a week if that's what she wanted. She liked the idea, and said she would work on her lessons and do as many assignments as she could, submitting them to me whenever I was there. When she got up to go to her room, she kissed my head. I almost passed out and couldn't say a word. The next day, I brought her a bouquet of flowers and she loved it. Then I kissed her hand. She only smiled, and it was the sweetest smile you could ever see. That was it! Since then, we hold hands and kiss each other's hand every day, until today.'

"'So, what did you do today?' I asked him. He could not answer at first, but finally, with tears in his eyes, he said, 'I touched her breast.' He paused, searching my face. 'I did a most horrible thing, didn't I?'

'Yes, you did! Why did you do that?'

'I don't know, but haven't you seen in foreign movies when the man touches the woman's breast and they show that they like it?'

"I was horrified and furious with him. 'You can't use movies as your guide in life!' I shouted at him. 'What did she do?'

'I don't know, she just looked at me and shivered, then she jumped up and ran into her room.' By then, poor Shayan was crying like a little boy.

"I rushed back to Minoo's room, knocked on her door, and asked her to please let me in. After a few minutes, she opened the door. Her eyes were puffy; she had obviously been crying. I asked if she was okay, and she replied with the sweetest smile, 'I am fine, how is he?'

'Well, he is very upset and worried sick about you.'

'Oh, he is so lovely and sweet, Payvand. I think I love him very much.'

'You are not angry with him?'

'No, I am angry with myself. But mostly, I am angry with my father, because when he paid his debts to Ahmad's father, I pleaded with him to leave Ahmad and return to Tabriz. He said, 'You will be a divorcee; who is going to marry you?' He did not fight for me. I am angry with this cruel world that has me, a young woman with three children, just now learning about love and how it feels to be touched, and how delightful is the sensation.' I asked her, 'And? How is it then?' Minoo blushed, then held me and said, 'You have to experience it yourself, as I have now.' "

Ragusa is laughing so hard she can barely breathe. "I cannot believe it! In the seventies! Oh boy, so different the lives we had. I was engaging in sexual activities all through high school with Dragomir, and we had our own adventures in learning about our bodies. Oh dear! But then again, it was so short-lived. Look what happened." Ragusa sighs. "Ah well, my drama is told. We're hearing your story now. Oh, such sweet innocence. Perfect! Do go on, please."

Payvand has a sip of her wine, leans back in her chair, and chuckles with Ragusa as she reminisces. Then she continues to recount Minoo's response. "'No, I am not mad at him. Actually I'm embarrassed about how little I know about these things, although he is inexperienced too, isn't he?' Minoo giggled. 'The problem now is what am I going to do with him? Yesterday, he told me that as soon as my divorce is finalized, he would love to marry me.'

'Well, that's nice! What did you say, Minoo?'

'Nothing. I just smiled at him. His family will never let him marry me, a divorced woman with three children.'

'You are right. That could be a problem. But never mind that for now. Tell me, why did you run away after he touched you?'

"She blushed again and said, 'At first I was shocked, but then I felt this warm sensation all through my body, and I didn't understand it. It felt so nice. Then, I felt bad about myself and ran to my room. I breastfed my girls so many times and never felt anything. I mean, why should I? The breasts are on my body to feed babies, right? But when he touched me, it was so different and electric. I didn't and I don't understand the feeling.'

"Would you believe me? Minoo with three kids was almost twenty-two, I was twenty-three, and Shayan was twenty-six and becoming a physician, yet none of us could comfortably talk about these natural feelings; some of the most beautiful emotions that any human can have and enjoy."

Ragusa finds this highly amusing and again has tears of laughter streaming down her face. "I believe you," she says. "With what you have told me so far, I believe you."

Payvand makes a face at her, and then she laughs too.

"So, do continue," Ragusa says with a smile.

"Well, I didn't know how to calm these two passionate, enamoured people. I decided to ask Shayan to leave for the day, and Minoo and I spent the rest of the day playing with the kids and cooking for them.

"The next day, Shayan apologized to Minoo and said, 'I love you and your children, and everything else starts from there.' He said he would wait for her divorce to be settled, and they would talk about their future then. It took a few days of awkward discomfort, but eventually Minoo and Shayan got back to their daily routine of studying, playing with the children, and continuing to learn each other's ways.

"Soon summer was over, and Minoo reiterated that she would not accept any other tutor but Shayan. So Shayan came twice a week to continue her lessons. And every Friday he would test her on what she had learned, and thus he prepared Minoo for school district exams.

"Time was passing beautifully for Minoo and her children, and for Shayan. While we were preparing for our revolution, they were having their own mini-revolution of the heart in their little heaven in that safe house. Minoo decided to stay with us so that she and her girls would be safe until her divorce was finalized.

"As the months went by, she patiently waited for her freedom from that monster. Because she was with us for so long, we decided to occasionally drive her parents to the safe house late at night where they would stay with Minoo and the kids for a couple of days. Then, we would drive them back home also late at night. Minoo loved the safe house's yard, and took care of the garden in the same way she took care of her children.

"I, conversely, was in and out doing my work: participating

in rallies with my team associates, pushing for our revolution, talking about our manifesto, and encouraging the advancement of the country as a whole and its people in particular. The cruelty of the Shah's regime, his neglect of the majority of the people and his unfair distribution of wealth in the country, had the people of Iran in rebellion, as one, calling on him to leave-so that a new democratic country could be created where people might vote and choose legislators.

"We believed that oil and other resources belonged to the citizens of the country and not to the elite or foreign corporations. Furthermore, the Shah had built and developed the tourist cities in Iran beautifully, but only for the benefit of wealthy visitors and to glorify Iran's grand historical past. Many of the smaller and more remote cities and villages had no electricity, no clean water, and no proper schools. The majority of Iranians wanted a change.

"At the University of Tehran and at other major universities throughout the country, there were tables where young university students displayed their books and magazines and preached their ideology. The problem was that all of this could be accessed by other university students but not by the illiterate. Accordingly, one important focus for our group was teaching people to read so that they could learn for themselves. This way the revolution was happening because the majority of Iran's population was participating in one way or another, not just the intellectuals.

"There were many different political groups trying to recruit people to their cause. Each group had their own ideology, and sometimes they would clash here and there, but they all were united on two points: that the Shah had to go, and that we wanted no more 'overnight monarchies.'

"What is an 'overnight monarchy'?" Ragusa asks.

"Well, basically it means the Shah's family had no royal ancestry. But I'll talk about that later," Payvand says and waves her hand at Ragusa. "I would just like to concentrate on Minoo today. I'm talking a little about the details of the revolution just to show how the social upheaval of the time affected Minoo's situation. I promise to give you more information about the 'overnight' royal family later."

"Fair enough," Ragusa nods.

"As all this was happening, I filled Minoo in daily with information about what I was doing. As soon as I came home, tired and hungry, I could do nothing until I had satisfactorily answered all her questions. She would read anything she could get her hands on and she developed a passion for debating her beliefs, becoming an even stronger advocate for those beliefs than many of the busy activists in the universities. She had learned enough that she could tell you in thirty minutes why Russia's revolution failed and why it was now nothing more than another kind of dictatorship. She could clarify why and how China's revolution failed, and would sarcastically explain that, 'Their role model was Russia, so how could they do any better than to create another type of dictatorship?' She checked in with everyone around the home and charmed them with her newly acquired knowledge and the sweet way she had of expressing herself.

"She felt right at home with us, and she became much more knowledgeable than many of the people out on the street who often weren't clear on what they are talking about because of a lack of thorough research. Every day, Minoo gained more and more knowledge from all kinds of books, newspapers, TV news, and her friends, who daily kept her apprised of events.

"It was a few months before the revolution that the court finally granted her divorce and gave her custody of her three children. Her husband did not contest that, primarily because they all were girls, which, of course, was yet another reason why he had been beating her — she wasn't providing boys for him. What an idiot he was.

"Despite that, he continually delayed signing the divorce papers. Many of the government offices were shutting down as a result of chaos on the streets, and he was taking advantage of the situation by using it as an excuse for not signing the papers. I think this brought stress and anxiety back to Minoo, and she started becoming pessimistic again, fearing that he would never grant the divorce and would eventually find her and take her away by force. We all tried to keep her upbeat with busy days of study, political discussion or playtime with her girls, but we weren't very successful. From time to time, we would find her crying softly.

"On the political scene, with pressure from the people becoming too strong to resist, the West decided to go with an alternate plan of control and whisked the Shah and his family away into exile. For a brief time, this actually provided us with some breathing room to work harder to establish a new democracy.

"Unfortunately, after the revolution, there was a change in direction that none of us anticipated, which eventually resulted in the establishment of an Islamic regime. We were frightened and appalled that the country was falling into the hands of the most backward and ignorant ranks of our society."

"You were right to think that it was frightening. Time has proven that!" Ragusa says.

"Meanwhile, Minoo was losing her mind, convinced that the divorce would never come through now. Shayan was even more upset than she was. He would not come to our meetings, or if he did show up, he was disoriented and distracted. Eventually, I believe it was six months after the revolution, Shokat, the lawyer working on Minoo's case, called and said that Ahmad was at long last ready to finalize the divorce. She gave us the date and time that Minoo was required to appear in court to sign the papers in front of the same judge who had begun her case. He was actually trying to close as many cases as possible prior to the whole court system being refashioned into a new Islamic one, whatever that meant, so at least we had that going for us.

"We were happy that soon this would all be over. The night before the big day, Shokat was to come and fill us in, so we prepared a dinner for the meeting. This was overseen by Minoo, who was, not surprisingly, a wonderful chef. Ah, what a cook she was! How I miss her hearty meals.

"Shokat arrived right on time, and as soon as she came in, she stopped, took a deep breath, and said, 'Well, something smells very delicious.' Yes, that was pretty much everybody's first reaction when Minoo was cooking. We all loved her food.

"Minoo said, 'Oh just a few things, and the best is for you! But nobody gets anything until I know what you did or what the judge did to make him come and sign the papers.' We all laughed, and Shokat held her tight and said, 'Sure. Let's go sit and I will tell you all about it.'

"Apparently, judges, lawyers, and others working in the justice system knew that things were changing for the worse. Many of them were trying to close cases that they believed were the most sensitive, or that they had worked furthest toward completion. They understood that their profession was being refashioned and that they would have to leave their jobs when the new Islamic justice system set about demolishing the few rights women had at the time.

"In Minoo's case, not even Ahmad's lawyer liked Ahmad. Hoping to make this ugliest of cases his last one before retiring to teach, he wanted to get the divorce finalized before Islamic law was set up and made the divorce unlikely, or even forced Minoo back into the marriage. So the lawyer formulated a package that Ahmad would like, appealing to his ignorant traditionalist biases about wanting a son, and to his love of money. He also used Ahmed's present infidelities with his mistress and his past beatings of Minoo to show him that it would not be wise to go before a judge and they should instead settle now.

"The package presented to him read, in general terms, like this: 'With this new revolution, we do not know how the new laws will deal with a man who hits his wife. You may have to pay a large penalty. Minoo and her lawyer have agreed not to ask for money, not even to give her back her dowry. Also, she and her father will raise the three children, and will not ask for child support. They will close the file and will not lay any more charges against you, even though your last brutal beating could allow Minoo's family to pursue you with a criminal case. Minoo's father has paid off his debt to you, so you have nothing to hold against him and his family. Your mistress is pregnant, maybe with a boy, and you should move on with your life with her.'

"'So,' Shokat concluded, 'he has agreed to sign the papers.' She was expecting Minoo to be happy, but was surprised to see a grim look on Minoo's face. 'I will believe it, when I see it,' Minoo cried, and then ran into the kitchen. She was terrified that something might still go wrong.

"Poor thing! Two years was a long time to wait for this day, and she felt the last day would never come. We got her back out to the table where we tried to cheer her up with compliments about her wonderful meal and with optimistic talk about court the next day, but both Minoo and Shayan were quiet and worried. Their devotion to each other was now well known by everyone on the team, and we all hoped for the best for them.

"The next day, Shokat, Minoo, and Shayan went to court. Shokat had arranged that Minoo could present herself to the judge first so that she didn't have to be in the same room with Ahmad. Then Shayan brought Minoo home, and we all anxiously kept ourselves busy while Shokat attended to the rest of the proceedings. By noon, Shokat was back with a cheerful smile and handed the finalized divorce papers to Minoo. She grabbed them, read them, and then started screaming, leaping for joy, and simultaneously crying so hard that her children became confused and distressed. Someone took them outside so that Minoo could release all her emotions in this incredible moment of happiness. She was free at last.

"Everyone had invested so much into this day. Her father had worked two jobs to pay his debt to Ahmad, and Shokat, working as a member of our team, refused to charge Minoo. But there were court fees and other expenses for her and her children who had been living at our safe house for two years. Each one of us had chipped in, and now that Minoo's freedom had been granted, we all felt generously repaid.

"Shayan quietly watched Minoo with tears of happiness in his eyes. Then Minoo looked around to find him, and threw herself on him. They held each other tight and cried passionate tears of contentment.

"Shokat laughed, 'Okay, cool it down you two. You have to wait for three months, and then you can get married if you wish.'

"'What?' Shayan gasped. 'Why three months?'

"'It's the law. You have already waited two years, so three months won't kill you.' Then she went into the kitchen to look for leftovers from the night before."

"Did they get married?" Ragusa asks impatiently.

"Sure they did. But my satisfaction was not only in their marriage, but in watching that ridiculous Ahmad's anger and disbelief."

"How?"

"I'll tell you. But first let me give you a few details about the monster and what he had been doing the past two years while we were taking care of his family.

"As soon as he realized that he had really done it this time and that he had battered his wife so badly that he may never see her again, he went and got himself a 'temporary' wife."

"Now what do you mean by that?" says Ragusa.

"Well, here in the West, married people cheat or have mistresses and love affairs, right? They cannot really do that in Muslim countries, because if they are caught there are extremely serious consequences. However, patriarchy is patriarchy and an accommodating Muslim rule was crafted whereby, with the reading of some Koranic verses, a legal conjugal contract with a woman can be drawn up for the period of an hour or two, or a day or two, or a year or two — whatever the man fancies. Thusly, Ahmad had contracted a woman to be with him.

"Of course, it was another poor divorced woman, coming out of a miserable life with her first husband, only to get involved with a man like Ahmad because she needed financial support. We called this kind of arrangement 'legal prostitution.' Recall that this 'mistress' was pregnant when Minoo's divorce was finalized. We found out later that the unfortunate woman gave birth to twin girls! How ironic is that? Minoo's father said that Ahmad was going insane. Now he had five girls! So, he promptly discontinued his contract with that unhappy woman, who now had, counting one boy from her first marriage, three children and no income.

"Later, determined to have a son, he picked up a fifteen-year-old girl, twenty-two years younger than him, from a small nearby village and married her. If only we had possessed today's technology back then, we could have somehow steered that featherbrained Ahmad to a doctor for a quick test that would probably have shown that he was naturally short on the Y chromosome needed to produce a boy. We could hope that this would have perhaps stopped him from torturing women for boys, but maybe acting on scientific information would have been too much to ask of that sort of man."

Payvand smiles slyly, "Now let's get back to Minoo. But keep the monster's tale in mind. We'll come back to it, my dear Ragusa.

"Three months passed, and finally Shokat could provide Shayan and Minoo the legal papers they needed to get married. We prepared a beautiful ceremony, attended by our team and the immediate families of Shayan and Minoo. Shayan's parents had been spending some time with Minoo and her children over those three months to get to know them, so they took the kids for three days, and then Minoo's parents took them for a week, so that our lovebirds could go on their honeymoon.

"As soon as they came back, I took Minoo aside and asked her, 'So, how was it?' She blushed and said, 'We didn't do anything but hug, kiss and talk. We both were inexperienced and anxious about doing anything more.' I too was inexperienced, but I knew enough to know that this was a bit much and that they should seek some therapy if they wanted their relationship to survive, so through our contacts we set them up with an appropriate psychologist. After a few months of sessions, everything came together beautifully and the two of them developed a wonderfully romantic relationship.

"Shayan graduated and started his residency at a hospital. Our team had a meeting, and all of us that were involved with Minoo's case had to participate. We were to vote on whether Shayan and Minoo, who already had become a staunch activist, should stay in the team or be removed for some time. The vote was ninety-five percent that they should no longer be part of the team. We felt that with the kids just starting to grow up, they should have a happy, healthy, and stable family, with a loving mom and dad who would always be there for them. Strong activist work would add stresses and long absences that might take a toll on the children, not to mention the dangers of arrest or death that could destroy the new family."

Ragusa smiles and says, "How thoughtful. But did they accept that the team made that decision for them?"

"Of course not, but we convinced them both. We asked them to trust our judgment just for a year or two, to allow the team to work without worrying about the safety of their precious family. We wanted them to wait until their children were older and more independent. Then we could consider having our two brave humanitarians join us again. I think Shayan was very worried about those kids and didn't want them hurt, even unintentionally. He agreed and convinced Minoo as well. To be safe, we then had to leave the house to them, and move our group to another safe house so that there were no traceable links to them."

"What do you mean, how many houses did the organization have?" asks Ragusa.

"There were a few, and much of the money came from Behrouz's inherited wealth. I will tell you more about this when we get to Behrouz's story.

"Minoo's parents joined them to help with the kids, and they all lived together. Minoo went back to school at night to earn her high school diploma, and then she wanted to go to nursing school. She also worked as a volunteer during the day while her parents took care of the household. Shayan was making good money as a doctor, and Minoo's father did not need to work anymore. They were all quite happy."

Ragusa sighs, "How wonderful!"

"Wait!" Payvand lifts a finger. "I'm not done yet. At the beginning of Minoo's story, I told you about our team and that later I would talk about our involvement with the revolution and I will. But for now, I should tell you that our happy couple had less than a year to enjoy their new circumstances. After the new regime consolidated power, they created a new guard called Basij to patrol the streets to generally control people, suppress rallies, and force women to conform to the new codes of dress."

"You mean force them to wear the scarf?"

"Yes, but the scarf was only the beginning. They later forced women to cover up head to toe!"

"A pure dictatorship," Ragusa comments.

"Yes. Furthermore, they created a police force called 'Sepah-e Pasdaran,' which was used to defend the new regime and the Islamic system. They stepped up the Islamic Assembly squads, which were teams of fundamentalists working in schools, universities, factories, hospitals, government offices and other institutions, to control people's smallest movements. For instance, the hospital where Minoo volunteered and Shayan worked also had its own Islamic Assembly committee that monitored everyone, including our couple. They knew where they lived, but they didn't yet have any details about their marriage and children. It was the beginning of the forging of a huge frightening system in order to find out who was working against them, and especially who were the leftists.

"We were not surprised to learn that that monster Ahmad was head of the Islamic Assembly in the factory where he worked. We also found out that his third wife was giving birth soon. We didn't think anything of it, but when she went into labour, we were taken by surprise when she was brought to the very hospital where Shayan and Minoo worked. How coincidental was that?"

"The hospital staff immediately started helping the new patient because she was so young and frail. Complications soon arose, so they paged the doctor on call, who was Shayan. He had to do a C-section and he found the baby unresponsive and in critical condition. In fact, she died the next day. The mother explained that her husband had become angry when she accidentally burned some food, and he had kicked her hard. She fell onto her stomach, and after that, she did not feel the baby move. As they were talking, Ahmad arrived and his first question was, 'Where is my boy?' As soon as Shayan discovered he was the husband of that young woman, he stepped up and pushed Ahmad to the ground, shouting, 'You hurt your baby girl when you hit your wife!' The nurses helped the monster get up, but he was so angry at hearing that he'd had another girl that he did not even realize he had been pushed down.

"Meanwhile, Minoo got word that her husband was fighting with a patient's husband, so she rushed into the room, threw herself onto Shayan, and ordered him out of the room. As she pulled him to the door, she came face-to-face with her ex-husband. He stared at her with his wild eyes, and then decided that the most relevant thing to say was, 'Why are you not wearing your chador?'"

"What was the chador again?"

"Remember, I told you that before the revolution women were dressed much like European and other Western women. However, there were always some very religious families that never allowed their women to appear in public without being encased in a long black robe that covered them from head to toe. The only thing you could see of them was a part of their face. That is the chador. When Minoo married Ahmad, she had to wear one. But then with us, and later when married to Shayan, she never used the chador again. At the time of our story, the Islamic Assembly had started to enforce these new dress codes. So far they had pushed women to the stage of requiring head scarves such as hijabs, but not everyone was following the rules yet. In the hospital, Minoo typically wore a long and loose white nurse's dress and a small white head scarf. This was not enough for her ex-husband, or the new regime. The chador is meant to cover a woman from head to toe in black.

"Later Shayan told us, 'When I realized he was Minoo's ex-husband, all I cared about was removing her from there as fast as possible. We hurried down the hall, but he ran after us. The staff stopped him and asked why he was running after us when his wife was waiting in the room. He seemed confused and said, 'She is my wife too,' which surprised the staff. As they debated who was his wife, the delay allowed Shayan and Minoo to get away. Shayan returned to the hospital afterwards.

"So now the monster knew about Minoo's marriage, and when Shayan left at the end of his shift, Ahmad was waiting for him at the hospital entrance. He approached Shayan very calmly and hissed, 'I want my children, and I will go to court and take them.' Of course they got into a fight, and the police had to come to get them apart."

Ragusa is shocked, "Could he? Did he take the children?"

"Of course he could take them. It was an Islamic rule. A father has automatic sole custody of a son from birth, and of a daughter from age seven. Two of Minoo's children were over seven already."

"So then what happened?" Ragusa asks, agitated.

Payvand holds her hand, smiles, and says, "Good things happened. Shayan's family loved those children just as much as they loved Minoo, and they were well-off and willing to help. We knew there was no way we could win this battle in the courts, but none of us could bear to think of giving those children to that crazy man. The monster was simply angry that his ex-wife was married to a rich and handsome doctor, and that she was healthier and more beautiful than ever. We knew he just wanted to use those innocent children to torture her.

"The borders were still safe, and passports were prepared post-haste. Before any court proceeding could be called, all seven of them left Iran for Greece. From there, they went on to Norway."

"Ah!" shouts a happy Ragusa. "How wonderful! I could not bear another battle. I am so happy. Norway, ha! Good!"

"Minoo wrote to tell us that they were settled and had a nice home. She was back at school while Shayan took his examinations for becoming a surgeon. She also talked about how beautiful Norway is, about its nice beaches, and how in that cold country people really knew how to appreciate their summers. So, after a few months, I asked Minoo to send me photographs of those beautiful beaches and of the family wearing bathing suits at the beach.

"What? Bathing suits? Why?"

Payvand laughs hard, then puts her hand up to stop Ragusa from asking another question. "Wait, I am going to tell you. Be patient. Minoo did send me a few photographs. What a beauty! There was no way anybody could ever believe that body belonged to a young woman who had given birth to three kids. I chose one showing Shayan holding Minoo's gorgeous body in his arms. Two of the kids hovered near his lap and the oldest hung over his shoulder. It was a picture of an absolutely beautiful family. And everybody was content in Dad's arms. I put that one into an envelope and sent it to her ex-husband."

Ragusa slaps Payvand's hand playfully. "You little devil. I love it! Who but you could think of that?"

Payvand says, "Ooooh, yes. He went to every official he could think of showing them the photograph and begging them to bring her back. Well, that was an impossible thing to do, and it never happened. You know, there simply was no justice for all that he had done to that poor girl Minoo, and to the other women after her. He was not punished nor did he ever apologize. So, this was my way of punishing that monster. Hee, hee! He was tormented for years.

"Today, Shayan is a retired surgeon, and Minoo is a retired head nurse. Their parents have passed away and the three girls, plus their own two boys, are all building their own lives. As Minoo says, 'Now, we are on our second honeymoon!'

"And, my dear Ragusa, since you liked my trick so much, I have one more. I sent Ahmad two more photographs later. One showed Minoo with her two boys, again in Shayan's arms, and the other was a photo of the five sisters and brothers. This envelope had a note in it saying, 'See, you could not make a boy for Minoo, but her husband did — two of them.' The only sad part of this was that I was not there when he opened the envelope. That took half of the fun away."

Ragusa is all keyed up. "I cannot believe this! This is grand!" She is tickled pink and gets up to pour herself some water, laughing and shaking her head. "You are right, it would have been something to be there and see his face when he read that note. So, are you still in contact with the family?" she asks.

"Of course," Payvand gets up and goes to the study. Ragusa follows her to a bookshelf filled with photo albums. Payvand pulls one out and gives it to Ragusa. "Here are their family pictures, from the day they left Iran to today."

They sit on the floor and go through the album as Payvand introduces the family and explains each photo. Ragusa puts her head on Payvand's shoulder and they enjoy the moment as they trace the growth of the family.

"She is so beautiful. I remember you said she was only one or two years younger than you, right? She looks ten years younger than us even though I am younger than both of you," Ragusa says, laughing. Then she remembers something. "I'm curious. What did you sing to Minoo in the hospital?"

Payvand is quiet for a few minutes as Ragusa patiently sits motionless.

"Ahh, yes, that was Nima's poem. I don't think I remember it all," Payvand says. She then starts to sing, her voice like velvet, this time to her dear Ragusa, her new friend:

The moonlight is flowing
The fireflies hover, shimmering
My body exhausted, yet not able to sleep
I watch the slumbering crowd
And it breaks the sleep in my tear-filled eyes...
My heart hurts as I feel the thorn
I fear for the tender delicate blooms
With love I planted,
With love I watered
Alas, it breaks before my eyes....

Payvand stops and puts her arm around Ragusa. "I have forgotten the rest; it was well over thirty years ago."

Ragusa looks into her eyes and says, "I feel it. Your voice is mesmerizing. It pulls at my spirit. What a delicate, warm voice you have. Yes, I can believe it was a good tool. Who are you woman? I love you."

Payvand laughs and pushes her away. "Come on, don't you go mushy on me please." She gets up, and helps Ragusa up too. They walk back to the yard to enjoy the beautiful roses and drink some more wine as they talk more about Minoo's successful life.

Ragusa asks, "When will you talk about you? Can you start now?"

"I'm afraid not," Payvand says. "It's two-thirty. Nada will be here soon. Let's start fresh tomorrow." She gets up and cuts one of the red roses that Ragusa likes so much and hands it to her with the warmest smile. "For you, and for a new beginning." Then she pauses, and adds, "Listen, I do not want you to think that I will ever directly prevent you doing what you wish. However, I would love to encourage you to an adventurous life in company with me, instead of a cold, boring death in the depths of the ocean. You can live and share your experiences to awaken that 'slumbering crowd.' Who knows? Maybe you can help make some sense of the ongoing atrocities and struggles and wars raging as we speak all across Africa in Syria, Iraq, Palestine, and Israel. Right now, people are going through what you experienced. Can you ignore that? Maybe, together, we can find ways to stop all the suffering."

Ragusa looks at her but says nothing, deep in thought. Then her face brightens. "Well, I really am looking forward to hearing some more stories from you."

Payvand looks at her kindly. "And I am looking forward to sharing more of my life with you. I want you to know that I understand how you have had the most difficult of lives. However, you should know that you never were and never will be alone."

The doorbell rings bringing a stop to their conversation. They quickly set up a time for the next morning then Payvand opens the door and welcomes Nada.

Ragusa reaches into her handbag and touches the present she bought on the island for Payvand. *I hoped we would be done today and that I could give her this present and go on my way. Do I want to be here tomorrow? Yes, I do, it is my wish! I like her so very much. Last night, I looked forward to seeing her again and I woke up happy to come here. Am I backing away from my determination? Oh well, let's see what this world has been hiding from me in this mysterious woman.*

"Ragusa..." Payvand calls. "Nada is in a hurry. Where are you?"

Ragusa rushes to the door, greets Nada, and kisses Payvand on the cheek. "I cannot wait for tomorrow. Today's story was very sweet, and I am looking forward to tomorrow's tale." She kisses her again, this time on the other cheek, then turns and follows Nada.

Payvand cleans up a bit, then gets ready for her appointment.

CHAPTER 5 **PAYVAND**

P AYVAND'S CLIENT ARRIVES on time for the appointment. They go to the study for their counselling session, exchange ideas, look over the client's progress chart for the past three weeks, and then conclude their meeting. As soon as her client leaves, Payvand goes to her garden and sits by the fountain. She is upset with herself as she was not as prepared for the appointment as she usually is.

Soon, Brian arrives and joins her in the yard. He greets her with a kiss and asks about her day. "But before you tell me, I could use some wine. Would you like a glass too?" he asks.

"No, I had enough wine today."

"You had wine today. Well! I assume you had a good day."

"Yes," she smiles. "It was fun today, but I don't know how to go about it tomorrow. What should I tell her? I really don't look forward to digging into my past."

"I know," he says, sitting in a chair next to her. "Well, your plan was to tell her one story a day to draw her into a habit of daily companionship, and ultimately convince her not to end her life, right? Maybe you only have to tell her a few things to illustrate your points, and not dig too deep. What do you think?"

She frowns. "Yes, you're right about the plan, but most of what I want to tell her won't make sense unless I revisit some nasty things that I have locked up inside. I don't know if I want to do that."

He moves his chair closer, and gently takes her hands. "I am sorry," he says.

"My appointment didn't go as well as I had hoped today, and that upsets me as well. I would rather have cancelled, but it was too late."

"Why cancel? You said you had a good day."

"Yes, perhaps that's the reason why I didn't want to see anyone after Ragusa left. Oh well. It's over now."

"Are you going to introduce Ragusa to your friends?"

"Not now. I don't want to talk about her with anyone; not without her permission. Soon, if she's up to it, I may introduce her to my friends. However, it has to be her wish."

He nods then goes inside to get his glass of wine.

Payvand listens to her murmuring fountain as she looks around the garden. She gets up and starts trimming yellowing leaves and deadheading the flowers.

Brian returns to the yard, but when he sees that she is working on her plants, he is pleased. *Good, this has always been healing for her,* he thinks, and quietly turns around.

He takes his wine into the kitchen and starts to prepare dinner, looking in on Payvand from time to time. An hour passes before the meal is ready and he calls her in.

"I'm not hungry," she says. "Will you forgive me? Why don't you bring your food here and join me in the garden. I'll pick at your food."

He knows her well enough not to push her, so he fills a plate with her favourite fruits and vegetables, and joins her in the garden. She looks at the plate and smiles. *Handsome and smart. Ah, I love this man so much!*

He sets the plate on the table and settles into his comfy chair. She sits on his lap and kisses him intensely. Then, she sips his wine before handing it back to him.

She looks at him lovingly, nuzzles his ear, and lays her head on his shoulder, whispering, "You know, I never believed that I could ever find a true love, and then you came along and lightened my life. It has been like a sweet dream, the two of us growing old together." She hides her face in his strong neck, "I'm sorry if, with Ragusa, I have brought a new quandary into our lives and imposed it on you."

He holds her tight in his arms and says, "You have brought a world of happiness to my life, and I cannot imagine it without you. And, there is nothing to be sorry about. You have become a gentle light in Ragusa's dark days, and if you, my love, are the one making this broken soul happy, I am only proud of you."

They hold each other for a time, listening to the fountain. She takes a bite of his food, then slides off his lap, picks up her scissors, and says, "You eat while I finish with these flowers."

The next day she wakes up to the sound of birds chirping outside her window, Brian's arms wrapped around her. She kisses his arm and turns to him smiling, "You up?"

"I was listening to your breathing," he says, then tenderly kisses her shoulder.

"I am still worried about today," Payvand says. "I don't know which part to begin with this time. I bought a day by talking about Minoo, but today where should I start?"

He smiles and gets out of the bed, "I am sure you will manage fine, as you did yesterday. You have many compelling stories to tell. Start from a part you feel comfortable talking about and see how many days you can bring her here willingly."

She seems encouraged. "I hope I can keep her interest up, and in time take her to meet my friends and see if we can rejuvenate her interest in life again."

"I hope so too. Ragusa was devastated when we first met her, and now she seems noticeably different. I can even say she looked happy yesterday, and I'm sure with your help she will steadily improve."

She gets up reluctantly, then rummages in her closet, and picks out a bright, colourful dress. Brian loves it. "That's my girl! That alone will boost her spirits another notch. You know people always compliment you on your inspired taste in clothing." She is pleased by his remark and gets ready for the day.

After breakfast, Brian hugs her and wishes her a pleasant and successful day before leaving for work. He walks cheerfully to his car, and considers himself a very lucky man.

Payvand sits in her garden waiting for Ragusa to arrive. She is late and Payvand starts to worry. She heads for the telephone just as the doorbell rings. "Ah!" She hurries to the door and is beaming as she ushers Ragusa into her home.

They hug and Ragusa apologizes for being late. Payvand shrugs it off. "You are here now and I am so glad to see you." Then, she turns and adds, "What would you like; tea or coffee?"

"Wine, please."

Payvand laughs. "Wine in the morning, again? Wow! Let's hope we aren't picking up bad habits," she says, and goes in search of one of her finest wines.

They settle into their chairs in the garden and fill their glasses. "What a pleasant day," Ragusa says. "So fresh and nice!" Then she takes a beautifully wrapped box out of her purse and gives it to Payvand.

"What is this?" Payvand says, smiling bashfully. "Is it a present? Why?"

"Open it. The day you left me on the beach, I thought that for all your kindness and understanding I should postpone my doom a bit longer. I felt I owed you that. So I walked to the fishing village near your cottage, perhaps to get you some flowers, but then I discovered a jewellery store with some magnificent little pieces."

"This is the Dove of Peace!" Payvand exclaims. "That was a signature I shared with another activist back in Iran."

"What do you mean?"

"Well, remember I told you I used to contribute material to our underground magazine, as did another woman. We wouldn't use our real names, so we drew a little dove as our signature beneath any short stories or articles that we wrote. A small dove with open wings, just like this one! Except of course ours was a little drawing. But this is so shiny and brilliant. Just beautiful!"

Ragusa is delighted to see that Payvand likes the pendant. She describes the story of each gem as the shopkeeper told it to her and that the pendant was handmade by an artist who collected the stones on journeys to the most remote areas of this planet.

Payvand is excited and inspects the pendant so thoroughly that she soon notices the inscription on the back. She reads it out loud: *You have conquered my spirit with your unconditional love.* Then she looks at Ragusa humbly. "Thank you, Ragusa. I do not know what to say."

"Say nothing. It suits your spirit, and I mean every word of it. I'm so happy you like it."

"I love it! Help me put it on."

"Of course," Ragusa says as she gets up and helps to clasp the pendant's chain around Payvand's neck, thrilled that Payvand so obviously enjoys the gift.

"Thank you so much," Payvand says as she gently pats the pendant that is now lying against her skin. "But really, you shouldn't have. This was obviously very expensive."

Ragusa smiles happily, "Why not? You deserve it. After all, what do I need money?"

Payvand looks up and frowns at her.

They sit quietly for a few minutes. Ragusa right away regrets what she has said. The distressed expression on Payvand's face is such a contrast to her previous excitement. She tries to find some way to make it right. "What an impressive dress you have on this morning! Such a beautiful pattern and eye-catching colours. Every time we meet, you impress me with your outfits. I like your taste very much."

"Thanks. I do really like colours and funky patterns." Payvand says as she gets up and fusses around her garden.

Ragusa looks at her and laughs. Payvand turns to her, "Why are you laughing?"

"You know, I can barely distinguish you in that colourful dress from the flowers around you. You become a part of this garden when you walk around in it. If it wasn't for your black head, I could lose you in here." They laugh, and Payvand playfully splashes her with water before returning to Ragusa's side.

Ragusa seizes the moment, and says, "I'm so sorry, I didn't intend to spoil our moment. I didn't really mean what you think. I'm just a person to whom money is not particularly important. That's all I meant."

Payvand reaches out to hold her hands. "Perhaps it's just that I worry too much, and I sometimes interpret things wrongly. It's okay."

Ragusa is relieved and places her hand on Payvand's shoulder. "I miss you when I am not with you. It's as if I have known you for a long time, and I feel very comfortable around you."

Payvand smiles affectionately. "Why don't you stay with me for some time? You know I would be thrilled if you could stay with us."

"Are you sure? What about Brian? Would he be all right with it?"

"Of course! He likes you very much. Who is picking you up today?"

"My brother, but I told him I would call him when I'm ready."

"Well, let's ask Brian to talk to him and assure him you just need a change of scenery and are safe with us."

The women agree on that, then make themselves comfortable in their seats and raise a glass to their new friendship. While they savour the wine, Ragusa says, "Well, I think it's time you tell me all about you, your past, and everything that led up to today. Also, how did you meet Brian? You are so compatible. Tell me about everything. I want to hear from your 'true beginning,' from when your 'real life' started, just like you asked me."

Payvand sinks into her chair, and over a long pause gathers her strength. Then she looks deeply into Ragusa's eyes and begins. "Let's see, how do I start? Umm ... I am in my late fifties, though usually I don't feel it. I have lived an active and adventurous life, tasted love and despair, peace and anger, struggle and achievement, defeat and challenge side by side with my comrades. I have fought against tyrants and fought for those who could not fight for themselves. I have made many good decisions, and I have made plenty of bad ones, doing my best always to correct them. Through all those years, I have never stopped examining myself carefully to see how far I have come, and what I have done with my life."

She sighs. "I always valued the advancement of my education and applied myself to it, yet I never allowed my schooling to get in the way of learning from life. I read widely; I experimented with and experienced the changes and challenges in life; I probed the histories, sciences, and literature that came my way; and I explored other cultures and their worldviews. I never seemed to rest in one place for too long, and I learned as I travelled. It's important to note that my life never was a solo project. It always involved many others, all committed to what we believed was right. I had little tolerance for people who abused their power over others or took advantage of a given situation exclusively for their own gain, or somehow saw themselves as superior to others.

"You see, I have worked and lived in different parts of the world, and I've noticed a common type of structure in all societies; one that exists on scales both small and large, whether within a company or a country. No matter where you turn, you have serfdom within fiefdom within kingdom within empire, like a set of Russian dolls. One lord of the line rules over his or her crew with a hand that is kind or cruel. That lord answers to a baron of the business who jealously guards his power over his collection of lords. The baron answers to the king of the corporation, and on it goes.

"Somewhere in there are the governments we think we voted for. Do you think they answer to us, the voters, what with all those powerbrokers whizzing around peddling their influences? Have a look at the daily news to find revelations of a fresh scandal in some unfortunate nation somewhere. At the political level, it begins with the almighty parties that shatter and trash one another, desperate to win top prize in the House. Why? To work for us, the people? Perhaps we enjoy small accidental benefits when politicians pay necessary lip service to the public good. But that's not why they are paying their dues. They are more interested in looking at how well a few years of fame brands their names and positions them for the real prizes to be collected after public service.

"In all that turmoil, do we step back and look at the Earth as a whole, the only planet in our solar system supporting our precious human race? And what about that one human race? How did that become subdivided into more races? Where does any 'superior race' nonsense come from? What does 'racism' mean if we are only a single human race? What could possibly be the motive behind the hate crimes and racist acts that happen around us from time to time?

"All this can be explained with one word: 'Ignorance.' That toxic condition is the fundamental cause of most conflicts on this planet."

She pauses, looks at Ragusa, and adds, "Okay, maybe I am off topic. But my ideas and passions are part of me, so we're still talking about my life, right?" She playfully punches Ragusa's shoulder. "Sorry, let's get back to my story."

"I never really feared failure, yet I had my share of ups and downs. I always worked hard to change what I believed was not just or noble. For instance, after I came to Canada and completed my first college degree here, I worked many years in a technical setting in a career where I made good money. But I didn't feel that this profession could contribute positively to human society or the planet's health. As a consequence, I shifted careers to one that aligned more with my principles: helping people live and work in healthy ways, as well as encouraging them to form networks to build sustainable and successful communities.

"I have never used anyone for my own gain and have always tried to help others. Thankfully, I always had a good circle of wonderful people around me. Having said all that, I am not always happy."

Before she can continue, Ragusa interrupts her. "Why?"

"Why? Look around you. If you examine the societal structures controlling this world, you see how corrupted and dysfunctional they are. It seems as if they are designed solely to facilitate resource extraction with no regard for local livelihoods, or to support free market abuse of labour through sweatshops or the unnecessary migration of peoples. There is so much suffering because of this flawed world. I have heard about your own pain and agony, and you are just one person."

Payvand is up and vigorously seeking out more dead leaves in her garden to remove, trying to throw off some nervous energy. "Yet, does this vast and violent attack on humanity make any impression on the mindset of those around us here in the comfortable heart of that empire? The majority are submerged in the legions of distractions provided to occupy our attention. Television, Internet, sports, and hobbies —these things keep millions of people throughout the world focused on fluff and indifferent to the agendas of their governments or to the exploitative nature of commerce. Can you see how offensive that is to the human intellect?"

"Yes, sadly I see your point," Ragusa says. "And if you try to reason with people, they let you know that bringing up these issues disturbs their cozy life. They just don't seem to care."

"Exactly! Although having said that, I don't want to suggest that people are not supposed to have fun and enjoy life. No, no. If we humans do not have pleasurable moments and pursue personal interests, we cannot be productive. Happiness and the enjoyment of life are essential ingredients for healthy human minds. My concern is that most people have lost the ability to differentiate between the pursuit of pleasure and careless indifference to realities. And the consequence of this apathy is that there is not enough attention paid. True, daily democratic oversight occasionally exposes those opportunistic jackals forever hovering and seeking any opportunity to exploit individuals, communities, and ecosystems. Ah, they would consume the Earth if such an act would enrich their estates! We need to hold them to the responsibility that they, and all of us, have to care for this planet now and leave it a better place for subsequent generations.

"Maybe I am tired of questioning why our world, with such advancements in science and technology, does not support a dignified life for all. It seems that the whole world is labouring just to support the world's elites, and to maintain the bloated Western, capitalist economies that are sucking the life out of our biosphere. It saddens me greatly that I am here, contributing to the planet's abuse by supporting this system."

Payvand shifts in her seat restlessly, looking for a distraction. "How is your wine doing? Would you like another glass?" she asks.

"Oh no, I'll just have some water for now."

Payvand gets up and walks into the kitchen, her face grim.

Ragusa follows her and looks sympathetically at her. "Don't be so sad."

Payvand shakes her head. "I can't help it. We who live in the Western world are such self-serving egocentrics. We live our lives without any concern or regard for how our careless, wasteful habits are affecting the rest of the world's population." She pauses, thinking briefly. "Of course, I have to acknowledge that there are many responsible intellectuals out there. They have written fine books and articles, created documentaries and independent films, and given powerful speeches and lectures for the purpose of increasing awareness about the man-made disasters threatening our world.

"The question is, how can they compete with the vast and wealthy industries that produce overwhelming volumes of entertainments that crowd out all else and effectively numb people to the problems in the world requiring everyone's attention? Furthermore, there are so many who, even if they could access such information, engage in self-censorship. They do this to protect their loyalties to a religion or a way of life that might be threatened by a paradigm of reduced or shifted consumption."

They take their glasses of water outside to the patio table and admire the garden quietly for a while.

Then Payvand turns to Ragusa and continues. "Do you know what story I would like to tell now? I'd like to start with Iran's ancient history. We can take a tour through the ages to see if we can develop some insight into how and why Iran ended up with such a hideous, barbaric regime as the present one."

"That should be very interesting," says Ragusa. "I'd like that!"

Payvand gathers her thoughts, then begins. "Iran is one of the world's oldest major civilizations, dating back more than three thousand years. Over the centuries, the land was ruled by many different dynasties. The most well-known of these, the Achaemenid, was forged by the famous emperors Cyrus the Great and Darius the Great, each recognized in world history for his unique achievements and method of governing. Nonetheless, as with any other expansionist emperor of the age, the extent of their territories was determined by the fortunes of war. That was the narrative of the time: an empire's range waxed and waned with an unending series of victories and defeats. These were set down in the annals of antiquity as the glories and disgraces of kings, but in reality, and as always, they actually were the miseries of the masses. Such was the game all through Iran's history as dynasties rose and fell, bringing us to modern times.

"A good starting point for recent history is the 1908 British discovery of oil in the south of Iran, one of the first big petroleum finds in the Middle East. By the beginning of World War I, they had built a refinery in Abadan, the largest on earth for fifty years and it made Iran's rulers incredibly rich. The Anglo-Persian Oil Company was established, which developed the petroleum industry and exported the oil. The Iranian government had little control over this process and there was no benefit to the Iranian people.

"Now, remember all those dynasties Iran had through the ages? Well, a new one started up around this time. I like to call it an 'overnight monarchy,' and it took over from the previous Qajar dynasty. This takeover involved Reza Khan, a military commander who, due to an agreement between the Soviets and the British, was anointed with the title of 'Mir Panj,' which means a lieutenant general. In 1921, with the help of the Anglo-Soviet overlords, he staged a coup and became Iran's leader. Then he was declared Prime Minister and oversaw the last years of the Qajar dynasty from 1923 to 1925. In 1925, Reza Khan extinguished that dynasty with the stroke of a pen and invented his own, changing his family's name from 'Khan' to 'Pahlavi' and declaring himself 'Shah' or King of Iran. There was no war or military campaign, just a lieutenant general taking over power. That's what I mean by an 'overnight monarchy.'

"Of course, the Anglo-Soviet strategists were just using him for their own purposes, which was to secure Iran's oil fields. They needed that oil to power the British Navy and Soviet Army after World War I. But the new Shah was uninterested in the goals of foreign powers, except where they could help him consolidate his power. As the years went by, he became more nationalist in his policies, thus annoying his keepers. So after only sixteen years, the Anglo-Soviet occupiers swept him aside and installed his son, Mohammad Reza Pahlavi. It was that easy!

"The pleasure or whims of the powers of the day reigned: One day a soldier; the next day, a Shah. Sure, other ancient monarchies, such as the British or Swedish, may have begun hundreds of years ago with some similar usurpation of power, but the appearance of the Pahlavis within living memory just highlights its overnight character and guides the critical mind to a reasoned rejection of monarchies themselves.

"The history of these Pahlavis coincides closely with the history of petroleum in Iran. With the disobedient Reza Shah gone, his young son continued the family enterprise of acquiring wealth and power from the proceeds of oil with the permission of the new lords of the universe, the CIA. It seemed like 'oil' was synonymous with 'rich,' and so one could be excused for thinking our oil must be a good thing. I say, no! We were cursed with that oil. That ill-fated resource has brought little but trouble since its discovery: trouble for us and for other countries in that region. That wealth has meant nothing to large sectors of Iran's population. Ironically, one of the richest countries in the world was host to some of the poorest people, living as they were in backward and difficult conditions. The monarchy, therefore, did not have the support of much of Iranian society. And so the stage was set, only fifty-five short years after its inception, for the downfall of the Pahlavi dynasty, and the overnight creation of a new set of autocrats."

Payvand stops and looks at Ragusa, "Am I making you tired?"

"No, no, please go on. I am fascinated."

"Good, I just wanted to give you a short history of one of the oldest states in this world to show you how we got to the point where such a horror of a government gained power. That government is the reason that so many Iranians are living in the diaspora all around the world."

Ragusa has a bitter smile, "Of course. As you said yourself, that pesky oil puts you on every major bully's radar."

"Yes, you got that right! Well, we'll return to the big picture later, but for now let's bring the focus back to me and a bit more of the history of my own family....

"I was born in Tehran and, as with you, I had loving parents. I was their only child and they indulged me. They had me later in life, partly because their marriage was a forbidden one. By the time they were married and had me, my father was in his mid-forties and my mother was in her late thirties. Anytime I asked them why I had no siblings, they would say, 'This brutal world does not need more children.' Nonetheless, they were generous people and were actually paying for the education of several young students who could not otherwise go to university. In a way, those young people became much like sisters and brothers to me."

"What fine people," Ragusa says. "Why was their marriage forbidden?"

"Well, my father was born to a Muslim family, and my mother was born to an Armenian family. In a country where about ninety percent of the population is Muslim, such a relationship is taboo, and their parents did not agree with the two of them marrying. When my father graduated from university, his parents wanted to send him to Switzerland to pursue his Masters and PhD in his field of study. Their main ulterior motive though, was to separate him from my mother and hope that by the time my father returned she would be married to an Armenian. They had no idea of the depth of the love my parents had for each other or that they already were married when my father left for Europe."

Ragusa chuckles. "How did that happen?"

"For one thing, my mother threatened her family, telling them that she would commit suicide if they didn't let her marry my father. My father also went to my mother's home and asked for her hand, promising them that he would take her away with him so that his own intransigent family could not bother her. He assured them that he would take care of their daughter to the best of his ability. My grandpapa accepted that, and they held a small private ceremony at my maternal grandparents' house, before sneaking off to Zurich."

"I love that. How smart."

"They certainly were smart and very much in love. My father studied some sort of Political Science although I'm not sure what the program was called in those days. My mom studied History and Anthropology. When they graduated, my father announced his return and sent a picture to his family of himself and his wife of six years. He warned them that if they did not respect his wishes and his wife, he and his wife would stay in Switzerland.

"Well, his parents missed their only son, so they accepted his ultimatum without argument. They also had five daughters to keep them happy and busy but, as is sadly the case in so many other cultures, the son held prime importance in their hearts. So, in 1949, they returned to Tehran."

Ragusa looks bemused. "Yes, unfortunately that's still true about gender preferences in so many places around the world. What these ignorant people do not appreciate is the importance of women in creating and raising each new generation. It would be an empty world without women."

Payvand smiles ruefully in agreement. "Sure, if only that was the sole problem in this world. Ignorance of every sort can at times seem far beyond comprehension. Anyway, my parents were both professionals and soon started working. My mother worked for the University of Tehran, and was among the first of professional working women there. They were both young and wanted to establish themselves securely in their own home before starting a family; although I've always had the feeling that they also had some problem getting pregnant. Eventually, eleven years into their marriage, I arrived on the scene."

"What a wonderful tale. Come on now, don't leave me waiting!" Ragusa demands impatiently. "Skip ahead to how and where you met Brian? Was he your first love?"

"Hey, hey, allow me to get there in due time, you pushy lady." Payvand gets up and stretches her legs. "My parents were one of the first leftist activists in Iran, and it's because of them that I became acquainted with my first love. You have to let me walk you through my life in the order that events occurred."

"You're right, I'm sorry ... so Brian was not your first love?"

Payvand gawks at her open-mouthed, and Ragusa doubles over with suppressed laughter. "Okay. I'll wait. Go on. Sorry, I'm in a mischievous mood. Please, do go on."

Payvand laughs as she goes into the kitchen. Ragusa shouts after her, "Where are you going?"

"I just want to prepare something to eat! Come in here. I can work and talk!"

Ragusa quickly gets up and follows her to the kitchen. "Okay, please continue."

"My dear, you are very impatient! I still have many other thrilling parts to share. Are you pushing me so I will arrive more quickly at the specific parts you are interested in?" She winks at Ragusa and brushes her hair with the tip of her fingers. "You naughty girl. You just like love stories."

Ragusa laughs as she prepares a kettle for boiling water. "Would you like some tea?"

"Sure," says Payvand as she continues her story while preparing their meal.

"I saw many broken people such as you, Ragusa. Some were very close comrades of mine, whom I lost to the cruelties of this world. They were young and devoted people who were among the most brilliant this world has ever known, and they all worked hard for the progress and development of their beloved nation of Iran. Their belief was that Iran's oil and other resources belonged to its people, and it was those people who should benefit from those natural resources. They believed that if there was a profitable trade in oil, then those profits should be spent on the country's development and on improved infrastructures of every sort.

"The Shah combated those ideas and those people with all his vicious might. However, fighting his own people only destroyed his legitimacy, and he eventually could not resist the pressures of the various oppositions. Unfortunately, the strongest component of our alliance of opposition groups was itself autocratic and it took advantage of the revolution to take control and once more burden Iran with a junk government.

"That government is certainly a problem, but its influential enemies portray it however they wish. Currently, Iran's regime is 'terrorist.' Oddly, I would even agree, as it has been terrorizing the Iranian people for over three decades and has been involved actively with several wider Middle East quarrels. However, the Iranian people themselves cannot be characterized that way as they are quite detached from Iran's regime. Those people are suffering economically, physically, and emotionally in the country-sized prison of theocratic Iran. Not that the soulless globalized corporate culture cares about that; the captains of industry are only distressed that they don't have access to a market of seventy-five million people. Their only concern is that Iran's consumers be free to accept the exploitations of the marketplace. Well, the finest tried-and-true method of freeing an oppressed people is, as with Yugoslavia and Iraq before or Syria today, through war. No other technique results in such lucrative reconstruction contracts."

Ragusa is angry. "Hypocrites! That whole mainstream system is a wasteland of insincerity, my dear Payvand. They don't attempt to construct any socially equitable peace. They only use force to maintain an illusion of calm, yet, as you mentioned by way of example, neither Tito nor NATO could strong-arm a lasting and meaningful harmony in my Yugoslavia."

Payvand agrees. "That's right. All we see are policies that facilitate the appropriation of markets and resources. What people actually want, whether in Syria or Mali or Sri Lanka, is peace. But all they get are market extremists and religious extremists battling it out over loyalties to their destructive causes.

"Take the example of Mali, a country rich in gold, and thus attractive to whatever group can control that nation. The religious fascists who are already there are happy to control that wealth, also making some of the country's population miserable with imposed piety. The multinational market overlords, with the help of NATO and French troops, who would rather be the ones to control that wealth, are also making the country's population miserable with imposed minimum-wage slavery in the service of resource exploitation. Does it look like the people of that country have much to say about which misery they will endure? Do we ever know what other agendas might be active behind the scenes there, or do we just take their word for it that they are 'bringing freedom to the people?'

"Doubly so for Syria; can you look at that situation with anything but confusion? Who is motivating Arabs to kill Arabs? Are they trying to draw the entire region into a self-destructive war? I believe we have to educate ourselves about any conflict in order to understand who is benefiting from it so that we can challenge it. No war of any kind can ever bring peace. That can only be achieved by patient education and debate, which can provide insight and understanding into how and why we should all live in global accord."

With the lunch and tea ready, they sit at the kitchen table and eat. In between bites, Payvand continues. "I left Iran a few short years after the revolution and never returned, but I had a taste of the brutality of Iran's government before I left. Its savagery is why I and so many others like me had to get away from that country." She looks at Ragusa, analyzing her mood. "Are you still up for more?"

"Sure, go on."

"I would like to take you back to Zurich where my parents spent about six years. They were there to pursue a higher education and to gain a greater understanding of our world and how it was operating at the time. My father had a very close friend in Zurich — another Iranian student who was also there with his wife. They all shared a house and were living, studying, and working together.

"Make sure you pay attention as this can get a little confusing. My father's friend and housemate had two other brothers in the country who were both already surgeons working at the University Hospital of Geneva. My father eventually met his housemate's brothers at a leftist conference in Bern, and the four gentlemen, along with their wives, soon became inseparable as they pursued their common interest in social justice. Remember this was happening after World War II when the whole world, and certainly Europe, was suffering in one way or another. Nations were struggling to recover from the global conflict. As you know, 1949 is the year the North Atlantic Treaty Organization was formed, the same NATO, you may recall, which bombed your Yugoslavia.

"My father and his friends debated whether NATO was a good thing or whether it was established only to better serve wealthy elites seeking to guide the evolution of the worldwide capitalist economy. So they attended many European meetings and conferences, learning and discussing. Eventually it came time for them to return to Iran. So the four friends, with their wives, went back to their homeland, eager to put their skills and scholarship to use.

"There, the four men kept their promise to one another and started an organization dedicated to educating people. They accomplished that in any way they could, whether that meant actually teaching, or financially supporting like-minded associations. Their wives did the same for women and girls.

"By the mid-fifties I was born, but that didn't slow down my parents' busy life. I had their attention, and they always made sure that I knew: 'You were the best addition to our lives' they would say. However, they maintained a committed schedule of social activism, and I grew up in that environment with many 'aunts and uncles' in the parlour or around the dinner table. For instance my mom established and operated a small school for orphaned girls and divorced women who did not have the finances, education, or skills to commence a new life."

Ragusa nods. "That must have been hard work."

"Are you tired, dear Ragusa? Would you like to take a break? Let me clear away the dishes."

"No! I mean, yes! I'll help you with the dishes but don't you stop."

"Ha! You are a sweet, funny woman. Okay, I will go on.

"Let's go back in time a bit more. Remember we talked about oil and the huge refinery built around 1913. Well, that was the beginning of British control over Iran. The British required stability so they put serious effort into Iran's politics. They needed to maintain and expand the petroleum industry there to serve the increasing Western demand; especially for the war effort during World War II.

"In that era, however, there was a very well-educated man called Mohammad Mosaddegh who was a strong Iranian nationalist. He had a law degree from a political science institute in Paris and a doctorate from Switzerland. My father and his three friends knew him and respected him very much. Doctor Mosaddegh was a founder of the National Front of Iran party. When my parents and their friends returned to Iran, they joined him, supported him, and worked with him. Mosaddegh strongly believed that Iran's oil belonged to its people. Through much of his political career, his main goal was to nationalize Iran's oil for the benefit of its people.

"He worked for years on this policy and developed a strong following of people who appreciated his agenda. Finally, in 1951, he was elected as the Prime Minster of Iran, loved by his people and even well-respected by the young Reza Shah, who you remember had been installed in his father's place some ten years earlier by the wartime Allies.

"Mosaddegh and his colleagues tried hard to reform and transform Iran's political culture, modernize its social security, and improve compensation for employees. As a result, factory owners had to pay benefits to their employees, and peasants were freed from forced labour on their landlords' estates. Most importantly he moved forward with nationalizing the Iranian oil industry, controlled by the British for many years. Mosaddegh cancelled the agreements imposed by foreign powers and confiscated the industry assets."

Payvand raises her hand in indignation. "If you can believe it, the British took Iran's government of the day to the international court. They challenged Iran's *Oil Nationalization Act* of 1951 as contravening a 1933 convention, which granted the Anglo-Persian Oil Company a sixty-year license to mine oil in a large area of Iran in return for a small royalty. Imagine the hubris of one country going into another and imposing a one-sided contract to pull out the wealth of that land in return for a pittance. I cannot even comprehend that, can you?"

Ragusa shakes her head solemnly.

Payvand sighs loudly and drops her exhausted body into a chair. "You see how sad it is? Back then, they didn't even have to spout lies about doing it for 'freedom' before coming in and taking your wealth. To intervene in Yugoslavia or Syria, they now must chant 'Free the People!' Hypocrites, just like you said before.

"So there we were, finally free of foreign control. Mosaddegh was democratically elected by those who supported nationalist policies, and he worked hard to develop and modernize his country. In only two years, he moved Iran toward a democracy that the country had never seen in its history. Unfortunately, he was not strong enough to resist the manipulations of MI6 and the CIA. In 1953, his government was overthrown."

Ragusa is surprised. "Ah, what a shame!"

Payvand turns to face her, and shrugs her shoulders. "Read the histories on that particular tragedy. If we could have kept the democratic system and economic strategies that Dr. Mosaddegh introduced to the people of Iran, and if they had continued to develop through all these years to today, what an advanced and flourishing nation we might be now. There would have been sixty years of progress, and our present leadership would be sane. Instead, the imperialists of the day said, 'How dare you want to keep your own oil for the progress and improvement of your own people? We will tell you what you are allowed to do.'"

Payvand sits up straight and continues. "Removing Mosaddegh as our Prime Minister involved both the Shah, who had to sign the decree while hiding in Rome, and the CIA, who spent a million dollars hiring an ignorant mob to take over the streets and attack that fine man's house. So you see how far the bullies will go to obliterate the aspirations of a nation and claim its wealth from across the world. Iran has never enjoyed the leadership of such a person as Mosaddegh before or since.

"Looking back, what bothers me more than those bullies are the people of Iran. Didn't they elect him? Indeed! Then why did they not rally to his side when he was forcibly removed? Why did they not fight for their own beliefs? What really happened?"

Payvand rises abruptly and paces around the kitchen in frustration. "The bloody history of the CIA did not end with the 1953 overthrow of Mosaddegh in Iran. That 'success' only seemed to encourage them. Much has been revealed about the CIA's involvement in actions around the world, such as the 1954 toppling of Arbenz, the popularly elected president of Guatemala, and the subsequent refashioning of that country's army into a gang of thugs used against its own people. Over the years, the list of murderous CIA interventions around the world has become a long, depressing one. These kinds of tactics are used to police the world, and the apathy of people busy with entertainments, debts, work, and raising families allows the world's elites to continue doing whatever pleases them.

"Anyhow, after the overthrow of Mosaddegh many people were arrested. They came for my father, but he and my mother and a few others fled to a small city where they hid for some time. The two brothers that my parents had met in Geneva left Iran again to resume their work in Switzerland as surgeons.

"After a year, my parents returned to Tehran and started working to reorganize the National Front party. However, in just a few months my father and his friend, the younger brother of the two surgeons, were arrested. What my father and his comrades didn't fully understand was that, just like in Guatemala, Iran's army and policing system had been revamped to align with the best practices of the CIA and MI6 in working against its own citizens and protecting whoever pays the bills.

"This all occurred right before I was born. So I came into this world with my father in prison for taking an interest in the well-being of his country."

Payvand stands quietly at the kitchen counter staring thoughtfully into the distance. Then she shakes her head as she tries to gather her thoughts. She turns the heat back on for the kettle, and says, "How about we put together a nice tea and go back to the garden?"

"That's a good idea," says Ragusa.

Payvand assembles the teapot and some sweets on a tray, along with an empty vase and two of her favourite small glasses. She then reaches out the window to cut a rose for Ragusa and places it in the vase. "Do you like this one?" she asks Ragusa.

"You know I do," says Ragusa, smiling at her.

Once the tea is ready, they take the tray to the garden and take their places at the patio table. Payvand pours tea and passes the sweets, then leans back and looks at Ragusa intently.

"A few months after I was born, my father was released from prison. My mother remembered that he was a changed man. He didn't quite have the same positive outlook anymore. Mind you, even though my father was a political prisoner, I cannot ever compare the treatment of prisoners at that time with the situation in my time. The daily lives of the common citizenry of Iran are worse now than they were then. Well before the 1979 Revolution, there was a modest level of freedom in most facets of day-to-day life in Iran. Today there is widespread social control and ideological suffocation. I think even into the early years of my own activism, people could openly debate issue in their own homes. I had a healthy and exciting upbringing, surrounded by those kind and cool 'aunts and uncles' who filled our house on so many evenings with laughter and debate.

"I have many exciting memories of trips to Europe in the 1960s. My parents and their friends always took me with them as they travelled to different European cities, conferencing with various social democrat organizations. There was a rich exchange of ideas among the many progressives and advocates of the day, and as a teenager, I could sense the deep respect they had for one another. They strongly believed in 'All for one and one for all for a better world.' It did not matter that they were from different ethnicities and many different walks of life. There were many educational lectures and meetings, not only on social and political topics, but also on wider interests such as space and science. The sixties were an inspiring time with interrelated political and cultural trends happening across the globe."

Ragusa jumps in. "And don't forget the Beatles!"

"Right!" Payvand chuckles, and returns to the kitchen for more pastries. "We took many trips to Paris, Berlin, and England, but not to Switzerland. Then, in the summer of 1971, I graduated from high school early and..."

Ragusa interrupts her. "You were one of those smart ones, weren't you?"

"I don't know if I was. I didn't feel that smart after I met one particular man." Payvand looks away bashfully. "So that summer, I was finally taken to Switzerland for the first time, where in Zurich I met Malahat and her son. Malahat was the sister of my parents' best friend; the one they met in the forties. Do you remember? They lived and studied together."

"Yes, I remember. After the overthrow of Mosaddegh, his two surgeon brothers went back to Geneva."

Payvand nods. "Malahat had a son, and the two of them where living in Switzerland with those two brothers. My mother spoke of the son as a university student, but I would hear some people calling him 'doctor,' so I asked my mother about that. My mother said, 'He is working on a PhD in Philosophy, but he actually already has two other PhDs in Economy and Political Science!" We were in Zurich for his conferences on the world's economy, NATO, and the influence of the West on third-world countries. We also attended a conference on colonization in Africa. A few weeks later my mother informed me that we would actually be accompanying him to Paris for another conference on world poverty and that he would be giving the speech.

"He was only twenty-four and obviously very smart. All my life, because of my high marks and quick understanding of subject materials, I thought I was a bit of a 'wunderkind,' until I met him. I mean, he was getting his third doctorate, in *philosophy*, so he was a very unusual young man. Furthermore, his skill at languages was phenomenal. When he spoke with French people, one would assume he was French. It was the same with German and English, both of which he spoke fluently. My mother was especially impressed that he spoke, read, and wrote Farsi impeccably, even though he had left Iran for Geneva when he was not even two years old. He picked up both French and German so quickly that he was tested as a gifted student. As a result, he started school at age four. My father would say, 'They pushed him too much, the boy is not sociable.' One of his uncles would say, 'He was their guinea pig.' Another said, 'Who goes to university at age fourteen?' His own mother would challenge all of them: 'He is happy. He likes it and he never complains. He always wants to learn more. He soaks up knowledge faster than they could throw it at him. Let him be!' By the way, in addition to his brilliance, it's important to note that he was absolutely handsome!"

"Ha! Devil!" Ragusa reaches over and smacks Payvand's leg. Payvand laughs, happy with the expected response.

"I always thought my parents indulged me and loved me unconditionally, but it was nothing when compared with the unreserved love Malahat had for her son. It was an unusual attachment, like nothing I have ever seen. She knew intuitively when he needed a glass of water or needed to be alone or when he was happy or sad; sometimes she knew these things even before he knew it himself. She was attuned to him, as if she could smell his feelings and his needs. I have never met anyone like her to this day."

Payvand is teary and stops. "Shall we stop for now? I'd like to start getting some dinner ready."

"Sure, let me help" Ragusa says. "Are you all right, Payvand?"

"Not really. But after dinner we will begin the real adventure, and you will see how everything in my life changed direction with him and his mother. Ah, that brilliant young man was the essence of intelligence in our species and a living embodiment of how we all ought to be. He represented human integrity as seen in the depth of his devotion to humanity. Well, well, the rain has started. We had better stay inside."

"Yes, good idea. What is it you're making?"

"A vegetarian dish with Iranian spices. I hope you like it."

"I know I will like it. What do you call this dish?"

"We call it ghormeh-sabzi. It is made with kidney beans, chopped spinach, fried onions, dried lime, some herbs like parsley and cilantro, and some other secret spices…. It's a stew that you serve on top of rice. Of course, it's supposed to be cooked with lamb, but I am a vegetarian, so I have eliminated the lamb."

"My mouth is already watering," says Ragusa.

CHAPTER 6 **BEHROUZ**

AYVAND PUTS ON some classical music, and they talk quietly about favourite foods for a while as they prepare the meal. Once the stew is simmering in the pot and they are tidying up, Ragusa is eager to ask more questions — *was this man her first love, hmmm...?* But the look on Payvand's face makes her back off.

"This smells so tasty!," she says instead. "You have to give me the recipe."

Payvand smiles and cheerfully says, "For sure!"

Ragusa is happy to see that smile again. Payvand begins setting out some dishes and Ragusa helps her. Then Ragusa goes to look at the books on the shelves in the study, where Payvand joins her a few minutes later.

"You have such a wonderful collection of books."

"You can borrow anything you want, anytime you wish!"

Ragusa says, "I already have one of them in mind. And of course, don't forget that recipe."

Payvand's heart squeezes as she thinks, *It's only been a few days. Is she regaining an interest in life?* She shrugs her shoulders, and smiles. "No problem," she says. She moves to one of the corner shelves and pulls out a photo album that she opens to a particular photograph, then passes the album to Ragusa.

"Oh, is this them? The mother and son?"

"Yes!"

"Ah, you're right, he is quite handsome. Look how they hold each other. They are obviously so close. I see what you mean."

"Yes. As I said, I never met the likes of them; they were so kind and considerate to one another."

Ragusa smiles playfully. "Malahat! Meaning of her name please!"

Payvand grins. "Hmm, I think it means 'pretty,' or 'charming.' But forget her name or her looks. She was one of the strongest women I have ever met in my life. These two people became important parts of my life for over a decade. So, if I want to talk about my life, first I have to elaborate a bit about their past."

"I understand. After hearing Minoo's story, I can appreciate the role others can play in a life."

They sink into the armchairs in the study and make themselves comfortable as Payvand continues with her story. "Well, Malahat was from a small town near Tehran. Her father owned half the town, as well as several surrounding villages and their farms, along with their residents. Malahat was a younger sister of the two surgeon brothers I mentioned earlier. There was also an even younger sister, and when she married, it actually made it more difficult for Malahat to find a husband. That's just the way things worked in old Iran back then, maybe even now, in some villages. If a girl passed twenty, it was very difficult for her to marry. So, it was remarkable that she was in her thirties when she finally got married.

"In the town where Malahat grew up was another rich man who owned the other half of the town and surrounding countryside. That man was already married to three other women. His first wife gave him three daughters, and in those days, a wealthy man responded to such a curse by marrying a second woman, hoping for a son. That wife gave him two more daughters, and he was so damned worried about his wealth and who was going to take care of it after he was gone, that he married a third time. His third wife was only sixteen years old and hated him so much. The young bride hit him with a brick on their wedding night and ran away. Of course, her own family captured her, beat her, and returned her to her lord. As time went by, it became apparent that she could not give him any child at all, so the rich man cast his eyes on Malahat, the older daughter of his competitor.

"He considered how easily that family produced boys, since Malahat had five brothers and only one sister. And that sister had already produced two boys. A grand patriarch can never consider a perceived problem to be his fault. So, with arrogant ignorance, he secured marriage to Malahat in his continuing pursuit of a son.

"Malahat despised him, but she wasn't the only one. Her father did not like him either, and Malahat's brothers disagreed with the whole idea. They asked their father to let her be or to allow her to live with them in Switzerland. Well, in those days not many people would let their daughter go to a European country unless accompanied by a husband." Payvand has a cynical smile. "A single girl; in Europe? That was out of the question. However, in her father's mind, Malahat was already too old to find a husband, so he forced her to marry the fiend. A simple ceremony was performed, and as Malahat always said, 'They sent me to my death chamber. But from that horrible place emerged this magnificent treasure, my son.'"

Payvand sits back and sips some water.

"Those days were brutal," Ragusa says, "when people could do anything to their daughters. I gather from things you told me here and there that Malahat is not married to him anymore, right?"

Payvand is gazing off into the distance, lost in sad thoughts. "What?" She flinches slightly in her chair. "Sorry, did you say something?"

Ragusa looks at her anxiously, "What happened to you? Are you okay?"

"Yes, yes, I'm fine. Give me a moment." She reaches for her water and takes another sip, as Ragusa repeats her question.

"Oh no," Payvand says. "She is not married to him anymore. Though when she was, she had awful days with him. Also, the two older wives did not like her and caused problems for her. However, the youngest wife became close to Malahat and called her 'Momoni.' Malahat protected that young child who, like her, was trapped in that house with the two witches and their fiend of a husband."

"What does 'Momoni' mean?"

Payvand laughs and gets up, "Come on, the meal should be ready. So 'Momoni' is a term of endearment meaning 'sweet mother' or 'dear mother.' In other words, a cute version of 'Mom' that you can even use for someone who is not your mother, but who you respect for her kindness."

"How sweet! I am so glad they could find some good in that terrible situation and provide support for one another."

In the kitchen, Payvand arranges the gormeh-sabzi on a beautiful platter and the friends settle comfortably at the table there for their meal.

"Yes, and she actually told Malahat why she was not getting pregnant. She said, 'Anytime that ugly beast comes near me, I throw anything that comes to my hand at him, even if it's a sharp object. When he and his stupid wives took away all the sharp objects, then I bit him on his ears, his nose, his lips, even his head. So they called me "crazy" and he left me alone.' She told Malahat that so far she had never let him touch her. Malahat tried that strategy too, but he beat her so badly that she did not dare try it again. In addition, the other two wives prevented her from eating for two days.

"So, within a year she became pregnant, and in due course, she gave birth to a beautiful little boy, whom she called Behrouz. Don't ask! I'll tell you!" Payvand laughs.

"Behrouz means 'better day.' For Malahat, he was the start of better days. Cruelly, she was only with her boy for four months when the insensitive brute sent Malahat back to her father's house, like he was returning a watch. He said, 'I wanted a boy which I have now, and I don't want your daughter anymore. She is disrupting life with my other two wives.' It was actually a malicious way of exacting revenge on Malahat's father for whatever petty feud was going on between them.

"Malahat was devastated. She did not eat or sleep; she just cried and pleaded with her father for help. He did fight for her and was soon able to force an arrangement whereby Malahat could at least breastfeed the baby twice a day. When he couldn't do more, he expressed his regret to his two older sons in Switzerland and admitted his mistake. They both were furious with him for forcing her to marry the fiend.

"Malahat's oldest brother returned to Iran with a plan, but he didn't show his face in town. In Tehran, he prepared passports and other documents for Malahat and her son, while a trusted friend of his, who was visiting at the time and was to return to Paris, went to Malahat's family to arrange things there."

Ragusa is on the edge of her seat, "Oh, oh ... that's when Malahat and her son moved to Geneva, right? I love it!"

Payvand smiles mischievously. "Every morning, one of the older wives would bring Behrouz for his daily milk. She would wait in the courtyard during the feeding, which Malahat would drag out for as long as possible, and then whisk the baby away without a word.

"One morning, she arrived as usual, and Malahat's mother took Behrouz in to his mother. Then, for the first time, Malahat's mother went back out and asked the witch to come in and have tea. The wife hesitated at this change of the routine but decided not to be rude. She went in and the two chatted for more than hour before the visitor realized how much time had passed. She began to ask where Malahat was.

"They called Malahat, but there was no answer. Malahat's mother went to look for her and hurried back in agitation a few minutes later. 'I looked everywhere, and she's not in any of the rooms!' she exclaimed. The woman ran out into the street to look for them and encountered a strategically placed neighbour who asked who she was looking for. She said 'Mala-hat,' to which the neighbour replied, 'Oh, she jumped into a car about an hour ago with her baby and left with a man that I've never seen before.'"

Ragusa jumps out of her chair and claps her hands in glee. Payvand laughs at her little dance, though with a sad expression on her face, which does not go unnoticed by Ragusa.

"Well, the gossip began! Word spread around town that Malahat had run off with a strange man. Malahat's father made sure to join the earnest search for the two in order to prevent Behrouz's father from believing that her family had anything to do with the disappearance. The trusted friend took them to Tehran, where her brother had already made arrangements for them to leave the next day for Zurich.

"For their first year in Switzerland, they lived with my parents before they returned to Iran. This was so that Malahat could join my mother in learning French. Also, Malahat's brothers wanted their sister to become a little more comfortable in her new country before living with them and being alone with their French and German wives.

"Behrouz was about a year old when he started displaying his gifts. Everyone around him said they had never witnessed any baby like him. At fifteen months, without passing through a baby talk stage, he was speaking articulately. If he was in the mood or engaged with something that interested him, he would talk non-stop. However, if he didn't like someone or the subject, he was completely mute. He hated being put on display and would become silent if he thought he was just the entertainment."

"So, from a young age people knew he was different," Ragusa comments.

But Payvand continues as if she does not hear her, as though she were miles away, lost in the intensity of her past, and dig-ging for stories worthy of keeping her new friend with her in this world. "As I said before, they lived with my parents for about a year because my parents remembered that they were still in Geneva for Behrouz's third birthday. As I said earlier, he started school at age four, and by age fourteen he had entered university. When I met him in Switzerland, he was twenty-four and already had those two PhDs under his belt with the third one on the way."

Ragusa smiles. "Well done! I like them both, and I cannot wait for more of their story. Tell me you two became an item! Say it was so!"

"Oh, you are incorrigible. Give us a chance to get to know one another, woman." Payvand laughs as she lightly pinches her on the arm. "As I told you before, we went to his first lecture, which I did not understand because it was in German. So I was left only with the pleasure of sitting there and watching him as he spoke. I did also notice though how everyone was listening carefully and admiring the quality of this young man's presentation. We were there for a few weeks and went to all of his conferences or lectures. How proud was his mother as she humbly accepted compliments about her beloved son!

"We then all travelled together to Paris for his next lecture. We went by train, and I put myself in his way as much as I could, asking questions and talking to him. I knew he liked me; but not in the way I wanted, as he kept calling me 'kid,' 'little girl,' 'pretty girl,' or 'the smart one.'"

"Well you were only, what, seventeen? He was twenty-four, so of course he would look at you as a little girl."

"Well, I was a very mature seventeen-year-old, I'll have you know!" Payvand says as she makes a face and laughs.

Ragusa smiles, shakes her head mischievously, and teases Payvand again. "So, I gather he was your first love?"

Payvand avoids the suggestion with a grin. "I tried to ask intelligent questions, formulating them carefully in my mind to make sure there were no mistakes. He was so darned smart that he knew I was doing that and would read the direction of my thought before I even finished the question. But he didn't seem to read my feelings.

"To be fair, he was like that with all the young women around him. He had no girlfriends and was not trying to find one either. He was so respectful, and he wouldn't treat us as sex objects or talk down to us, as so many other men did. He just loved an intelligent conversation no matter whom he was talking to.

"That being said, he wasn't blind to the appreciation of attractive women. When he first met Minoo years later, he reacted like everyone did: 'What a beauty! Nature has done right by her.' But that was it. He treated her, me, and all other women the same way he treated men. He was resolute in regarding every person as, first and foremost, a human being, each of whom has a different perspective, a unique look and shape, and a set of valuable opinions. He loved and respected everyone for who they were and not for their gender or status or wealth or nationality."

Payvand gets up and stretches, then stands beside Ragusa while they look at Behrouz's photograph. She takes the photo, has one last look, puts it in the book, and returns it to the shelf. Ragusa asks her if she is tired. "Yes, a bit, but I can go on a little more.

"That trip was a wonderful experience. It was great fun, with lots of sightseeing as well with him and his wonderful mother. Finally, it came time for me and my parents to return to Iran, while our companions went back to Geneva. I felt a lingering sadness for a few months, missing in him that vast ocean of knowledge and perception and distinctive kindness. But soon I started university and buried myself in my studies though from time to time I thought about him.

"As for Behrouz, he completed his third PhD and then entertained several good offers, one of which was to teach in a French university. There were a couple of others, apparently from Zurich and Geneva. All I knew was that he was a respected academic, and gaining fame as he lectured around Europe. It wasn't long before the University of Tehran heard of him and they offered him a teaching position there. I believe that was in 1975. His dream had always been to pursue his career in Iran, as he had always wanted to be active in the progressive movement there. From afar he had been diligently keeping up with events in the country. In fact, since 1973, he had been making brief trips to Tehran, trying to develop an organization to do political and social work for the benefit of the people of Iran. He probably knew Iran better that many Iranians who had lived there all their lives, so when that wonderful opportunity at the university came up, he took it without hesitation. It was a welcome chance to become more intimately involved with the action in his homeland."

Payvand sits upright, stretches her body, and decides to take a little sidetrack again. "It was in 1973 when the Shah decided to reinstate some national control over the oil industry. He announced that the capital gain of our oil should be used for the modernization of Iran. However, it became apparent that his idea of modernization was mainly to increase military spending, and soon, Iran had developed the region's strongest armed forces. Yet again the wealth provided by oil was not invested in improving the livelihood of the average Iranian citizen or developing the economic diversity of the country as a whole. The success, fame, and wealth of Iran's government only benefited a small group around the Shah and the men who worked for them.

"It was this state of affairs that Behrouz wanted to address more fully as he began teaching at the University of Tehran. One of his first projects was to develop a magazine as a forum for publishing his group's ideas. He then embarked on organizing his group to be more active but in a fashion not typical of other leftist groups of the time. He knew that nothing was stable and that a revolution was inevitable, but he was sure that the outcome would not be what most progressives in Iran expected. Behrouz strongly believed that it would take years of education to make the people of Iran understand that they were being robbed and that they could take charge of their own destinies. He also knew, as did we all, that Iran was too important to the world's bullies to be relinquished easily.

"For my part, I didn't realize at first that Behrouz was teaching at the same campus where I was a student. I had heard rumours about a new, exciting, young professor, but I was too busy to care about who he was.

"One day, I was having my lunch in the cafeteria when he sat at my table and said, 'Hey kiddo, you're all grown up.'

I looked at him with disbelief, 'What are you doing here? Are you living here? Are you the young professor everyone is talking about?'

"He smiled and said, 'Yes, I live here. And yes, I teach here.'

"I was a bit annoyed. 'When did you arrive? Why didn't you let us know? Where is your mother? Oh, I have missed her.' I guess I was bombarding him with my questions, as he looked taken aback.

He held up his hand and stopped me. 'Whoa. Okay, you're quite right. I should have let your parents know, and I apologize. I've been very busy though, so I hope you can forgive me. My mother is here too, and we live together.'

"He had returned with a few of his closest comrades, the gang all having grown up and gone to school together in Geneva. One of them was a young doctor and his wife Fattaneh, the nurse activist in Minoo's story. Do you remember Fattaneh?"

"Yes, I do!" says Ragusa.

Payvand pours some water into her glass and reaches over to fill Ragusa's too. She then leans back into her chair, with that fleeting expression of sadness that is worrying Ragusa.

"He talked about his group as well as the that magazine he was using to publish his ideas and the program he was planning to start with a few others in different factories. He spoke with such an excitement that he looked like a little boy, and I remembered how he had been just such an enthusiastic lecturer when I saw him in Europe.

"A few weeks later, I was introduced to a few of the young members in his group, and I was invited to contribute to their activities. I was a strong-willed woman in my early twenties, and I sympathized with their ideals and goals. It was thrilling to participate in some small way in such a dedicated activist group, and it was like a dream come true to also be working with Behrouz."

They have finished eating, and Payvand gets up. "I'm tired now. Let's take a break."

"No! Why now? Tell me a bit more, about you two. Come on!"

"There was no 'we.' He did not know anything about my feelings. He never knew. Let's take a break for now. I need to stop for a while, please."

"All right, you go rest in the living room while I clean up here, then I'm going to go raid this wonderful little bar you have here and make drinks for us. You relax and I'll whip us up some martinis."

Payvand goes and settles on the sofa with a smile, "I love martinis!"

Ragusa walks around the kitchen and soon she is banging cupboards and opening drawers as she searches for the ingredients she needs.

"I have a workshop tomorrow!" Payvand calls out, chuckling to herself at Ragusa's frenetic activity. "Would you like to go with me?"

"Workshop? Sure, but what about our stories? Do we have time for them after your workshop?"

Payvand rejoins Ragusa in the kitchen so they do not have to shout. "It starts at nine in the morning and should take about two hours. We can have lunch afterward, rest a bit, and then start again."

"Is presenting workshops your job?"

"One of them, yes. But I do not present them too often. You know, I am semi-retired."

"Neat! What kind of workshops?"

"I have developed all kinds of them over the years. Recently though, I mostly present workshops on general human history, society and its cultural diversity, and some specific topics in psychology."

"I like that. Sounds like an interesting job. Sure, I would love to go with you."

"Okay then. Oh, our martinis are ready."

"Yes, here we are," Ragusa says as she carries two beautiful, ornamented glasses out of the kitchen. "Let's go back to the study," she says.

They get comfortable in their chairs, and Payvand takes a sip from her glass. "Mmm ... wonderful! Now *you* have to give me *your* recipe. Just what I needed!"

Ragusa is pleased and executes a little bow. "Cheers!" she says, and they raise their glasses in appreciation of finding one another and of their time together.

For a time they sit quietly, each with her own thoughts. Then Ragusa eyes Payvand cautiously. "Are you better now? Can you start again? Not that I want to push you. Just letting you know I am ready when you are."

"No, I'm fine. Where was I?"

"You had just been introduced to other group members and started to work with them."

Payvand takes a deep breath and exhales slowly, stretches her arms, and then nods. "Mmm, you *are* listening."

She smiles and continues. "Yes, I had begun a very special chapter of my life, full of interesting and educational activities. The team's ambition and primary purpose was educating people: teaching them to understand Iran's history, both ancient and modern, and how petroleum had defined Iran's relationship to the world's superpowers over the last century. But first, it was sometimes necessary to teach them to read and write. So, most of us worked in areas that had large illiterate populations.

"Each member of our team, independent of the group activities, already had a job or was a student. After getting home from our mainstream occupations, we each had a project that we pursued for the group. Many of us would scout factories and other workplaces and apply for jobs there, especially team members who had specific trade experience or skills for those jobs. Our tactic was to set up a new team from among the employees at each of these places. We would then educate them about their rights to fair and proper pay, benefits, and most importantly safe working conditions; and as soon as they were operating independently as a kind of functional union that could hold their own in negotiating reasonable and improved conditions of employment, we would move on to the next workplace.

"To make it easier for Behrouz to get into such places, he took the initiative of learning skills as a repair technician for heavy and light machinery. It was amazing to us how quickly he became proficient at working with all kinds of mechanical and electronic machinery.

"After a few months, he had organized two strong activist groups of professors and students in the two campuses of Tehran University. As with our group, they published pamphlets for distribution and held workshops and study groups to educate people about social issues. When those groups were self-sustaining in their activities, Behrouz stepped away and cut back on his teaching hours, which allowed him engage in the front-line activities of the labourers in an effort to apply his ideas to the real world. He gained employment in an electronics manufacturing company where he was a part-time repair technician, which enabled him to visit most sections of the facility so he could get to know as many people as possible.

"He was very good at gaining the trust and respect of his fellow workers. He was friendly and spoke their slang as if he was a child of the streets. Nobody could imagine he had all those PhDs. Soon, he had his first union set up there, had the labourers choose their own leader and new members, and then guided them to a new contract with their management. Then, he quietly terminated his employment with that factory and moved on to the next one, only to repeat the process elsewhere."

"What a remarkable man. What is he doing now?"

"Yes, he was absolutely unique and I haven't met anyone like him ever." Payvand then looks at Ragusa pointedly and says, "Ragusa, please allow me to work through the stories without skipping ahead. Trust me. It would ruin everything if I tell you where he is right now."

"Ah, I am sorry Payvand. I'm acting like an impatient child."

Payvand has another sip of her martini. "This is really good." Then she continues. "We were so proud of what we were doing. We had meetings three times a week to report our progress and accomplishments. And Ragusa, you'll remember Minoo. As soon as she arrived at our safe house, we began to have more and more of our meetings there, just for Minoo's cooking."

"Oh, yes, Minoo. She was helping your group too?"

"Of course. She read, listened, discussed, and gradually became more and more involved with our teamwork. In one of our meetings, I announced that I was changing jobs and transferring to a different factory, but Minoo got very upset and had a strong opinion about the safety of that new location. Her arguments and reasoning were cogent and strong enough to convince Behrouz to have two of his male friends go and look into it. Sure enough, they found that place too rough for our group to be working there just yet."

"She really was a budding little activist, wasn't she?"

"Yes, and if you remember, eventually for her safety after her marriage to Shayan, we asked them to pull back from involvement with us. Soon after the revolution, they had to escape."

"Right, I remember. But it's nice to hear about her again. I loved that story."

"Yes, it was one of our happy endings. Anyway, we continued our work in factories and workshops, and we made similar efforts in colleges and universities, hospitals, and other institutions. Our members were working everywhere among the people, sometimes at two or three tasks; and, of course, we were also working at our regular jobs or studying at school. For example, Behrouz taught in the university, oversaw our magazine, and worked in factories. On top of all this, he regularly translated the best of the newly published books coming out of Europe. They were in German, French, or English, and he would simplify them to a readable language so that everybody could understand them. I too could be thought of as representing the typical workload of our membership: I was a student, then I worked in a factory, and I provided essays and poems for our magazine."

"What an active life. I can certainly understand your pride in it."

Payvand nods. "Yes, I really enjoyed things then. Well, about a year before the revolution, as the political situation in Iran intensified, new tasks were added to everyone's plates, such as rallies or university and street gatherings and discussions. It was at one of those university gatherings that we learned that Behrouz was not a communist, at least not as we understood the term.

"Previously, I and everyone else saw communism through the lens of its manifestations in China, Russia, or Eastern Europe. There were activists who would promote those examples as goals for our country. On this particular day there was a huge debate. Many people were gathered, listening to three men discussing Iran's situation, and what we, as progressives or socialists, should do to guide our nation's political future in a promising direction.

"Behrouz was one of the three men and was seated in the centre. The other two men supported, respectively, the Soviet and the Chinese systems. None of the three could find any common ground. Behrouz argued against the two established communist states: 'Both countries have failed their people and are not trustworthy. Why should we emulate a doctrine that has already failed? We can't just copy other countries. Instead, we must understand and appreciate our own people's needs, and develop our own ideas accordingly.'

"The two other debaters liked him and wanted his support for their own cause. He refused to give it to them as he disagreed with both. He said neither the Soviet Union nor China could be looked to as mentors. We should instead look to Iran's unique politics and culture as the basis for developing our own form of a just society and for seeking what is good for our people. He argued that we should learn from the mistakes of history, not repeat them. He tried to illustrate that we should all work together within our own cultural context to form a more insightful understanding of our people, from which an appropriate social structure could then be tailored for the country.

"They wouldn't listen to what Behrouz said, as they were locked into their commitment to the Stalinist, Leninist or Maoist theories that they promoted. In the end, the other debaters simply asserted that if he did not accept their communist manifestos, he must be religious.

"He would only smile at such faulty logic and ask why we should even assume that communism was the only theory worth looking at. He argued that we could examine a variety of political ideas in our pursuit of a formulation suitable for Iran.

"Much of his time was spent in such forums as he worked hard to convince other political activists and socialist groups to strengthen their causes by combining all their efforts instead of working against one another. He tried not to be discouraged, but his message seemed to fall on deaf ears. He never judged his colleagues because he understood how strong the political fashions of the day were. He could see that building a united front was important to combating the Shah's vision of a modern Iran based as it was on American-style militarism and a market economy. In a way, the Shah promoted those values as a way of combating religious and political extremism. But he picked an unfortunate model to emulate because many Iranians saw America as a place that had no mercy on its own people, with its ghettos and homelessness. It was thought of as a state that had no respect for other countries, with the way its CIA bullied and subverted national self-determination all around the world. It seemed reasonable to many that if China and the Soviet Union were opposing American-style democracy, then they must be better.

"That is why Behrouz had a hard time convincing people to forget about what the Soviet Union and China were doing and to concentrate instead on the needs of the people of their own nation. Even the most intelligent theorists and activists had a form of ideological tunnel vision that locked them into a combative defense of their chosen dogmas. Behrouz would come home from these encounters disappointed though not disheartened.

"He continued to write, translate, and distribute publications. For instance, in one of his handouts he persevered in his call for unity: 'While we the people of one country are divided, belligerent, and hostile towards each other, our opponents are using all we have against us, including our resources, our intelligence and our spirit.'

"He wrote for people of all walks of life: professionals, students, labourers, homemakers, workers, and even soldiers and police. Of course no publisher would print his material, so we printed the pamphlets and magazines ourselves and distributed them at night. They were great! I loved one of his children's books in particular. It was a story in which he portrayed a group of kids having lunch in a schoolyard. Two of them conspired to goad the remaining five or six into fighting each other so that they could run off with everyone's lunches. He would tailor all his materials like that to particular audiences, as he encouraged people not to let scheming government agents manipulate them into arguing with each other on every street corner. He encouraged the activists to see that their main goal was to engage the actual working people, who were really the basis of their ideologies, so that they could, all together, develop a political plan for the country.

"He wrote about various revolutions and why each of them failed when its leadership succumbed to policies of control and intolerance. He would ask why, if China and the Soviet Union succeeded in their revolutions, did they have so many political prisoners? Behrouz contended that diverse political voices must not be locked out but must gather around the table so that all proposals and recommendations for the advancement of the country's welfare could be heard and could contribute to formations of policy. He challenged those who supported systems that utilized all, if not more, of the tools of control used by the Shah. But who would listen? With their threats of, 'If you are not with us, you are one of them,' he sometimes feared certain activist groups more than the Shah's guards, or SAVAK, his secret police. Some days, their ignorance crushed his spirit."

Payvand looks exhausted and shifts her position in the chair. She has a sip of her martini. "So my dear Ragusa, history proved him right! Our revolution failed as well because the people of Iran were not united and left the matter to 'God's good will.' So God took over, and since then the chasm between classes has grown much wider, the demolition of women's rights is complete, and the increase in the number of political prisoners has required the building of more prisons. The factional bickering among leftist groups is now irrelevant as the new regime has crushed them utterly, imprisoning or executing all who oppose it. Today in Iran, the amount of fear, unemployment, drugs, prostitution, child abuse, and child labour defy belief."

"What about your group?" Ragusa asks with a worried look. "I know Minoo is in Norway, but how about the rest?"

Payvand takes her hands and looks down at them, "Be patient. You don't want to rush to that part." She pauses momentarily, and then looks into Ragusa's eyes. "So that was the scene in the year leading up to the revolution. As divided as the opposition was, they did all have in common the goal of bringing down the Shah's regime. They cut away at the legitimacy of the monarchy itself, showing how Reza Shah was a mere creation of British foreign policy, and his son a mere stooge of the CIA. They criticized the Shah for leading the country toward Western models of continuing to allow concentrations of wealth in the hands of the few, which we felt would lead to the exploitative abuses of capitalism in the hands of a self-centred bourgeoisie, while still maintaining ancient systems of feudalism that continued to exploit the peasantry. Newspapers and pamphlets flooded the universities and streets, but the proletariat, the theoretical foundation of so many of the leftist groups who were pushing the proletarian revolution, had no idea what was being said. The leftists were disconnected from the reality of the worker's life. How ironic!

"I have to tell you, Ragusa, this period was the most interesting time of my life, yet it also turned out to be the saddest. Great ideas were being formulated and debated, but I watched Behrouz getting worn out as his daily efforts exhausted his strength. He was not as happy and enthusiastic as I once remembered him in Europe. It was excruciating for him to watch the spectacle of so many devoted, honest, intelligent, young people working so hard for their country yet scuttling their own efforts by blindly following pre-set dogmas. They didn't listen to one another, and most importantly, they didn't learn from history.

"Watching him hurt like that only hurt us all, and it hurts me to this day." She sighs and gets up to go to the bathroom where she splashes water on her face. Refreshed, she returns to sit beside Ragusa. "You see, my darling Ragusa, your people weren't the only ones who didn't listen, read, and investigate.

No, my people didn't listen either, just as the scattered, inattentive peoples of this world today are deaf to the lies all around them."

Ragusa takes Payvand's hand and strokes it. "I'm so sorry. Oh, this story is becoming dark. I can hear in your voice that there is much pain and conflict coming." She pauses, then quietly asks, "Did you tell him that you loved him?"

"No. He never noticed how much I cared for him personally, but he knew that we all collectively cared for and respected him deeply. I got used to my love being unrequited; nevertheless, in time, I learned that my feelings for him were not really romantic but more of deep respect and admiration." She smiles briefly, and quickly moves on with her story.

"We all questioned him from time to time, sometimes seriously, sometimes teasing, 'What is wrong with you? Why can't a devoted, passionate person like you love a woman or share your life with someone?' or 'Did you ever have a girlfriend?' or 'When are you getting married?'

"He always had this sweet smile, saying 'No, I never had a girlfriend because I haven't fallen in love yet.' Then, with a wink and a laugh, he would add, 'Since you seem to have so much time on your hands for examining my personal life, let me give you some more work!'

"But finally a day came when he did fall in love. Unfortunately, he suffered as I secretly suffered. The girl did not know, or care to know, that he was madly in love with her."

"Wow," Ragusa cries as she rises from her seat. "What an irony. Who was she? Was she one of your team?"

"Not at first, but she eventually did join us and become one of our best activists. She was the sweetest young mother and had a story similar to Minoo's, except that we did not help free her from her arrogant and conceited husband. She was capable of doing that all by herself, despite facing the challenge of laws designed to give no advantage to women. That strong-willed young woman even took custody of her son, an amazing achievement in a country where patriarchy ruled strong; and still does. For a second time, I witnessed a deep bond between mother and son, similar to the relationship between Behrouz and his mother Malahat."

"So you never let Behrouz know that you loved him. Oh, that's so sad."

"No, and I have never regretted it."

Payvand suddenly snaps her fingers as she too rises. "Okay Ragusa, it's about six o'clock and Brian will be home soon. He has had a long day. Let's take a break for today and we'll continue after my workshop tomorrow."

Ragusa crosses her arms and glares at Payvand. "Oh, you always stop at such exciting points!"

"Don't be like that, my dear Ragusa. Look, I'll give you her name and its meaning as a bonus for today. How's that?"

"Fair enough. What was her name?"

"Her name was Shabnam, which means 'dew,' and she really was as pure as the early morning dew on a blade of grass."

"So, even though she had your love's attention, you loved her too?"

"She had nothing to do with any of that. For most of the time they worked together, she was never aware that he loved her; and yes, I loved her very much. She was a wonderful and unique woman, and everybody loved her. She was also sweet, with a most beautiful smile and a kind laugh. I appreciated her pure innocence, her devotion to her son, and her tireless efforts on behalf of battered and abused women. I think, though, none of us understood her as well as Behrouz.

"She took the attention of my other favourites as well. Malahat and Minoo fell in love with Shabnam as soon as they met her, and with the help of Shokat our lawyer, they formed their own women's organization to assist battered women. Shabnam turned out to be a born leader, filled with great and sometimes dangerous ideas. She used any method, simple or dangerous, to achieve her goal of helping a particular woman out of a bad situation. We began to think her brain didn't detect danger, just like a child."

"She seems an interesting, kind of mysterious woman. Do you have a picture of her too?"

"I do, but let's get to know her first. Tomorrow, please!"

"Sure. So what about her boy? How old was he, and what was his name?"

Payvand laughs. "You and names! Okay, his name was Shaheen, which is a type of bird. Some Iranians say it's a falcon, while others say it's a phoenix-like bird, a legendary creature in our culture. His mother had the phoenix in mind when she named him."

Ragusa refills the martini glasses, hoping to keep the discussion going or to have more fun with names and their meanings; but just then Brian arrives. "Hello, ladies!"

Payvand and Ragusa both call out their greetings at exactly the same time: "Hello Brian," "Hello darling!" in a bit of jumble.

They all laugh and Brian is pleased to see they have had a good day. He enters the study and Payvand gives him a good long hug, and then asks Brian to call Ragusa's brother and convince him to accept Ragusa's wish to stay with them for some time.

"Sure, as you wish my ladies. I think that's a great idea."

Brian goes to the other room to call Andelko while Payvand quietly sorts through the mail that Brian just brought in. Ragusa heads for the kitchen, "I'm going to make a martini for Brian too."

"Thanks. He'll like that."

Brian returns and takes a seat next to Payvand. He reaches for her hand, and brushes it with his lips. "How are you?"

"Not too bad. She's very sweet and is following my stories attentively. She even sometimes pushes me to skip ahead to parts she is more interested in. She loved the lunch I prepared for her, and even asked for the recipe. What do you think of that?"

"No surprise there; you're a great cook! So it's going well then. Her brother agrees with Ragusa staying here, and he thinks she is much more positive since she has met you. Apparently, at dinner last night, she was joking and laughing with everybody. She hasn't displayed such behaviour since her son passed."

"Good! That is very encouraging." Payvand's eyes are glowing. "I'm so glad he is okay with her staying here. I am taking her to the workshop with me tomorrow, and I'm thinking of taking her to our Friday meeting as well."

"Friday.... So, you think it's time to introduce her to your friends."

"Well, today is Tuesday, so I have a couple of more days to present her with a few more shattered lives such as her own. Hopefully, this will give more meaning to my plan of exposing her to the way traumatized people best cope with their ordeals. I can only hope for the best in her case."

Ragusa enters the room with Brian's drink. "I would like to know what you think of my martini."

Brian has a sip. "Mmm, I do like it very much. What's the secret ingredient? It tastes so different?"

"I'll give the recipe to Payvand. I'm glad you like it!"

"Now, how about if I take you lovely women out for dinner?"

Ragusa and Payvand look at each other, smile, and say, "Sounds great!" Then, they burst into laughter as they once again have spoken the same words at exactly the same time.

"Have you been practicing synchronous speech as performance art?" Brian chuckles contentedly, "You two are scaring me!"

Payvand says, "We had a small meal not long ago, but I think it would be wonderful to go out tonight. By the time we change and get to the restaurant, we'll be ready for a little something."

"Good," says Brian. "I'll take my time." Then he goes to take a shower and change for their night out.

Payvand giggles and says, "Did you see Brian's face?"

Ragusa chuckles and nods.

Then Payvand links her arm with Ragusa and leads her down the hallway. "Come on, let's go to my room and find nice dresses for tonight. I believe we're the same size." They act like two teenagers as they scamper off to try on some finery. They have each picked out a dress by the time Brian emerges from the bathroom.

"Would you like to take a shower?" Payvand offers.

"After I finish my martini; you go first."

Payvand goes, and Ragusa returns to the study to pick out a book, then returns to the living room and sits on the sofa. Brian joins her. "So, I hear you two had a good day."

"Yes, a great day. It's so nice to come out of my shell and see the world from someone else's perspective and through someone else's experiences."

She then asks Brian, "What do you think of that fine man?"

"Which one are you talking about? You mean her husband?"

Oh, Payvand was married?

Ragusa is confused, so she does not pursue the topic. "No, I mean the guy who learned many languages so easily."

"Ah, you mean Behrouz. Yes, he was quite a phenomenon! I wish I could have his brain on my lab table so I could find out how it allowed him to gain complete fluency in any language so quickly. Quite mind-boggling, I have to say. I tried to learn Payvand's language for years, and I have learned the grammar well enough. Payvand says my accent is fine, and some Iranians have told me that my Farsi is good, but it's a far cry from Behrouz's ability to master a language to perfection."

"Yes, he sounds rather exceptional."

"I never met him, but I really wish I had. I heard so much about him from Payvand, Shayan, and Minoo. Our world needs more people like him."

Ragusa agrees with him and thinks, *He knows about Behrouz. I wonder how much he knows about Payvand's feelings for him. I'll have to ask her tomorrow.*

"Would you like more of the martini?"

"Sure, I actually liked it very much. The restaurant is within walking distance, so I'll be all right." He gives his glass to Ragusa and she goes to refill it.

When she returns, Payvand is emerging from the bedroom, all dressed up and ready for their evening.

"Aren't you looking fresh and gorgeous," says Ragusa.

"Oh, thank you! I'll give you some towels and you go get ready too."

Ragusa follows her into the bathroom. "So what is Brian's job?"

"He's a biologist, doing research."

Ragusa laughs. "That explains why he wants Behrouz's brain on his lab table."

"You talked about Behrouz? Mmm, yes, Brian is funny that way. He always says that he wishes he could inspect Behrouz's brain. Come on now, go get ready."

She then returns to Brian. "You look great!" he says, and when he leans in close to kiss her, he sees the necklace.

"Wow, what is this? So beautiful."

"Yes, isn't it? Remember on our return from the island when she stopped in the village to pick up something from the store? This is it!"

"She really likes you. This is a wonderful gift."

"I'd like to get her something too. Any suggestions?"

"You know I'm not good at gifts. I'm sure you can find something suitable for her. Ah, look at you! It's so beautiful, Payvand." As he leans down and kisses her, he chuckles, "And it sits so agreeably on your beautiful bosom!"

It is a quiet evening with a fresh breeze in from the ocean, and their table by the window gives them a splendid view. It is getting dark, and the cargo ship lights complement the shadowy water. They dine leisurely, enjoying their meal in the dimly lit room as waiters silently glide like ghosts behind them from table to table. They say little as they rest from the intensity of the past few days though Ragusa occasionally whispers appreciations for the food or the view or the ambience.

They finish their meal and walk slowly home by a longer route to enjoy the mild evening air and to talk more about each other's lives. Eventually, as is their habit, Payvand and Brian turn the conversation to politics, with Ragusa listening eagerly.

"You know," Ragusa says, "I have learned much from you two. My Dragomir was just like you, Brian. Calmly analyzing the faults of our civilization and expressing great hope that humans would learn from their past mistakes."

Brian shakes his head. "Unfortunately, our history shows that we haven't learned much. We keep the Great World Wars in mind on Remembrance Day, but newly fallen soldiers are added to the lists all across the world every year, as conflicts rage unabated. Doesn't seem like we're learning any lessons, does it?"

They discuss solutions and how these require long-term commitments to enriched universal education and widespread reforms in justice and government. They talk about the reasons for people's distrust of their political systems: national and corporate leaders concerned only with the next election or with maintaining their status or income streams; public promises to tackle world problems that only last as long as the cameras are on or until all the ballots are counted; backroom wheeling and dealing that resumes as soon as the promises are forgotten; and bureaucratic mazes that are strengthened to make public scrutiny as opaque as possible.

They return home tired, so Payvand quickly makes sure everything in the guest bedroom is in order for Ragusa. She gives her a photo album to browse through and then wishes her a good night.

Payvand goes to her bedroom and drops her exhausted body on the bed thinking, *I will get up in a minute and change,* but then she drifts into a deep sleep.

Brian comes in and smiles tenderly. He removes her shoes and clothes, and covers her with a warm blanket. He sits in bed reading for some time, then puts the book away, slides under the blanket, and wrapping his arms around her, he goes to sleep.

CHAPTER 7 **SHABNAM**

THE WORKSHOP IS OVER. Ragusa sits at the back of the room, watching Payvand as she answers questions and says farewell to the participants while packing her materials. Eventually, everyone leaves.

Payvand looks at the time and then looks for Ragusa and sees her watching from the back. They exchange smiles. "Sorry, it always takes a little longer when people have many questions. Did I tire you out, my dear Ragusa?"

"Not at all. I enjoyed your topic, "Deskilling of Skilled Workers." Who knows about that better than me? My overseas credentials meant nothing here and I never could find work at my level of proficiency. It was very interesting to hear you explain it, and I got to know another Payvand through your words."

"Well, I know this is a serious issue for many new immigrants to this country. I should have invited you to share your story! I hope I spoke to the experience well and didn't disappoint you."

Ragusa gets up and approaches as Payvand finishes packing. "Don't be silly. I appreciate you even more."

"Good, then you are stuck with me." She hugs Ragusa fondly, and says, "It's sunny and bright! We should eat at the beach before going home."

"You lead. I don't know this area. Lunch is on me though, and no arguments," says Ragusa as they walk out into the bright sunshine.

"I'm not going to challenge you on that. I think we should go to the same place we went last night. It was so dark then. We can enjoy the ocean better in daylight like this." As they walk toward the car, Ragusa asks, "Do you hold all your workshops at city hall?"

"No. I provide workshops for several different organizations with diverse employees, and the location usually depends on where the organization itself is located."

They get in the car, drive to the restaurant, order their food, and are soon admiring the beautiful tranquil ocean. Their lunch is delicious, but neither of them is very hungry and they bring much of it home. When they get there, Payvand stores the leftovers from lunch in the fridge, then puts the kettle on. "Tea or coffee?"

"Coffee, please!"

Ragusa goes to the garden and sits in her usual chair to wait for Payvand. It is several minutes before Payvand emerges from the house with coffee and pastries on a colourful tray, only to find Ragusa sleeping soundly. She quietly slips back inside the house, puts the coffee on low heat, and returns to the yard with a book to sit next to her friend. Soon, she too falls asleep.

The phone rings and wakes them both. Payvand jumps up and goes inside to take the call. She returns to report that Brian will be late tonight. "Brian and his sister take turns shopping and cooking for their parents. Tonight his sister is not well, and Brian has to take her shift."

"Well, maybe this is a good thing. Do you know what time it is? We slept for over two hours, and we have untold stories to tell!"

Payvand laughs, "Okay, but I have to throw out that coffee and make a new pot!"

"I'm sorry. I was tired."

"Don't be silly. I slept too, you know. I'll go make that fresh brew now."

"Can I water your plants? They look thirsty."

"Sure, thanks!"

Ten minutes later, Payvand is back in the garden with fresh coffee and sweets. As she arranges the table, she thanks Ragusa for watering the plants and cleaning up some dead leaves.

"Oh, no problem, it was relaxing. Mmm, I love the smell of fresh coffee."

"Me too," says Payvand. "So, where were we?"

"Shabnam. You stopped after telling me about her name."

"You have a good memory. Let's see. How about I start from how we met her."

"The beginning is always the best place to start."

"Right. Did I tell you that my activist group went into the mountains once in awhile?"

"Maybe you did, refresh my memory. I remember you mentioned your outings, but not the mountains. Tehran has mountains?"

"Yes. We usually went to the Alborz Range, where Mount Tochal is situated, to enjoy nature and the outdoors while having our discussions. Have you seen any pictures of Iran? Tehran is surrounded by mountains. Some of them are quite difficult to climb, and they make for excellent hiding places. We held some of our meetings in a few of our favourite secret locations in those mountains."

Ragusa smiles. "How nice! A meeting and a picnic...."

"Yes, it was quite pleasant. There was one location that we all liked the most, but we had to drive about an hour and then climb about three hours to get there. It was a unique and absolutely beautiful area where a very tall waterfall had been carving its way through the mountainside perhaps for thousands of years, and, in doing so, had created seven magnificent pools of water. The height between each pool varied from two to five metres. Beautiful lush vegetation had grown between and around the pools, which were each between five and perhaps fifteen metres wide. Most had a depth of well over two metres, except the middle one where I could stand up with the water below my chest."

"How was the current? If the waterfall was so high, the water must have been moving fast. Wasn't it dangerous?"

"Not really. Only the top one looked a bit scary where the water cascaded into it. It was the biggest and deepest of all and the best for swimming and playing around. Standing at the top of the falls looking down over the seven-pools ... yes, it did look scary, but it was gorgeous.

"So, there we were one day, gathered in our secret place behind some bushes between the two highest pools. We were enjoying the warm summer day, having our tea, and talking away about the accomplishments of the past week. Suddenly, we heard a loud splash, and we carefully peeked through the bushes to see what had fallen in the water. It was a girl climbing out of the second pool, looking around to make sure she was alone, and then jumping into the next pool with a tremendous splash. She was obviously enjoying herself and didn't seem to care that her clothes were soaking wet. She climbed out of the pool, but when she prepared to jump into the shallow one I got up to yell a warning. Omid stopped me and said, 'Wait, she seems to know what she's doing.'"

Ragusa interrupts. "Wait. Who was Omid? Did you tell me about him?"

"No, I guess I didn't. He was another comrade; a very nice man." Payvand reaches for her coffee and has a sip, her voice trembling. "He was right; she knew the area very well. She climbed the wall down to the shallow pool and sat on a big rock under the sun to dry. We chuckled quietly at her crazy antics, but Omid said, 'I think she was brave.' I added, 'I loved the way she swam around, very calm and cool.' Behrouz saw something different and was frowning. 'She was reckless. It looked as if she didn't care that she might injure herself.' The girl wasn't putting on any more of a show, so we all got back to our work and forgot about her.

"The next Friday we were there again, around the same time. This time we heard laughing and what seemed like the playful voices of two children. Again we peeked through the bushes, nervous about being discovered. Omid said, 'It's the same girl who was jumping in the pools last week. Look, her hair has those distinctive long thick braids, and I recognize that same cheeky attitude.' I chuckled to see everyone in our group hiding behind a tree or bush spying on the youngsters. They were coming down the cliff, and the girl was very protective of the little boy. She had one foot back to support her body and the other foot bent for the boy to clamber down onto. They dashed around playing and chasing each other.

"Behrouz was surprised that she had brought the little boy that high up into the mountains. Omid said, 'They both seem familiar with the area.' Someone else chuckled, 'They enjoy their day much better than we do. We have worked so hard here over the course of the year since we found this place, and none of us have enjoyed the pools the way she does.' We continued watching the two playing and enjoying each other's company. Behrouz commented, 'She is more alive than all of us together.'

"The girl finally asked the boy to come and eat his lunch, but he was too riled up and wanted to keep on playing. He said, 'No, open your hair and play Rapunzel with me.' She smiled, climbed up a tree and sat on a branch. The boy looked so happy, and shouted, 'The valiant knight is here to save you, my princess! Let down your hair.' Then the girl opened her braid and let her long raven hair tumble down. The boy climbed the tree pretending that he was using her hair to get up to the 'castle.'

"They were so funny that I and a few others laughed, but they heard us and looked sharply in our direction. The boy lost his balance and fell, and the girl rushed down to help him up. Behrouz also rushed out to help, and then all of us emerged from the bushes to make sure they were all right.

"'Are you okay?' Behrouz asked.

"They both stepped back and stared at us, the boy slowly tucking himself behind the girl as she looked at Behrouz and replied, 'We are fine, thank you!'

"'Sorry, we really did not mean to bother you,' I added, 'We were just here on a picnic and we saw you two playing.'

"'Well, we thought we were alone,' she said and she took the boy's hand to pull him gently away so they could leave. 'Where were you guys?' she said.

"I tried to calm her fear and said, 'We just arrived here, but when we saw you two playing we stayed behind those trees so as not to bother you. Please continue with your picnic, and we will leave you to it.'

"I think our numbers overwhelmed them, and the boy said, 'Let's go, Mama.' This surprised us, as she seemed too young to be his mother. The boy looked about seven or eight but she didn't even look twenty. We didn't retreat to the trees as we promised, but just stared at them as the girl began to pack her things. Then Behrouz blurted out, 'We have tea. Would you like some tea?'

"The boy then placed himself right in front of the girl and said, 'Thank you, my Mama doesn't like tea! You can go now!' He glared at Behrouz like an eagle, ready to attack. We all stepped back in surprise and then burst into laughter, as did his mother. But not Behrouz, who looked at the boy seriously and said, 'I am sorry. We don't know you, but I just thought it was only polite to offer tea. But I understand if some people don't like tea.' Then he turned and walked away.

"The boy looked at us for a bit, and then said, 'You go! This is our place!' We laughed again, but this time Behrouz frowned at us, pretending to be angry. 'The knight is here to save the princess! How dare you argue with him!' Then he turned to the boy and bowed, 'We will leave soon, sir. Please forgive these peasants, they do not know better,' and started to walk backward. The boy looked at him, smiled, and said,

'Well, today we can share this place with you for a bit.' We all quietly watched this sweet little game Behrouz had started with the boy. 'Thank you, sir. We have fruit. Would you like some fruit instead of tea?' The boy said, 'We have grapes, would you like some?' Behrouz bowed again. 'Thank you sir, I would love that. We do not have grapes in our village.' The boy giggled with glee and said, 'You are silly. Everywhere has grapes.'

"His mother frowned at him, 'Be polite.' The boy looked at Behrouz and smiled again. He had the cutest little dimple on his left cheek when he smiled.

"Behrouz agreed to stay, so we all settled ourselves at the edge of the pool and began talking about the hot topics of the day as we shared our food. I noticed we all were chatting, but not Behrouz. He was sitting back a bit, his eyes fixed on our guest in a way that I had never seen before. She was talking with such passion about the strikes that were being organized and the dangers that the religious factions posed, all the while braiding her long beautiful hair. She asked us, 'Do you attend any discussions around the universities, or the street rallies being held in the city?' We kept to our story about just being working people and too busy for such things. She looked at us reproachfully and said, 'What do you mean? It's our duty to work for a better country!'"

Ragusa's loud laugh stops Payvand. "What? Why are you laughing?"

"It's funny! There she was criticizing you guys, the hard core activists, about not being political."

"Well, she didn't know us."

"I know, I know. But it's still funny."

"I need more coffee. I'll go put on a new pot, and you laugh it out." She gets up, tugs Ragusa's hair gently and giggles, then goes into the kitchen.

Ragusa follows her, "Don't stop. Work and talk."

"Yes, Ma'am!" Payvand laughs as she puts the kettle on.

She regards Ragusa quizzically. "You really are interested in all these lives, aren't you?"

"I am! As you talk about them, your feelings and memories reflect on your face, and it makes me feel as if I am there with you."

"Oh, my dear Ragusa, I told you, you were never alone. If you look at our troubled world, in many ways, people are facing the same turmoil you and I experienced. Each story may be different in its details, but the feelings of loss are the same."

"I suppose. Well, for my part, I certainly am happy that I picked your walking path for my last day of life. It gave me the opportunity to meet you."

"Wow, a bit of an odd comfort, but I appreciate the affection! Thank you darling, now don't get mushy on me again." They laugh as they work around the kitchen. Payvand decides to start preparing a few things for dinner. "No leftovers for you, my dear guest.

"Well, let's see, where were we?"

"You were sitting under the trees being lectured by the young lady."

"Oh, she was the sweetest little thing. Fattaneh asked her how old she was, and when she said twenty-three, nobody could believe that she was a year older than me; she looked five years younger! I asked the age of her boy, and she said he would be six in a couple of months. He was tall for his age and looked older, which is why at first we had all thought that they were brother and sister. Fattaneh turned to me and whispered, 'Another Minoo?' So we started trying to find out more about them.

"I asked why she was alone without her husband, but she said defiantly, 'We are not alone, we are together!' Her stern reply made us all quiet for a bit, then she said, 'My name is Shabnam, and my son is Shaheen.' As soon as the boy heard that, he got up and went to each person to shake his or her hand and ask for a name. When he got to Behrouz, he said,

'My name is Shaheen and I am not a knight now. I am only a knight when I play with my mother. Or if I have to protect her.'

"Everyone laughed, but Behrouz asked him, 'Why do you have to protect her?' That was when his mom got up and said, 'Okay now, we have to go.' We apologized and asked her to stay, insisting that we did not mean to make her uncomfortable. She said it was getting dark soon and they had to go. As she started to pack, Fattaneh went to help her and gave her a card. She said, 'I really like you and your son, and I have a little girl as sweet and as talkative as your boy. If you ever want a playmate for him, please call me. We can meet in a park, and they can play while we watch and enjoy them.'

"Shabnam looked at her distrustfully, but took the card and looked at it. 'You are a nurse,' she said.

"'Yes, I am.'

"Shabnam smiled and continued packing. Shaheen said, 'Mom, can we stay a bit longer, that man has a book I like.' That man said, 'Omid. My name is Omid.' Then Omid turned to Shabnam and said, 'I can read a bit to him, if you don't mind.' Shaheen said, 'But I want your book, and I want him to read it to me.' He pointed at Behrouz.

"Just as Malahat had always melted for Behrouz's requests, so Shabnam was with her boy. 'Okay,' she said, 'you can have ten minutes,' and then continued to pack the boy's toys and their other belongings.

"Behrouz started reading to Shaheen, and Shabnam watched them from the corner of her eyes. She was so protective of her son. I seized the moment and asked her if she was working. She explained that she was studying for her second writing of the university entrance examination next year.

"I asked her what her mark was the first time, and she replied, 'I wrote it this year, and my marks put me at the teacher profession.' I congratulated her and she said, 'Thanks, but I'm having fun testing my ability, and I'm trying for higher scores.' I wished her luck, and then she turned and looked at her son, who was listening so intensely to the story and enjoying the different voices Behrouz was providing for each character.

"With the storytelling done, we all started down the mountain, talking and enjoying the forest trail. Eventually, we separated from Shabnam and Shaheen as we all headed home.

"The following Friday ... remember, Friday is our weekend...."

"I know," says Ragusa.

"Okay then, on that Friday only Behrouz, Omid, and I went to our mountain hideaway, where we sat behind our green bushes, reading and working. Less than an hour after our arrival, we heard a familiar splash. We all smiled, got up, and peeked out from the bushes, not surprised in the least to see Shabnam jumping from pool to pool, alone without the boy. Behrouz urged us to be quiet, afraid that she may start to wonder why we were here week after week. We watched her for a while longer as she swam and splashed about. Then we returned to our place to continue our work but we found ourselves mostly talking about her and how much she enjoyed those pools.

"The Friday after that, we did not see her there, but talking about her took a good chunk of our time. So we planned our next meeting somewhere else in hopes of refocusing our minds fully back to our work.

"A few weeks passed, and one day I was with Malahat, cleaning vegetables for a big gathering we were having that night, when Malahat asked me if I had seen Shabnam. I told her I had and asked her how she knew about her. She said that Behrouz had been going back to that mountain where we had met her, and he kept talking about her. I asked Malahat if the two were talking, and she said they were!"

"What, how?" asks Ragusa.

"Apparently, Behrouz had been going there on his own for the past few weeks. The first day, Behrouz joined her as she jumped from pool to pool and swam about. She ignored him and they never spoke. And when she was done, they went their separate ways.

"The following Friday, when she saw him there again, she told him, 'If you like it here, please let me know and I can find another place. I do not like company and I want to be alone.' Behrouz apologized to her and promised he would not bother her and that she would not see him again, and he left. After that, he kept going there, but hid himself well and only watched her. I asked Malahat, 'That was the extent of their conversation?' She said it was, and that he was quite worried that the girl seemed oddly sad and troubled."

"Oh, Fattaneh was right! She was another Minoo," says Ragusa.

"Well, we finally managed to establish a relationship with Shabnam when she called Fattaneh for an outing in the park. While the kids played, Fattaneh explained a bit about our group and our main goals of education and awareness among average people. She told Shabnam that people in our group could see that she was passionate about such issues, and we wanted her to join our organization and contribute to it directly.

"Shabnam said she needed to think about it, so Fattaneh told her to look us up where we first met, second pool from the top, should she ever want to learn more about us. She then gave Shabnam a few of our magazines and handouts to read and consider. Shabnam accepted them, but gave her a sly grin and said, 'You sneaky people! I like how you protected yourselves so well that I didn't even suspect you were political. That may mean that it's safe for my son. I will see you there if I decide that this is good for me.'

"After Fattaneh reported the encounter to us, she sighed and said, 'Safe for my son. I like that. My own poor daughter is so often with a grandparent or a friend or an aunt, that I sometimes think she forgets who her real parents are.' Fattaneh was right. Our own personal lives were suffering, and it felt good to hear someone care about family ahead of the group.

"The next Friday, we made sure that the only people at our meeting were those she had already met. We proceeded with our reports and discussions as usual though Behrouz was not himself and kept looking around to see if Shabnam was coming. He asked Fattaneh, 'Did you give her the time?' 'No,' Fattaneh said, 'I only told her we will be in the same location all day.' But before she finished her sentence, we heard soft footsteps on the pebbles near the pool, and then saw Shabnam's face peeking through the bushes.

"Behrouz jumped up and called her in, welcoming her with shining eyes and an innocent childish excitement that convinced me he was hooked and in love. I sighed in resignation, realizing I had no chance in the presence of this vibrant woman. But I felt a heavy look on me and turned to see Omid regarding me intensely. He moved closer and whispered, 'How does it feel to care for someone who doesn't even know you exist,' and he smiled kindly and went out near the water."

"Omid loved you?" Ragusa clasps her hands together in exasperation. "Oh, you people! How many of you guys loved someone else in the group without the other knowing about it? It's funny, and yet at the same time, cruel and heartbreaking. How did you feel?"

"Well, to be honest, I felt relief. I'd had a thing for Behrouz since I was sixteen and was tired of him looking at me like his little sister. Also, we all, including his mother, were thinking that there was something wrong with the man if he could not find someone close to his heart among all those well-educated and beautiful women around him at the university. So I was happy for him, yet at the same time, I was trying to understand what was so special about Shabnam that she had captured Behrouz's heart.

"Then I thought about all that Omid had said and done for me over the past two years. I ran things through my mind: the way he never forgot my birthday; how he would bring me flowers from time to time; how if we were on a trip, he would give me the best seat on the bus and the most comfortable camping site. There were endless other affections that played out in my memory. Oh....

"I decided I had to talk to him, so I joined him near the water where he was sitting and throwing pebbles. 'I am so sorry if I hurt you, but you have to know it was unintentional. When we finish here, let's talk.' I put my hand on his shoulder. He took my hand, kissed it, and said, 'From the moment I was introduced to you and you said, 'What cute curly hair,' you have squeezed my heart daily.' He then got up and faced me, and we looked at each other for a time. Then we heard someone say, 'What the hell, say it, Omid!' and the rest of them laughed. We were being watched, so we stuck our tongues out at them and rejoined the team and its new member."

Suddenly, Payvand jumps and says, "What is this smell? Oh, no! I burned the onions I was frying!"

"I'm so sorry," Ragusa squeals. "It's my fault. I am pushing you too much. But it's fine. I'm really not hungry, and you can have the leftovers from lunch. Don't worry about it!"

Payvand turns on the fan and opens all the doors and windows. "Ah, it smells terrible. No, no, it's my own fault; I should have turned the heat down. You know what? Let's go for a walk and we'll have a bite out. We'll walk and talk; what do you think?"

Ragusa gladly accepts the offer and is at the door right away. Payvand laughs at her cheerful and impish behaviour as she checks that the windows are all locked and the stove is off before following her out. "Okay, let's go."

"Did you lock the door?"

"Yes, I did."

"Go on then. Tell me about that poor boy who loved you ... loved you for how long? Hey, you haven't told me about the meaning of his name!"

Payvand laughs, enjoying their game. "Omid means 'hope.'"

"Hope? Just hope?"

"Yes, what else do you want? Yes, it means hope."

"Oh, just like our Nada. I like it!"

Payvand nods her head. "Well, I knew Omid for a little over two years, to answer your other question. I had always liked him, and he was very attractive with his green eyes, which is very rare in our culture. Nonetheless, as you said before, there were some in our group who might like another, but we were shy or we told ourselves that it was not important or was inappropriate for such a serious political group. We would read a book and discuss it for weeks, submit our weekly reports, and keep ourselves informed about the latest events around town, but we purposely kept personal and romantic elements out of the mix. It was an unwritten rule, because we wanted to focus on goals we felt were more important than ourselves as individuals.

"We were all young and energetic, but our intense daily work kept us from considering that perhaps there should be more to life. The dangers inherent in what we were doing day and night kept us close to fears of arrest and far from thoughts of love. In a way, we missed out on our youth as we huddled behind those bushes in yet another meeting. Maybe that was why everybody liked Shabnam — we saw in her someone who could enjoy cool pools of fresh water or whimsical warrior and princess games with her spirited young son. She was living for all of us; she was so alive and full of energy.

"So that day, she came to her first meeting and put in strong contributions to the discussions and observations. After that, she faithfully attended subsequent gatherings and very soon began working with us. Often, as we trekked up the mountain, she would sing lovely songs with her wonderful singing voice. At the waterfall, she encouraged us to overcome our fear of jumping into those pools. 'Trust me, it's no more dangerous than what we do daily in the city,' she would say. However, she also had to have her solitude with nature, leaving us occasionally to dance with the breeze among the leaves and birds as if she were part of that magnificent forest.

"Shabnam also managed to coax Behrouz into reciting for us. He knew many poems by heart, and he was often mumbling his way through one as we walked along the trails or relaxed by one of the pools. Eventually, Shabnam couldn't take it any longer, 'Eh! What is wrong with you?' she said. 'You know all these mumble poems, so why don't you share and turn them into spoken poems?' Behrouz stared at her not knowing what to say, and he tried to humbly excuse himself, but she scolded him with such a firm voice: 'Well, go on!'

"Hey, what do you know? After that, we had poetry sessions. Ha!

"Soon Behrouz's mother heard a lot about Shabnam, so she very much wanted to meet her, and she finally got the chance at the next meeting held at Malahat's home. Everybody gathered on time, but Shabnam was a bit late. She arrived wearing a beautiful red dress, greeted everyone, then looked around the house, complimenting Malahat on her taste in décor and art. Then her eyes fell on the piano, and she asked, 'Who plays this?' Malahat pointed at Behrouz, so Shabnam swept her arms toward the instrument. 'Well play then!' Malahat clapped her hands in delight at Shabnam's strong will and the straightforward and innocent way she spoke to people. Her effervescent spirit was loved by all, and I certainly did not want to compete with her. She was a bright light in our group, and we valued her merits."

"So, did Behrouz play?" Ragusa asks.

"Yes, and I will be forever thankful to Shabnam, as we all had no idea until then what a great pianist he was. He started to play, and we gathered around and watched those beautiful fingers fly over the keys and produce gorgeous poetry in sound. He played for about twenty minutes, and then we all stood up and applauded, thanking him for the concert.

"Somebody asked him, 'Why didn't you play before?' and Shabnam piped up with, 'Well, maybe nobody asked him before.' Then she asked him, 'When do you play?' But his mother answered for him: 'Almost every night before he goes to bed.' Shabnam put her hands on her hips and looked around at us. 'You guys should be doing more of this. Music is food for the soul as is nature. If you constantly sit around and do nothing but discuss and plan, your soul will dry out and you'll forget why you were all inspired to these efforts in the first place. Before anything else, your spirit has to be uplifted with life's enjoyments, so that your hearts are strong when you're working so hard. You have to appreciate life. Your devotion is admirable no doubt, but don't forget to play.' She looked at us once more, then went to Malahat and said, 'Do you need help, Mother?'

"We all stood there looking at this petite woman, smiling at how we had just been chastised by her. We didn't mind a bit, and loved her even more."

"She called Malahat, 'Mother?'" Ragusa asks.

"Yes, right from the beginning. I asked her once about that, and she said that Malahat was the mother she had always wished for."

"Do you know anything about Shabnam's mother?"

"Yes, and that will be the story for tomorrow. I'm hungry and have just realized that I have no money on me. How about you? Did you bring your wallet?" Ragusa has nothing in hand and Payvand has only her house key. They laugh, realizing that they had locked the door and left the house empty-handed.

"It's getting late. We have to go back home, eat something and go to bed. You see, I didn't stop on a sensitive point this time, did I?"

"No you didn't, and I thank you for it!"

They walk swiftly back to Payvand's home, chatting about the people in her group, and how Shabnam had been right to tell them to stop and smell the roses.

Brian is at the door when they arrive, "Where *were* you two? I've been home for some time, and I've been worried!"

They tell him about how they burned the food and so went out to eat something, but had forgotten to bring any money with them.

Brian chuckles and says, "It must have been an exciting and distracting day for you two, and I'm happy to see you so cheerful and content. Don't worry about food because Setareh decided to visit Mom and Dad tonight, and she's been cooking up a storm."

Just then a young woman steps out of the door and says, "Hi Ragusa, I have heard a lot about you, and I'm so pleased to meet you." She reaches out her hand to greet Ragusa.

Payvand says, "So good to see you darling! Ragusa, this is our daughter."

Ragusa's face lights up, and instead of taking the proffered hand, she grabs hold of the young woman and squeezes her tightly. "I was so much looking forward to meeting Payvand's daughter."

But Setareh does not respond, and only smiles. Then she says, "I have dinner all ready for you. Come in, come in!" She scurries into the kitchen.

Ragusa is a bit confused at her lack of response and at the way she speaks. Brian takes her aside to explain. "You have to talk with her face-to-face because she cannot hear you and has to read your lips."

Setareh calls out, "Food is on the table, everybody!" and they go to take their seats, with Ragusa wondering how she will converse with Setareh.

It turns out not to be a problem. Ragusa speaks slowly, and she and Setareh, who is sitting right across the table from her, have a good chat about Setareh's work, her partner and friends, where she lives, and so on. After dinner, Setareh shoos everyone out to the living room and cleans up the kitchen. Brian goes to take a shower while Payvand and Ragusa get comfortable.

"She is so beautiful!" exclaims Ragusa. "How old is she?"

"She's twenty-five years old, and I agree, yes, she is beautiful and very bright."

"Do I have to ask you, or are you going to respect our game and tell me the meaning of her name?"

Payvand looks quietly at her and hesitates.

"What?" Ragusa asks worriedly.

Payvand sighs and looks down at the rug. She is a 'star' just like your Danica." She looks up and tries to read Ragusa's face. Ragusa has tears in her eyes and Payvand gets up right away to sit next to Ragusa on the sofa, where she holds her hands for some time. "I thought about this when you told me about the meaning of Danica's name and I was hoping you would never ask me about Setareh."

"Why not? I find this very interesting. And, actually, I love this coincidence."

"You're not upset?"

"No, it's beautiful to find us connected in such ways." They sit back again and continue chatting for about an hour, and eventually Payvand dozes off where she is sitting. Ragusa is worried that Payvand will wake up with a sore back, so she gently slides Payvand's head down to the armrest where she has placed a couple of throw pillows, and then straightens her legs out along the length of the couch. Then she rearranges the blanket so that it covers her completely. *Now, that's better. Sleep tight, my darling friend.* Ragusa stretches out on the other sofa, and is soon sleeping as well.

Setareh finds them like that, and she goes to her father in his bedroom. "Dad, they are sleeping on the sofas. Should I wake them up?"

"No, no. Let them rest. They'll be fine there." In a few minutes, Brian gets up and goes to the living room with extra blankets. He looks at the two tired faces and gently covers both women with the blankets to make sure they are warm. Within an hour, the house is quiet and dark, with only the soft sounds of rhythmic breathing. Through an open window, a breeze sneaks in to silently dance with the curtains.

Night slinks away as daylight gradually enforces its dominance, and the full yellow moon slowly slips below the horizon. Ragusa moves uncomfortably on the sofa and wakes up feeling tired and sore. She gets up, rubs her lower back, and looks over at Payvand still sound asleep on the other sofa.

She lies down and tries to fall back asleep, but she tosses and turns and cannot doze off. She looks out the window and realizes that dawn is approaching, and decides she will head to the garden to watch the sun rise. She picks up the woolly blanket from her makeshift bed and Minoo's family photo album, and goes outside to lie on one of the long, soft, deck chairs. She covers herself with the blanket, and slowly flips through the album again, enjoying it much more now that she knows something of the lives of the people in it.

It is after eight when Payvand wakes to the smell of coffee. She opens her eyes to see Setareh sitting cross-legged on the other sofa, watching her. Payvand opens her arms and Setareh folds herself into them, arranging herself for a snuggle. Payvand holds her tight and kisses the head lying on her chest. She wants to say something but is loathe to break the warm embrace in order to facilitate lip-reading, so she just holds Setareh tighter and smells her hair.

Brian comes into the room, kisses Payvand, then faces Setareh to ask her if she wants a ride on his way to work. She nods, kisses her mother and says, "I like your friend. She made a bed for you." Payvand lifts herself up, and sees how Ragusa had settled her. "Ah, I was that tired that I didn't feel her doing this? Where is she?"

"She is sleeping in the backyard!" Setareh says.

Payvand gets up and looks out, "Oh, look at her! What's on her lap?" She goes out to find that it is Minoo's photo album being held tightly by Ragusa in sleep.

She chuckles to herself then goes to the kitchen to sit with Brian and Setareh as they finish their breakfast. She then walks them to the door, kisses them goodbye, and sends them on their way.

She assembles a tray with a pot of coffee on a small candle heater, along with some toast, jams, and other items she has learned Ragusa likes. She quietly places it on the table in the yard, gets herself comfortable, and watches Ragusa sleep.

Payvand is reading a book when Ragusa yawns and opens up her eyes to see the flowers already awash in bright sunlight. Then she sees Payvand smiling at her. "Good morning, sleepyhead."

"Good morning. So, I fell asleep again, did I?" She stretches and gets up. "Oh look, breakfast in Payvand's beautiful little heaven!"

Payvand pours two coffees, and hands one to her, then selects a few items from the tray and puts them on a plate in front of her.

"Go ahead, indulge me! You may never get rid of me!" Ragusa laughs and sips her coffee.

Payvand smiles. "You deserve it."

Coffee in one hand and a small sandwich in the other, Ragusa sits down again. "Are you ready to begin? You wanted to tell me about that singular young woman, Shabnam."

"Yes, yes, Shabnam. Now, I don't want you to confuse all these different stories: Behrouz, Fattaneh, Minoo and Shayan, and now Shabnam. They were all a part of the same group around the same time, but I felt it best to talk about each individually. Remember, we met Shabnam before the revolution."

"Don't worry; I understand that all these little stories are around the same time. I'm fine, and if I find myself losing track, well, I have always asked you right away, haven't I? So, go on; I'll stop you whenever necessary."

Payvand's eyes shine with satisfaction. "Thank you, I like that. Stop me whenever you have a question. Okay now, let's see; we had just brought Shabnam into the group. Well, the two of us became friends very quickly and worked together occasionally, but our most important joint effort was our magazine.

"Behrouz read one of Shabnam's early poems and shared it with us. It was a short ten-line piece with a simple message, but it had a strong structure and good delivery. If we had not been told that she wrote this when she was only twelve, we would have thought it was the work of an accomplished poet. It was beautiful work from a child, and we all agreed that she should be one of the writers. Within a few months she became our best, and she even oversaw my work.

"Shabnam never talked about her personal life with anyone, not even with Malahat who was closest to her. Malahat liked her very much and knew that her son was quite taken with her, so she wanted to know her story.

"One day, Shabnam went to the Malahat's home, where we had all our publishing machines, to drop off some flyers and perhaps some of her work. She gave the materials to Malahat and was about to leave, but Malahat thought that she didn't look right so stopped her to ask her what was wrong. Shabnam acted bravely as usual and tried to leave, insisting everything was fine. But Malahat convinced her to stay for tea and then sat her down for a talk. Shabnam had just come from court where her husband had yet again not shown up to sign divorce papers.

"Apparently, after that day they talked a lot, and Shabnam was grateful to have someone to confide in. But she made Malahat promise not to talk about her life to anyone, not even her son. Malahat assured her of that, and they soon became like mother and daughter.

"I remember once hearing Malahat tell her son, 'Don't even think about telling her how you feel. She will hate you and never come here again.' He asked her why, and she said, 'Just take my word for it. I have promised not to share anything she tells me with anyone, and that includes you.' He agreed

and did not ask again, and Shabnam and Malahat grew closer every day. Malahat would say, 'She is the daughter I have
always wished for.'

"So our busy lives went on, without knowing more of Shabnam's personal details. We never even saw her son anymore;
she was so protective of him. Any time she didn't attend a
meeting or showed up late or left early, it was because she had
something arranged with her son. Once, and only once, I don't
know which one of us said, 'Our work is very important. You
cannot just leave like that.' She looked at him in such a way
that I honestly feared that she was going to attack him. She
said, 'Last week, I transported our material accompanied by
my six-year-old son because somebody here suggested children
are a great cover. I used him as cover, and I could have been
arrested in front of his eyes. That was a crime on my part and
I will not ever do it again. I still have nightmares about it. We
should not have to involve our children. Also, if I need to be
with my son or I feel he needs me, I will leave. A young life
depends on me, and I am a mother before any of this here.'
And she was gone. I looked around to see every eye staring at
the door that she had just slammed behind her.

"Somebody said, 'That was intense.' After a few minutes
of silence, Kaveh said, 'She's right, we tend to neglect our
children. My daughter doesn't know if Fattaneh is her aunt
or her mother.'

Ragusa pounces. "Wait, what? Who is Kaveh? I do not recall
that name! Man or woman?"

Payvand laughs at the question. "This is true; the names are
strange to you, aren't they. Kaveh was Fattaneh's husband, the
doctor who was taking care of Minoo at home, remember? He
and Behrouz grew up in Geneva and went to school together.
They returned to Iran at the same time to start the organization we were working in. Good enough information for you?"

"Yes, yes. Proceed please." Ragusa holds her head up and
moves her fingers like a queen.

"Yes, your majesty," Payvand smirks and continues. "After that day nobody said a thing. Shabnam came and went according to her time, and we found that we couldn't really object. Her writings for our magazine were always ready on time, she had already set up two unions in two separate factories that she had worked in, and she was very popular among the workers she was mentoring and teaching. She gave us no reason to complain that prioritizing her son had made her any less effective as an activist."

"I like her," says Ragusa. "Perhaps she sacrificed her own time, maybe even herself, to the team, but not to her boy or to her responsibilities."

"Yes, that boy was everything to her. One night, she didn't show up at all to a meeting, which was odd because if she couldn't come, she would always call. Also, Malahat seemed worried and distracted, so Behrouz asked her, 'Do you know where she is?' She replied, 'No, but if you are worried about arrest, I don't think so.' We had no choice but to go on with our work.

"The next day, Malahat told her son that she was leaving to visit a friend and then disappeared for several days. When she returned, it was with a thin and pale Shabnam. Behrouz was going mad not knowing what was happening; he was frustrated that his mother, who had never hidden anything from him before this, remained silent about Shabnam's problems.

"That night, before our Friday meeting, Behrouz asked Shabnam if she was okay. She growled at him and said, 'I am fine, and I want you to go on in and tell everyone that I do not want a barrage of questions asking how I am.' Behrouz relayed the message to us, and we had a very sombre meeting as we all did our very best to ignore the thin and pale elephant in the room. When the meeting wrapped up, everybody left. But I was very tired and I rested on the sofa before driving home. I guess I fell asleep for a second, and I woke to hear Behrouz's voice, trembling and upset. Until that day, he had respected his mother's wishes and said nothing, but now he was at the end of his rope.

"'What is going on, Mother? I have respected your privacy with her so far, and have not asked you about her life, and I have not said anything about my feelings to her, all just as you requested. But considering how much I care about her, please do not keep me in the dark about what is happening with her. Please, I cannot function as I am too worried about her.' He was begging her for an answer, but Malahat used me as an excuse, 'Payvand is here.' I pretended I was sleeping as he peeked into the room where I lay. 'She's sleeping,' he whispered."

"Ah, you sneaky girl you, why did you do that?" says Ragusa, sitting upright.

"Well, I cared about her too, and I had not been able to take my eyes off her during the meeting that night. I wanted to help her, so I needed to know what was going on. Unfortunately, Malahat and Behrouz moved into the other room and closed the door, so I threw off my pretence along with the blanket. I knocked at their door and went in.

"They both looked at me. 'We thought you were sleeping,' said Malahat. I said, 'I was, for a bit, but I overheard Behrouz's concern for Shabnam and I need to know what is going on with her too. Malahat, you have known me since I was a little girl, and I have loved you like my own mother, and in all that time we have never kept secrets from one another. I know you trust me, and I need you to trust me now. Shabnam has become my close friend, and I want to help her. And if the only way to help her is to help you help her, then let's work together and perhaps solve Shabnam's problems even faster.'

"Malahat looked at me long and hard, then said 'Maybe you can.... No, no.' She paused a bit, 'No, I don't think so, though I am so concerned.'

"Behrouz said, 'Maybe you can start with where you have been the past few days.'

"Malahat said, 'I was taking care of her.'

"Behrouz, agitated and pale, asked, 'Why? Mother, you're killing me!' I sat down feeling frightened, and asked Behrouz to calm down and get his mother some water. He rushed out, and I grabbed a moment with Malahat. 'Please let us help! You cannot take on this responsibility all alone. It's obvious she is in distress and those who care for her most should all be working on this.' Malahat had a sad and hopeless smile, 'But she will not allow that. If I talk about it, it's because I cannot handle the burden alone anymore. But nothing can change in how you interact with her, because I am sure if she knows I have talked to you, we will never see her again. I promise you that.' Behrouz was listening at the door, and he came in. 'Why?' he asked again in despair.

"Malahat sighed with resignation, and said, 'If you want to hear, come and sit.' Behrouz looked at her intently as he sat next to her, then asked his mother if someone was threatening Shabnam. Malahat held his hand and said, 'She has been walking on a tightrope for the past seven years, and she trusts nothing but her own instincts.' I asked Malahat if she had a family. 'Of course, but like many of us, not a responsible one. Remember how my own marriage was set by the one who was supposed to protect me, not hastily marry me off because he thought I was getting too old? Also remember Minoo? Many families are that way. Shabnam has a sister and two brothers, and she has nothing to do with any of them. None of them know what she is doing, or how she is managing. They are busy with their own lives, and if they think of her at all, it's only to judge her. I really am the only one she has to talk to.'

"'How did she come to trust you?' I asked.

"Malahat explained. 'Well, anytime we were alone together, piece by piece I would tell her my own life story. One day, she took me to my doctor's appointment, and after that we had lunch. That's when she opened up about how she felt about me. She told me how different I was than her own mother. She talked about being mystified at how some women, who may have had very difficult lives, instead of using their experiences to become strong and more knowledgeable, become more cruel, selfish, and thoughtless.'

"Malahat told us that from then on they shared stories and observations, and deepened their mother-daughter bond. In time, Malahat found out what was causing Shabnam so much stress. Behrouz and I jumped in, 'What is it?' Malahat asked us to bear with her because she was going to have to organize a fair number of stories that she had heard from Shabnam over the course of the past few months into a coherent and chronological account.

"Behrouz and I could not contain our impatience, and were tripping over each other in a babbling plea to know various details and how we could help. We regretted it when we saw Malahat's broken and tired face, and we realized that she must have endured a few very bad days with Shabnam. Malahat glared at us in silence for a moment until we shut up, then she closed her eyes briefly, and continued: 'The day she didn't show up at your meeting, she had called me in the morning and said she was not well and needed me to be with her. We arranged to meet the next day, and that's when I told you I needed to go see a friend. That day, I accompanied her as she went for the third time to court, attempting to finalize her divorce. There, her husband did what apparently he always did, which was to prepare for signing the documents, and then say, "The divorce is yours if you just leave my son and go." You know her; that is simply not an option. So the court once again rejected her petition, and she had to reschedule another court date to continue her endless battle to be free.'

"Malahat had a bitter smile as she said, 'It was all ridiculous because for years she had only been married on paper. Since the second week after the wedding, that little woman has not let that man touch her again, ever!' I could see there was a long story here, so I said, 'Okay Behrouz, your mother's right. Let her start from the beginning and let's not interrupt her.'

"Malahat sat on the floor and leaned against a wall, 'Yes, please do. I'm not young anymore, and I forget things, so let me say this once and get it over with. Leave your discussion of what you want to do or how you can help until after I am done.' We both agreed, and waited for her to start.

"After some moments she gathered her thoughts, then began: 'Shabnam's parents were a piece of work, fighting all the time with no regard for how the tension they created in the household might affect their children emotionally and psychologically. Her mother hated Shabnam's father, and it was no secret that she didn't like living in his house. But she was a weak, lazy woman who preferred that arrangement to putting any effort into improving the relationship, or leaving for a better life on her own.' Malahat shook her head sadly, 'To be fair, as you know, the patriarchal restrictions on women in Iran are such as to make the latter option unviable, so she was forced to remain in her loveless marriage and just be toxic. Shabnam's father was a very religious man and a strict disciplinarian, so our little girl grew up in an edgy and aggressive environment.

"'Shabnam was fifteen years old and in grade nine when, out of the blue, her hand was requested in marriage. It seems a twenty-seven-year-old man was about to leave for France to go to university. His mother was adamant to find him a wife here before he went off and picked up a French bride, so she paraded a steady stream of prospects past him. No girl was good enough, but one day, while visiting his aunt, he spotted our Shabnam playing volleyball in the neighbouring yard and took a fancy to her. He asked his mother to go explore that option, but she disagreed, saying that the girl was too young. He considered that an advantage in the project of moulding her into a proper wife, so he declared his choice final or he would leave for France immediately. That afternoon, negotiations began with Shabnam's parents, and when the details were settled, Shabnam was informed.'

"Even though I was not supposed to interrupt, I yelled 'No' angrily. I apologized and said, 'Sorry, Malahat, but she was only fifteen and such a callous arrangement just wasn't right. I recall how my own mother was always there in all my serious decisions to guide and advise me. What a crime to consign Shabnam to marriage at such a young age without even consulting her. Why did her parents do that?'

"Malahat said, 'Yes, I understand your anger, and it's true that our highest calling as parents should always be to protect our children and equip them with sound knowledge and good common sense. Shabnam's case goes back to the discussion we had about the unfortunate prevalence of bad parenting. Her mother apparently was a narcissistic, selfish woman. When she started hearing more and more complements about Shabnam's beauty and fewer about her own, she saw Shabnam as a threat. When that mother and son appeared at her door requesting Shabnam's hand, she jumped at the opportunity to be rid of the rival to her title of household belle. What could be better than marrying her off, especially to a man based in another city?

"'When Shabnam objected to this imposition, her mother worked away at her, telling her to be a hero and go set up a safe refuge for her beloved sister and brothers, 'where they can go when I leave your horrible father.' Shabnam had no one to counsel her and the enticing idea of pulling herself away from that poisonous household strife seemed like a good plan.

"'At that young and impressionable age, her natural kindness and her naïve belief that she might be helping her mother and siblings convinced her to go through with the wedding. As was traditional in the marriage of underage girls, first they performed a dedication ceremony and then the new groom went to France for a year to complete his school.

'When he returned, they staged the formal wedding and our now sixteen-year-old Shabnam was moved to the city where her husband worked. She soon realized that her mother and siblings would never be joining her there. She was now all alone in a strange place, unprepared for the role of a wife, and in no way willing to submit to its intimacies. Terrified of her husband and his intentions, she rejected his advances for two weeks. Then he came home one night drunk and in no mood to be rebuffed on his prerogatives. They wrestled and fought, and he overwhelmed the efforts of her tiny body. What should never happen to any child of that age, happened. When she could, she dragged her broken spirit and bloody body from under the drunken man, and fled to the next room where she hid herself for the night. The next day, as soon as the man left for his work, Shabnam went out and hired a locksmith to install a lock on the inside of the door to one of the big rooms.'"

Payvand looks at Ragusa's pale face, "I am sorry dear. I know how dreadful you must feel. Do you want me to stop?"

"No, no," said Ragusa with tears running down her face. "Please, let's get past this part."

"Well, as Malahat continued to describe Shabnam's lonely, frightening time in that stranger's house, all I could think about was how tiny Shabnam was now and wonder how small she must have been seven years ago. I felt angry and I did not know what to do with myself. I looked up to see how Behrouz was doing. He was purple and tears filled his eyes as he bit his hand to restrain his voice. I don't know how much I missed by the time I shook my head and refocused on Malahat's account. She said, 'Shabnam knew she could not return to her father; what good would that do? Tradition dictated that he would be obligated to send her back to her husband. Besides, she had always wanted to run away from that hellhole. She knew that, at such a young age, she was on her own to either live a life with this despicable man or save her soul with whatever resources her inner strength could provide.'

"'She needed a plan, but first she worked on making sure she never encountered her husband again. She would come out in the morning to eat and clean and walk around the house, then she would retreat into her room and lock herself in before he returned from work. He tried to be nice and sweet-talk her out from behind the door, but she wouldn't even respond to him. A few weeks passed, and one day he surprised her around noon, walking in the door with flowers and a present. He apologized for what he had done, promising that it would never happen again, and that they would be husband and wife only when she was ready. She accepted on the condition that at night they sleep in separate rooms and that she be allowed to go to night school to complete her high school diploma. He accepted, and they started to live a peculiar but somewhat less confrontational life. They each had their own room, ate together sometimes, talked occasionally, and even went out as a couple a few times.'

"'This went on a few weeks. Then, one night, he quietly crept into her bed. Shabnam had suspected this might happen, so she always kept a pair of scissors with her under the pillow. As soon as she awoke to his presence in the bed, she spun around and stabbed him twice. He jumped away, shouting curses and screaming out that she was a crazy fiend. The wounds were serious enough that he had to go to the hospital, but he didn't reveal to the staff what had happened to him. He retained a certain level of affection for her and didn't want to involve the police. But now she was back in her locked room, and he didn't see her again for a couple more months.'

"'Then she felt a movement in her belly, and she went to the doctor and said, 'I have a worm in my belly; is it because I'm not eating well?' They ran tests and found that, yes, she was pregnant. She left the hospital in tears and wandered the streets all night, oblivious to any dangers that may lurk there. In the morning, she returned to the house where he was waiting at the door for her. But before he could scold her, she spit at him and screamed with all her might, 'Come near me, talk to me, or touch me, and I will kill you with my bare hands and teeth!' Then she fled to her room and slammed the door in his face.'

"The emotion of the story was taking a toll on Malahat, and she had to pause at this point to catch her breath. We helped her to her feet, and she continued more comfortably around the table. 'Shabnam told me that she sat in that room and talked to her child, promising the baby that no matter what happened she would never leave him alone in this world, and that she would make a life for the two of them away from that man.'

"'In due course, a son was born to her, and soon after that she asked for a divorce. He agreed, but only if she gave the baby to him and left. Having full custody of her son was not a negotiable item, so she continued to live in her barricaded room for two more years, going to night school and caring for her child. During that time, she tried to make the other resident in the house understand that this would be the extent of his life with her, that she would not be his wife. With her son now two years of age, she thought that perhaps this man might have had enough by now, and she again requested a divorce. Her husband set the same condition, that she leave the boy with him and go, probably knowing full well that she would never do that. Thus, he trapped her for another year, at the price of not having a woman in his bed or in his life. Over the next year, Shabnam finally decided to just pretend there was no marriage, and after months of preparation she moved out with her son to live on her own. She left him saying, "I do not care for your divorce paper or your support. All I want is a life without you always there on the other side of the doors and walls."' Malahat paused for a moment then continued.

"'She moved back to Tehran and began preparations for university, working and becoming more and more independent every day. It's amazing to think how well she did over the next couple of years, living life as a single mother in a male-dominated culture with so many barriers to such a lifestyle. Then, a few days ago, her husband found her as she was shopping and tried to force her back to his house. She screamed that she would die before that ever happened, so apparently he grabbed the boy and threatened to take him. You would think he would know what a mistake that was; Shabnam attacked him and they fought, with the result again that he was injured. In such a public place, this time the police were involved, and that's when I left home for a few days to be with her and help her out of that situation.'

"'While I was there he came by again, demanding to see his son. Shabnam gave them time together, then as he was leaving, she told him, "You have known me long enough to know that I care nothing for the divorce papers, and I care nothing for a life shared with any male animal ever again. As long as I don't see you, I will be happy living my life. It is you that is suffering with only a hateful wife to your name, and it is you that is torturing yourself as you get older and older with no stable life." She spoke wisely I thought, and it seems he reached a turning point there, as he began to fully realize there was no way this young woman could ever love him, or forgive him for what he did.'

"'It finally sunk in that her stubborn refusal to live with him meant he could never bring her back to his home, so yesterday he agreed to sign the divorce papers. They went to the court for the final time to end that drama of so many years.'

"'Outside the courthouse I hugged her and congratulated her, but Shabnam showed no sign of happiness or relief. She just sighed, "These papers will not heal the scars from what I have experienced over these past six or seven years; those long fearful nights, and those stressful long days full of anxieties and hatreds. They fill my mind, and I don't know if I can make them go away. You know, I never really cared about the divorce itself. I had done that in my head and heart years ago, and I didn't need a man behind a desk in a courtroom to grant it to me. I simply didn't want to see him ever again. I dream about going back in time to when I was three, and magically being the child of different parents. I know it sounds crazy, but I wish somebody could just make all those frightening, lonely nights disappear." Ah, she looked so sad.'

"Malahat was exhausted as she concluded, 'Well, as you can imagine, the last few days have been difficult for her. So there, now you know her story. She, as with so many other children in this chaotic world, was betrayed by the ones who were supposed to protect her and give her a safe and nurturing environment in which to grow. For years now, even her own family has not been aware of how she has been managing and coping in her marriage. Just look at the three of us, or others in our group. I'd say we are closer to her than anyone, but could any of us have guessed what she was going through? No; she always seemed so happy and cheerful that one might believe there were no problems at all in her life.'

"Behrouz stopped her at that point and said, 'I don't think she is putting on an act or a brave face. I think she really is naturally carefree and lighthearted, but the world she was born into has conspired to try its best to take that away from her. I think she may have some kind of strong ability to push that world aside and live as herself in the moment. Yet, have you noticed how she flinches if someone accidently touches her or pats her on the back without warning? She jumps aside as if she's being attacked, and that's obviously the product of years of trauma. I knew there was something about her by the way she would react with such disgust toward any man that even looked at her the wrong way, never mind express any interest in getting close to her. I sometimes suspected that she had been through a lot, and has been dealing with it all alone. But as you say, she masked it so well that I would just tell myself I was imagining things. I know she is strong and stubborn, but somehow we should be able to help her.'

"Malahat became agitated, 'How? No! You promised to let her be! You know for a certainty that she will leave us if she even suspects I told you all this, and most importantly she will trust no one ever again.'

"We all sat there in dismay, not knowing how to proceed. Shabnam was so very private, and even hated it whenever we asked her to help with another team member's problem. She would say, 'If they need help, they will ask. Don't put them in an awkward situation.' Yes, she was very independent and stubborn."

Payvand looks despondent and tired, and she sits back studying Ragusa's cheerless and weary face. "We will stop here. You look exhausted."

"No, I don't want you to stop. I want to know, did you guys mention anything to Shabnam? How was she after that?"

"My dear Ragusa, it has been almost two hours, and I see such sadness in your beautiful face. That hurts me, and I blame myself for it. Let's take a break and go for a walk, and I will tell you the rest later. For now, just know that we took Malahat's advice and we said nothing to Shabnam. The three of us had a long discussion and concluded that we should accept Shabnam's capacity to deal with her own problems herself as she had already been doing for too long. Besides, she was now free and clear of that marriage and living on her own with her son. We thought that, as a group, it was best to just be there for her like a family, providing a space where she could work and play with people she could trust. So, we acted as if we knew nothing about her."

Ragusa gets up, "You're right. We stop here. I haven't even washed my face since I woke up."

"Oh, that's true," says Payvand. "I certainly need to freshen up too." They go inside, wash up, change their clothes, and head out for a walk by the ocean. They chit-chat on the way, but as soon as they are on the seawall, Ragusa says, "Okay! Now start!"

Payvand laughs so hard that she has to stop and lean against a tree. Then she playfully pushes Ragusa ahead. "What am I going to do with you? At least give me a chance to first do some deep breathing and fill my lungs with fresh air."

"Oh sure, that's your excuse, as if you were back in Iran working in a factory? The whole morning we were sitting in your beautiful garden taking in all the fresh air you'll ever need, along with the wonderful aroma of the roses. So stop procrastinating and start talking. How was Shabnam after the divorce?"

Payvand laughs and shakes her head. She gives Ragusa a big hug and a kiss on the forehead. "You are so sweet. I love you my dear new friend."

Ragusa sighs. "Thank you, but I doubt I will ever be able to compete with your old friends. You all had such a deep connection to one another. I mean, we had our weekly discussion group at university in Sarajevo, but the bonds forged among your team members, what with the daily activism and dangerous conditions, must really have made your group feel like an extended family. Yes, remember? You alluded to that briefly just now regarding Shabnam's relationship to you all."

"That's right. But you know, it felt like more than a family because, for quite a few in our group, their own families were very uncomfortable places where fathers ruled like tyrants. For instance, even though Minoo's parents loved her, her father felt entitled to sell her off for his debt. Though he had regrets later, the mess was made and it was just too late. Did Shabnam have a family? What family lets a fifteen-year-old child marry? Such situations are failures, not families. What term should I use? We were devoted to each other, and would go out of our way to support one another, and that's why calling it 'comradeship' meant more to us back then. The term sounds dated now, but at the time, it captured the sense of mutual respect, selflessness, devotion and, most importantly, trust, that we all had for each other. These were qualities so many of us wished we had in our own families. Our fellowship was a great one for people like Minoo and Shabnam."

"Yes, I like it very much, and I envy you! I wish I had been part of a group with such magnificent connections."

"Oh, we don't need to look to the past. Look, I feel you and I have that kind of relationship now. You will soon meet some of my friends, new ones, just like you, who all form quite a similar group with similar deep bonds, I think."

"I will? When?"

"How about Friday?"

"My dear Payvand, look at where you have me now. A week ago I wanted nothing to do with anyone. Now, I am meeting your friends. A few days ago, I would not have thought this possible. I would be honoured to meet your friends."

They arrive at a bench looking out over the water and sit down to enjoy the view. "Good, I'm glad," Payvand says as she takes a deep breath.

"Well, everything I heard from Malahat was just shocking. How could one as young as Shabnam face all those dilemmas and all that pain alone yet keep her head up and live life daily looking so happy and strong? I imagine her son kept her going through all those lonely days and nights.

"Since becoming part of our group, she had introduced poetry sessions or storytelling at the end of each meeting. She made us sing as we hiked up the mountain or walked in the forest or at the end of each meeting, and she had us jumping into the seven pools like carefree school children. She would run, jump, and dance in the forest like a wood sprite coming home after a long absence. Behrouz said she was like a cornerstone of nature and a daughter of the forest.

"She would sit motionless under a tree and stretch out her arms, making them like two more of its branches. With bread crumbs in her open palms, birds would be sitting in her hands within minutes and peck at the crumbs as her eyes shone with joy at watching them feed. Observing such beautiful scenes, we would gain inspiration and strength as we prepared for another week of hard work. She would bring joy to everyone and laugh at every little thing. Behrouz and I marvelled, knowing what was concealed behind that happy demeanour. We were amazed at her strength in dealing with what was hidden inside her and at her nobility in taking such pleasure in her son as if he had nothing to do with the man whose arrogance and selfishness had ruined her young life."

"Will Shabnam be there too on Friday?"

"No, unfortunately she will not. And don't ask why. I'm trying to finish all the stories by Friday my dear one, so you be quiet now!"

They get up from the bench and continue their walk, holding hands and matching each other's strides.

"After our discussion with Malahat, Behrouz was more attentive to Shabnam, but also more careful than ever to avoid doing or saying anything that might chase her away. When she sang for us, in the mountains or after our meetings, with that most beautiful voice, she was oblivious to Behrouz sitting close by, gazing in admiration."

"How difficult it must have been for that poor young man," Ragusa says.

"Yes it was, though he never let his feelings distract him from his hard work within the group or his commitment to all of us. Now, let me shift gears and tell you a bit about Omid and me."

"Yes!" Ragusa says happily. "I almost forgot about him."

"After that day up in the mountain when I discovered his long-time affection for me, I let myself relax around Omid and allowed my feelings for him to flourish. I loved the way Minoo and Shayan looked at each other, and I realized I wanted to feel the same type of joy. So, from time to time when we weren't very busy with our responsibilities with the group, we would go out together. He was so sweet and funny and I enjoyed being with him. He was not versed much in the literature and poetry that I loved so much, but I was happy to find that this wasn't important to me. He had many other wonderful qualities, and in just a few months, I found that if I hadn't seen him for a day, I would be cranky. I guess he was the same, and to make a long story short, he soon asked me to marry him. His parents were religious and did not agree with his choice, but he was a man, and in that patriarchal culture of ours, he had relatively little problem getting his way. We had our wedding just a few months before the revolution."

"So you were able to marry that easily?"

"What do you mean? How else does one get married? It was easy enough. We loved each other; my parents loved him; his parents hated me; we got married anyway. Done! I'm sure there are stories like ours everywhere in the world. Romance? We had plenty! We went away for a wonderful two-week honeymoon though it was rather different than the one Minoo and Shayan had. We knew what we were doing and enjoyed every moment of it, but don't think I'm going to tell you what we did..." says Payvand as she tickles Ragusa, and they collapse on the grass screaming and laughing.

"What do you mean," Ragusa complains, when they regain their composure. "You have to give me all the details. I had to bear all those sad stories, now you have to balance that with some saucy stuff too. Are you censoring this part? Come on, it's important to hear about a nice, normal, uneventful, lovey-dovey marriage and...."

Ragusa suddenly sits up abruptly and looks at Payvand, who looks back at her. Both of them are now two steps ahead in the story and not wanting to be there. Tears fill their eyes as Ragusa whispers, "Ah these brutal stories of yours. The revolution is imminent and I am going to hear more of them, aren't I? Oh, I'm so happy that you had a cheerful and romantic wedding but knowing that today Brian is your love, I see something dreadful must have happened to Omid. Oh, dear, oh dear...." Ragusa sighs and puts her arm around Payvand, who trembles.

They sit quietly for some time gazing over a serene beach and out at the storm clouds brewing in the distance over the shimmering, tranquil Pacific Ocean. Ragusa now holds Payvand's hand. "You can stop anytime you want. I know how difficult it is to remember the loved ones we have lost. You have made your point. Yes, I appreciate better now that in this troubled world people may have lived very painful lives, some perhaps worse than mine, yet they do carry on and survive. I know you want me to set aside notions of self-destruction and go on, and I will try. Being around you certainly gives me strength because I feel how much you care. But this is hurting you too much, so I do not want you to remember anymore. Please stop!"

Payvand smiles softly and says, "Really? You aren't curious about everyone you have come to know over the past few days, and what happens to them or where they are right now?"

Ragusa puts her head on Payvand's shoulder. "Well, not knowing the ending would bother me I suppose, but I don't want you dredging up the pain I know is coming." They sit silently for a few more minutes.

"Honestly Ragusa, I tried the path of concealing all those memories of Iran's disastrous revolution, and everything we lost. It was a painful and difficult journey, and ultimately, not a successful one. As you well know, we will never forget what has happened to us. We may try to keep the past in the past, but our past is what made us who we are today, isn't it? I don't really want to forget it all.

"The imperative now is that we who have experienced such soul-shattering events should support one another to, yes, heal or recover in some small way, but more importantly, to work together. We must push back against the forces that not only conspire to inflict that pain through these nonsensical, immoral wars, but also try to convince everyone that such situations are normal and inevitable. We must challenge the impostors who govern us, and we must expose their policies of exploitation.

"But we can talk about that later. The point is, those of us who have lived through and witnessed such destructions can more easily understand one another, and we can share our stories in order to learn from each other and develop a strong united voice for change. I still live with my past — anything can trigger a memory — and I cannot stop it as much as I might like to.

"My new life in Canada has helped me significantly, especially with Brian, strong like a mountain behind me, never letting me fall. I have kept busy, going back to school, working and raising a family, and in time, I have come to a kind of compromise. One can never completely forget everything, and I still have nightmares about my fallen comrades, that devoted bunch that had forgotten how to live until Shabnam came along. Meeting you and hearing your story, it was inevitable that I should compare it to my own experiences.

"I haven't reminisced about my group in such detail for a long time, and now that I have come this far, it's okay to continue honouring the memory of all those wonderful, dedicated, faithful chums of mine. And who better than with you, Ragusa? Who better can understand what I have endured?"

They sit at that beach for almost an hour without saying a word. Then, sprinkles of rain start to fall, bringing the women back to the present. They get up and walk quickly back to the house, getting through the door just before the downpour begins.

"Well, there'll be no sitting in our lovely garden today," Payvand says. "I'll make some coffee, and we can settle into the sofas." Ragusa joins her at the kitchen counter, and Payvand takes up her story again as she works.

CHAPTER 8 **REVOLUTION**

"LET'S SEE IF I have talked about all of the key members of our team. You now know Behrouz, Shabnam, Fattaneh and her husband Kaveh, Minoo and Shayan, and I have briefly mentioned Shokat, and, of course, Omid. There were several other people as well who had different responsibilities, but I didn't work all that much with them.

"So, there we were, all carrying on with our routines in our team, along with other activist groups, and indeed the entire population of Iran as the country drifted headlong into the upcoming catastrophe."

"Will you be talking about Shabnam anymore?"

"No, not now; I will later. I introduced her so that you would know which member of my team I was closest to; she was my best friend, really. We'll come back to her and most of the others as events unfold."

"Sorry, I keep interrupting you."

"That's fine; I don't mind. So, as I said, it was before the revolution. We all were busy conducting our educational classes, planning rallies and demonstrations, participating in political discussions at universities or wherever we could, and also working and organizing in factories. Over the course of the '70s, I myself had been taking minimum course loads at the university in order to spend more time with the group. Actually by the late '70s, most of us were working in factories except for Kaveh and Fattaneh, who worked in two different hospitals.

As it became evident that we may actually soon have a major change in the Iranian government, most of us abandoned our university studies. We focused all our energies on activism and helping with what we hoped was the refashioning of Iranian political and social culture. My schooling could wait until after the revolution.

"Behrouz taught very little at the university now and spent much of his time working in a few factories as an electrician fixing machinery, something he had become very good at by then. At this time, he was pretending to be Azeri and was learning Turkish. He even spoke Farsi with a Turkish accent.

They take their coffee into the study and get themselves comfortable under blankets on the two sofas. Payvand smiles at Ragusa, then she looks down into her cup. "One night, we were all gathered at the home of Malahat and Behrouz for our meeting. But Behrouz was not there yet. We were worried as he was well-organized and never late for anything. His mother was agitated, informing us that he had planned to come at around two in the afternoon to take her shopping for that night's dinner. His absence made us fear that he had been arrested, so a couple of people rushed out to the university to see if he had attended the class he taught that day. It was agony for the rest of us, waiting. They finally came back at midnight to confirm that he had been arrested. Behrouz was heavily involved with two groups he had organized at the University of Tehran, and of course an ever present concern was that SAVAK was always infiltrating organizations and institutions to monitor people's activities."

"Refresh my memory; what is SAVAK?" Ragusa asks. "Did we even talk about this?"

"Briefly. I think I described it as the Shah's secret police. Well, I'll explain it better now. SAVAK was like the American CIA or the British MI6. It was Iran's intelligence agency, developed with the help of the CIA and MI6 to control political activity and destroy any opposition in Iran."

"Oh, we had something like that too in Yugoslavia. How awful that our governments always seem to feel such an urge to control everyone everywhere, and we all put up with it for the most part. Why?" Ragusa asks dejectedly.

"I feel the same. Really, why? Imagine being so afraid of what people think that you set up an organization dedicated to being afraid of ideas! What does it say on their business cards: 'Professional Cowards?'"

They sit quietly for some time, enjoying that insight. Then Payvand sighs. "It was a sure thing that they had a SAVAK agent acting as a member of one of the groups, because when the police showed up at the university that morning, they knew exactly where to go and who to arrest, including Behrouz, five other professors, and over thirty students. To make matters worse, we found out that Kaveh had also been arrested, and Fattaneh was frantic with worry for her husband.

"The next day, Malahat ran from jail to jail and from one police station to another, showing pictures of Behrouz and demanding to know, 'Where is my son?' She found herself in the company not only of Fattaneh, but also of quite a few other mothers, wives, and siblings who were on similar searches for their loved ones. Fortunately, at this time, the Shah feared what was coming his way, and was trying to improve his image by not treating his political prisoners quite as harshly as he had in former days.

"I don't remember clearly, but perhaps several weeks passed before Malahat found Behrouz. He was in Evin, one of the Shah's newest triumphs. It was his special prison for political prisoners, equipped with all the latest tools of torture. To think that Behrouz was there gave us goosebumps.

"It was a few more weeks before she was finally permitted to see him. He had lost a considerable amount of weight, and he was walking with a limp, most definitely a consequence of torture. He was pale, though he actually seemed upbeat and excited. He told her that Kaveh was in this prison too, along with many other political prisoners who were all keeping each other's spirits up with lively discussions. He was even acquiring a new language — Russian — from another prisoner."

Ragusa laughs with joy. "What a guy, how admirable. There he is, even in prison, picking up another language. I am sure he mastered that one too, didn't he?"

"Yes he did. He also wrote a lot in there, and at every visit, he would find a way to pass papers to his mother, which she brought to us for printing and distribution.

"He also reported a disturbing division among the prison population. The religious clique there treated the socialists badly, walking away from them as if they were filth. He wasn't particularly surprised at their behaviour, but he gained an appreciation for the difficulties that might lie ahead in the transition from the Shah's dictatorship to some form of democracy. He wondered how much of a problem the religious faction of society would be during the revolution.

"He encouraged us to not give up and to continue doing what we had done so well before. But he also asked us to be more cautious about the people around us. So we carried on with our work and waited for his court day when he was to be put on trial with eight other people. We organized a huge demonstration for that day, but events conspired to make that unnecessary.

"Demonstrations and civil resistance had been increasing not only in Tehran but throughout much of the country. In early 1978, strikes and demonstrations paralyzed the whole country, and there followed a steady series of strikes in many private and public organizations. It crippled the economy and put the government on notice that people wanted change. Army tanks were on the streets, but people interacted with the soldiers, so there was a nervous but friendly balance between them.

"After months of protests and strikes, this pressure prompted the authorities to allow the release of some political prisoners. That was not long after Malahat had discovered where Behrouz was being held. On the day of the release, she and many other people gathered at the prison to see who would emerge. Some went home happy with their loved ones; the rest went home devastated and fearful of the worst. We were among those returning home heartbroken. Malahat was distraught, thinking that Behrouz would never be let out. However, a few weeks later, just days before Behrouz's trial, an angry crowd attacked the prison, broke down the doors, and freed everyone inside. Behrouz escaped, and he came right home to his mother.

"Our group was unaware of the prison break, and at the time, Shabnam and I were with Malahat, comforting her as we often did after Behrouz's arrest.

Malahat was sitting in the yard staring at the wall in front of her when Behrouz walked through the gate saying, 'Hello, Mother.' Malahat stared at him, then turned to me to ask, 'Do you see him too or am I dreaming?' Before I could say anything he helped her to her feet, kissed her hands and head, and said, 'It is I Mother. I'm home.'

"Shabnam was sitting on the stairs leading to the yard, watching the mother and son reunion with such joy that her eyes brimmed with tears. Behrouz noticed her and went over to stand before her, where they smiled quietly at one another for some time. Then Behrouz bowed, kissed her hand, and said 'My lady,' and before Shabnam could react, he smartly turned to his mother and said, 'I am starving; what's for dinner?' Shabnam looked a bit shocked, so to keep the mood light I jumped in and said, 'Hey where is *my* hug?' He gladly gave me a hug and, as we went inside, he asked about Omid and how everybody in the group was doing. Shabnam sat back down on the stairs and looked off into the distance, so I excused myself and returned to the yard to sit beside her, asking if she was all right. After a few moments she said, 'Did you see the look in his eyes?'

"'No, what was it?' I asked.

"'When he stared at me, his eyes, though kind as usual, were filled with tears...' She turned to me and said, 'He cannot be like other men. Does he feel something for me?'

"I placed my hand on her shoulder gently and asked her, 'And if he feels something, what of it? He is human and one of the best, don't you think so?'

"'Oh, I believe so,' Shabnam said. 'That's why I am surprised. I always thought of him as a serious and devoted visionary, whose purpose in this world is to help guide us to a more just society for all. So then I assumed he was not supposed to act like all those other shallow, dim men.' I took her hand and thought for some time, and then I said, 'Shabnam, you say Behrouz is one of the best men you know. Well, being human, he will have all the feelings any human has. You can't expect him to act like some sort of robot, so don't be so hard on him. He means well; he has just been through a difficult time in prison, and he is probably very relieved to see the people he loves again. Why can't you see he is suffering?' Then I left her there before I became too emotional myself, and she sat on the stairs for several minutes before coming inside.

"The word got out, and in a matter of hours, everybody in our group arrived and we gathered for a joyful dinner together as Behrouz told us all about the events of the prison break. Shabnam listened quietly and from time to time looked at him in despair. We had many questions, and Behrouz answered what he could, but he wouldn't talk about the torture or the interrogations he endured.

"All he would say was that he was sure they would have killed him if the Shah's regime had not been under such pressure. They would never have released him either, given all that SAVAK knew about him and his ideas from his lectures and activities in Europe. Only the prison break allowed for that. We were all so happy that he had survived the ordeal although his injured leg never fully recovered. He couldn't walk properly any longer, and one of his favourite activities, hiking through the mountains, now became a difficult task for him.

"That same evening, another member joined us just as we were sitting down to dinner. It was Kaveh, who had been arrested on the same day as Behrouz and was now also free. They greeted each other with the ecstatic enthusiasm of long separation, which surprised us because we knew that they had been in the same prison all those months. They explained that Kaveh had pretended to be a religious fundamentalist so that he would be taken to a different wing than Behrouz. This ruse had allowed him to gather valuable information about that other great camp of opposition to the Shah. What he had learned was disturbing to him.

"In the days and weeks to come, Kaveh and Behrouz began talking more and more about a black evil that was on the way. They believed the Shah would soon fall, and they were afraid that those who would take his place may prove to be far worse. Behrouz was concerned that machinations behind the scenes were preparing Iran for a far more theocratic future than any of us had ever imagined. He paced the room anxiously and said, 'Those with autocratic tendencies who seek power, whether here in Iran or anywhere, have one primary requirement: an ignorant population. Plans are afoot to use the tool of religion, as has been done across the world for so many centuries, to seize control of people's minds and actions. In the West, there is room for freedom of thought. Keeping politics and religion separate has proved to be effective there. If the two instead become fused here once the Shah falls, Iran will regress instead of moving forward.'

"We were rather shocked that religion might have anything to do with our revolution. We understood that most people in the country habitually observed Muslim traditions, much like a smoker was inclined to continually light up cigarettes without really examining why. We trusted that, following the revolution, widespread education and access to knowledge would temper religious activity to the background noise seen in many other countries. But we had to seriously question our assumptions when we saw Behrouz's troubled expressions. He would ominously shake his head and say things like, 'This revolution will be bloody, before and after and for many years to come,' or 'Watch who you are talking to, and trust no one.'

"He talked about several clerics he had met in prison, a few of whom were intelligent and interesting, but the majority of whom were filled with malice. They were focused on getting revenge for their loss of power and influence under the Shah. Above all, they were quite intolerant and despised whoever didn't share their opinions. They talked about an 'Islamic Revolution' and showed no signs of being open to negotiation or compromise. Behrouz reminded us of the new group seen around the university and in the streets, their female activists covered head to toe in black. Behrouz had been in prison less than a year, but he was changed. He was not as positive and excited about the future as he had been previously. He was fearful for our safety and dismayed at the forces arrayed against us. He spent a lot of time quietly walking and thinking, with far more frowns than smiles on his face.

"Behrouz immediately returned to work, eager to apply the lessons and insights he had learned in prison. He had lots of new ideas and set about organizing himself and the group with renewed purpose, refocusing our activities and having us gather more frequently to talk and report.

"One night, after we had concluded a meeting, Shabnam asked Behrouz to play the piano. But he said he was tired. She persisted, suggesting that it would make him feel better, and help others to wind down and relax. But Behrouz seemed to have lost patience with our companionship, and he walked to another room. Shabnam followed him, took his shirt, and gently turned him around. He visibly relaxed, as if deflated slightly by allowing exhaustion to ease his guard. He smiled at her serenely, his eyes glowing with affection, though they were tempered with caution and restraint. She held his hand, and with a kind but practical voice said, 'Pull yourself together; we need you! I know something horrible happened in that prison, and I know you feel overwhelmed by your fear of what is coming, but we need to be together right now, at this moment, supporting each other even more firmly. You're acting like you are not with us anymore.' He looked disoriented, and glanced down at the hand that she was holding. Looking intently into her eyes for a few seconds, he kissed her hand and said, 'You are right. Please forgive me.' He returned to the room and sat at the piano, 'I will play three requests. What shall they be?' I still remember that night fondly. He played more than three pieces, and not only the classics. He delighted us with material we didn't even realize he knew when he pounded out some lighthearted traditional Iranian dance tunes."

"He was full of surprises, wasn't he?" said Ragusa. "I like him, and I like Shabnam of course. Did those intense looks get them anywhere?"

Payvand smiles. "No, not really. We were all busy with the revolution, and Shabnam was so moody that Behrouz told me later he simply didn't want to ruin any trust he had gradually gained with her. We could never be sure what Shabnam was thinking or what she may do.

"From the summer of 1978 onward, in many cities, there were frequent mass demonstrations though protestor demands varied depending on particular factional interests. A general strike that October paralyzed many vital industries and weakened the country's economy. Several countrywide demonstrations were so large that some analysts have described them as the largest ever recorded worldwide. Modern history had never witnessed so many people with differing ideologies demanding one thing only, 'The Shah must go!' The police and army began to deal more harshly with the mass demonstrations, with thousands of people killed over the course of the uprising, mostly young adults.

"Eventually, by January 1979, the Shah had no choice but to leave the country. January 16 is a day no Iranian in the country at the time will ever forget. It seemed like the entire population was in the streets, chanting and celebrating and parading their joy that the people had forced the dictator out. What they did not know on that day was that we were replacing him with a new dictator. You see, very soon after the revolution, the clergy took control, and they quickly began the elimination of those not strictly pro-Islamic. There were arrests and imprisonments and mass executions.

"The fast pace of events surprised the people of Iran. It surprised observers in the rest of the world, who were trying to make sense of where the country was going. Seemingly overnight, our society transformed into a full-blown theocracy, rigidly controlled by arrogant clerics who believed, and still do, that because of their religion and their positions as Islam's representatives, they are imbued with a God-given superiority above the rest of the nation. They have found themselves on very high horses, and have been enjoying the view ever since, heedless of the destruction their iron-shod steeds have been wreaking.

"After the revolution, Behrouz did not want to go back to university. Because it had been a hotbed of secular activism, it was a prime target for theocratic revolutionaries seeking opponents. He knew that there was a thick file on him in the Shah's prison that was now in the hands of the new dictators, so he worked only in factories. He even changed his name and documents. When he confirmed with one of our young Turkish team members that his Turkish was flawless, he forged a new identity as a native of Tabriz.

"The new political reality did not slow him down. He continued his non-stop work organizing labour, translating and simplifying important political research and articles from different languages, and conducting political workshops for whoever cared to learn. He would get three or maybe four hours of sleep; some nights he got none at all. It was distressing for many of us to see the effort and devotion he put into his hard work, and the pain and disappointment he experienced at not getting the results he wanted."

Payvand takes a deep breath and exhales loudly. "Please allow me to stop for a bit, and you rest while I prepare dinner." She gets up and goes into the kitchen, but Ragusa, as usual, follows her. "Let me help you and then, when you are ready, we can continue to talk."

Payvand opens the fridge and takes out what she needs for dinner, arranging things on the counter and giving some vegetables to Ragusa to clean and chop. "Okay, if you wish." They work in silence for a time, each with their own thoughts. When things are simmering, they sit at the counter and Payvand continues her story.

"Well, as you probably know, it was a disaster not a revolution. Soon the rights of women were severely curtailed as well as those of some ethnic and religious minorities.

"There was a short period of exciting social reform and active debate among all the revolutionary groups about how the new government should be fashioned. But soon, the religious factions took over the machineries of power and within a year opposing views began to be suppressed and their champions prosecuted. If socialist or secular groups were seen distributing their newspapers, holding meetings at team houses, or making such criticisms as, 'Our revolution has failed,' they were arrested."

Ragusa shakes her head. "Indeed it failed, if you went from one dictatorship to another one. It's impressive how much determination there was to achieve a goal: a revolution. It's so tragic that after the goal was accomplished, such a calamity ensued."

"Precisely!" Payvand says. "Sadly, many things contributed to the problems: widespread illiteracy, feverish religious devotion, disparity and disagreement between political activists. The leftists, in their flyers and newsletters, busily tried to analyze the new system. Was it feudalist? Was it micro-capitalist?

Was it lower middle-class? Was it a working-class theocracy? These were ridiculous arguments. The working class had no understanding of these distinctions and had nothing to do with any of it. As the imams took over, our group adopted even more precautions, determined to keep firmly out of sight of the new authorities.

"You know dear Ragusa, when people are not in control of what they are allowed to read and how they are allowed to think and can only whisper with the ones they trust, they won't grow intellectually. In time they really forget how to think critically and lose any desire to seek out alternate theories about what is right and what is good. The Shah had censored pretty much everything, so even though he always seemed to be trying to make Iran more westernized, he didn't allow people to develop modern political habits of critical thinking. Therefore people maintained old fatalist traditions of leaving everything to God's will. Thus, after the revolution they did just that, and the clergy took over in God's name claiming to represent God's will. The people just accepted that and returned to their routine lives.

"After the coup against Mosaddegh decades ago, many books were banned. Do you know Maxim Gorky?"

"Of course. I am Eastern European, and we know all the Russian writers."

"Well, his books were banned by the Shah's SAVAK. For instance, if they found his book, *The Mother*, in your home, you found yourself in prison for seven years."

"What? That was just a little story about a mother and her devotion to her son, and her son's devotion to revolution. Why would one go to prison just for reading that?"

"Ah, tell me about it. In addition, any Marxist book earned you ten years in prison, and any history book criticizing monarchies got you even more. That was how the Shah and SAVAK kept people in the dark about the marvelous political events and historical movements happening simultaneously in the sixties and seventies worldwide. Mind you, not everything was censored. Everyone seemed to know about all the actors and actresses of the time or the latest European fashions.

"Of course, there were always brave ones who could not be prevented from finding books, and reading and exchanging them with others. But that was difficult and frightening. Most importantly, not everyone could even read, and thus benefit from even that limited access. In my opinion, in a truly liberated society, all books about history, politics, science, and new discoveries, have to be in the bookstores on the shelves, and people must be free to choose material based on their personal interests. We did not have that because the Shah considered knowledge to be dangerous. It was quite ironic that the Shah was kicked out and replaced by a regime that had been nurtured by the very ignorance he nurtured.

"A few months after the Shah's fall, a referendum was called wherein the uneducated and religious majority voted to confirm the new Islamic regime. That was why and how the Iranian party of Hezbollah took over the post-revolutionary process. If ordinary people had understood or foreseen what an Islamic fundamentalist government would bring their way, they would not have voted for them, and we, perhaps, would have had a successful revolution."

The door opens, and Brian is home. He hears the women in the kitchen and goes directly there. "Hi, Ragusa," he says, and then kisses Payvand. "Hello, my love." They both greet him, and Payvand asks about his day.

"Fine, but I should ask how you two are and where you went today."

"Well, we had a great day," Ragusa says. We had a wonderful walk by the ocean, and I got to know about a couple more of Payvand's friends."

Brian nods, "Yes, amazing people they were."

"Dinner will be ready in thirty minutes," says Payvand.

"I'll take a shower then," Brian says and leaves the kitchen.

Payvand sets the table as she talks. "So now the theocrats began ruthlessly suppressing all opposing political groups, or, for that matter, anyone who disagreed with them. Then, the number of political prisoners increased.

"As I mentioned before, our group was now back underground, and we altered our policies regarding communication between sections of the group. Only the leader of each section would know the identities of other leaders, and no one outside a section, not even other leaders, would know the identities of section members. If one section leader was arrested, the rest of the organization had no way of contacting his section. Behrouz and Kaveh thought that was the only way to increase security for the members.

"Where before our meetings were held at various locations, they were now held only in the mountains, disguised as usual to look like family picnics. Sometimes, we would go higher up a mountain than usual, where the police did not have the manpower to check on us. However, that was time-consuming and difficult for Behrouz as his leg had not healed properly. We no longer had a safe house, and we all moved into different accommodations. Only the ones who worked together knew about each other's locations. All these precautions and protections had to be implemented within only two years of the revolution. Additionally, when we went out to distribute printed materials, one person carried the materials and another one followed to make sure nothing happened to the transporter. If she or he was arrested, it was quickly reported and anything connected to that person was changed."

Payvand pauses. "Now, our dinner is ready. How about we continue after that?" She calls Brian for dinner.

"Wow, it's so scary!" says Ragusa.

"What is scary?" Brian says as he enters the kitchen.

They sit around the table and talk about how frightening Payvand's activities had been and how difficult life became for all Iranians at the time.

After dinner, Brian says, "I'll clean the kitchen while you guys go on with your stories. Enjoy your time together. Go on. Once I'm done I'm going to read for a bit before bed. I had a long day."

Payvand kisses him, then follows Ragusa into the study. The two of them get settled amidst a comfortable arrangement of pillows and blankets. But before they can begin, Brian returns with two glasses of wine. "For my ladies," he says, and wishes them a good time as he leaves them to their talk.

Ragusa smiles. "Such a gentleman!"

"Yes, he is kind and considerate. Well, where was I?"

"After the revolution."

"You always remember. Thank you for listening so well." Payvand pauses briefly. "Yes, soon after the revolution, a split between Islamic and non-theocratic intellectuals began. The new regime branded whoever disagreed with their tactics and strategies as 'western-style intellectuals,' or 'imported intellectuals.'

"Before long the regime published a new constitution, which had no tolerance for non-Islamic theories, ideas, or processes. They called liberal and left-wing groups 'counter-revolutionaries' and issued fatwas against them for being anti-Islamic. That was kind of like putting a price on someone's head, making life intolerable for the victim.

"Soon, opposition newspapers were banned and anyone who took issue with the new reality was declared a 'conspirator against the Islamic Revolution.' The National Democratic Front rallied a mass demonstration to protest all these measures, but it was viciously attacked by Hezbollah thugs wielding rocks, clubs, chains, and iron bars. Hundreds were injured and an unknown number killed. Shortly thereafter began a steady barrage of arrests. The authorities detained thousands in retaliation for that day's demonstration. They also attacked and looted the offices of liberals, leftist groups and anybody else who disagreed with them.

"More and more institutions came under theocratic control. All universities were closed after they were labelled breeding grounds for western-style thinking, and they were not reopened until their codes of operation had been aligned along Islamic principles, whatever that meant. Then, a dress code for women appeared, and women were forced to completely cover themselves head to toe when out in public.

"While these lunacies were being perpetrated, we passionately continued our work underground. All other political activists were being arrested, executed, or forced to flee the country. Yet, for four years, we continued functioning well, most certainly due to our precautions. Behrouz and Kaveh had witnessed the Islamists first-hand in prison, and experienced their hatred towards non-Islamic ideologies. They knew we should have no contact with them. With the increased stranglehold by the Islamist regime, we had decided that we would only work underground; so, our organization continued unchanged without any arrests.

Brian comes back once more, sits down next to Payvand, and puts his arm around her. He says, "Ragusa, please don't look," and plants a kiss on Payvand's lips. They laugh at his silliness. "I just came to say good night. I am going to bed," he says. "It looks like you guys are going to stay up."

"I may turn in too," says Payvand, but she sees the eager look in her friend eyes.

Ragusa shrugs her shoulders. "If you are tired we can go to bed and start again tomorrow."

"Not with that look! You want me to go on! I can see it in your face. Okay, let's see how far I can go." She kisses Brian again, then says, "I will join you as soon as this woman falls asleep." They laugh, and Brian leaves the room smiling.

"Thanks Payvand! Tell me just a bit more. I truly care to know what happened to your team members."

Payvand sighs. "You are not going to like it!"

"I figured that out already, but I still care to know."

"Okay. Let's sit closer," says Payvand. They push the chairs into a position that allows them to hold hands and to feel each other's warmth and support. Payvand begins. "What happened to those team members of mine is no different really than what happened to you in the Baltic and what is happening right now in countries experiencing conflicts, such as Mali or Syria. The power-seeking elites simply don't care what happens to the people, land, and ecosystems that fall under their sway. They just devise their plots and then move in and take over by whatever means necessary. You and me, the people of your country and the people of mine, we have little say in how we are treated. The result, as we know all too well, is fallen friends and family, and destroyed lives.

"The latest empire to wreak this kind of uncaring havoc on populations is America. The character of American hegemony is interesting because 'regime change' has been its preferred technique lately. In contrast, the favoured method of empire building over the past thousands of years was direct occupation. For example, when the Europeans came to North America, they simply took the land and pushed back or wiped out the people they found there. I mean, most nations grow larger over time, but the indigenous populations of North America decreased over the years and were decimated in order to replace them with the new settlers. Not many years have passed since then, but the latest North American generations forget what their grandparents or great-grandparents did to the First Nations of this continent. All my life I heard that America is the land of opportunity. Do you believe that? History has shown that America is the land for opportunists!

"But my point about all this is that, back then, the British and the Americans didn't install a local puppet to control the native population, and then leave. By contrast, since World War II, the American empire has used regime change as a normal policy for domination. Examples are CIA-supported coups in Chile and Iran, the American invasion of Grenada, and the implementation of the Cuban Project. Then, of course, there was the removal of Mosaddegh in Iran. These were all ways of keeping countries in line without the long-term military occupations imposed by the likes of the old Roman or British empires. Of course, occupation is still on the table if necessary. First, blame the victim for forcing an attack; second, set up sanctions to weaken the target nation's fabric; third, create a little rhetoric about freedom from tyranny for the poor benighted population; then fourth, go in and try out some new military technology or tactic, like depleted uranium or 'shock and awe.' Meanwhile they trot out the propaganda to train their own people to believe that everything the government does is for the national interest. These conscience-soothing falsities make it easier for people to not concern themselves with what their governments do. And thank God that they can sleep peacefully and enjoy the protection of their 'wise government.'"

"Well, Yugoslavia didn't really have much in the way of oil or resources, so what was the war in our country for?" asks Ragusa.

"Oh, resources are not the only inspiration for domination and control. Perhaps they want to keep a region weak using a policy of divide and conquer or maybe a region has geostrategic value. At times I wonder if the only reason for warmongers is a sick desire for power." She sighs. "Ah sorry, Ragusa. I went off on a tangent again, didn't I. Forgive me."

"Don't worry. I appreciate at times having a look at the larger view. In any case, when we finish your story I can see our next step will be to apply what we have learned through our experiences. We must examine what is really happening behind the scenes around us and in places such as in my Yugoslavia in order to work out solutions."

Payvand smiles weakly. "You are a quick study, my dear. Yes, we are living in a greed-driven world of blood and suffering, and it will be hard work finding ways to make things different. Well, for now I suppose I should get back to my compatriots, as they watched in horror while the imams slowly transformed Iran.

"Before the theocrats could take full control of the country, all the Shah's political prisoners were released and SAVAK's offices fell into the hands of the people. Activists discovered many gruesome photographs of tortured young women and men who had been killed in the most inhumane ways, just because their political beliefs put them in opposition to the Shah's greed. We all went to see the pictures when they were posted on the walls of the University of Tehran. Ah, such atrocious evil!

"After that brief 'access to information' by popular decision, the clear view into the abuses of power went opaque once again. The new regime took over SAVAK and changed its name to SAVAMA and used it for exactly the same purpose. The very tools used by the Shah's secret police began to be used by the agents of 'holiness' to torture and kill the very same people; young activists who disagreed with or objected to the government line.

"These new secret agents of the clerics got off to a running start in their enterprise of oppression because they had in their possession the SAVAK files on many old activists. My father was one of them; if you recall, he had been imprisoned in the Mosaddegh era.

"Omid and I were living with my parents at this time, but we were out when they came for my father. My mother said the first thing they asked when they invaded the house was, 'Why are there no pictures of the prophets on your walls?' Faced instead with a wall covered in books, these vacuous new guards, protectors of the revolution, turned to my father in bewilderment with, 'Did you read all of these?'"

Ragusa laughs out loud, "You are kidding me!"

"No, I am not. Without waiting for an answer, they grabbed my father and dragged him to the door. As my mother pleaded, 'Where are you taking him? He is ill!' those bullies pushed her to the floor. My father tore himself away from them and rushed to my mother's side to help her up, but the goons knocked him down with their rifle butts and hauled him away. Two weeks later, they called my mother to come get his body."

Ragusa tightens her grip on Payvand's hands. "Oh, dear! I wasn't expecting that. Your father! They killed him!"

"Yes, it was that simple. Why they had to kill a man who worked all his life to help others, financially, educationally and ethically, I can never know. There can be no valid reason. He certainly was defiantly opposed to them philosophically, but he was not active at all anymore due to his age and bad state of health.

"After my father's arrest, my mother asked us to stay at my aunt's until she heard something about him. But after they killed him, my mother sent a message and pleaded with us not to come home in case the thugs returned. You see, after they closed the universities the authorities had even more information about those who were active before the revolution. In addition, any non-Muslim former guests of the Shah's jailhouse were diligently sought out for a return visit to prison.

"Anyway, when my mother went with some relatives to get her husband's body, they demanded bullet money."

"What type of money?" Ragusa asks.

"Bullet money. After the revolution, when they executed people, they required money from the family of the victim to pay for the bullet 'wasted' on the 'traitor.'"

Ragusa's voice is shaking, "Oh! It's infuriating that some people have such diseased minds that they not only feel entitled to take other people's lives, but they have to dream up ways of insulting their families as well. Sick through and through!"

"You know, I couldn't even say goodbye to my father. Not knowing how he died has haunted me for years. Did they torture him? Did he suffer before they executed him? My mother became ill soon after, and I'm sure it was from sleepless nights wondering the same thing. Fortunately, she died in her sleep only six months after my father's death. My aunt said she took pills, but that didn't matter. I was relieved in a way that she was not there to see the things that later happened to me and Omid."

"Oh ... I don't know if I want to hear it anymore!"

"I'm sorry. Would you like me to stop?"

Both sit quietly, holding hands in the dim light of the study. "No, no, I feel selfish. You listened to all the misery I went through. Sorry, please go on."

Payvand leans in closer. "I was pregnant and due in a few weeks when my mother passed."

Ragusa is startled. *Oh, no! What is happening? It can't be Setareh; she is too young for the time she is talking about. She only has Setareh now.*

Payvand lifts Ragusa's chin up. "Are you all right? Are you talking to yourself?"

Ragusa is agitated now, though she is trying hard not to let it show. "No, no, sorry. I'll be okay; I want you to go on please."

"Don't worry Ragusa, I'm right here, so you need not be worried about me."

They hold each other's hands in silence for a bit. Ragusa says, "I am here too, but I am far from all right."

They sit for a few minutes, each wrapped in their own thoughts, then Payvand continues. "Behrouz and his mother left their home for the second time and moved to one of the busiest parts of Tehran. Shabnam also moved to a different place, as did many of us, a tactic for safety and precaution.

"Not long after that, Kaveh's life took a dreadful turn. Remember I told you he pretended to be a religious man while in the Shah's prison?"

"Yes, yes, I remember!"

"Well, here we were, a couple of years later, and he receives a call from a revolutionary guard asking him to help them!"

"What do you mean? How he could help them?"

"I'll tell you. Kaveh was a doctor, right? Since 1981, Iran's new secret police, SAVAMA, also known as the Ministry of

Intelligence and National Security of the Nation of Iran, had been stepping up its work of identifying political activists from before the revolution, both Muslim and non-Muslim. The Muslims were used to help them identify any non-Muslims they may have seen in prison. Those non-Muslims, in turn, were then arrested and tortured psychologically and physically to elicit more names.

"If prisoners wouldn't talk, they were badly beaten, and for that doctors were needed to keep them alive as long as possible. So Kaveh was flagged as the perfect candidate for this work; he was a doctor and supposedly a former Muslim prisoner."

"Oh dear, Oh dear! For someone like him? So what did he do?"

"At first, he didn't know why they had called him, so he went in to talk to them. He said they were no more than twenty minutes into the conversation before he realized what they were asking. Of course, he refused at first, but they said, 'We must protect our revolution. Aren't you with us?' He tried to reason with them and said, 'There is a difference here, in that we are not torturers! These kinds of methods had the people of Iran screaming for the Shah to leave. We should not do what his regime did.' But they weren't happy with his answers; they were rough people who had no mercy and were not there for a debate. So he told them he had a family and a job that kept him busy, and that he had to think about it.

"We had a group meeting right away. Kaveh was devastated and didn't know what to do. Each one of us had a suggestion. One said, 'Well, being there will help us to see how they are torturing people,' while another said, 'Why do we need to know how they are torturing people? It's enough to know that they're doing it. Even one slap is an attack on a person's dignity!' Yet another said, 'Leave the country; they won't let you be.' Behrouz finally turned to Kaveh and said, 'What do you think? We really cannot tell you what to do. Your decision will have full support from all of us. Tell us how you feel.'

"Shabnam was sitting in a corner quietly. She had on her pink flowery dress — a bold refusal to don the long black gown that was the new requirement for women. She looked different that day, as if primed to battle whoever dared to cross her. She went and sat beside Kaveh and held his hand. 'Do they bring these mutilated people to a general hospital or do they have their own location?' Kaveh responded, 'Well, I think they have a hidden corner wing of a jail or something.'

"She looked at him intently, 'Then you should take this opportunity to find out what exactly they want you to do and where they are doing their disgusting work. I hear their torture is more psychological, in which case they wouldn't need you much for patching up. But don't you think it would be helpful to know what they are doing and how far they have gone only a few years after this bloody revolution? With you or without you, they will torture to get what they need; however maybe, just maybe, you will be able to help even one prisoner, or perhaps a few, or even be there with them at the end.'

"Kaveh and Behrouz listened thoughtfully as Shabnam got up and continued, 'The main point is, we won't know what they are doing if you don't look into it. Right now, you are the only one who can gather information and let us know how far they have developed their techniques for tormenting people. They trust you for now. See what is going on. If it turns out you cannot do it, you may have no choice but to hide or leave the country. They will not let you be after you have stepped through their door that far, and you know that.'

"Behrouz wanted everything to be clear, and said, 'Think about this carefully. Are you sure you can see yourself responding to even one of their requests?' Kaveh was quiet and thought for a while. Then he got up and said, 'I will let you know,' and left. The rest of the group talked nervously about the issue and left for home one by one. Most were happy that they were not in his position. We did not see Kaveh for a week. Not even Fattaneh heard from him."

"What do you mean? He didn't even go home?"

"Oh, I forgot to tell you this little part. As we just saw, Kaveh's file identified him as a Muslim revolutionary man, and thus, he was respected by the present regime. Fattaneh, on the other hand, was a black sheep where she worked, and no one there was under any illusion that she was a religious woman. So as much as they loved and respected one another, their public face was one of disagreement and conflict, to the point that they were putting on a show of separation and divorce. So, at this point, they were not living together. They would see each other at our meetings, or from time to time, they would stay at my home or Shabnam's."

"Oh, what an agonizing situation," says Ragusa.

"Don't worry, they were happy. They said that because it was so challenging to be together at all, they were back to their passionate loving days as a newlywed couple. Those two were always ones to look on the bright side.

"So, yes, where was I? Not even Fattaneh knew where he was. Eventually, Behrouz sent Malahat to the hospital where Kaveh worked to see if he was there and he was! He was happy to see Malahat because he wanted to get a message to us. He wanted us to know that he could not risk visiting us as he was sure he was being watched and followed, and he did not want to put any of us in danger.

"He told Malahat that the prison guards had not yet called him to help heal the tortured ones for which he was truly thankful. He asked that we wait until he found a way to contact us himself.

"Well, for us, that was relatively good news, so we all went back to our tasks more relaxed in spirit though still constantly tired in body. Shabnam was now going to a new location to work, but by then, the religious dress code was fully in place. We all had fun trying to convince her that she simply could not go to the new factory with her brightly coloured pants and blouses. Fearful for her safety, we tried to convince her to comply with the dress code and wear the required long black robe, or chador.

"She didn't strictly comply, but she did compromise. Before going to work, she came to see us with her new style, announcing, 'I wear this ridiculous Islamic outrage under protest!' It was a very stylish navy blue dress with dark blue pants, and scarf. She had made sure there was no dark grey, black, or brown, and it looked quite good."

Ragusa chuckles. "How stubborn she was! I like her so much."

"Yes, that was our Shabnam. I too was moved to another location, and Behrouz continued fixing machinery in various locations. As always, he was popular among the workers.

"Not long after this, Behrouz's love for Shabnam came to a head. It had become like a tumour growing inside him, and now it was causing him such a pain and anguish that he was seriously thinking about revealing his feelings to her. But he always prevented himself from saying anything to her for fear of throwing off the balance she seemed to have achieved for herself. Shabnam valued her personal life and the time she spent with her beloved son. At the same time she was firmly loyal to the group, treating everyone equally in her usual strong, positive, and caring way. She showed no hint of favouritism to Behrouz or anyone else. He risked losing her friendship and admiration entirely if he told her how he felt. Also, we had begun to gather for meetings much more rarely by that time as it was not safe anymore, and this only made him miss her more.

"After a particularly long stretch, we all finally had a get-together at Behrouz's home. It was not a meeting but an opportunity to have a relaxing evening and wind down a bit. Malahat arranged it because she thought it would be nice for everyone to have a good meal and a good night's rest. She wasn't sure who would be able to attend but about ten of us showed up. Shabnam was there too. Her son was at his weekly visitation with his father, where he could play with his cousin, and she was thrilled to be staying the night with her beloved Malahat.

Fattaneh also came, but Kaveh did not show up. As a matter of fact, we hadn't seen him for quite some time."

"So, Shabnam had reconciled enough with her ex-husband to allow him those weekly visits?"

"Well," Payvand adds thoughtfully. "He wasn't a bad father to his son. He was an arrogant product of a patriarchal culture and she just hated being married to him through the machinations of her family. So, yes, she agreed to the weekly visits."

Payvand continues. "We had a wonderful time that night. We had a great meal, read poetry, listened to Shabnam's melodic voice as she sang for us, and, of course, enjoyed music played by Behrouz. By midnight, everyone had left, except Shabnam, Omid, and I. Malahat and Shabnam would sleep in the same room, as they occasionally did from time to time, such as when Shabnam was particularly sad or under stress. She would come and stay with Malahat for a night, or Malahat would go and stay with her for a few days.

"In the morning, Omid and I left for work, leaving Malahat, Behrouz, and Shabnam in the kitchen having breakfast. Before we got out the door, Malahat came and told me that Behrouz was adamant about having the big talk with Shabnam today. I was happy to hear that and suggested to Malahat that she let him do it. I felt that Shabnam was so involved with the group and all her activities with us that she could not just leave. I said, 'Let him get it off his chest; he is suffering.'

"'I know, you're right,' Malahat said. Then I left for my busy day with my love Omid.

"In the afternoon, I received an anxious call from Malahat asking if I knew where Behrouz was. I responded, 'You all were home when I left. What do you mean?'"

"What?" asks Ragusa. "Wasn't he at his house talking to Shabnam?"

"That was what I had thought, so I hurried back to Malahat's home. She was rather upset, so I calmed her down and asked her what was going on. She said that after Behrouz had talked to Shabnam, they had both left for work. I jumped in. 'Oh, they did talk? Do you know what Shabnam said? Was she fine with it?'

"'Yes, yes,' said Malahat. 'I heard everything. I left them alone in the kitchen, but stayed behind the kitchen door in case she got angry or stormed out, and I might be able to stop her. Shabnam began preparing to leave for her work, so Behrouz stopped her by reciting a poem that he knew Shabnam especially liked.' I asked which one it was, so Malahat tried to recite it to me:

> I am the cold ashes,
> yet within me, there is an inferno of bonfires.
> I am the tranquil sea,
> yet within me, there is a hurricane.

"Then Malahat continued. 'Shabnam was surprised to hear Behrouz break into poetry like that, but she had the sweetest smile as she listened. She stopped him to ask if he was not going to work, but Behrouz didn't respond to her question and continued reciting the poem. So she joined in and they finished it together; one line him, one line her, alternating back and forth:

> You are dancing in my dreams,
> with everyone but me.
> You are in my heart and soul,
> yet seem so far away.
> You are with me,
> yet that love is shared with all.

"'Oh, I tell you, Payvand, it was so wonderful watching them share that beautiful poem. After they were done, she asked him again why he was doing this. I watched my poor boy standing there, looking at her lovingly, yet so terrified at what her reaction might be.' Malahat was crying. 'My boy was never afraid of anything, but at that moment I had never seen him so petrified, and yet also somehow so happy as he searched her face to know her mind.'

"'Now wait a second,' I said to Malahat. 'How do you know all that?'

"'Oh, I've been waiting for my son to find his soul mate for too long. I watched him fall in love with this angel but suffer for years in silence with the strain of his affection for her. If my boy was about to find happiness, I had to witness it. So when I left the kitchen, I found a corner where I could hear them well, and peek to see them from time to time.'

"Impatiently, I asked her what had happened. Malahat said Behrouz began by quickly asking Shabnam to listen to what he had to say before she stormed out. 'Shabnam smiled and said, "What is it? Why would I storm out?" He made her sit on the floor and he sat down facing her and said, "For years, I have changed your bodyguards whenever you asked me; and why? Because if they liked you as more than just a friend or looked at you the wrong way, well that upset you and I could not have that. There were times when I actually changed them myself before you even noticed. I just wanted you to stay happy and cheerful. I am most content when I see you dance with trees and birds and when I admire how you love everyone equally in comradeship. When we played music, I always wanted to dance with you, but I never did. I loved your singing voice, but I never told you that. I delighted in your curt and biting retorts to whoever opposed you. No matter how dangerous some of your actions were, I didn't hold you back. I supported you. I have long loved you and ached to say how much I admire your brave and daring manner. I just don't know how to express my feelings for you as words are failing me. All I can do is recall everything I have seen while in your presence. You never judge others by their colour, accent, how they dress, where they live, or how much money they make. I loved that about you, but I could never mention it. You love everything around you so easily, and you give to everyone so freely, yet you never expect anything from anyone. Because you are sure you can do it all without help, you seem to radiate a purity of being."' Malahat said that he paused then, for the briefest of moments.

"I looked up at Malahat and she had tears in eyes. She said, 'Then, he went on. "I have delighted in how much you enjoy playing with your little boy; there were times that I wanted to hold the both of you and somehow be part of those beautiful moments. For years I have watched you attend to that boy of yours so carefully that I wanted that bundle of joy to be part of my life too and for you to be my partner and my comrade in life. But I respected your feelings and acknowledged your distrust towards men, all men. I understood that. But by now I am sure you can trust Omid, Shayan, and Kaveh, and know that they are nothing like what you experienced. I am not one who has hurt you, and I am nothing like what your tragic experiences have led you to expect. However, even now that I am telling you how much I love you and want you by my side, I am not expecting much. I just want you to know what my heart holds; that from the first time you jumped into that pool of water, I have been watching the vibrant life within you and have loved and admired it. All I am asking is for you to consider whether you have room in that beautiful open ocean that is your soul for a comrade, a friend, a lifelong companion, and, in time, a lover." He paused, unsure what to say next. "If not, then I would want to be your friend as long as I live."'

"Malahat stopped and held her breath behind a smile as she looked at me. I spun my hand in close orbit around my impatience, urging her to continue. 'Well,' Malahat said, 'Shabnam was shocked. She stared at Behrouz as he talked nonstop. When he finished, she sat there quietly for so long that I wanted to burst in and shake her, and tell her, "Why you can't love him? He would never disappoint you, my dear!" But I didn't dare.'

"'He sat there staring at her, tears in his eyes, and after rather some time she reached out and caressed some hairs off his forehead and with a trembling voice said, "I have kind of noticed you following me around recently. And I noticed that you played more of my favourite music lately. Last week, Payvand actually got a little angry with me, calling me blind and insensitive and asking me how long I wanted to torment you. You have to know that never in my life have I had a high respect for any man, nor counted on them for anything. Yet you and the other men in our group have helped tremendously in changing my perceptions. Your love, belief, and devotion to other people is admirable. I know you could live a luxurious life in Europe, enjoy your studies and fame, and forget about Iran; but you are here living a difficult life, and doing it for the people of this country. I love that about you. As for the idea of a life partner, I don't think I'm ready for that, and I do not know if I ever will be. I do not see inside me the ability to love a man. You are right about my love for nature. When I dance with the wind's melody through the forest boughs, I seem to lose myself in the surroundings. I can feel the vibrancy of life all around me, and I can easily imagine myself flying among the birds or being one with a waterfall. I can relate to all of it and release myself into oneness with nature. It's a technique I have used to help me survive all these years. I shut out everything but what I want to hear, and see nothing but what I want to see. For a long time, I had nobody to talk to, and only my wild imagination for company. Over time, I have picked up some unhealthy habits, and I am sure I will need lots of time to pull myself away from them, for example, my rude and hateful behaviour toward men. I have even trained my brain to see certain men as women, just so I can to talk to them and work with them.'"

"Malahat said that Behrouz stopped her at that point, and said, "'I understand all that. But would you allow me to help you correct those feelings. You do trust me, don't you?'

"She said, 'Of course, I trust you, but I need time to think about what just happened here.'

"'He said, "Can we go out and take a walk in the park and talk some more?" She shook her head. "No, no, not today. Let me absorb this first." He said, "Okay. We don't have to go out. We can stay home and I can play the piano for you, or maybe we can read some more poems together." She got up smiling and said, "You are sweet, but not today. I have to go." Then, he got up too, and replied, "Fine, I promise not to bring this up again, until you are ready to talk about it."'

"Malahat said Shabnam smiled then, a really warm smile. She said, 'He wanted to hold her, but she stepped back. So he smiled and said, "Whenever you are ready, I'll need one of those hugs you give my mother or Payvand." This time she laughed and came out of the kitchen to where she could see me around the corner. She stared at me a bit then, as if she understood me as a mother, she gave me the nicest smile ever, and then she left.'

"'I went to the kitchen where my boy was sitting in the chair thinking, not unhappy with how the talk had turned out. I told him that she would come around and that she had not seemed angry.'

"'He said, "I know. We'll let time take care of it." He held me and said, "Ah, Mother, I love her so much, and have for so long!" I kissed him and told him to be patient, and then he too left for his work.'

"Her smile suddenly vanished as she remembered that Behrouz's whereabouts were in question. 'Just before I called you, Omid phoned to ask how I was doing. He sounded quite agitated, and I felt that he was not himself. So I insisted, and demanded he tell me what was going on. He admitted that he thought Behrouz had been arrested, but was not sure. After I hung up, I called his work and asked for him, and they said he was busy. I was so confused and getting desperate. I tried to find Shabnam or Kaveh. I was finally able to get a hold of you.'

"We were still talking when Kaveh suddenly arrived, looking wild and disheveled. 'You look horrible!' we said. 'What is going on?' He dropped into a chair and replied, 'How I look is not relevant right now! They arrested him!'

"Malahat turned pale and went weak in her knees, slumping into a nearby chair. I asked, 'How? We were clean! What happened?'"

Payvand gasps for air. Ragusa looks at her with concern. "Are you okay?"

But it is as if Payvand does not hear her, "We could not believe it. You are not going to believe it! You do not want to believe it!"

"What? What can I not believe? What are you saying? Are you with me?" says Ragusa.

Payvand breathes rapidly. "He did it! The hatred that man had for him! It was someone who knew him, and he went up to the management's office and reported him. Do you remember, I told you there was an activist who often debated with Behrouz and knew of his knowledge and energy and wanted him to work with his own group? Behrouz always rejected the idea because he was strongly against any attachments with Russia. That man was a member of an old activist faction in Iran that faithfully followed Russia's lead in all they did. Many of them were educated in Russia, trained there, and strongly believed Iran should follow in Russia's footsteps. This man knew Behrouz well from his work in Europe and at the University of Tehran, as a professor and as an activist. He had even been in prison in the same wing as Behrouz.

"As you just heard, that morning, Behrouz had gone to work in a pleasant mood. He had been working on a machine with a few other workers, chatting cheerfully, when that monster arrived and saw him. This man was an engineer who inspected machinery installations at factories. In front of everyone, he called him 'Doctor,' and used his last name. Then he went up to management and told them that the man down there at the machines is a university professor who knows several languages, and suggestively asked why he was working as a mechanic. That was all it took. The Islamic Assembly agent for the facility hurried down to look into it.

"Behrouz knew this man and his vindictive personality, so he immediately attempted to leave the building. There was some chasing outside of the factory, but they eventually caught him. Kaveh found out about it through a team member who worked in the same factory and witnessed the whole thing. He left his work, went to Kaveh's work, and reported the incident.

"Malahat listened to Kaveh tell the story, biting her finger and shivering the whole time. Then she turned even more pale and collapsed where she sat. Kaveh was prepared, knowing she might fall ill at the news. He injected her with something to calm her, then held her tight, kissed her several times and said, 'I want you to be strong for me; we have to find out where they took him. We have to get him out, do you hear me? Do you understand? He got out last time, so you have to be strong for him again, for all of us!'"

Ragusa holds Payvand's hand tight as she continues. "I lost my father to them. Six months after that, my mother passed because the pain was too much for her. She couldn't understand why they had to kill an old man who was living a quiet life. Now, it killed me to look at Malahat's lifeless face, and I felt a sharp pain in my stomach. I held my belly and thought, *No, baby stay in! Please not now, this is not the time!*

"Kaveh left to find more information, and he returned a few hours later to say that he had found out where they took Behrouz. Malahat had recovered somewhat by then, so he asked her to go there. She was to tell them that she had just heard from her son's work that they had brought him here, and she wanted to see if he was all right.

"Right then, Shabnam and Omid arrived. Omid had told Shabnam all about it, and she looked dark and different. But, of course, we were all worried. Shabnam offered to go with Malahat, but I said that in my pregnant condition it was safer if I went. Omid agreed, saying that he would follow us to make sure we were okay. Kaveh debated that for some time, not wanting too many of us in a dangerous area all at the same time. Shabnam pointed out that we would be going in separately, alone or in pairs, so the authorities wouldn't know we were all together. We agreed to the plan, and Malahat and I headed out.

"We found many families at that police station, showing IDs with names and pictures of their loved ones and begging for answers. I couldn't believe there were so many; we seemed lost in a sea of desperate people.

"Kaveh had told us that the traitor used Behrouz's real name at the arrest. That meant that the authorities knew everything about him, so Malahat used all his legitimate information to ask for him. I pretended to be Malahat's neighbour who was helping her out, and I hoped that maybe my huge belly would gain us some measure of sympathy and respect. I was so wrong! The guards there were rude and uncaring goons, and they cursed people at will as counter-revolutionary and against God and Islam. They dismissed everyone there as undeserving of anything good for having raised infidels that had never been instructed to live a proper, godly way of life.

"I felt that sharp pain more and more, but I was afraid to say anything as I noticed that Omid and Shabnam had arrived now and were anxiously watching us. Malahat literally pleaded with whoever came around for any details about her son. But the effort was too much for her, and she suddenly fell. I wanted to help her up, but a soldier pushed us both, ordering us to stay away from the door. I was exhausted and in pain, and I shouted at him, 'Watch it and have some respect for your elders!' He yelled back, 'I have no respect for her, and if you are here it is because there is a traitor in your family here! We have no respect for anyone who is against our Islamic revolution,' and he kicked me in my belly. I have never experienced pain such as that in all my life, and I fell on my back. Now it was poor Malahat hovering all over me, trying to help me get to my feet. I heard loud noises and a commotion all around me and I tried to find Omid, knowing he must have seen what had happened. Yes, he was in there fighting with the soldier who had kicked me down. I gathered every ounce of energy I could find to get up and pull him away, and then I heard a gunshot.

"There was a sudden silence, and I looked to see my sweet, kind love lying on the ground. They shot him in the face, with one eye completely gone and the other one open and lifeless. I don't remember how I got up, and I don't remember how I got to the soldier with the gun. He was standing over Omid smiling proudly, and I was all over him screaming and scratching. Then I heard another gunshot and a sudden sharp pain in my back and stomach."

Ragusa breathlessly watches Payvand with her eyes wide and one fist at her mouth, not daring to say anything.

"Apparently, after I was transferred to hospital by Shabnam and Malahat, there was a war at that police station. People were outraged at the brutal behaviour of these new revolutionary guards, and they attacked them for throwing down an old woman and shooting a pregnant one. The next day's newspapers described a titanic battle between infidels and devoted revolutionary guards, but they didn't say how many people had been killed or injured."

Payvand sits up, looking pale and breathless. "My love was killed and so was our child. I was in a coma for a week after they removed my uterus and one of the ovaries, and I remained in hospital recovering for about three weeks, with Shabnam and Malahat taking turns caring for me day and night. One of my aunts took me home. My husband was already buried, as the authorities would not allow us any ceremonies for our loved ones."

The room is dark and quiet, and dawn is just breaking. The two broken women lean on one another, drawing long deep breaths as they sit in a daze for some time. As the morning brightens, Payvand regains some strength. "I awoke from my coma during the second week to a world without my Omid and our child. Kaveh and Fattaneh came to see me, but Kaveh looked so thin that I was surprised he could still walk. He was extremely morose, saying that he could not forgive himself for allowing me to go with Malahat that day. He felt so guilty. I asked him if he knew where Behrouz was.

"His only answer was tears in his eyes, and he left soon after. It was a dark and hopeless day. Shabnam was there to help me out, and also care for Malahat. We asked Fattaneh to explain what was going on. She said that Kaveh had been neither eating nor sleeping for days. 'He has accepted that position as their doctor in their prison hospital, and he has seen what they are doing to people.' She said, 'He is very upset because most of the prisoners are young adults, but there are also children and many teenagers there. They are executing daily; they fill the prison's wing, torture at will, and then execute their broken bodies. No, he is not doing well at all. He accepted the position mainly to find Behrouz, but also to see if he can help any other prisoners. He cannot really help anyone; the guards watch him and don't really trust him. They needed a doctor; he is a doctor, but that is all. He is another tool to use in their daily disgusting activities. Kaveh is losing his mind, and he hasn't yet found Behrouz.'

"Fattaneh sat down and cried so hard. 'Did you know Kaveh and Behrouz have been together since grade five?' She then held my hands, 'And you my dear darling, when he found out that Omid was shot, and how bravely you attacked that soldier for which you too were shot, his reaction was indescribable. He cried, and he paced the room all night long.' "

Brian pokes his head through the door of the study and sees that the girls have not slept yet. He takes one look at Payvand's face and returns to his room to call work and let them know he is not coming in. He then goes back to the study and gestures at Ragusa to come out. She pulls herself away from Payvand who is sitting motionless, barely aware that Ragusa has left. She is still talking in a soft monotone, but she is not making sense.

"Which part is she talking about?" Brian asks.

"We are at the time when she lost her child and her husband!"

"How about Behrouz? Has she said anything about him yet?"

"Just up to the part where he was arrested. I'm kind of worried; she looks so sick. Is she all right?" Ragusa asks.

"No, she is not all right. Could you please draw her a nice, hot bath?"

But suddenly Payvand calls out for her. "Where are you, Ragusa? I'm not done yet."

Brian pats Ragusa on the shoulder and says, "Okay, you go back, and I will draw the bath myself later." After going to the kitchen to put the kettle on, he returns to the study. "Can I join you?"

Ragusa is sitting there quietly listening to Payvand, so he settles into a chair near the door. He hears Payvand say, "Ragusa, do you know the story of Spartacus?"

"Yes, dear Payvand, he was..."

But before Ragusa can say anything else, Payvand continues, "You see, Behrouz for us was a supreme symbol of bravery, love, kindness, and devotion. He recognized his place in this world, and he wanted to be a free man with free will and to share his vast knowledge as much as he could for the betterment of his fellow citizens. Behrouz could have lived a happy and successful life in Switzerland, making a name for himself in Western society. However, he saw that in the land of his birth, a tyrant king exercised abusive powers over his people, and he wanted to use his knowledge and skills to help create a new and better society there.

"Spartacus too did not want to bend to an emperor's will by killing other gladiators just to satisfy imperial bloodlust. Spartacus fought the system that prized exploitation and human degradation. Now we have to try to understand why, thousands of years later, our advanced civilizations still operate under the same program of manipulation and destruction, thus requiring the rise and fall of still more Spartacuses all across the world. Over and over again, people who see the problems of humanity try to speak out and strive for change, but they are immediately shut down because their voices are always up against the ruthless tyrants of the day.

"Behrouz despised both the Shah as a puppet for the West, and the Islamic regime that forcefully destroyed all who opposed it. He loved his homeland and dreamed of seeing a free Iran with its people living in their land and benefiting from its resources in an equitable and just way. Both regimes refused to allow that, and the one presently in power killed him in the most cruel and unimaginable fashion."

Ragusa looks apprehensively into Payvand's face, then holds her hand tight and listens.

"You know, Kaveh finally found him; or no, it was actually the authorities that asked Kaveh to come in. One sunny day, Shabnam and I were sitting in Behrouz's home while Malahat was out at Evin prison begging to see her son. She had been going there for the past three weeks. I was so weak and tired, and Shabnam kindly helped me to keep comfortable as we both waited for Kaveh. He had said he had news.

"He finally arrived and immediately asked for Malahat. When we told him she was at Evin hoping to see Behrouz, tears filled his eyes, and he whispered, 'Poor mother.' We knew that was not good. Shabnam fell back in her chair and in a frantic voice said, 'Please say he is okay.'"

Ragusa is all ears as Payvand's voice subsides into a monotone. "They called Kaveh that day to go to the same location he had been going for the past couple of weeks, where he helped them revive tortured prisoners while hoping incidentally to find Behrouz. He said they did not trust him much as he had lately been delaying his response to them, so he thought he had better go in quickly this time. As soon as he arrived, they informed him that they had a man who had been in the Shah's prison previously. They told Kaveh that the man was well-educated but had been working in a factory in order to turn ordinary people against the regime. They said, 'The engineer that reported him to us knows him well as a man who can speak many languages, and we think he is a spy who wants to topple our revolution. We know he has his own organization, but he hasn't revealed any information about it yet, so we cannot let him die. Fix him up! We are almost there. Just a few more hours, and he will give up.'

"They brought Kaveh to a semi-conscious, severely beaten, broken body. Kaveh threw up. The guards made fun of him. They jeered, 'What kind of doctor are you?' Kaveh responded, 'The kind that heals, not destroys!' They told him, 'Ha! You think you are better? We are protecting what we have fought for. He is against Islam and our revolution.' They looked at him viciously and ordered him to 'Do your job and get out of here. We want him up and conscious as soon as possible.' They then left Kaveh there, with the bloody mess that resembled a human body.

"Kaveh looked out into the yard to make sure Malahat was not home. He said, 'The smell of infection was nauseating. The cuts and bruises were so bad that I couldn't be sure I recognized him. I looked at him closely thinking that the description they had given me made it likely it was him, but part of me hoped that it wasn't. The ruined body moved and tried to reach for my hand. He was whispering something. I put my ear close to his mouth, and he asked me if it was daylight. I said yes. Then he said another word — a little joyful childhood memory of ours. It was him! In that shattered condition, it was him! What they had done to him was revolting. His jaw was completely broken, his arms and legs were broken, and he was emaciated. He definitely had internal bleeding, and the sounds coming out of his throat with each breath told me he likely had hemorrhaging around his lungs.

He was badly damaged, and there was no way under those conditions that I could restore him to any level of comfort. He motioned me to come close again, and said, "You cannot fix me nor take me away from here. Be the friend you have always been and end my pain."' Kaveh stopped talking then, and sobbed like a little boy.

"I was shivering and had difficulty breathing, and Shabnam was so pale that it distracted Kaveh. He had come prepared with medication, knowing the news would affect us. 'Take this, it will help.' We did as he said, then he held both of us, crying and repeatedly saying, 'I am so sorry, I am so sorry! I couldn't do anything better. He was in such bad shape! It took him minutes to say a few words through the relentless pain. Two of the torturers returned and asked me if he was saying anything. I told them of course not; I wasn't sure if he was even breathing. I said he was hemorrhaging badly and that there was no way he could make it. I took the guard by the shoulder and forced him to look at his abdominal region, showing him the swollen and bruised areas and telling him, "Too much blood has gathered there. He may bleed out from these areas at any moment. Do you understand?" But before they could react or do anything, Behrouz exhaled one long rough breath and settled into a very shallow breathing rhythm. I was happy.' He repeated, 'I was happy that my old friend went quietly. The guard demanded to know what had happened and why he had gone quietly. I told him that he had gone into a coma and with that level of internal damage nobody could bring him back. The guard started screaming that I was a traitor too and that the other doctor would arrive soon to take care of this. He ordered me to stay and keep trying, and then he left me there. I wanted to pick Behrouz up and hold him, but I knew touching him would only give him more pain. I wanted to run out and get a gun to kill them all, but there were many of them and only me. All I could do was to make sure they could not wake him for a few more minutes of torture. I was sure he didn't have more than an hour or two to live, and I feared that in that short time they might hurt him more. So I injected him with an overdose of morphine to end his suffering. I wet his lips with some water, and was surprised to see him open his one good eye and look at me. I bent close to his mouth and he said, "Thank you." Then with much difficulty he said, "Tell my mother ... I am sorry I didn't listen to her ... I love her so much...."'

"Shabnam interrupted him, 'Do you know what Malahat had told him?' Kaveh looked at her wretchedly, 'Well, last year Malahat begged him to return to Switzerland, but he said he would not go anywhere without you. So Malahat told him that all four of you — that included you Shabnam and your son, should leave immediately. He disagreed, promising that he would build a life here for all of you.' Shabnam stared at him as tears ran down her face. Weakly, she said, 'Go on.' Kaveh again said how sorry he was before he continued, 'Behrouz was quiet for some time, then he said, "Tell Shabnam ... I wish I could hold her just once." He exhaled roughly, then tried again but only said "Shabnam," before sinking into a coma. I kissed his hands and his forehead, sat there for a bit to make sure his heart had stopped, then left the room certain that nobody could hurt him anymore.'"

Ragusa's pale face is fixed on Payvand, who is staring off at nothing and breathing in slow but sharp gasps. Brian sits at the door, anxiously looking at her. He knows that there will be days of silence again, and a tormented woman crippled by the past and desperately worried that the future of this world will see no relief from more stories like hers.

Payvand finally notices that Ragusa is anxiously looking first at her, then at Brian, uncertain of what is happening. "I'm so sorry. I know this upsets you terribly. I will always remember my time with that great human being and how much he contributed to this world in his short life before being taken so brutally. He only wanted to help others, but there are those who see that as a crime, and are driven to silence any voices of justice and virtue."

Brian brings Payvand a tall glass of water, and she takes it with a look of tender love and appreciation. He leans over and kisses her. "Would you please stop now and rest a bit?"

She looks at him for a few seconds. "No, if I stop now I won't be able to come back to it. You know there is not much left. I'm okay."

She then turns toward Ragusa. "You know, what we heard from Kaveh that day seemed unbelievable. Shabnam said, 'If I hadn't said no that morning, and we had gone out for a coffee, this wouldn't have happened. The inspector would have come and gone and Behrouz would be here now. It was my fault.'

"Kaveh stopped her, and said passionately, 'Stop it! Look, he was not a yearly inspector. He was working for the company and he came to that factory regularly. It was only a matter of time. Imagine if he had not told you about his feelings and had gone to work as usual; it would have happened anyway. What he should have done was not work at all anymore. He should have left that place. Think about me and how I feel! I killed my best friend because I didn't try hard enough to convince him to quit working out in the field.'

"Right at that moment we heard a loud thump outside of the door. We rushed out to find Malahat collapsed on the floor. She must have heard Kaveh's last comment. Kaveh shouted, 'Here, I killed his mother too!' Malahat's eyes were open, but it seemed she was not seeing us. Kaveh took her pulse, looked into her eyes and ears, and came to the conclusion that she had suffered a stroke. Shabnam and I took her to the hospital where that diagnosis was confirmed. Three days later, she passed away. We were sure she had overheard the news of her son's death, and it tormented us to imagine how she must have felt at that moment.

"I saw Kaveh a couple of more times after that, and every time I saw him he seemed thinner and sicklier. He had quickly sent Fattaneh and their daughter back to Switzerland, and he was planning to join them soon. We had a heartbreaking farewell, and I never saw him again.

"With Behrouz and Kaveh gone, any connection to other sections or branches of our organization was severed. We were automatically cut off. We knew no one but the ones we had been working with. Minoo and Shayan were living in Norway with their children, Omid had been murdered, and Shokat had not been involved with us for a few years as she was not practicing law anymore. So there only remained Shabnam and me.

Brian interrupts and says, "Excuse me my love, sorry. I just want to know if you would like me to draw a bath for you."

"No, I'd rather have a hot shower, thanks! Do we have tea?" Payvand asks. "I can make it right away!" But she stops when she sees Ragusa's sad weak smile. Payvand wraps her arms around her. "Oh, my dear. Yes, life for people from your region and mine has never been easy. The suffering is real, but we must be strong and use our experiences to inform our actions and help others to be strong too."

Ragusa agrees with her. "It's just that I knew you were going to lose a few of those wonderful people in your group, but I couldn't begin to imagine the manner in which you lost them. Your husband didn't deserve to die like that. Behrouz didn't deserve to die like that! Such a devoted visionary, as your Brian said the other day. This world needs more people like him — and Omid — and losing them like that is heartbreaking and simply a crime against humanity. I am so sorry. What eventually happened to Shabnam?"

"She ended up in hospital. Nobody could convince her that it was not her fault. She was sick for some time. To this day, she wonders about her last day with Behrouz, and if he she had stayed with him that day, what the outcome would have been."

Brian comes in with tea and some toast and puts them on the coffee table.

Ragusa gets up and hurries to the bathroom, hiding her tears.

Brian sits beside Payvand and folds her into his arms. Her hands are cold and shaking. "How are you?" He rubs her hands and kisses them. "I'm so sorry. Maybe you shouldn't have gone that far."

Payvand is quiet. She lays her head on his comforting chest. Brian says, "I called work, and I'll be staying home today. Maybe we can all go for a walk by the ocean. What do you think?"

Payvand gets up unsteadily and says, "Let me take a shower. My breathing is difficult. Maybe I'll feel better after I get cleaned up and changed."

"That's a great idea." He supports her arm and walks with her to their ensuite bathroom and leaves her to stand under the full force of the shower, which masks the sound of her sobbing as she leans against the wall.

Brian returns to the study to find Ragusa has returned from the bathroom though she still looks miserable. "She'll feel better after her shower. Don't be worried." says Brian.

"Well, I certainly did not want to make her that upset. I now understand you better."

"In what way?" Brian asks.

"You said she has nightmares."

"Oh yes, she has. She is going to have a few of those for the next few days. But she has become quite a bit better lately at controlling her emotions."

"Where is Shabnam now, do you know? Oh, and how did you two meet?"

"Shabnam and her son are in Norway. They live in the same city as Minoo and Shayan. As a matter of fact, Shabnam's son married one of Minoo's daughters a few years ago."

"How beautiful!"

Brian smiles. "And as for how we met, that happened in Greece. In fact, I met Payvand and Shabnam at the same time. I was a tourist visiting Athens. You know, in Greece people love to sit out in public cafés and in parks, often listening to live music. It's a nice custom. My friend and I were sitting in a café, and there were two women and a little boy sitting nearby. The two women both looked sorrowful, and the boy, who we later learned was called Shaheen, was trying so hard to make them smile or bring life to their faces. He was practicing his English and hoped to make them laugh at his mistakes. He kept pestering one of the women, 'Mom, please come and dance with me...' and she would smile at him but wouldn't get up. Finally the boy gave up and sat there sadly. It wasn't long before his mother noticed that her behaviour had saddened her son, so she got up and pulled him out onto the patio to dance together. They were so cute and had everyone's attention, so I dared to go over to Payvand and say, 'Let's go help your friend, all that attention is making her uncomfortable.' She smiled and got up hesitantly, but that smile had me, as did everything about that mysterious young, beautiful woman. There were just the four of us on the dance floor, all of us unfamiliar with the bouzouki music, but doing our best. It was delightful. Do you know that music?"

"I do love it too. Dragomir and I had travelled to Greece, and yes, we loved their food, their music, and the friendly people. As nice a place as any to meet your future love."

"Ha! Well, after a bit my friend joined us and tried to dance with Shabnam, but she was not as friendly as Payvand. She gave my friend a withering look and went back to her seat, so my friend danced with her son instead, and the boy did not mind at all. I asked Payvand out for breakfast, and we agreed to meet at her hotel in the morning. Shabnam did not come, but she allowed her son to accompany us. So the next day, Payvand, Shaheen, and I had a very enjoyable time seeing some of the sights and getting to know one another.

"You know how they say when you meet the right one you know it? Well, I fell for her hard, so I called my work in Canada and extended my vacation. My friend returned to Canada, and I stayed there to spend more time with Payvand. By the fourth day, I had learned much of what you have heard about these past few days: how Payvand lost her husband of only two years, as well as her baby, to the violence and ignorance of their revolution; the tough life Shabnam had endured; and, a good understanding of her team members, including the legendary Behrouz. She had already applied for immigration to Canada, and I stayed with them two more weeks to confirm that the process was going well and to make sure I had won her affections.

"I also met Shayan and Minoo and their children, who had come to see their old friends. Such a wonderful family and the kids were so smart, polite, and knowledgeable. Shabnam's son had a great time with them, which allowed his mom to be alone with her thoughts. I made friends with Shayan right away, and since both of us were in the medical field, we had a lot to talk about. I took all his contact information and invited him for a drink if he ever came to Canada." Brian looks over his shoulder and drops his voice to a whisper. "Truth be told, I also thought it was a good way to make sure I didn't lose track of Payvand."

Ragusa laughs out loud, and Brian says, "Well, I'm glad I could entertain you. What's so amusing?"

"You stayed there to make sure she cared for you? Of course that is funny. You are funny, Brian! Then you secured Shayan's information in case Payvand did not contact you? You were like a hunter after his prey, weren't you?"

Payvand comes through the door drying her hair with a small towel. "He's funny, is he? What is he saying?"

"I'm telling her how I fell in love with you, and how I forced you to love me back." Ragusa and Brian laugh, and Payvand smiles and says, "It was coercion of the most beautiful and persistent kind, I must say! Everywhere I went you were there, with flowers or baklava, and lots of sweet talk."

"What happened when you came to Canada, Payvand? Did he have to pursue you or did you look him up?"

"Ha, I didn't even let him know I was here. I actually forgot all about him as soon as he left Greece. We were upset. We had been displaced from our homeland and were busy with our problems, and I had no time or inclination to think about starting another relationship with a man. We were dealing with a lot of emotion after leaving the disastrous situation in Iran. For our first two years in Canada, Shabnam and I slept in the same bed so we wouldn't be alone."

"Why?" asks Ragusa.

"Why? Just to wake each other up when we were having nightmares or talking in our sleep. We were both emotionally ill for some time, and found that it greatly helped to be together in our struggle to survive the worst effects of our traumatic experiences. We had lost our families and the most important people in our lives. There was no way, so soon after losing my love, my best friends, and my child, that I had any thoughts of looking for another man. No, I was too damaged to even think about Brian. When he left, he was out of our lives."

"How did you find her again Brian?"

"I waited for several months, and when I hadn't heard from Payvand, I contacted Shayan in Norway. He was glad to give me her contact information in Canada; as a doctor he believed that Payvand and Shabnam were both depressed. They needed a good companion.

"I called Payvand and introduced myself, and she said, 'Brian? Sorry, I don't know anyone by this name; you have a wrong number.' I thought she was teasing me, but she wasn't. So I talked about Greece and reminded her of the guy with the flowers and baklava. Then she remembered and apologized. At first, she didn't want to spend much time with me, but I tried to take advantage of whatever opportunities I could to make her laugh and help her forget. It took me two years of hard work before I dared propose to her. Well, I eventually took my chance and here we are, twenty-seven successful years later."

"How beautiful! What about Shabnam? How is she doing now?"

"When her son married one of Minoo's daughters, he moved to Norway, so Shabnam moved there too. She has her own place and travels around the world, volunteering and trying to help others. So she tries to enjoy life as much as she can. She never married again."

Payvand smiles as she sits listening to Brian and Ragusa talking about her life. Ragusa turns to her and puts her hand on Payvand's. "I hope my questions aren't bothering you."

"No, not at all. And I'm sure there is one more question you are dying to ask. What about Setareh, and how could she be our child if I lost my womb in that shooting?"

Ragusa looks at her sadly. "No, no, I'm so sorry. I do not need to know. Why do you think that?"

"Well, I don't mind. Actually it's a very nice story...." She pauses and looks at Ragusa slyly. "And I'll bet you would never guess! It was Shabnam who helped us. She knew how much I loved Brian and how much both of us wanted to have a child, so she offered to carry our baby. If you remember, I still had one ovary, and I was young and healthy, so Brian and I thought about it and we decided to go ahead with it. Shabnam gave a wonderful gift of life to us, and Setareh has two moms who love her very much."

"What a special friend! Oh, how I envy you. That's unconditional love right there! I truly wish to meet her."

"You will. We visit each other twice a year. One time I go to Norway, and one time she comes here. Each time we spend about a month together. She will be here soon."

Ragusa sits back and leans in her chair. She smiles, but at the same time is holding back tears. "I know that I cannot be with you all the time, but I feel I cannot be alone either. I do not want to forget my family, yet I also don't want to be thinking about them compulsively, which at times I do. They were my love and my life. They are gone; all gone.

"I am so tired, Payvand, and I don't know what to do with myself. Oh, I appreciate so much that you went to such painful depths into your past, and I realize you did it for me, to help me see I am not alone in this kind of pain. Finding you and getting to know you does make me want to live, but I still don't know what I would do if I found myself at the water's edge again."

Payvand sits in front of Ragusa and takes her hands. "I want you to stop thinking about that moment. I am sure you felt completely devastated and it was a moment of frightful confusion. I am sure you did not really want to do it."

Ragusa cannot hold back the tears now. "No, my sweet and kind friend, it was not a momentary bout of depression that suddenly came upon me. It was all calculated and premeditated. I did not feel there was anything productive in my life anymore. I felt all alone, missing the ones who could never be part of my life again. There was no reason for me to live."

Payvands holds Ragusa's hands tightly. "Not even now, with me? I am you, you are me, and don't ever think you are alone. Not anymore! I cannot ever replace your loved ones of course, but I will be here for you, from now to the time of departure."

"Payvand, if I say 'I love you' would you believe me?"

"Yes, of course, because I love you too. We met only a week ago, yet I consider the bond between us to be deep. We have shared our painful experiences so vividly that it's like we are old souls, or friends since time began. I think we have a strong mutual love, and I just want to have you by my side always. Am I selfish, Ragusa?"

"No, you are not selfish. I certainly feel the same way and I enjoy being with you tremendously. However, I will choose my departure time and I want you to understand and accept that. Now that I know you, I have gained a strength that does make me want to continue. I want to be with you and work with you, but if some day I decide it is the time, I want you to come to terms with that now."

Payvand looks at her grimly. "So you want to keep that fear over my head do you? That one of these days you may not show up?"

"No, no, don't get me wrong! After hearing you and learning about your life story, I feel truly excited that there is much in life that we can do together. There are people that have suffered even more than I did. I'll accept that the single fact of my brutal life is not reason enough to dispatch myself. And, as I said, I want to work with you. But I do not wish to get to a point of dependency as I have no one to take care of me."

"You mean when you get infirm and needy?"

"Yes, exactly. I do not want to go to a senior's home to just waste away."

"Oh, don't worry about that. I'll put you down myself if you get there."

They all laugh at that sinister joke. Brian says, "Well for now, I think you should both go have a sleep of the temporary kind. I'll wake you in a few hours, and we can go for a walk, and then I'll take you out for lunch."

Ragusa hugs Payvand warmly, then retreats to the guest bedroom and lays down her exhausted body.

Payvand waves from the door, "Sleep tight my dear friend," she says, then holds Brian's arm for the walk to her bedroom. She goes to her jewellery box and picks out a necklace, "Do you think she would like this?"

Brian takes it and says, "What are you doing? You love this!"

"Yes, I do, just as much as I love Ragusa! I want to give this to her right now!" and she hurries over to Ragusa's room. Fatigue has her walking unsteadily, so Brian follows her and supports her arm. Ragusa sits up when she sees them come in. Payvand sits at Ragusa's bed, opens her hand, and gently places the golden necklace in it.

"Oh, such a beautiful gold dove! Is this an olive branch in its beak?"

"Yes!" says Payvand. "I hope you like it."

"I do! I do very much!" Ragusa says as she squeezes Payvand in thanks.

Payvand puts her tired head on Ragusa's shoulder and holds the hand holding the dove. "Remember I told you that the Dove of Peace was the signature of Shabnam and me on our writings? Shabnam started that tradition. She signed her first story in our magazine with a drawing of just such a dove. Her story was absolutely beautiful, and everyone was delighted with her dove signature. On her next birthday, Malahat gave her a golden chain adorned with her signature dove."

Ragusa pushes herself back and says, "No, this is a reminder of your dear friend! This is her necklace; I do not want this!"

Payvand smiles. "No, no, please let me finish. It isn't hers. When Shabnam received that beautiful present, I was delighted and told her just how appropriate it was, and then I kissed Malahat for her wise decision. What I did not know was that Malahat had ordered two of them to be made, one for each of us. When my birthday came around a few months later, she gave me mine; Shabnam and I had earned our signature. It's mine, and I want you to have it. You are part of me now. I love you, and I want you to have a part of me."

Ragusa sits up, wearing the biggest smile Payvand has yet seen on her face. Payvand puts the necklace on her, and Brian says, "It suits you very well Ragusa, and I am sure she means it!"

The women relax in each other's arms, enjoying the trust and affection they have for each other. Fearing that they'll fall asleep in this potentially uncomfortable position, Brian puts his hand on Payvand's shoulder and helps her rise. "Come on, you need to rest. Let's go." Payvand kisses Ragusa once more and follows him out of the room.

Ragusa lies back in her bed with a faint smile on her lips, holding the dove, and as she gradually falls asleep, she looks through the window at the backyard full of flowers beaming brightly in the noonday sun.

Brian holds Payvand's hand and guides her to their room,

where he helps her lie down. Suddenly she sits back up. "Oh, it's Friday! My group meeting!"

"Don't worry, I will call them and let them know you are not well today." He then lies down next to her, holding her gently and whispering in her ear his love for her. He recites "The Road Not Taken" by Robert Frost, kisses her lovingly, and waits for her to fall asleep.

Brian listens to Payvand's fitful breathing as she sleeps, then kisses her gently and quietly leaves the room. Before he closes the door, the phone rings, and he jumps on it, fearing it may wake her. He picks it up and moves quickly to the living room.

"Hello," says Brian. After a pause he says, "Oh, hello Andelko, how are you?" He talks to him for a bit and then invites him and his family over for dinner. When he hangs up, he makes the call to Payvand's friends to let them know she is not well and will not be joining them today. Then he turns off all the phones just to make sure the women get the rest they need.

He goes to the garden to pick a few of the roses Ragusa likes and puts them in a vase, then fills another vase with Payvand's favourite flowers. As he is putting Ragusa's flowers beside her bed, she wearily asks, "Was that my brother?"

"Yes, he wanted to know how you are. He wants to see if you would like to go home. I told him you are sleeping and then invited them here for supper. You can tell him yourself, if you wish to stay longer or go home."

"Brian, I haven't met anyone like you and your lovely wife. Thank you for all your patience and care."

Brian smiles kindly. "Don't worry about it. You are a wonderful and wise woman. I am sure you and Payvand will have some marvellous adventures and a full and rich life ahead. Payvand is adept at recognizing the jewels of this world. She believes you are her best discovery."

Ragusa smiles. "Thank you, you are kind. I also overheard you phone her friends, so we are not going to ... um...?"

"You need to sleep now. You can meet them all on Wednesday evening. I'll be there too. We're having a special gathering for some beloved friends who are in town visiting. Actually, I am going to invite your brother and his family too. It should be fun."

Ragusa mutters a few words before she falls back to sleep. Brian puts the vase on the table beside her, pulls the blanket up to fully cover her, then quietly slips out of the room.

He returns to the bedroom and places Payvand's vase at her bedside, then sits beside her in the armchair, and watches her sleeping. He picks up a book and tries to read, but he cannot concentrate. He frowns as he watches Payvand squeeze her lips tight, mutter from time to time, then even grind her teeth. It is heartrending for him to see her like this. Payvand moans and mutters, derailing Brian's train of thought. "Oh my darling," he says. "How can I take all your pain away?" He has tears in his eyes as he watches her in despair, knowing that her memories will not go away easily. He murmurs softly, "I am here for you my love." From time to time Payvand tries to open her tired eyes and sees Brian sitting next to her, then relaxes with a weak smile and goes back to sleep. The hours pass as he continues to try and read, but mostly he is thinking about how painful memories can be for those, like Payvand and Ragusa, who have lived through such horror and tragedy.

The doorbell rings and, startled, he looks at the time. "Oh boy, have I've been sitting here for over six hours?" he says out loud to no one in particular. He rushes to the door. Andelko, his wife, and daughter are there smiling at him.

"Hello, Brian! You know my daughter, and this is my wife Anica."

"Hello, hello, welcome!" says Brian. "Come on in! Sorry, the women are sleeping. Come in and make yourselves comfortable. They will be up soon."

"Oh, when I called you six or seven hours ago you said they were sleeping then. Are they all right?"

"Yes, yes! Don't worry. They didn't sleep at all last night because they were talking right through till morning."

Ragusa enters the living room yawning, "Good morning!"

"Good evening, dear sister!" Andelko says. He smiles at her and hugs her. She hugs him back, then says hello to her sister-in-law and niece, and asks Brian if Payvand is still asleep.

"Yes, she's still sleeping. How about you sit with your family while I prepare some beverages for us. What would you like everyone?"

Just then, Payvand comes in, sleepy and yawning. "Why didn't you wake me up, darling?"

"I never wake you up! You wake up when you are rested and your body decides the time is right."

Anica steps forward. "Now there's a kind considerate husband. Hello Payvand, I am Anica!"

"Hello dear, welcome!" says Payvand.

Ragusa starts to tell her family about her hosts' sweet and loving relationship, though Brian and Payvand turn the compliments to jokes and fun. Brian offers to take them out for dinner.

"Could we please stay at home for dinner? You have lots of food in your fridge, and I don't think Payvand and I have any energy for going out," says Ragusa as Payvand smiles at her in appreciation.

Brian looks at Payvand and reads her mind, "Right! You're right. You do still look tired my love. Okay, we'll do that. You ladies sit and chat, and Andelko and I will put something together." He goes into the kitchen as Andelko follows him.

"What is going on?" asks Andelko.

"Don't worry. They just had a long, rough night. Let's see what we can do for them."

Ragusa comes in and announces she will make a round of her famous martinis for everyone.

CHAPTER 9 **FRUITION**

BRIAN AND PAYVAND arrive at the airport, and Payvand is so excited she already has her seatbelt off. "Please drop me off at the international arrivals."

"But we're thirty minutes early!"

"We didn't check the computer. Maybe she's early."

"Okay, you go on in, but don't make me look for you in there. Stay at the arrivals screen and check the landing time while I park the car."

"Okay!" She leaps out of the car and rushes inside. Brian parks the car, and hurries toward the entrance, thinking that not for a million dollars would he miss the excitement of the two seeing each other again. He smiles and walks into the lobby to find Payvand standing at the arrivals monitor looking unhappy. "Oh, this doesn't look good. Has there been a delay?"

"Yes, by forty-five minutes," says Payvand pouting.

Brian kisses that pouted lip. "She'll be here soon, and you are going to have a month of laughter and excitement together."

"Get a room, you two," someone says behind them. "It's a busy airport you know. How about you guys stop smooching in public!" Brian and Payvand turn to see their beautiful daughter smiling at them. Together they grab her and hold her tight.

Payvand steps back so Setareh can see her. "What are you doing here?"

"I thought we were going to see you at the house," says Brian.

"Hello, Mom, hello, Dad. Well, I had time and I thought I would surprise you all. Besides, Shaheen and Mina are coming, and I'm taking them to my house."

"Okay, but have you talked to them about where they are staying?" asks Brian.

"Yes, and they love the idea. Shaheen said our two noisy mothers are better off staying together in one nest." They laugh at her remark.

"Fine with me!" says Payvand.

Brian walks to the gate followed by Payvand and Setareh. Before they know it, the door opens and passengers are filing out. Payvand, excited and happy as a child, moves closer to look for her beloved friend.

"I don't understand them, Dad. They see each other once a year and each time they are so happy to see one another again, as if they haven't seen each other in years."

"Shabnam is the only living link to your mother's past, my dear. They have shared a brutal life. It's as if they rejuvenate when they are in each other's company, and they remember their lives with the loved ones that they have lost." Brian holds his daughter and kisses her on the cheek. Then, he steps back to face her again and says, "For us who live in safe regions, it's difficult to understand them or their connection to the land of their birth. It was a place of horror, yet also a place where they developed exceptional friendships under exceptional circumstances.

"Oh, look, there is Shaheen! Ah! And there's Shabnam! Let's watch them…" But before he finishes his words, Payvand is flying to the door and Shabnam is flying to her. They reach for each other and hold tight, then twist and turn, laughing as if they are hearing some shared music in their head. Their movements, like a dance, are full of light and joy.

"To be honest, Dad, I'll never get tired of watching them like this. Just these first few minutes are so candid and full of vitality."

Shabnam sees Setareh and runs over to give her a big mother-ly hug. "Hello, baby. How are you? Do I need to say how much I have missed you?"

Setareh kisses her heartily. "No, Mother, you don't need to. I'll never doubt that, and I too have missed you a lot. Welcome back!" She kisses her once more, and then she turns to Shaheen and his wife Mina for more hugs. When they have all finished greeting one another, they head to the cars, Shaheen and Mina with Setareh, while Shabnam accompanies Payvand and Brian. On the way home, they report to one another about the past few months.

As soon as Shabnam steps in the door, she closes her eyes and takes a deep breath, "I have missed the scent of your home and your flowers ... aah.... Oh, and my favourite room." She makes a beeline for the study to settle in. The two women continue to chat, even talking non-stop throughout dinner. Then Payvand shows Shabnam the necklace that Ragusa gave her. They sit side by side on the sofa as Payvand tells her all about her wonderful new friend Ragusa.

Shabnam listens carefully to Payvand's account of Ragusa's experiences in Yugoslavia, offering only the occasional remark: "Wow, we think we had it bad," and "Ooooh, brutal," and "Oh, my heart goes out to her," and "Ah, I like her already...." By the end, they have made their way under a blanket to be more comfortable as they talk.

Brian eventually arrives with some wine only to find them both fast asleep under the blanket. He smiles to himself and thinks, *Here we are again, I may as well be the roommate when Shabnam is here.* He smiles to himself as he enters his bedroom to turn in. He is happy. *This will be such a wonderful time for Payvand after what she has been through for the last couple of weeks. Shabnam is the best medicine for her.* He lies down and tries to sleep, but he misses his love, feeling as if a piece of him is missing, and making it difficult for him to fall asleep.

A couple of hours pass but he still can't sleep, so he reads, watches some TV, reads again ... but nothing works. Then, he hears Payvand tiptoeing out of the study and coming toward him. She talks quietly, and sweetly, the way Brian loves. "I heard your restlessness. Oh, darling you cannot sleep. I'm sorry. We fell asleep again. Let's just let her sleep. I don't wish to wake her up."

Brian gets up and closes the door to the study so that Shabnam will not be disturbed. Then he joins Payvand in the bedroom and closes that door behind him as well.

"Why you are closing all the doors?" asks Payvand. Brian pulls her into his arms and kisses her passionately. Payvand pulls back. "Are you crazy? We have a guest."

"We'll be quiet, I miss you..." He is kissing her neck as he undoes her clothes. He holds her in his arms, and they wrap around each other with joy.

A morning breeze caresses Payvand's face as she opens her eyes. Brian's face is smiling over her. She kisses him and then playfully nips his nose.

"Good morning, my love," he says, nuzzling her neck.

"No, no, let's go. I hear her. She's up and in the kitchen."

"No, she's sleeping. You're imagining things," he says and pulls her back into his arms.

Payvand pushes him away gently and gets out of the bed laughing. "Time to get up, we have a busy day."

She goes into the kitchen where Shabnam is preparing breakfast. "Oh, smells good; Malahat's special omelette ... you still make that," she says as she hugs Shabnam and kisses her on the cheek. "Mmm ... feels like old times."

Shabnam smiles at her, "Of course, it's the best omelette ever, and I enjoy thinking about her while I am making it."

Payvand sighs. "I envy the sweet way you remember our past without letting it crush you."

Shabnam kisses her and says, "The best and most productive time of my life was working in our group with its wonderful and devoted members; I cannot ever forget them. I have many positive memories of the things we did together back then, and it makes me feel I am still connected to them, at least in spirit. I have also kept all the recipes I gathered from Malahat, and I use them whenever I miss her."

Brian joins them in the kitchen with a cheerful, "Good morning, Shabnam."

"Good morning, Brian. I am so sorry. Every time I'm here I seem to fall asleep with your wife on the sofa. Forgive me?"

"You can sleep with my wife anytime and anywhere you wish, as long as you give her back to me at bedtime. As long as my love is in my arms, I can even fall asleep on nails." They laugh at his silliness.

They sit at the table and talk, much of the conversation involving compliments on the marvellous omelette. Shabnam also tells them about her lastest trip and its accomplishments and adventures. Then, she goes on about her plans for her next trip. Brian looks at her smiling.

"What?" asks Shabnam.

"Oh, nothing. I just thought you might enjoy these travels more if you had a companion to share them with."

Shabnam looks at him long and shrewdly. "You have known me for about thirty years, and you know that I love my life this way. But I forgive you because I understand your concerns, and I assure you that I am fine. I did try dating a couple of fine gentlemen I recently met, but when they got close to me and asked for more, I couldn't help but remember Behrouz's loving eyes on the day he told me he had loved me all along, the last day I ever saw him. First, I become angry at myself for my indifferent behaviour to him; then, I think how he lived a life without ever touching anyone and, as he put it, never falling in love. And when he finally did, it was to unapproachable me. In a way, I think I did love him too, but I could not deal with it at the time. So, I am not really interested in anyone else. He died without touching anyone, and I will do the same."

Payvand tries to say something, but Shabnam raises a fore-finger at them. "I don't want to talk about this, thank you!"

They complete their breakfast tranquilly and then Brian leaves for his work. Payvand calls Ragusa to give her the address for the evening's event, after which the two women return to the study so that Payvand can finish telling Shabnam the rest of Ragusa's life story.

It is about seven o'clock and everyone is gathered in the meeting hall, a beautifully designed modern community centre with large windows that let in the bright evening sun. There is a wide variety of food and beverages from various cultures arranged on the tables. Some people are wearing traditional outfits, and some are dressed casually.

Payvand and Shabnam arrive and greet everyone gathered there one by one. Brian remains outside to make sure Ragusa and her family find the place and to escort them in. When Ragusa arrives with her brother's family, she is happy to see Brian at the entrance. They walk into the meeting hall together and look for Payvand, "There she is," says Brian. "Let's get her over here so she can introduce you to everyone."

Payvand sees them enter before he can call her name, and she rushes over to hug Ragusa, then greets her family and welcomes them. "Come on Ragusa, I want you to meet all these dear friends," and before long Ragusa has met a wonderful array of friendly and interesting people. As Ragusa moves among them, she notices a woman standing in a corner with a glass of wine in her hand, who seems to be looking at her curiously. Ragusa approaches the woman, and notices that she is wearing the same dove necklace that she herself has on. Now she knows it is Shabnam, who greets her with a lovely smile.

"Hello sister," Shabnam says, and they hold each other warmly.

Payvand appears beside them and says, "Ah, you found each other!"

Shabnam laughs. "How many people here could possibly have exactly the same necklace as ours? I have heard a lot about you, my dear, and I think it is wonderful that Payvand gave the necklace to you."

People gather around the tables, drinking, talking, and engaged in enthusiastic conversations. The teenagers start dancing, and tease the older folk playfully. After dinner, they all move into a relatively big theatre where the public settles in for the evening's presentations. People are taking their seats, and Ragusa is excited as she watches with fascination the liveliness of the people moving around her.

Eventually, the program begins with Payvand introducing some of the topics for the evening: Climate change and global warming, wars and conflict, and displacement. The speakers are from various walks of life, and Payvand emphasizes clearly that, "None of the speakers have any suggestions as to specific actions that we should take next; this is primarily an information session. Each speaker has worked hard to bring to your attention some basic facts about important problems afflicting our world. It is then our responsibility as citizens of this world to investigate the issues closest to our heart. We are all mature, clever people who can research, learn, and educate ourselves about what is going on in our world, and from that develop our own contributions to making our world a safer and better place for all.

"We discourage the top-down model where one individual or team directs the actions of the rest. We wish to provide information and then the actual heavy lifting is on each one of us. It is up to each of us to take the actions we deem appropriate to develop solutions for effecting positive change. We should all be proactive in caring for this planet of ours and leaving to the next generation a safe and healthy place to live. The key is knowledge about the world's issues and dilemmas."

The first speaker introduces himself as a world citizen born in Belgium and raised in Canada. He has put together a slide-show that he uses to guide the audience through an array of well-designed graphs, statements from scientists, visuals, and research analysis. He uses these slides to illustrate his concerns about the effects humans are having on Earth's biosphere, and he speaks passionately about the harmful, gradual changes in the climate caused by a slow but steady increase in the temperature of the Earth's atmosphere. He talks about the scientists who have been working for decades on this urgent and threatening issue, and who have assembled an impressive body of research that has examined natural cycles and other relevant non-human factors, and concluded that the warming is caused by human activities.

From time to time, he reminds the people in the audience that they do not have to take anything that he or anyone else says on faith. Each and every person should edify themselves as best they can to satisfy him or herself of the validity of his claims.

Step by step he brings forward his evidence. He notes the various symptoms of the global warming trend: record drought and heat waves, extreme storms, alterations in rainfall patterns, unusual flooding, and the accelerated melting of glaciers. He explains how the warming trend can be linked to greenhouse gases such as carbon dioxide, which is emitted when we use electricity and run our cars and trucks, or in the course of industry's activities. He concludes by exposing the serious public health concerns of global warming: increases or invasive shifts by tropical viral and bacterial microbes into northern zones; crop failures, desertification, and other ecological stresses. He warns the audience that they must not allow their daily hectic lives to minimize their response to this phenomenon and thus cause the problem to become much worse.

He opens the floor to questions, and several people rise to ask for more information or to augment the discussion with additional data and perspectives. One woman gets up and firmly encourages the audience to educate themselves, reiterating the importance of the speaker's challenge that everyone seek out more information independently.

The next speaker presents a powerful collection of remarkable photographs. They depict scenes from brutal wars and conflict zones, demonstrating the destructive face of modern warfare and the frightening conditions endured by peoples displaced by the fighting. She asks the audience to consider why we should still have such terror and violence all across the world, when all of humanity has seen so clearly the catastrophic effects inflicted by past travesties: the Vietnam War, the Iraq Wars, and World War II which culminated in atomic devastation. She shows the amazing work that these skilled photographers have done to demonstrate the harm that wars do to human beings and their communities, and she wonders how it is that we still find ourselves witnessing raging battles and civil conflicts.

She also highlights the bravery of these people, some of whom have lost their lives to bring these disturbing and otherwise hidden realities to the world's attention. The images speak loud and clear to the pain and suffering of people afflicted by warmongers, and they tell an unimpeachable story of man's inhumanity to man.

She speaks with passion while working through the pictures, and responds thoughtfully to questions from the audience. She mentions various scholars who have written masterfully about world history, especially after World War II, to expose the criminal and unnecessary wantonness displayed by belligerent leaders and factions of all stripes as they wreaked havoc on communities, cities, countrysides, and entire nations. These tyrants, ever hungering for more power and control, imposed ridiculous and often self-serving agendas on populations that had not put in requests for their services. She asks the audience to consider why we, as the people of this world, cannot stop these atrocities. She questions how it is that we are not able to change the direction our world is headed, so that instead of war, we aim for global peace and security.

As did the previous speaker, she emphasizes that education is the key. People must know about their world and be aware of who is responsible for preventing them from it being a healthy and safe planet. She concludes by urging everyone to commit him or herself to working actively in some way to promote world peace and to combat government policies that support war and exploitation.

Payvand now rises to speak about a topic that highlights how citizens of a supposed democracy cannot necessarily trust that their leadership is honouring human rights. She gives a brief overview of an institution called the U.S. Army School of Americas, which is run for the sole purpose of training Latin American police and military personnel in the techniques of counter-insurgency, and which is known today as the "Western Hemisphere Institute for Security Cooperation (WHINSEC)." The academy is known popularly as the "School of Assassins" because when its graduates return to their countries and set about actually countering insurgency, they regularly engage in activities such as kidnapping, intimidation, murder, and assassination. However, their targets — the "insurgents" — turn out to be peasants, human rights activists, labourers, land reformers, organizers, and other citizens who are fed up with being ruled by dictators. They are people who want a chance at living in a free country that is governed by its own people.

The operators and instructors of this School of Assassins simply assume that such people are insurgents, and their training manuals explicitly teach the students to ignore principles of human rights and do whatever it takes to destroy those working in opposition to the elites in power.

Payvand asks the audience to imagine what form of evil would be capable of creating a school dedicated to teaching how to torture, murder, rape and terrorize civilians. It demonstrates that the governments of the client countries are so enslaved to power that they will allow these kinds of atrocities to take place in their countries and to their own citizens. Those are the puppets, but it is the puppet master who must be taken to task. By operating a school that preaches anti-democratic principles, the U.S. has failed to uphold its own rhetoric about democracy and human rights.

Ragusa is enjoying all the discussions. She admonishes herself for allowing her own situation to prevent her from connecting with others and seeing how they live. She peruses the pamphlet in her hand, and then perks up her ears when she hears Payvand introducing Shabnam as the next speaker.

Shabnam uses the School of Assassins example to take the discussion from the topic of abuses of power to the related one of regime change. This includes the topic of puppet dictators whose only function appears to be ruining their own people in order to stay in power.

"A major factor that allows such phenomena to exist," she says, "is Ignorance with a capital 'I.'" She pauses for a few seconds to get the audience's attention, then says firmly, "Make no mistake, Ignorance is our greatest enemy and a most deadly weapon! It is our enemy because populations that are uninformed can be ruled, deceived, and used by anyone. If a School of Assassins exists and operates in a host country, it's only because the citizens there don't care about how their government works, and are Ignorant of its undemocratic habits. They are acculturated to think like this.

"That deadly weapon of Ignorance also supplies the thugs who attend that School of Assassins. Those unsavoury characters don't care about human rights. They only care about the money and power they can get from what they learn. What is the result of a world filled with such selfish and reckless people? Madness!

"I am truly grateful that the speakers here are directing us to self-education. A well-informed citizenry is the only antidote to Ignorance. I have researched resource-rich countries.

Consistently, it is the lack of education that allows them to be exploited. Without education, populations remain in the dark about the way their resources are stolen from them by local elites and foreign interests.

"Iran, where I was born, is a good example of a country that has had to endure a lot since the discovery of oil there a century ago. Since then, Soviet, British, and American foreign interests have instigated regime change. They installed or supported puppet dictators, just to maintain privileged access to Iran's oil.

"Thus, the Pahlavi Shahs, both father and son, were tools used by the major powers of the day. Through them, the foreign power could administer this strategic, resource-rich country. Any ruler that didn't co-operate was swept aside and replaced. For instance, when the older Pahlavi declared Iran neutral in World War II, the British and Soviet governments forced him to resign in favor of his more compliant son. Later, when Prime Minister Mosaddegh unexpectedly initiated a program of democratic and social reform, he was taken down by the CIA, which allowed the Pahlavi son to be a tool once again.

"The price of maintaining favour with the West was steep. Many people were killed, tortured, or imprisoned. This instilled fear in the population and made sure people did not organize political opposition or pursue knowledge. Thus, the ignorance that autocratic and secretive governments needed was maintained. And who was actually killing and torturing Iranians? Other Iranians! The overlords didn't even have to do the dirty work. It is the same in any exploited country. The immoral native elites and gangsters are happy to preserve their power and wealth at the expense of their own people.

"Then the regime in Iran changed again in the 1979 Revolution. What happened there? Two important factors were at play. First, the people were thirsty for knowledge. There was such a resurgence of intellectual inquiry that it threatened the autocrat's requirement for an Ignorant citizenry. This brought about a violent campaign of repression by the Shah's secret police. That only redoubled the efforts of political activists to bring down the Shah.

"Secondly, the opposition that was pushing for change in Iran was unusually diverse. There was the usual array of infighting between intellectual and leftist groups battling the regime, but there was also a strong religious camp. They were protesting their weakening influence in the country. Support for this religious elite came from the vast majority of rural folk and urban workers; the very people who had been kept Ignorant by religion. The weight of those numbers gave power to the clergy. It allowed them to transform Iran into a theocratic dictatorship. Those clerics have stayed in power now for over three decades, and we can once again thank Ignorance for that. The new theocracy destroyed all opposition voices and intellectuals quickly and brutally; and so, Ignorance was guaranteed.

"Iran is a theocratic dictatorship and a socio-economic failure. The government maintains its power by a complete control of media, public spaces, and workplaces. It controls education from preschool through to university. It forcefully suppresses any movements or protests against it. Ignorance has become the puppet master."

In conclusion, Shabnam continues to emphasize self-education and the learning of lessons from world history. "These," she says, "can help prevent us from making the same mistakes and allow us to move forward with effective policies and actions. We must reform the political and economic structures that presently produce instability and destruction."

An intermission is called, and people get up to stretch and mingle with lively discussions breaking out everywhere. Payvand approaches Ragusa and asks, "Would you like to share some of your experiences?"

"Oh, I don't know. I have never spoken in public!"

"Just focus on me. Think about the past couple of weeks. Speak clearly. Believe me, it becomes easier as you go on and gain more confidence."

Ragusa smiles. "Do you think I can do it?"

"Yes, I think you would do very well, and you would give our audience good food for thought." Payvand looks at Ragusa encouragingly. "I'll introduce you after the next speaker."

After the intermission, Payvand introduces another speaker who is a frail-looking, shy young woman. She begins her talk by saying, "We are witnessing a new round of turmoil and chaos in the Middle East. It seems that the elite have somehow lost control in the area, and many of the dictatorial managers installed in the past to help govern the Middle East are not good enough anymore and are being removed. Why? What happened that all of a sudden there is civil strife throughout the Middle East?"

She looks out at the audience with her young, innocent face. "As you know, conflict in that region is nothing new. I am a child of war. I am twenty-five years old now, but until we came to Canada two years ago, all I can remember are fearful days and nights growing up in a war zone with regular clashes between heavily armed combatants. After one of my brothers was killed, my father decided to leave, and I have only recently become accustomed to a life where I can relax and not worry all the time. The nights are good here and I feel rested when I sleep, and rejuvenated the next day. Where I come from, you are on guard even when you sleep, or you are constantly being startled awake by the sounds of bombs and artillery. One can never relax, and everyone is agitated and frightened."

She pauses and sighs. "When my dad went to work, I feared that he would not return home. And when he came home, I always feared we would not see the morning. I wondered when all of this would be over, if ever."

With a trembling voice she says, "I am here now. I am safe but not happy because I remember my friends and cousins. They are still living in fear and I know what their sleepless nights are like. I feel guilty, as if I have abandoned them."

She talks about the ongoing conflict between Israel and Palestine and how the world has become numb to it. She presents horrific photographs of the area and of the conditions in which many people are living. Such scenes seem unimaginable here in Canada and the photos sadden the audience. She too urges the audience to take it upon themselves to learn more about the dreadful lives of children in war zones and to think about them as they might care for and think about their own children. Tears fill her eyes, and emotion chokes her voice, and she cannot go on. But before she leaves the stage, with heartening effort she offers her sincerest wish: "Who knows, maybe one of you can come up with a better solution than your politicians."

There is quiet in the room as Payvand guides the young woman back to her seat and then returns to the stage to preside over a question and answer session. There is much discussion about the emotional damage done to children growing up in such conditions and the trauma that will stay with them for many years if not a lifetime. Several people rise to share tragic stories they have witnessed of lives ruined by the Korean War, by Vietnam, and by many brutal conflicts here and there in Africa, the Middle East, and so on.

Payvand then raises the topic of Yugoslavia's terrible war and introduces Ragusa as one whose life was shattered by that conflict, and who would now like to share the perspective she has gained from her tragedy.

Ragusa, pale and nervous with so many eyes staring at her, steps to the microphone. She looks back at the audience and says, "It broke my heart hearing that young lady just now who spoke about her dreadful childhood fears, her dead brother, and her feelings about the ones she left behind. Do you think she will someday get used to it and go on with her life?" She pauses as she looks over the audience. "She may come to some sort of compromise, but she will never forget. I certainly cannot forget how I lost my loved ones, one by one. I will always love them, and I will also never forget nor forgive how a country as beautiful and flourishing as Yugoslavia could be torn apart in a matter of a few years."

She asks if there are any Serbs in the audience, and a few hands are raised. She asks about Croatians, and a few more hands go up. Bosnians? Slovenians? A few more hands appear. She smiles. "Wow. So why are we all here in Canada?

Someone in the audience calls out, "It wasn't safe anymore." Another says, "I disagreed with what was going on, and I tried to involve people in finding solutions. But they were so deeply drawn into their hate for one another that I felt there was no use. But as the young lady previously said, I feel guilty too. Perhaps I could have tried harder."

Ragusa looks at the woman who said this respectfully. "I didn't want to leave either. My husband and I tried to make it. After all, it was our birthplace. All our memories and our families where there." She sighs, "Ultimately, though, we too had to leave after I lost my mother and my daughter to violence." Ragusa explains that she did some research surrounding the breakup of Yugoslavia and how its own people tore it apart. She pauses and takes a deep breath. "I'm not going to get into details about who did what to whom. All I ask is that we all look at the weaknesses and failures of the human spirit that occur when people succumb to petty ethnic rivalries. I ask that we try to learn our lesson when we see that such events do nothing more than devastate lives and massacre innocents. It disappoints me that I just do not see much evidence that we do care to learn. If we did, then how is it that the world is still producing victims, such as the young lady who spoke previously? She reports that Arabs and Jews continue their childish quarrel and that Arabs are killing Arabs over trivial differences in theological interpretation. Who is benefiting from these upheavals? What will it take for us to wake up and appreciate how little benefit there is to any wars in comparison to its human cost?

"How many children must lose their parents? Why must we hammer ecosystems with depleted uranium and other such chemicals? And don't forget the aftermath of war's pollution such as horrifying birth defects and sterile croplands. Yesterday, I read about Fallujah and was overwhelmed. The residents of that area have endured high rates of birth defect due to depleted uranium; these rates are higher than those in Hiroshima following the nuclear bomb attack.

"I wonder how anyone can live a carefree life when there are people living in this same world who are suffering that badly. I myself just lost my son to medical complications. They were the result of breathing war's fumes and suffering war's stresses while I was pregnant with him. I lost my mother, my daughter, my husband, and, at last, my son, to a useless, nonsensical little war."

Ragusa takes a deep breath. "I could live my life in a bitter sadness, or simply decide not to live anymore. But I am seeing a different path now. I want to find out who benefited from the conflict in my old country, and why it really happened. I want to know and I will do so, not for revenge, but to prepare myself to join the ever-growing community of activists who are working for a just world and striving to end future wars and conflicts."

She concludes with a powerful offering, "I did not prepare to speak today, and I don't have pictures or articles or documents to share with you. But I have my broken soul for you, and I have the lives of my lost family to share with you." Ragusa controls her emotions as Payvand comes up to hold her and help her down from the stage. The audience stands up to applaud.

People gather around her with many questions, but she raises a hand and says, "I am still alive, and I'm still here, and I am eager to learn from you all. All our speakers had brilliant presentations with the goal of awakening our minds, so let's begin to learn. Let's work to choose politicians who share our desire for justice and peace. Let's learn from each other's struggles and work together to provide a safe and healthy world for our children."

Ragusa is tired and breathless, and Payvand takes her to the back of the meeting hall, where she offers her a glass of water. Shabnam joins them and wants to know if Ragusa is all right. They rest there for a while, then move closer to the stage to listen to Kathleen, the next speaker, an old friend of Shabnam's and Payvand's. Kathleen is a Canadian sociologist who works hard to educate people about the psychological cost of war. She lost her American husband in the Iraq war. After his passing, she joined Shabnam to travel around the world and provide workshops on the social issues surrounding conflicts.

Payvand sits with Ragusa and whispers, "Oh Ragusa, I know you would love this woman; she is great. But if you are worn out, you should go home, and I can tell you all about it tomorrow."

"Oh, no. I want to be here. I definitely want to hear her." They hold hands and listen carefully.

Kathleen is presenting slides depicting life in Iraq over the last ten years, and the ways that residents there have been coping with the upheavals in their lives. She also spends some time explaining the psychological problems many soldiers have adjusting to family life after returning from that war of occupation. She uses as a very personal example her own husband's painful difficulties before he eventually died at a very young age.

Ragusa is sitting between Shabnam and Payvand and each are holding one of her hands. She feels she is part of a strong and caring friendship, and she relaxes her body in her chair and feels content. She thinks about Dragomir, as well as her son and daughter, and then she turns to Payvand who is listening intently to Kathleen. Then she turns to Shabnam who is looking kindly at her. Shabnam leans over and murmurs softly, "Everything is going to be fine, I promise you!" Ragusa smiles back and looks down to hide her tears.

Brian comes close to Payvand and whispers, "I would like to do the closing remarks. I have a few words of my own." Payvand pulls him close to kiss him. "Go darling, you do the closing; I am sure you have plenty to say."

After Kathleen finishes her talk, Brian climbs up to the stage and takes the podium. He thanks all of the speakers for their powerful and insightful presentations. "I would also like to thank everyone for attending this event. We are fortunate to be living in a land where discussions like this can take place without fear of harassment by the government. But that doesn't mean we have a perfectly righteous society here. The problems and pains you have learned about today are a result of injustices and inequities. We live in a world where governments give lowest priority to the most important policies: lifting people out of poverty, protecting ecosystems, implementing sustainable economies, and resolving disputes peacefully and maturely. They ignore these policies even though they are in the best position to enact them.

"We in the developed world have a privileged standard of living but we choose to ignore the effects this has on others. We demand the resources required to maintain our levels of consumption, and we insist on the lowest prices for anything and everything. As a result, we ally ourselves with the warlords and dictators willing to help us take what we need, and thus force people elsewhere into poverty. The institutions that facilitate these conditions are corporations, which are in an endless war for profits that translate into conflicts on the ground in the resource-rich regions of the world. Such wars are impositions on the populations of both belligerent and victim states, creating displaced peoples and refugees, causing brain drain from war zones, and destroying farm lands and other food resources.

"Will the people of this planet ever realize that war and corporate greed are only tragedy and disaster? If they fully understand that, then they will strongly advocate for the peaceful coexistence of the peoples of our planet. We, as an obviously intelligent species, should be able to learn to live together and share the Earth's resources. But we are prevented from living in harmony because selfish greed overrides our compassion and intelligence and is permitted to be the guiding principle in controlling the world's resources.

"Fights that break out over those resources are justified as being 'in the national interest,' without the populations of those nations having any idea what is actually happening under their noses. Whose fault is that? How have people been trained to look away and say, 'I don't want to know' or 'I don't care?' If we continue to turn our back on these issues, our own politicians will not feel obligated to reform our economies and our foreign policies. These must be reformed, so that assumptions of justice and sustainability are built into how we relate to each other and the rest of the world.

"I am sure the other speakers join me in urging you all to live your lives as ethically and honourably as you can, by always being aware of how your actions affect other people and Mother Earth. In addition, we should make sure we put pressure on our elected representatives in Ottawa, Washington, and all other seats of power. Let them know you are opposed to economies and governments that are structured to favour conflict, destruction, and human misery over justice and peace.

"Again, thank you all for being here. Talk to the people around you, form alliances and work together to change this world for the better."

With that, the program is over and conversations bubble up all around the room as people get up and prepare to leave. Ragusa is talking to her brother and letting him know that she would like to stay with Payvand for a few days. Andelko is glad to see his sister so happy and energetic, and he kisses her and wishes her a good night before leaving with his family.

The little group arrives home still discussing the evening's revelations. Brian declares, "I am exhausted and I'm going to bed. Good night everyone." The women prepare the sofa in the study as a bed for Shabnam, then Payvand kisses the other two and apologizes for being so tired, leaving the two of them to relax together.

The two women sit in the study quietly. Then Ragusa asks Shabnam how long she is staying. "Six weeks, and then I will go on a trip for three months with a group of twelve people."

"What will you be doing?"

"Well, have you heard about organizations like Education Without Borders, or Builders Without Borders?"

"Well, I have heard of Doctors Without Borders, but I don't know exactly what they do really."

"There are actually many doctors, nurses, labourers and builders, and educators working with those kinds of organizations in developing countries. They form teams of people who want to use their specialized skills to help disadvantaged communities around the world. Of course there are also organizations, such as the Council of Canadians, working here. They try to change Canada and its corporations from being a problem in the world into being champions for social, economic, and environmental justice, both here and internationally. I'm considering focusing my efforts in that direction. It might be more effective in my effort to solve the roots of global disparity.

"Anyway, this time my team is going to a small farming village in West Africa to first develop a community centre, and then train the locals in a variety of useful skills. At the same time we can teach them about wider issues in the surrounding world, many of which affect them. Would you like to come with us? If you are not working and have no obligations here, you are more than welcome to join us."

Ragusa looks at her as she considers the offer. "So, are you with me?" asks Shabnam.

"Well, yes, it certainly sounds interesting. I would love to. What would I be doing?"

"Helping us; nothing big. We would guide you as you go. I will talk to the group tomorrow, and we will set you up. We have six weeks to prepare all your documents, so no worries."

Ragusa contemplates the amazing turn her life has taken. *A couple of weeks ago I was planning to leave this world, believing it had nothing for me anymore. Now, I will be part of a committed group of activists.* She looks at Shabnam who is regarding her with a smile.

"You know, last night, Payvand and Brian were talking about your city and also about a hiding place in the mountains where you and your family stayed for some time. They said you had a lot to say about that magnificent area and that you had wanted to provide Payvand with a map to it."

"Yes, yes, that is near Dubrovnik, my birthplace. Why?"

"Well, they were talking about going there with you!"

"Oh, how wonderful. I would love to be their tour guide. Are you coming too?"

"I was thinking about it, yes. If you want to join me in my work, I'm sure you will be quite exhausted by the time we return. A trip to your homeland together might be a marvelous opportunity to relax with each other. What do you think?"

"You mean after our humanitarian work, we would go to Dubrovnik? If so, that would be wonderful. You know I haven't been there since I left."

"Why?"

Ragusa has a sad smile. "My last memories there are of a dead child and my dying husband. I lost them both. Where do I want to go without them?" She sighs and dries her tears with a tissue. "I have missed my husband very much, and when I am happy I want him with me so I can share my thoughts and feelings with him. For instance, today I just wanted his presence so badly."

"Of course you miss him. You will always miss him, and that is good. You'll always have your sweet memories with him, but you cannot stop living. I'm sure he wouldn't want that."

"Do you miss him?" says Ragusa.

Shabnam knows right away who she is talking about, and she looks down and sighs, "Of course, but I cannot bring him back. For years I was angry with myself, wondering if he would still be alive if I had gone for a coffee with him that morning or for a walk. But in time I understood that he had been resisting the pleas of everyone around him to get out of those factories. I personally told him many times that he didn't need to work there anymore, and that his talents were best employed writing, translating, and doing other important work. I will always miss him and think about him, and I also hate the barbaric hands and evil minds that tortured him to death, killed him and many others like him. There were and are many devoted people everywhere who are killed in the worst imaginable way, simply for their beliefs and political activities, for their love of humanity and justice. They are crucified for their ideas. I ache for that day when all of humanity can work together in a spirit of love and community."

Shabnam sits quietly for a bit. Then, she adds, "I cherish my memories and life with, not only him, but the whole group. They were my family, and I miss them all. There are times that I am deeply saddened, remembering the extraordinary people I knew and worked with. But I can't stay in that frame of mind forever, so I try to do the best I can at helping people who don't have what we here take for granted."

She pauses, takes a deep breath, and slowly exhales. "What a waste. They have killed many in Iran since 1979, and still do. You know, when Payvand and I left the country, we were so frightened, wondering what was going to happen, where we would go, what to do, who to trust. Then we met activists in Greece who were working hard for a better society in their own country. Then, in Canada, we met Brian, Kathleen, Jean, Anna and that whole marvelous gang of speakers you met tonight. I left Canada to join my son in Norway, but I always love coming back here to these people. We have the honour of knowing so many who think just like we do and want to do their part to make this world a better place. Quite a few have their own terrible stories to tell, but what's important is that we find each other and work together in our never-ending struggle to bring our ideals to fruition." She pauses for a cavernous yawn. "Wow, I think we should get some rest. Then we can talk more about things tomorrow with Payvand."

Ragusa agrees and says goodnight. She goes to her room where she lies down and thinks about her husband and about starting a new life without him, and without her children. She realizes she no longer feels the same despair, nor is she lonely anymore. She has two sisters now, and many new friends. But her heart still aches, and she wishes her husband, her family, could be with her still. She smiles to herself and then whispers out loud, "I am ready for my new life." And as she falls asleep, she pictures her husband's smiling face and she thinks, *I am going on a trip, and I promise I will tell you about everything that I'm doing before I go to sleep every night.*

Shabnam is in the kitchen where she gets a glass of water for herself and one for Ragusa. When she peeks into Ragusa's room, she finds her already asleep, a tiny smile on her face. Shabnam sets the water down on the night table, but then realizes that Ragusa is whispering to herself, talking softly as she falls asleep with a faint smile.

Shabnam tiptoes out and goes to the study where she takes a photo album from the top corner of the bookshelf. She opens it and looks at a photograph of Malahat and Behrouz and caresses their image with the tip of her finger. She lays the album down, then opens her braids and lets her hair fall down as she looks out the window at the bright full moon. Then, she pulls the curtain over just enough to cover the bright light but not to prevent the caress of the breeze on her face.

She puts the album next to her on a pillow, looks at the photograph again, and softly recites a poem before she goes to sleep:

Someday people will find each other...
That day, each woman is sister to each.
Each man is brother to each...
That day, the meaning of each word is love...
That day, on each lip is the smile of kindness
That day, you, you will return home, forever...
That day, we will feed the doves
They will eat from our hands without fear
That day will come
I am longing for that day
Even, if I may no longer be here...

She looks out into the night and remembers her comrades. The breeze gently teasing her hair, she repeats quietly, "I am longing for that day! Even ... if ... that day ... I myself may no longer be here...."

ACKNOWLEDGEMENTS

To the people of our only home, Earth; to those devoted, dedicated and selfless ones who gave their lives for humanity, and continue to do so; to those who inspired me with their gentle love, self-sacrifice and altruistic living; and to those who gave me reasons to love life.

Again, I must acknowledge those who use, manipulate, injure, and take advantage of any given situation to satisfy their greed at the expense of this earth and its people; this book would be unnecessary without you. With my whole being, I dedicate this book to the world's political prisoners and the victims of wars and conflicts.

As well, I would love to thank Inanna Publications for recognizing the importance of the book and helping me to publish it. Also, with the love and support of my darling, Murray, and my dear sister, Jean, it became possible to work through those difficult memories.

Last but not least to my two beautiful children, Hooman and Payvand.

Credits:

Chapter 4, page 119, excerpts from the poem "Moonlight" by

Nima Youshij (1896-1960), from his *Collected Poems* (Tehran: Tala koob, 1983). Trans. by Nasreen Pejvack.

Chapter 8, page 240, excerpts from poetry by Ahmad Shamloo (1925-2000), from his *Selected Poems* (Tehran: Thunder, 1984). Trans. by Nasreen Pejvack.

Chapter 9, page 293, excerpts from the poem "The Bright Horizon" by Ahmad Shamloo (1925-2000), from his *Selected Poems* (Tehran: Thunder, 1984). Trans. by Nasreen Pejvack.